RESTITUTION

A SEAN COLEMAN THRILLER

JOHN A. DALY

BQB

North Carolina

Published in the United States by BQB Publishing Company
www.bqbpublishing.com

Printed in the United States of America

ISBN 978-1-952782-50-3 (p)
ISBN 978-1-952782-51-0 (e)

Library of Congress Control Number: 2021951548

Book design by Robin Krauss, www.bookformatters.com
Cover design by Rebecca Lown, www.rebeccalowndesign.com
First editor: Caleb Guard
Second editor: Andrea Vande Vorde

Praise for Restitution and John A. Daly

"I'd never met Sean Coleman until John Daly's gripping new thriller. Now that I know him . . . I want him on my side."

— Tom Nichols, author of *Our Own Worst Enemy*

"*Restitution* brings Sean Coleman fans the series' traditional strong sense of setting and mood, and clipped, realistic dialogue, and adds a refreshing, subtle sense of heart and hope amidst all the Vegas grit and Western landscapes of the Nevada desert."

— Jim Geraghty, senior political correspondent of *National Review* and author of the *Dangerous Clique* thriller series

"John Daly has a magical writing style, and his books keep you up late at night turning pages."

— Dana Perino, former White House Press Secretary

"You'll wish you could read faster just to keep up with and stay in the action."

— Lance Storm, former WWE Superstar

"*Restitution* offers hard-hitting action spearheaded by a badass protagonist who talks the talk and walks the walk in a brutal story of surviving an unforgiving territory. . . Written in the vein of old-school stories of revenge, familial bonds, and relentless action, *Restitution* is a definite must-read."

— Kashif Hussain, *Best Thriller Books*

"I started reading *Restitution* on my flight from Phoenix to O'Hare. I read without stopping for three hours and I wouldn't have minded if the plane circled the airport a few times. . . Riveting, with a great cast of flawed good guys and nasty, but believable bad guys, this was nonstop action from beginning to end. Highly recommended."

— Len Joy, author of *Everyone Dies Famous* and *Dry Heat*

"John A. Daly crafts a suspenseful thriller. . . replete against the developing plot is a moral and ethical interplay of emotions that juxtaposes fast-paced action with serious character development and changing perspectives. *Restitution* may be the fifth book in the series, but its solid attention to detail and action makes it a powerful read on levels that move beyond suspense alone, providing an especially satisfying story for those who like their thriller multifaceted, operating in arenas of personal assessment as well as physical struggles for survival."

— D. Donavan, *Senior Reviewer, Midwest Book Review*

"*Restitution* by John A. Daly opens with a scene so intense and heart-wrenching that I could not stop reading. . . Everything I read made me love this story even more."

— Rabia Tanveer, *Readers' Favorite*

"To the loves of my life, Sarah, Chase, and Olivia."

August 12, 1971
Chihuahua, Mexico

Chapter 1

Almost a week of scorching highs in the hundreds brought another day of eye-stinging sweat to a thirteen-year-old boy with a dirty face and black, unkept hair. He dribbled a worn-out basketball along the terribly cracked blacktop that was once part of a public court. The metal poles at either end still stood tall, but they were rusted and missing their hoops. One still had two-thirds of a backboard, graffitied with profanities and male genitalia. Tall, thick grass and loose trash from the wind covered much of the surrounding lot.

In a tank top, knee-high socks with stripes, and torn sneakers, the boy bobbed his head to mariachi music blaring from a rundown three-story apartment building across the street. He lifted his arm high to spike each bounce, trying to match his dribble with the song's proud guitar riff and trumpets. The under-inflated ball made it difficult. When he lifted his dark face to meet the above sound of a bird, his face tightened from the sun's glare. His bruised, swollen eye watered.

A shirtless elderly man with a tattoo on his dark shoulder, and a wide-brimmed straw hat, rode down the adjoining street on a bicycle. Its frame was rusted and its brakes screeched when he reached the adjacent intersection. The driver of a pale blue, early '60s El Camino stopped at a red *alto* sign, and waved him through. The sparkle of the driver's gold watch caught the boy's eye.

The boy stopped dribbling, holding the ball with both hands as he gazed at the gleam of the car's finish and its whitewall tires. When the driver turned right, the boy ran over to a patch of grass at the edge of the court. He pulled from it a well-used canvas backpack, jamming his hand inside and pulling out a gym whistle with half of a neck-strap. He shoved the whistle in his mouth and blew into it as hard as he could, arching his back and rising to the tips of his toes.

His eyes honed in on an open window on the top floor of the brick apartment building, where drying bedsheets hung on a line attached to the next window over. He squeezed the basketball into his backpack and nearly blew into the whistle again, when a younger boy with wavy dark hair appeared in the window. The boy on the court waved his arms in the air, pointing in the direction of the El Camino. The boy in the window had one arm in a sling, but it didn't seem to slow him down. He reached down and pulled a phone handset up to the side of his face. It looked huge in his hand, as did the coiled cord that stretched around his chest like a snake. He dialed a number.

The boy on the court threw his backpack over his shoulders and ran across the grass, leaping over a discarded planter and around a leaking fire hydrant on the sidewalk. He crossed the street and ran to the opposite end of the apartment building. On its wall was a large, colorful mural of a dog with big pointy ears and flowers on top of its head.

As he passed over the dirty narrow yard, a hairdryer blew from an open ground floor window. It competed with the sound of the mariachi music. The boy skidded to a halt when he reached the front of the building, carefully peering around its corner.

The man in the El Camino had parked along the street in front and had already stepped out of his vehicle. Sporting sunglasses with gold frames below dark, slicked-back hair, he took a moment to rub a blemish off the car's hood with the palm of his hand. A toothpick pointed down from his mouth as he scrutinized his work closely.

The man appeared in his late twenties or early thirties, a good-looking guy with a strong jawline, broad shoulders, and a thin waist. He wore a white long-sleeved shirt with a collar; the top three buttons detached. Cowboy boots poked out from under his brown jeans topped with a belt buckle so large it looked like some boxer's championship prize.

The boy had never seen him before, but he was sure it was the right guy. The car matched the description he'd been given to a T.

The man walked with some swagger up to the front door, holding it open for a middle-aged woman with boxes in her hands as she exited. She thanked him. He nodded in return before entering. The boy heard him start his way up the stairs before the door closed shut behind him.

The boy stayed put for ten minutes until a white pickup truck pulled up behind the El Camino. Three men stepped out, each wearing jackets that didn't match the weather. One of the men was older, probably in his fifties. He was bald and stout with a strong mustache and rough skin. The other two could have been in their teens, full heads of dark hair, sharing a fierce narrowness in their eyes.

The boy ran up to the men. The bald one glanced up and down the street before reaching into his back pocket and pulling out an envelope. He handed it to the boy and slapped him on the back before he and his partners made their way to the front door. The boy bent the envelope in half and shoved it into his front pocket. He watched the men enter and work their way up the first flight of stairs before the door closed. He took a few steps back, peering up at the flat roof of the building.

He waited nearly a minute but no one appeared. He cupped his hand to his mouth. "Alvar!" he said in a loud whisper.

Suddenly, there was a loud crash from above. Men shouted. A woman screamed. The boy's heart raced, his body shaking and his eyes wide as he stared intently at the roof. "Alvar!"

Another scream was followed by the loud pop of a gun. Three more pops came soon after.

The mariachi music went dead. An overweight man with his daughter in his arm barreled out through the door. Other tenants followed, panicked and confused—an old man, a teenager, a woman in a towel. Alvar wasn't among them.

The boy breathed hard. He swung his head to the street, watching his neighbors flee in different directions. He knew none would return to help. They were too scared.

With another pop of a gun, he clenched his teeth and ran inside. His backpack bounced off another tenant as he jogged up the stairs, skipping every other step. When he reached the third floor and entered the hallway, he gasped at the sight of one of the men from the truck lying motionless in a pool of his own blood. His head was pointed right toward the boy, wide eyes glaring through him. Part of his skull had been blown off, a gap in his hair leaving some brain exposed.

A man yelled from the open apartment door next to the body. Another man yelled back. One was threatening. The other was pleading. A woman screamed and whimpered.

In the dead man's hand was a silver revolver. The boy pulled off his backpack and set it against the wall. He quietly made his way forward, as the shouting and screaming continued inside. Two men. One woman.

The boy knelt beside the dead man, avoiding looking at his face a second time as he pried the gun from his warm fingers. He looked the weapon over before gripping it the way he'd once been taught. He peeked inside the doorway. There he saw the other young man from the truck. He was lying facedown on the orange shag carpet. Blood spattered the short wall beside him, along with a bullet hole that had torn off part of the drywall. Across the room was the open window he'd seen his younger brother standing in from the court. The phone on the stand below the windowsill had been knocked over. Its off-hook tone began screeching.

The boy swallowed and entered carefully as another tenant raced down the hallway behind him. He held his breath through a stench of cigarettes as he stepped over the man's body. The shouting belted back and forth, growing more aggressive. It was coming from the master bedroom to his left.

"Drop it!" repeated a man in Spanish.

"You drop yours or she's dead!" yelled another man in the same language.

Furniture in the small living room had been knocked over. A lamp and end table had been smashed in a scuffle. A picture had been knocked from its wall.

The boy made his way past a grimy kitchenette with a sink overflowing with pots, pans, and dishes. A half dozen bottles of booze and a large ashtray sat on the counter beside it. Children's crayon drawings hung from the dented door of an under-sized fridge.

On the other side of the narrow hallway was a small room, dark from pillows shoved in the window frame. All that could be seen inside it from the hallway light was part of a bunk bed, though its frame and thin mattresses more resembled military cots.

When the boy reached the master bedroom with its bright pink walls and white dressers, he peeked through the doorway. Inside, his mother's terrified eyes met his. The slender woman was being held from behind by the bald man, his thick arm around her throat and his pistol pointed at the temple of her head.

"No! Run!" she screamed at her son in Spanish, tears pouring.

Her long bleached-blonde hair covered half of her thin face. She was clad in white lace lingerie that came up past her hips, revealing long bronze legs that shook with fear. Other, more colorful nightwear of various styles hung on hangers in the closet beside her, its lattice door caved in.

When the bald man saw the boy, his eyes shot wide. The boy held his breath and stepped into the room, gun pointed at him.

"No!" came another man's voice to his right. The boy twisted his head to meet it. There he saw the driver of the El Camino with a gun in his hand, it too pointed at the bald man. He was dressed only in black underwear briefs and had backed himself into the corner of the room, on the other side of the bed, with his body in front of Alvar's . . . protecting him.

"Kid, I'm a police officer!" he shouted, keeping his eyes on the bald man. "You need to leave right now! Go to another apartment and call the police!"

"Go!" his mother screamed. Her captor yanked back on her throat before she could say more.

The boy hadn't known the man was a police officer. He'd assumed it had been about drugs—his mom turning tricks for a dealer and the cartel wanting to take out a rival. They said when they'd approached him a week earlier on the court that his brother wouldn't be harmed when it went down. But things had gone south. The cop had fought back. He'd taken out two of the men, and the third was now leveraging his mother's life.

Tears ran down his mother's face, dark makeup streaming with it. Her eyes pleaded with her oldest son to leave. The cop shouted at him again, demanding the same. Alvar glared up at his big brother, his charcoal-colored eyes desperate.

The boy's face tightened. His nostrils flared as he straightened his arm, training his focus on the man who held his mother. He suddenly swung his arm to the right and fired. The policeman's head imploded. Blood sprayed through the air.

The mom howled. Her captor, seemingly just as shocked, dropped his arm from her neck. She collapsed to her bare knees while he stared in disbelief.

The policeman, blood flowing from his skull, gradually toppled forward. The gun fell from his hand. His chest and face hit the carpet.

Alvar's face was covered with the policeman's blood—everything but his dark eyes that mirrored his brother's gaze.

The bald man's mouth remained open. His eyes shifted between the two boys and their mother, who sobbed on the floor with her hair dangling in front of her face. The boy walked up to Alvar and grabbed him by his slung shoulder. He pulled him up and out of the corner. Alvar cringed and whipped his arm free. He leaned forward to grab something from the floor with his good hand.

"Why?" the mom screamed, pulling her wet face up from the carpet. Her eyes washed over her oldest son's face without a hint of familiarity, as if she were suddenly staring at a complete stranger. "How could . . . how could you . . ."

"How could *you?*" he said, eyes expressionless. His voice had taken on an eerie depth.

A loud pop echoed off the walls.

"God!" shouted the bald man, stumbling backwards into the wall behind him. His gun fell from his grip. His eyes were as wide as his mouth.

The mother no longer cried. She lay on her side, her half-clothed body curled in nearly a fetal position. Blood oozed from under her bright hair. Alvar stood above her with the policeman's gun drawn straight. Smoke rose from the weapon's barrel as he glared down at her from behind his crimson mask.

The bald man's head shifted back and forth between the two boys, eyes blinking.

Ignoring him, Alvar turned to his older brother, who set his pistol on the bed and jammed his hand into his pocket. He pulled out the envelope. He opened it and flipped through the bills inside, dividing the sum in half. He handed Alvar his cut—restitution for hardships and abuse a ten-year-old shouldn't know.

The bald man launched forward and retrieved his gun from the floor. He nervously switched his aim between the two boys. His face had gone pale and his shirt was soaked with the mother's blood.

Distant sirens made their way out of the background.

The older brother lifted his eyes to the man. "You're taking us with you."

Chapter 2

"**M**ove it or lose it, buddy!" the stocky man with short, dark hair and a round face yelled out his window. He used a deeper, more exaggerated voice than his natural one, as if he were enacting a scene from a movie. His meaty hand laid on the horn. "We've got places to go . . . people to meet!"

"Easy, Dusty" a short, thin man advised from the passenger seat. Bald up top with trim hair on the sides, he shook his head in irritation. His eyes averted upward as he rubbed his knuckles along his scalp. "It's a crosswalk, and you took us right into a school zone."

Dusty folded his lower lip into a pout. "It was an accident, Chief."

"I know. And for the twentieth time, we're not in Winston anymore. We're in Vegas, so no more of this 'Chief Lumbergh' stuff. I'm just Gary."

A man's tattooed arm extended from the driver's side window of the '70s model black Camaro idling in front of them. His forearm went vertical, as did his middle finger. A reply to Dusty's horn.

Dusty winced. "Well, that was uncalled for, especially in front of the school kids." He turned to Lumbergh. "Hey, can you arrest him for that?"

"No."

"Write him a ticket?"

"No."

Dusty nodded. A few seconds floated by. He scratched his pencil-thin mustache with his finger. "Maybe the issuing of a stern warning or something?"

"God," Lumbergh moaned, his shoulders slumping. "You know what, Dusty? It's hot, and it's been a very long trip. Do you think we could just hold off on the talking until we get to the hotel? I just want a shower and a nap before—"

"Hey, check out this old guy," Dusty interrupted, pointing his finger through the dirty, insect-riddled windshield of the '94 Oldsmobile Cutlass Cruiser.

An elderly man with glasses, a baseball cap, and a wrinkled red face came into view. He slowly made his way across the street in front of them. Holding a Stop sign in one hand, he smiled as he motioned a sea of elementary aged students over from the sidewalk. Some of the kids wore backpacks. Others carried lunch pails.

Lumbergh sighed. "This is going to take a while."

"I thought we weren't talking," said Dusty.

Lumbergh's head dropped forward.

Dusty leaned forward with him, turning his body and twisting his head to more closely assess the expression on Lumbergh's face. His foot slipped off the brake and the car sprung forward.

"Dusty!" shouted Lumbergh, eyes wide as the back of the Camaro grew larger.

Dusty slammed on the brakes. A loud thud from the back seat rattled the entire vehicle.

"Fuck!" came a gravelly voice from behind them. "Hell's going on?"

Sean's head rose from the rear of the car, eyes blinking

and face stretched in annoyance. He'd begun to stir from all the noise up front, but the sudden stop had jarred him wide awake. His narrow eyes shifted between Dusty and Lumbergh.

"Sorry," said Dusty.

Lumbergh glared at Sean, his wide eyes and scowl telling a silent story of the aggravation he'd been put through while Sean was napping.

Sean grunted and took a breath, turning to Dusty. "It's fine," he said, stretching his broad back to a pop.

The rear of the vehicle wasn't built for comfort, especially not for a man of Sean's size. At six-five and close to 250 pounds, the last few hours had been a pretty rough rest. Still, rubbing his eyes with his large fists, he couldn't help but be amused by his brother-in-law's undeterred irritation with the driver. When Lumbergh shook his head, a chuckle escaped Sean's lips.

"Did you get any sleep?" asked Lumbergh.

"Yeah," said Sean. "No thanks to you two old ladies bickering back and forth. We almost there?"

Dusty erupted into obnoxious laughter, causing Lumbergh to jump in his seat. "Old ladies . . ." he snorted, nostrils flaring above multiple chins.

Lumbergh rolled his eyes and glared at Sean.

"He grows on you," Sean mouthed to Lumbergh, offering a wink. He glanced in the rearview mirror, meeting his own hazel eyes and short, dark hair matted down from his nap.

"It's too hot for this shit," mumbled Lumbergh, glancing back at the air-conditioning dial before returning his attention to Sean.

Unlike Dusty and Sean, who wore T-shirts and shorts, Lumbergh was in a shirt with a collar and khakis, a decision he was regretting.

Dusty loudly cleared his throat. In an artificially deep voice, he began to sing Jim Croce's "Time in a Bottle."

Lumbergh sighed. "You really owe me," he mouthed to Sean.

Sean's face straightened. "Like hell I do," he said aloud, breaking their discretion.

"What?" asked Dusty, bailing out of the song. He edged the car a few inches forward before locking the brakes again.

"Don't worry about it," said Sean before returning to Lumbergh. "Hey, I'm paying for your hotel. I don't owe you anything."

"What are you talking about?" Lumbergh asked.

"I'm a Winston taxpayer, aren't I? Isn't that who's picking up the tab for your little PD ass-kiss convention?"

Lumbergh let some air escape his mouth, shook his head, and returned his back to Sean. "Again . . . it's a national law enforcement convention for chiefs of police," he said matter-of-factly. "It's a learning and instructional opportunity that—"

Sean interrupted him with a blaring kissing noise, delivered through his puckered lips. The gesture drew another loud laugh from Dusty.

"Anyway," Lumbergh continued once the unpleasant sound fizzled. He took a breath. "You, personally, are probably only paying for about ten cents of it. I saved the people of Winston a heck of a lot of money by catching a ride out here with you two instead of flying."

"A simple 'thank you' would have worked," Sean said, his lips curled.

A few seconds floated by before a chuckle begrudgingly fell from Lumbergh's mouth. "Fine. *Thank you.*"

"You're welcome," said Sean, grinning. "And don't tell me you aren't looking forward to helping us celebrate Dusty's last days as a single man." He leaned forward and slapped the driver on the shoulder. "A lot of women are gonna be heartbroken once this guy's finally off the market."

All three men grinned, exchanging glances. It was the first real levity they'd shared since a few miles outside of Green River, Utah. Dusty's performative, overbearing personality had already been wearing thin on Lumbergh by then, but when the car blew a tire and it was discovered that the spare had been removed from under the rear floorboard to make room for party supplies that Dusty used for his job, Lumbergh had about lost it. Luckily, hitchhiking with an armful of balloon animals evoked either enough sympathy or curiosity for a family to pull over, and take the least threatening-looking of the three—Lumbergh—to a mechanic's shop in Green River.

The tension didn't ease, however, when Dusty gave Lumbergh grief after not passing on his business card to the family. Sean, to the surprise of both Dusty and Lumbergh, had taken the incident in relative stride. He'd learned a lot in recent months about not sweating the small stuff and turning over his life stresses to a higher power. He'd also learned about making amends with those he'd hurt in the past—a long list of individuals that included the two men he was traveling with. The lessons had come from a multistep program he'd enrolled in, at the urging of his family, to help deal with his alcoholism following a relapse that had begun a year earlier. He had remained committed to the cause, making the time to attend meetings when he wasn't taking on contract security work.

Sean could tell the program was genuinely helping. He'd managed, after all, to keep his cool in an enclosed space for nearly seven hundred miles. The old Sean Coleman would have tossed Dusty out of the car before they'd ever reached Grand Junction.

But there were times when his patience was still tested, and a second wave of students crossing the street ahead, without a single car being let through first, was starting to feel like one of those tests.

"What's the holdup here?" asked Sean, lowering his head and peering through the windshield.

"Just . . . school zone chaos," answered Lumbergh. "We came the wrong way at the wrong time."

Sean's eyes narrowed. A sour feeling tugged at his gut. "Wait," he said, leaning farther forward. "Where are we?"

Dusty turned to Sean, squinting. "Las Vegas," he said.

"No shit, Magellan," Sean said, drawing Lumbergh's attention back. "I'm sorry," he immediately added, tempering his tone. "I'm asking what road we're on."

"Oh, uh," Dusty began before Lumbergh cut him off.

"Wilmington. What does it matter?"

Sean's stomach clenched. His eyes shot wide and his pulse ticked up. "Are you shitting me?" His head swiveled between windows. His eyes shifted back to Dusty. "Did you come this way on purpose, asshole?"

Dusty's face tightened in confusion.

"Sorry," Sean caught himself again. "You're not an asshole, but . . ."

Sean let his remark dangle, gazing out the side window at a single-story brick building across the street. A large American flag hung high in front of it. Scores of students walked in every direction in the grassy area below a raised sign that read, "Patricia Bell Elementary."

"Wait, you *are* an asshole!" Sean shouted at the back of Dusty's head. "What, do you think this is some kind of joke?"

"I don't know what you mean," said Dusty.

"What's going on, Sean?" asked Lumbergh.

Outside, there was lots of smiling and laughter—kids excited about the start of their weekend. Some ran up to parents and shared hugs.

It was a sharp contrast from the tone inside the car.

"We need to get going," Sean said, out of breath. He turned to the long line of cars idling behind them. "Seriously, Dusty. Why did you come this way?"

"I missed a turn. And I already said I was sorry. Geez."

"Sean!" Lumbergh said with some volume, as if he were trying to wake his brother-in-law from a hypnotic spell. "What's happening? What's the problem?"

Sean felt his arms trembling. "The *problem* is that we're supposed to be at a blackjack table, or yanking on some slots, or doing some *Vegas-y* thing. Not stuck in a damn car in front of a school, in fucking ninety-degree weather."

Sean's eyes slid back and forth across the moving crowd. He wanted to look away—to force his eyes to the floorboard, but he couldn't quite bring himself to. And just as he had about convinced himself that the law of averages wouldn't allow for a face from the past to present itself at that very place and time, it did. And it was a pretty face at that.

Clad in a sleeveless white dress with a coach's whistle around her neck, a woman with glimmering blonde hair and an athletic build waved to a couple of students as they passed by. He knew the woman to be in her mid-thirties, though she still didn't look a day over twenty-five. When she leaned down to talk to a younger child who had approached her, seemingly with a question, the bright smile that formed on her lips stole Sean's breath and slowed down time.

"Whoa!" said Lumbergh, sitting up in his seat, his head now turned in the same direction as Sean's. "Is that . . . is that Lisa?"

Just hearing her name had always brought butterflies

to Sean's stomach, but seeing her in the flesh had left him speechless.

"Ooh! Who's Lisa?" asked Dusty, peering around Lumbergh's shoulder.

Sean and Lumbergh answered at the same time, Sean saying "No one," and Lumbergh saying "His ex-girlfriend."

"Ex-girlfriend?" Dusty shouted, his wide eyes taking up the rearview mirror. "Here? Where?" He leaned to the side, his left hand blindly searching for the automatic window lever.

"Don't worry about it, and don't you open that goddamn window," Sean growled. "Pay attention to the road. As soon as the kids are across, get us to the hotel."

"Is it the Spanish lady?" Dusty asked as Lumbergh's window steadily lowered at his command. "Hey!" he yelled, trying to grab the wrong woman's attention.

In a flash, Sean's arms lunged forward, one large hand going under Dusty's chin while the other pressed against the back of his head. With clenched teeth, he squeezed Dusty's skull as if he were trying to juice it.

Dusty wailed and snorted, his reddening round face shriveled like a prune. His hands left the steering wheel and latched onto Sean's wrists, unable to loosen his assailant's grip.

"Dusty, I've been kicking ass in recovery for almost five months and just drove seven hundred miles with you . . . without incident," Sean said. "Don't fuck it all up now. You wanted your bachelor party in Vegas, and I'm here because you're my friend. Don't repay me by being an asshole." He let a few more seconds tick by before he released Dusty, whipping his hands away.

"God!" Dusty barked, some drool dripping from his lips. He let out a couple of coughs as some color returned to his face.

The crossing guard waited on the last child to cross, waving to her as she passed.

"Sean, it's okay," said Lumbergh, his spread fingers facing Sean to urge calm. "She didn't see you. Everything's fine. There's no sense in getting any more worked up. We're going to go out and have some fun tonight, and forget everything else."

"Hundreds of thousands of people pass through this city every goddamn day," said Sean, as if he hadn't heard a thing Lumbergh had said. "And this dipshit . . . Sorry, you're not a dipshit, Dusty. But you drove us right up to the one person I wanted to avoid, and shouldn't have had any trouble avoiding. I mean, what are the odds?"

"I don't know," said Lumbergh. "But it's a small world and things like this happen."

"Sounds like *fate* to me," said Dusty, his eyes wide and his face still regaining its color.

"Jesus Christ, Dusty. Shut up!" snapped Lumbergh.

Sean saw Dusty follow up the remark with a wink through the mirror. He answered with a stiff slap to the back of his head.

"Gah!" Dusty moaned, his arm covering up his head.

"Sean," said Lumbergh.

The physical exchange caught the attention of the elderly crossing guard, who stopped on his way back to his post, lowered his head, and gazed through the windshield with a crinkled nose.

"Just get out of the road already," Sean pled, knowing the man couldn't hear him.

The man continued his way back toward the sidewalk, and Sean's head spun to Lisa again. She had just been approached by a young man with dark, perfectly combed hair and a chiseled chin. He wore a bright smile and held the hand of a little blonde-haired girl in a bright red dress who couldn't have been much older than one year.

The man appeared to ask Lisa a question. When she turned to face him, he leaned forward and kissed her directly on the lips.

"Oh God," muttered Lumbergh, his eyes shifting between the two and Sean.

Sean's heart stopped. His mouth dangled open, and he felt for a second as though he was going to vomit. His eyes lowered to the little girl. She had a button nose, pursed lips, and she squinted from the sun in her face. Lisa leaned down and hooked her hands under the girl's arms, lifting her up in the air and planting a kiss on her plump cheek.

"So . . . it's *not* the Spanish lady?" asked Dusty.

When a car horn honked behind them, Lisa and the man swung their heads to the street. Sean's back snapped flat against his seat. His eyes shot forward where there were no longer any pedestrians in front of the car.

"Go!" he demanded.

"Dusty, get going!" Lumbergh shouted.

"Okey dokey," Dusty said calmly, turning his attention to the road and pressing on the gas.

The car lunged forward and Sean sank deeper into his seat. His face was pale and he was having trouble catching his breath.

"So . . . when did you and her . . ." Dusty began.

"Nope," said Lumbergh. "Not another word. Just get us to the hotel."

Chapter 3

Sean hadn't uttered a word for the last two hours, and barely remembered taking a shower in his room or getting dressed. Now clad in beige Dockers and a short-sleeved aloha shirt his sister had found on clearance somewhere, he sat slumped forward in a worn leather chair in the small hotel lobby. There, he forced deep controlled breaths through his lungs.

His eyes were fixed to the tips of his new casual dress shoes; they'd also been picked out by his sister. Suede, light brown in color, and a bit wimpy looking in Sean's view . . . but he'd humored his sister.

Dozens of thoughts had traveled through his mind since the moment they'd left the school. They spawned questions and inconsistencies he continued to struggle with as the world moved around him. His gaze slid back and forth from the elevators across from him to a small clock and a short row of payphones along the adjacent wall. Clamor from nearby gamblers and slot machines shared the smoke-filled air, as a mixture of mostly college kids and senior citizens strolled by in opposite directions along the granite floor.

There was a young family at the front desk. A tall dad, a short and pretty mom, and two little kids—a boy and a girl. The children were arguing and wrestling around a bit until the mother got after them. Sean watched them for a while before his gaze drifted to a small, round end table beside him, where half a glass of what looked like whiskey sat. Someone had abandoned it there; most of its ice had melted. He noticed his knee shaking a bit before he drew his focus back to the payphones. Arching his back, he dug his fingers into his pocket and searched for change.

"702 . . . 518," he muttered, trying to recall a number he used to know by heart. "09 . . . " He almost had it.

"You got down here fast," came a man's voice.

Sean turned and saw Lumbergh standing just a few feet away, arms folded in front of him. His mouth worked a wad of gum.

"Hell'd you come from?" Sean asked.

"I took the stairs. The elevators were taking too long."

"Yeah, they're slow as hell."

Lumbergh had changed polo shirts. His new one was lime green. Beneath it were beige pants and brown wing tip shoes. The pants, more neatly pressed than Sean's, looked familiar.

"Did Diana get those on clearance?" Sean asked, lowering his gaze.

Lumbergh's eyes shifted between Sean's pants and his, the top of his head reflecting some light from the chandelier above. "They're the same, aren't they?"

Sean smirked, aware of his sister's affinity for sales. "Must have been one hell of a discount. Those shoes don't look cheap though. What are those?"

Lumbergh's eyes narrowed, seemingly unsure if Sean was making fun of him. "Oxfords," he said tepidly.

Sean nodded, his eyes sliding up and down his brother-in-law. "They make you look taller. Is that why you bought them?"

Now Lumbergh *knew* he was being made fun of. A subtle grin formed on his lips. "That may have had something to do with it," he said, shaking his head. "But they also have a casualness about them that I like."

Lumbergh was a short man—around five-six. He'd always been thin, but he'd formed a noticeable gut since his daughter Ashley was born. Diana used to refer to it as "sympathy weight"—a reference to the pounds she'd gained during her pregnancy. It wasn't the only change in Lumbergh's appearance in recent months. He'd also recently shaved his head, finally accepting his baldness. For years, his hair up top was so thin that it was virtually transparent under certain light. He'd never seemed to mind, but something had compelled him to take the plunge and succumb to the terms of the genetic hand he'd been dealt. Sean was still getting used to the new look, often finding himself scrutinizing a subtle bump at the top of Lumbergh's scalp.

"Why did you come down so early?" Lumbergh asked. "We don't have to head out for a bit yet. I figured you'd catch up on some more sleep."

Seconds slogged by before Sean answered. "It was too quiet up there. I needed a distraction."

Lumbergh nodded. "After the . . ."

Sean jumped in. "Yeah, after the shit show back there at the school."

Lumbergh's eyes slid to the drink on the table next to Sean. His face tightened.

"Don't worry, Gary. It's not mine. That's not the kind of distraction I meant. Just needed some noise. To do some people-watching and clear my head."

"All right," Lumbergh said, accepting the answer.

"So, why are *you* down here?" asked Sean. "You were more tired than I was."

"Well, I . . ." he hesitated, searching for the right words.

"You wanted to check on me, didn't you? Probably pounded on my door for a couple of minutes before figuring out I'd left. Huh?"

Lumbergh said nothing, biting down on his lip.

Sean continued. "Hey, I appreciate the thought, Gary, but there was no need. There's not even a minibar in the room. I made sure of that when I booked it."

Lumbergh nodded. "Why don't we do some walking around?" he said. He nudged his shoulder toward the casino. "Play a few slots, maybe a couple hands of blackjack. I know you think gambling's for idiots, but—"

"Sure." Sean shrugged. "Why the hell not?" He leaned forward, placed his hands on his knees, and pulled himself to his feet, grunting from the effort. "Lead the way."

The two left the lobby and crossed onto the thin, checkered carpet of the Dusty Nickel. It was an older hotel and casino, a couple blocks off Fremont Street in the downtown area some people referred to as "Old Vegas". Dusty had picked the lodging based on nothing other than the fact that it shared his name.

Slot machines flashed and whistled. Dealers in vests and bow ties stood over half-full tables. Women in cocktail outfits passed by with drinks on small trays. A cigarette haze hung in the air.

Sean dug his wallet out of his back pocket and pulled out a couple of singles.

"You serious?" asked Lumbergh.

"What?" Sean asked, returning his wallet to his pocket.

"Two dollars?"

"Yeah, those are nickel slots," he said, pointing his jaw toward a cluster of sparkling machines in the corner. "That's like . . . what, forty games?"

Lumbergh's brows angled inward.

"Oh please, Gary," said Sean. "You really think I need a second addiction?"

"You're too much of a tightwad for that to ever happen," quipped Lumbergh.

"That's true. Not all of us have high-paying government jobs," joked Sean. "Rent-a-cop security guards like me can't help but be a bit stingy."

"Except for when it counts," added Lumbergh with a wink, bouncing his knuckles off Sean's shoulder.

Lumbergh glanced around the room until his eyes stopped on a semicircular table in the opposite direction. Behind it, a middle-aged dealer with big, frizzy hair dealt a player a hand. She glanced at the other players as they considered their cards.

Lumbergh reached for his own wallet. "I'm going to try my luck over there. When you're done flushing your change down those machines, why don't you come on over?"

"High roller," remarked Sean.

"It's a five-dollar table, Sean," said Gary.

"Too rich for my blood. I can't expense stuff to the city like you."

Lumbergh sighed. "I'm not going to expense my gambling . . ." He stopped when he noticed the curl in Sean's lips. He shook his head. "Good luck."

"You too."

The men went their separate directions and Sean made his way over to the row of slots. An elderly bald man with a small bandage on his head and droopy eyes was collecting his winnings from a machine in the corner. Once he slowly trucked off, plastic coin cup in hand, Sean took his spot, plopping himself down in the still-warm chair.

Sean glared at the reels for a moment before sliding his first dollar into the bill insert, which swallowed it quickly. He sighed and tapped a button. Fruit and sevens spun loudly until they came to a mismatched halt. He hit the button again and let his eyes wander as the reels spun.

Across the room, Lumbergh sat at the blackjack table, his face comically tense and his eyes wide as he leaned forward clutching his cards. Lumbergh was a confident man when it came to just about everything else, but his gambling face made him look about as relaxed as a suicide bomber. The elderly woman in a loud blouse next to him pinched a cigarette between her shaky fingers. She eyed the dealer's movements, her smile displaying some missing teeth when the cards were turned over. Lumbergh bit his lip and shook his head in disappointment as the dealer collected his hand.

Sean plugged away at his machine, winning a few spins here and there but mostly losing. It was about what he'd expected, but he didn't care. His only disappointment was that the activity hadn't cleared his mind. He found himself thinking about the time he'd taken Lisa up to Lakeland on one of her trips out to Colorado.

The old gambling town in the mountains north of Winston was a far cry from the Vegas spectacle she was used to, but she seemed to appreciate it for that very reason. She found it quaint and with character, from the antique slots to a decades-old taffy shop, to an old bookstore that also sold music. Perhaps it was the same type of simplicity that had attracted her to Sean, at least once upon a time.

He loved watching her smile that day—the liveliness and curiosity in her bright blue eyes, especially when they aligned with his. They held a beauty that lifted his spirit high, but also stoked a sense of unworthiness in his gut. At times, things seemed so right and real that he felt obligated to convince himself that they weren't. After all, who was someone like *Sean Coleman* to find himself the beneficiary of such good fortune . . . after spending so many years of his life disappointing and hurting others—including those who loved him.

Sean couldn't shake the truth that they had only found each other through a traumatic series of events. It was an emotional bond that felt like it came with a looming expiration date, and likely would have even if Sean had been a better person. Still, he seemed to feel obligated at times to speed up the process.

That day in Lakeland was no exception. Lisa had pled with him to dress up like a cowboy for an Old West photo shoot of the two of them. In retrospect, it would have been a mild sacrifice—fifteen minutes of embarrassment for someone he cared about. Instead, he dug in his heels, deeming such a concession to be emasculating and a waste of money. No matter how much pressure she put on him— playful at first, but later more determined—he wouldn't budge. It was a stupid thing to get into an argument over, but they did, and his stubbornness ended an otherwise special day on a sour note. Other days and nights had ended similarly.

The memories played like a quick slideshow of failures through Sean's mind as he reached the end of his credit on the slot machine.

So far, Sean's first trip to Vegas had been a bust. The buildings and glitz on their way in—even in the daytime— had been impressive, but the city's allure wasn't what it was cracked up to be . . . at least not in comparison with the old 1970s show, *Vegas*, starring Robert Urich. Perhaps the nightlife would change his mind, but he was worried his psyche would continue to play the spoiler.

When he lifted his head, he saw Lumbergh on his way over, his pace slow, suggesting that he, too, was reeling from defeat.

"You lasted longer than I did," he said, raising his gaze up from the carpet.

Sean nodded. "How old did she look to you?"

Lumbergh's eyes narrowed. "The lady at the table? Hard to say."

"No, the girl. Back at the school."

Lumbergh's face loosened after a couple of seconds. "Sean . . ." he began, shaking his head. "There's just no way."

"That's what I keep telling myself, Gary. And I'm sure it has to be the case, but—"

"But nothing."

"No, but *something*. Lisa and I split up at the end of 2001, almost two years ago."

"Yeah. So?"

"How old do you think that girl is? Because if she's at least fourteen months, just add on an extra nine and the math works out."

"She wasn't that old, Sean."

"You sure about that? I mean, she was old enough to be standing and walking."

Lumbergh lifted his hands, his palms facing Sean to keep the peace. "Listen, you're getting *way* ahead of yourself. We don't even know if that girl belonged to Lisa."

"Do *you* kiss any little girls besides your daughter, Gary? And then, of course, she made out with the father."

"There!" said Lumbergh, snapping his finger. "Right there. Rewind that and listen to what you just said. The little girl's *father. He's* the father, Sean, not you."

Sean's nostrils flared. He let his eyes fall off Lumbergh as he took in a couple of deep breaths. "Are you saying she was cheating on me with him, then?"

"What?" Lumbergh said, his face recoiling. "No . . . God, no. I'm saying—again—that the girl's too young to be yours. You understand that, right?"

Sean glared at Lumbergh for a moment before the two realized that a half dozen spectators had stopped within earshot and were listening to their exchange. This included a drink waitress in fishnets and the old man whose machine Sean had taken over. The man's mouth dangled open as he waited for Sean's response.

Sean grunted and stood up. "Come on," he said to Lumbergh, patting his shoulder.

Sean led the way toward a gold-colored revolving door at the side of the casino, whisking his way past a young couple shouting at a roulette wheel. He glanced at a casino guard in a suit and tie who hovered beside the door. He leered over his shoulder to check if any of the eavesdroppers had followed them. When he saw that none had, he stopped short of the door and motioned Lumbergh over to the empty wall beside it.

"Okay," Sean began. "I'm not trying to be an asshole and ruin this trip, and I get what you're saying. And like you said, I'm probably dead wrong. But—"

Lumbergh jumped in. "But you unexpectedly saw Lisa for the first time in two years, and a lot of emotions came flooding back at once. It's perfectly normal to have some trouble processing it."

Sean glared at him. "Well, thanks, Dr. Ruth. But that's not what I was going to say. I was going to say that she wasn't wearing a ring."

Lumbergh's face twisted in confusion. "Lisa?"

"No, the old lady at your blackjack table. Of course Lisa."

Lumbergh rolled his eyes. "So, what are you saying?"

Sean bit his lip. "I don't know what the hell I'm saying." He gazed across the room emptily before returning his attention to Lumbergh. "I mean, they're a family of some kind. That's obvious. But Lisa would be wearing a ring if they were married. Trust me on this. She's big on commitment. She had a hard enough time just taking off Kyle's ring."

"Her ex-husband."

"Yeah, her *dead* ex-husband. The same guy who'd filled her head with bullshit the entire time they were married. The same guy who'd been cheating on her with Vincenzo Moretti's wife, which is *why* he's her dead ex-husband."

Sean noticed the security guard twist his head toward them. The guy was probably in his fifties—stocky with slicked back hair that was dyed black. Old school. He glared at them for a moment through tight eyes before tugging his focus back to the broader room.

"You probably don't want to be saying that name too loudly around here," said Lumbergh, lowering his voice.

"Why?" Sean asked. "He's behind bars."

"Moretti was a big deal in this town. Owned a lot of businesses. Multiple casinos. Hell, maybe even *this* one."

"So?"

"So . . . Former associates of his might not hold a warm view of two of the guys who helped put him behind those bars. Moretti was a crime lord. A lot of people here probably lost a hell of a lot of money when he went down."

"Whatever," Sean said, dismissing Lumbergh's concern. "What I'm saying is that if the guy at the school were the girl's father, Lisa would be married to him."

"That's a hell of a lot of speculation based on two people kissing," said Lumbergh, crossing his arms in front of his chest. "And think about what you're saying. If she would have married the father of her child, and you haven't heard from her in two years, doesn't that pretty much prove *you're* not the father?"

Sean stared at Lumbergh, letting his brother-in-law's words sink in.

Lumbergh leaned forward and put his hand on Sean's shoulder. "Listen. I get it," he said in a softer tone. "That scene back there was a lot to take. Dusty didn't help matters. But whatever the situation is between those people, that little girl isn't yours."

After a moment, Sean found himself nodding. Lumbergh was making too much sense to prolong the argument.

"So, why don't you just try your best to forget about it," Lumbergh added. "Let's get Dusty and get to the show. We'll grab a quick bite to eat over there before it starts."

Sean scoffed and shook his head. "Yeah, the show."

Lumbergh snickered, shrugging his shoulders.

"Of all of the entertainment choices in this town, he goes with that one," Sean moaned.

"Well, it was his call. Groom's privilege."

"Which is one of life's great miracles in itself. His fiancée's not even half bad looking from the pictures I've seen. No antlers sticking out of her head or anything."

Lumbergh chuckled. "Just be glad he didn't choose something at Circus Circus."

"Oh God," said Sean. "He would have handed someone his resume."

Lumbergh smiled, seemingly relieved that the tone and topic of the conversation had changed in a positive direction. "Let's go get him and get some food."

"Fine."

The two men made their way back through the casino toward the lobby.

"It's a good thing you're doing here," said Lumbergh. "Being a good friend and coming out here with him. It doesn't sound like he has many."

"Many what?"

"Friends."

Sean nodded, thinking back to when he and Dusty had first met in South Carolina a little over a year earlier. Sean had flown out to collect the body of his dead uncle, who he'd thought, prior to his death, had dated Dusty's mother. It ended up being a case of a mistaken relationship, not realized until after the two had begrudgingly spent a couple of days together—two very long days.

Lumbergh's *Circus Circus* joke had been on target, as Dusty was a professional clown—a birthday clown to be exact. Parents hired him for their children's parties where he'd make balloon animals, tell jokes, and perform tricks. Dusty took the job seriously—often too seriously. He had a habit of shifting into some obscure character in the middle of casual conversations and remaining in that character out of some artistic commitment to the craft. It used to drive Sean nuts and still did at times. Sean sometimes wondered how he made it through those two days in South Carolina without putting his fist through Dusty's teeth.

But Dusty had become a real friend, staying in frequent contact and checking in on Sean's progress during his rehab. It meant a lot to Sean, and like Dusty, Sean didn't have many friends to spare.

He was genuinely happy Dusty had found someone—a waitress from a seafood joint in Pawleys Island. Sean had never met her but felt like he'd come to know her from Dusty's descriptions. The two had only been an item for three months prior to Dusty popping the question. Sean hoped it would work out. If she'd managed to put up with his bullshit that long, perhaps it was meant to be.

Destiny. The word had been bouncing off the walls of Sean's head since the moment Dusty had used it back at the school. Dusty was just being obnoxious at the time, but he'd had a point. What were the odds of the three of them missing an exit in a faraway city, coming upon Lisa's school, and doing so at the precise time she was standing outside it? They couldn't have been any better than Sean winning a $1M jackpot on slots that weekend and flying back home in a private jet.

But Lumbergh was right too. Sean's relationship with Lisa was history. Part of his past, not his future. She now had a family, and judging by the smile on her face, she was happy. With Sean, she hadn't been.

Sean and Lumbergh had barely reached the lobby when a set of elevator doors slid open. From between them came a portly man clad in a loud, large-rimmed red cowboy hat and matching suit and boots. Sean winced and lowered his head, about to make a crack to Lumbergh about the getup. That's when he realized it was Dusty who was wearing it.

"Oh Jesus," Sean said loudly, stopping in his tracks. "Are you fucking kidding me?"

Dusty spun toward them, grinning and pointing both index fingers at Sean's chest. He snapped his hands up and down, emulating the firing of western revolvers. "Vegas, baby," he said with a wink and a snapping noise with his tongue.

Lumbergh turned to Sean, cringing as if a bandage were about to be ripped from his skin.

"Nope, we're not doing this," Sean said to Dusty, his jaw

clenched. "When I said to leave that shit at home, I was serious."

Dusty's smile shot to a frown. "You said to leave my *clown* clothes at home."

"That included *rodeo* clown clothes, dumbass," Sean growled. "Sorry, you're not a dumbass, but . . ."

"It's no big deal," said Lumbergh, placing his hand on Sean's shoulder. "There are lots of people around here decked out in crazy outfits."

"Yeah, they're called performers," said Sean.

"*I'm* a performer," Dusty insisted.

"You're an idiot," said Sean. "Sorry," he quickly added, gritting his teeth.

He took his eyes off Dusty and closed them after a moment. The memory of the Old West photo incident with Lisa was still fresh in his mind. Recognizing some correlation between the regrets he had and his current situation, he brought his clenched fists to his sides and forced them open. As if it were the end of a routine, he drew in a deep, calming breath.

"I can't control how others act," Sean whispered to himself. "I can only control how I act." When he opened his eyes two seconds later, he found both men glaring at him with furrowed brows. "Okay," he said, nodding and bringing more air into his lungs. "I'm okay."

Dusty's head receded above his chins, his eyes shifting back and forth between Sean and Lumbergh. "What the hell was that?" he asked, following the question with a boisterous chuckle.

Lumbergh shook his head at Dusty, seemingly worried his bluster would reignite a situation that had been diffused. "Okay!" he said with a surge in his voice, and an eagerness to change the subject. "Let's grab the car and get some dinner."

Sean nodded, taking in another deliberate breath.

"Okay then, partners," Dusty said in a western accent, puffing out his chest. "Let's get some grub." He placed his hands on his belt and led the way toward the glass doors at the entrance, the soles of his red boots clacking along the granite floor.

Lumbergh shook his head and turned to Sean. "Did you learn that in rehab? That was impressive."

"What?"

"That thing you said about not being able to control what others do."

"No, I got it from Diana. I think she heard it from that Dr. Phil guy."

"Hey!" Dusty shouted, spinning back around and pointing. His voice caught the attention of others in the lobby. "Do you know what this feels like?"

"Embarrassment?" said Sean.

"No!" said Dusty, his voice still uncomfortably loud. "It's like that show, *Crime Story*. Do you remember that?"

Sean did. He used to watch the NBC crime show pretty regularly in the '80s, and he hated that he was pretty sure he knew the specific comparison Dusty was about to make.

Dusty affirmed it. "During the opening song when those three cops are walking out of that old Las Vegas casino! Real badasses. Hey, the main guy's even from Chicago like you, Chief Lumbergh!"

"Gary," said Lumbergh.

"Hey, we should walk like those guys!" proposed Dusty.

"No," said Sean.

"Do you remember how that song went?" asked Dusty, head bouncing between Lumbergh and Sean.

"No," said Sean, though he did indeed remember. The song was "Runaway," a popular 1960s tune by Del Shannon.

Dusty remembered as well, puffing out his chest and adding some swagger to his step as the glass doors in front of them slid open. "I wonder . . . I wo-wo-wo-wonder," he loudly sang out in a high-pitched voice.

A couple walking in cocked their heads at the display. Dusty tipped his hat at the woman.

"Don't," Sean told Dusty, lifting his hand to the side of his face. He slid his eyes to Lumbergh, who was covering up as well.

"Why . . . why-why-why-why-why . . ."

Chapter 4

I n the shadows, dressed in black from head to toe, a large, towering man watched through a pair of binoculars from the garden of a neighboring property. The only outside lights behind the ten-foot-high steel gate and the two-story adobe home it protected came from the pool. They cast a calm green projection along the side of the home.

Tucked behind the sprawling trunk of a mesquite tree, he slipped his eyes down to his watch, tapping its side to light up its hands. 3:41 a.m. *He's running late.*

The street out front was filled with expended fireworks, liquor bottles, and other remnants of the weekend celebration. Most of it had come from the home's residents and guests earlier that night, while a couple of armed guards in sunglasses kept a discreet eye on things. When you're a man of Andrés Vargas's stature, you can make whatever mess you want on a public street and, rest assured, city workers will clean it up quietly and thoroughly the next morning without objection.

Inside the fence is where the classier gathering had taken place. Old men in expensive suits with young, hot wives in miniskirts to fluff their egos and demonstrate their wealth. Champaign toasts. Boasts of power and influence.

The faint sound of brushing caught the man's ear. He slid closer in behind the tree, watching the patio. A maid appeared from around the corner, her body outlined by the pool lights.

She wore a dark uniform and had a stocky build. She moved like she was in her sixties, resting her broom against a chair and carefully picking up glasses and bottles from a patio table. She placed them onto a tray.

When the man heard some rustling behind him, he spun around with his pistol ready, a silencer fixed to its muzzle. A man dressed similarly to him, with a similar build and height, approached from behind some bushes. A large canvas bag was draped over his shoulder. The first man relaxed and lowered the pistol. He turned back to the home, allowing the other to move in beside him and set his bag on the ground. Heavy metal objects clinked together inside it.

"Is it done?" the man with the pistol asked in Spanish, keeping his voice low.

The new arrival nodded. "Harder than I thought. Had to take out the rest of the block's phones too." He pushed up a pair of metal-framed glasses on his coarse face.

"Shouldn't be a problem," said the man with the pistol. He cupped his hand to his mouth and emulated a dog's subtle whining. The sound was eerie in its authenticity.

The maid didn't react. She continued filling her tray. Seconds later a man with a ponytail and broad shoulders casually walked up from the shadows beside her, glancing through the bars at the garden on the other side. The men hidden behind the tree stayed perfectly still.

It was one of the guards from earlier. He wore a nice blue suit minus the jacket. A shoulder holster with a pistol was strapped to his torso. The other guard was likely patrolling inside.

The guard outside nodded, acknowledging the maid. She returned the gesture. He walked around toward the front of the house, stepping onto the grass and tracing the fence with his eyes as he made his way to the opposite side. The maid watched him disappear into the darkness beyond some trees. Once he was out of sight, she slid her tray to the center of the table. Glancing up, she hesitated and then briskly walked toward a pedestrian gate at the fence that led out to the street. She looked around cautiously before punching in a code on a keypad at its center. When it chirped, she walked back to the table where she shuffled the tray around some more.

The two men in black left their tree and moved slowly around others toward the front of the property. They knelt down behind a shrub close to the sidewalk, the man with glasses scanning the street for activity and finding none. At the top of the fence, a few feet from the gate, was an automated security camera. It gradually moved from left to right. When it pointed to the east side of the street, about to change directions back the other way, the two men left the shrub and approached the gate. With the twist of a handle, they were inside. They quietly closed the gate behind them.

Lax security. Vargas was a cocky fool to think his competitors to the west were not a serious threat. Then again, until very recently, he may have been right.

The man with the glasses produced his own pistol, and the two dark figures walked past the pool and then the maid. She kept her eyes averted away, and went back to sweeping. The man with the glasses hugged his bag in his left arm, keeping the noise from the contents inside to a minimum. Around back was a brick patio and a well-kept lawn with a three-tier concrete fountain at its center. The splashing water and engines of a couple of air conditioning units helped conceal the noise they made as they walked up to a decorative row of hedges near the back entrance. There, they lowered themselves to avoid the eye of the next security camera.

They waited a good three minutes for the guard to make his way around. They didn't hear his footsteps approaching until just a second before he passed by the hedges. Once outside of the camera's view, the man without the bag shot the guard in the back of the head from ten feet out.

The guard never saw it coming. His body was subsequently dragged behind the bushes and disposed of on some wood mulch that ran along the house.

When the camera pointed left, the two men squeezed through the hedges onto the patio, the man with the glasses lifting the bag up high to get it through. The other twisted the doorknob. It was unlocked, signifying that the maid was two for two. They entered, closing the door behind them and locking it.

Inside was a long, open hallway that led across a marble floor to the front door. The banister of a staircase began beside the entryway, its railing curved inward. Upstairs were the bedrooms. To the right was a darkened living area with sprawling leather furniture and fine art and large family portraits on the walls. They were lit up with individual lamps. Vargas and his pretty wife had two daughters and a son, the most recent portraits placing them in their teens.

When the men heard footsteps down a hallway to the right, behind the back wall of the living area, they exchanged nods. The man with the glasses quickly set down his bag on the floor. It made a clank.

"Alejandra?" came a voice from the hallway. It belonged to a man. The footsteps grew closer.

The man with the glasses quietly holstered his gun and reached into his pocket as he walked toward a potted tree at the edge of the living area. He twisted his wrists and stood beside the tree, a knife with a large blade now clenched in his hand. His partner aimed his gun forward.

The guard emerged, dressed similar to the other but with a beard instead of a ponytail. His gun was holstered and he held a ceramic mug that steamed as he sipped it under the faint glow down the hall. He casually glanced at the back door, probably expecting to see the maid with a tray of glasses. When he was met instead with the outline of a large man, his eyes bulged.

Before he could further react, the man with the glasses lunged forward from the tree, grabbing onto the top of the mug with his right hand to keep it from falling. He swung his left arm above it. The knife went square into the guard's throat, jolting his body. The guard's arms flailed. He made a gurgling noise until his assailant twisted the knife out and let him collapse to the floor. He landed with a thud, arms and legs shaking as the marble on either side of his neck grew increasingly red.

The man who'd killed him casually lifted the mug to his mouth. He sipped some coffee from it and then dumped the rest of it in the tree pot next to him. He disposed of the mug there too.

The man by the door holstered his gun. The other returned to his bag where he knelt down, unzipped it, and reached inside. He moved aside some large bolt cutters and a handsaw, and pulled out a full-sized axe with a wooden handle. He handed it to his partner, and retrieved a second one for himself. They both stood up straight and gazed down the hallway past where the guard lay, eying the staircase.

It wasn't just about housecleaning. It wasn't just about freeing up the territory. It was about restitution. Vargas's wealth had come at their side's expense, and they needed to send a message to others who might think about taking his place. His and his wife's hacked-up bodies strapped to the front gate when the morning street cleanup crew arrived should deliver it.

They'd be sure to take the maid out as well, though less ceremoniously. She'd done what was asked of her for the safe return of her daughter, but she was still a witness. As was her daughter who, unbeknownst to the maid, had been dead for three hours. Vargas's kids would meet the same fate if they woke up before the men left.

The man without glasses turned to the other, their axes held firmly. "Ready, Alvar?" he asked.

Chapter 5

Dusty pulled the car into a parking lot outside of a run-down liquor store that advertised just a three-dollar fee for a space. When he found an open spot, he pumped the gas and then slammed on the brakes about a foot short of its concrete slab.

"Jesus!" Lumbergh shouted.

"Dan Tanna!" Dusty yelled as he raised his arms, evoking the lead character's name from the show, *Vegas*.

"Jesus, you watch that show too?" Sean asked, surprised Dusty had even heard of it.

"Oh, you bet!" said Dusty.

"You guys are like twins," joked Lumbergh.

"Only if he's Danny DeVito," said Sean.

"Vegas was a great show!" continued Dusty. "I like how they use a dollar sign for the *S*'s in Vegas. I used to do the same on my business cards . . . for the *S* in Dusty. But my mom worried it might make people think my services were too expensive though, so I changed it."

The three got out and waited for a break in the busy traffic before making their way across Krueger Drive. Harrah's hotel tower shot up to the sky beside them. On the other side of the street was the Venetian, a relatively new hotel and casino themed after Venice, Italy. It rose up much higher and took up more real estate.

They walked about a half mile past porn peddlers and street beggars to the Mirage casino on South Las Vegas Boulevard. The sun was lowering, casting colossal shadows from the buildings to the west, but the heat was still strong enough to draw sweat from the men—especially Dusty, whose wet hair glistened from under the rim of his hat.

Dusty was dressed too heavily for the temperature, nonetheless he seemed to revel in the attention his outfit was garnishing. Honks and whistles blared from passing cars. Pedestrians grinned in amusement. Even a homeless man with a missing leg and a pet rabbit offered him a low-five from his seat on the sidewalk. Sean hung back a bit, affording himself some plausible deniability from the spectacle. At the same time, he started to find a bit of amusement in it, especially after Dusty began handing out his business cards to random passersby. He even traded marketing materials with a Spanish-speaking man who was pitching female escort services.

"He has no reservations, does he?" Lumbergh muttered to Sean.

"No shame is more like it," Sean answered, shaking his head. "And does he think any of these people, wherever they live, are going to fly him out from South Carolina to put on a birthday show for their kids? He might as well be tossing those cards in the trash."

Sean knew it wasn't purely about ginning up business, however. Dusty just liked bringing smiles to people's faces, and there were worse goals in life.

The pedestrian traffic picked up as they neared the entrance of the casino, where a towering marquee sign rotated through digital images of current and upcoming shows.

"Are you kidding me?" shouted Dusty at one of them,

clenching his fists. "If we would have come a week later, we could have seen Billy Ocean?"

Lumbergh followed his eyes. "No way, Billy Ocean?" he said, echoing Dusty's disappointment.

Sean scowled at the two once he realized they were both sincere.

The sidewalk was cluttered with tourists from all over the world, speaking multiple languages and raising cameras up high to snap shots of the strip—everything from the buildings to the statues and water fountains. Up the street was a large replica of the Eiffel Tower, an elevator rising up through its center; it stood in front of another new hotel.

The volume of the crowd forced the three into a single-file line at the edge of the sidewalk behind Dusty, who was doing a decent job of needling his way forward. That was until he stopped in his tracks, forcing Lumbergh to collide with him and Sean to collide with Lumbergh.

"Jesus," Sean groaned, his new shoes pinching his feet. He quickly backed his pelvis away from Lumbergh.

"Oh my God," gasped Dusty, barely audible over the hundred different conversations that were taking place around them. He jammed his hands into the side pocket of his suit. "Chief, I need you to take my picture. It'll just take a second."

"What?" asked Lumbergh.

Dusty darted forward, in and out of people. Before long, the sidewalk widened into a larger footway. Finally with some breathing room, the three glared at a bronze statue that stood about fifteen feet high behind a short metal fence. Soaring, orchestrated music poured out from speakers behind it.

The statue was composed of three large faces. The top two belonged to men with high cheekbones and long, flowing hair that was trimmed at the sides. The face below was that of a tiger's, its fanged mouth open.

Dusty shoved a disposable camera into Lumbergh's hands and excitedly jogged up to the tiger, whipping his hat from his head and placing it against his chest of his suit. A large grin was plastered on his face as he positioned himself by the tiger.

"Is that Richard Marx?" said Sean. "And who's the other guy? David Bowie?"

Dusty's eyes bulged. His smile vanished. "Are you serious?" he asked defensively, as if Sean had just delivered an insult.

"The guy from Aerosmith then?"

"What? Come on!" Dusty protested, prompting a smirk from Sean, who knew full well who the men on the statue were. "They're just the most successful Las Vegas act in history!" Dusty added.

"He's just messing with you, Dusty," said Lumbergh. He held the camera to his face, closing an eye, and peering through the view finder.

"Say cheesy!" Sean shouted, his hand cupped to his mouth.

"Cheesy!" said Dusty with a big grin, missing Sean's joke.

Lumbergh snapped a couple of shots.

"Wait," Dusty instructed a second later. He lowered his head, hunched to the side and raised his skull up inside the tiger's mouth. "Go!"

Sean shook his head while Lumbergh snapped more pictures. An ocean of laughter suddenly roared out from behind Sean. He turned to see a few dozen tourists of Asian descent smiling from ear to ear as they worked their own cameras to capture the moment. Sean's gaze slid back over to Dusty, who had taken note of the unexpected attention. He reveled in it, keeping his hat pinned to his chest as he took a bow. The action drew another smattering of applause.

"What the hell was that about?" Sean asked Lumbergh as he handed the camera back to Dusty.

"A cultural thing, I guess," answered Lumbergh. "The French loved Jerry Lewis. The Germans, David Hasselhoff. Maybe Dusty has a big career waiting for him in Japan." His tongue slid to the inside of his cheek.

"Maybe," said Sean with a chuckle. "He'd be a perfect fit on one of their game shows."

The three negotiated their way through tourists and under spiraling palm trees to the main entrance of the building. To the right of a large, multitiered fountain and more trees was a flurry of loud taxicabs dropping off and picking up passengers along a curved driveway. Uniformed bellhops carried luggage to and from the cabs, holding open doors and wearing smiles as they extended their hands for tips.

Once inside the lobby, the coolness from the air conditioning drew instant relief. Dusty pulled a white handkerchief from somewhere under his suit and patted the sides of his head. He pulled off his hat to soak up some sweat from his scalp.

Sean gazed across the hallway at a large, bright arboretum area with a rock waterfall. It stood impressively underneath an enormous skylight. A handsome concrete walkway carved its way through its center.

"Oh!" Dusty hooted, drawing Sean's attention. Dusty quickly pulled his hat back on and jogged in the adjacent direction, nearly taking out a family of four as he made his way over to what looked like a wooden phone booth with glass panels.

"God. He's like a kid," said Lumbergh, glancing at Sean.

Sean shook his head, his stomach growling as he watched Dusty stop in front of the booth and stare at it like a child in front of a candy store window.

The two joined him. Once they were within a few feet,

Sean saw a female figure standing behind the booth's glass—a mannequin with long black hair and a dark bandana around her head. When her arm raised in the air and her head tilted mechanically to the side, jiggling her numerous necklaces in front of a shiny blouse, Dusty excitedly jammed his hands into his pants pockets.

"Do you guys have some change—fifty cents?" Dusty asked. "Please!"

The name "Syeira" read in an exotic font across the top of the glass. A recorded woman's voice poured out from a speaker, but the volume was too low, especially in the loud lobby, to make out everything she was saying. The word "future" was legible a couple of times, and it was clear from the figure's attire and the short table of tarot cards in front of her, that it was a fortune-telling machine. Sean had seen a similar one at a carnival when he was younger.

As Sean had remembered, there was a tray down below where a printed card with a "fortune" was dropped. "It's a waste of money," he said.

"Come on! Please!" pled Dusty. "I left my change back in my other pants. This is like that machine in *Big*."

"In what?" asked Sean.

"The Tom Hanks movie," answered Lumbergh. "Where the kid wishes that he was, well . . . *big*, and a genie in one of these boxes grants his wish."

"Never seen it, but Dusty's already plenty big."

Dusty ignored the dig and turned to Lumbergh, virtually out of breath. "Do *you* have fifty cents, Chief Lumbergh?"

"If I give you the money, will you start calling me Gary?" he asked, reaching into his pants pocket.

Dusty grinned. "I sure will . . . Gary." The sentence came out awkward enough to draw a wince from Lumbergh.

"People are going to be staring and laughing at your outfit the rest of the night," Sean abruptly said to Dusty, drawing his friends' faces. "There. That's your fortune. Free of charge. Can we get some dinner now?"

"I thought we were past the outfit thing," Lumbergh said, shaking his head and pulling out some change. He sorted through it with a finger and pulled out the smaller coins.

"Yeah," Sean said. "But that one wrote itself."

"You know," Dusty said, glaring at Sean with his hand on his hips. "You've been in a pissy mood ever since the school."

Sean's face tightened.

"Dusty," Lumbergh warned, shaking his head. "Drop it right now or you're not getting my change."

Dusty nodded, raising his hand to his mouth, pinching his fingers together, and sliding them across his lips—emulating a zipper. His face lit up when Lumbergh's palm revealed four quarters. Not wasting a second, he grabbed two, spun, and slid them into the coin slot.

A second later, the mannequin began moving again, her hands raising up and down and her neck twisting from side to side. More dialogue came from the machine, but again it was difficult to hear. A moment later, a small card dropped into a dish below the coin slot. Dusty quickly retrieved it, and held it under his gaze.

"A new business venture awaits, and it will bring you great riches." Dusty read it aloud with a grin.

"Great," said Sean. "You can buy dinner then."

"Can I borrow those other quarters?" Dusty asked Lumbergh just as he was about to return them to his pocket.

Lumbergh shrugged and handed them over.

"And now for friend Sean's future," Dusty said, plopping them into the machine.

"No," Sean said, unamused.

"O great Syeira!" said Dusty, raising his voice. He lifted his hands in the air as if he were summoning a spirit. "What lies in the future for one Sean Coleman?"

"Dinner," answered Sean. "I just want to eat."

Syeira went back through her routine, and when the card dropped into the dish, Dusty grabbed it and huddled with Lumbergh, keeping the fortune from Sean's view as the two read it.

Sean initially scoffed, but when he saw Dusty's face light up and Lumburgh's turn sober, his curiosity got the better of him. "Okay . . . What?" What?"

Dusty's eyes bulged. His hand covered his gaping mouth as he steadily shifted his focus to Sean. "Holy shit!" he shouted excitedly, grabbing the attention of some passersby. His lips spread into a huge smile.

"What?" pressed Sean.

Dusty opened his mouth to speak, but Lumbergh quickly cut him off.

"Nothing." Lumbergh grabbed the fortune from Dusty. "Just a stupid waste of money." He crumbled the card in his hand.

"Nothing?" said Dusty. "Are you kidding me? This is huge!"

"I swear to God, Dusty . . ." said Lumbergh, his eyes burning a hole through him.

"Enough bullshit," asserted Sean, having lost patience. "What's on the fucking card?"

"It's just a stupid game," said Lumbergh.

Lumbergh started to shove the collapsed card in his pants pocket, but Sean grabbed his wrist. Lumbergh fought him, squaring his jaw as Sean steadily raised his hand upward. Both of their arms trembled from the contest, but Lumbergh's strength was no match for his brother-in-law's. Sean's lips curled in confidence.

"Whoa," said Dusty, watching the battle. "This is like the beginning of *Predator*, where Arnold and Carl Weathers are—"

"Shut up, Dusty!" they said at the same time through their teeth.

Sean pulled Lumbergh in close, and with his free hand pried the card from his grip.

"Fine," Lumbergh finally conceded, whipping his arm away when Sean loosened his hold.

Sean uncrumpled the card and honed his eyes in on it.

An old flame will come back in your life, fulfilling your destiny.

His gut clenched.

"Bada-boom!" Dusty shouted, pumping his fist and slapping Sean on the back.

Chapter 6

Sean knew that a gypsy mannequin had no say in his life—no magical insight into his future. The thing was a glorified vending machine, not much different than those automatic crane contraptions kids grabbed for stuffed animals with. But Sean had become a reluctant believer over time in acts of higher intervention—strange moments of guidance that tended to come when he least expected them . . . but most needed them.

Back when he was still drinking, he'd write them off as mere coincidence—the accentuation of a picture that held a timely answer, or a book falling off a desk and landing on a relevant page, or a long-lost object suddenly reappearing and affirming or discouraging an important decision. But in times of clear-headedness, there seemed to be a genuine, even intentional wisdom behind them.

Once, when writing a note to himself about such an incident, as to not forget what he believed he was being guided to do, Sean referred to the phenomenon as "The Big Nudge."

Though Sean was a Christian, he couldn't say if it was God who occasionally *nudged* him in a particular direction. Part of him hoped it was his late father. Either way, he'd never spoken of the occurrences to anyone and likely never would. But he believed that he was stronger whenever he listened and paid attention to what was being said to him at those times. And as he poked at his buffet plate of ham, chicken, and potato chips, barely saying a word to his companions, he had convinced himself that not even a cheeseball fortune card from some hokey casino machine was something he should ignore.

What he wasn't convinced of was the role Lisa was supposed to play. She was happy in her life now; at least she appeared to be. Sean had trouble believing his "destiny" was to complicate or interfere with that happiness. The answer continued to escape him until just about the end of the dinner when he watched an elderly overweight couple at the next table guzzling down some cheap wine. The sight brought *him* back to his recovery program, and an important assignment he had yet to complete. Things suddenly made sense, or so he convinced himself.

"Give me a couple of minutes," he mumbled to Lumbergh and Dusty as the three left the dining area. When they didn't hear him over the slots and chatter, he repeated his statement. "I'm going to hit the restroom," he added. "Just wait here."

Sean made his way down a broad, crowded walkway, swiveling around people and more foreign languages. When he found the "Restrooms" sign he'd spotted on their way to dinner—one with a phone icon beside it—he dug into his pants, pulling out some change he'd withheld from Dusty earlier, along with a crumpled-up napkin from the buffet.

There were two payphones next to an ATM machine across the hall from the doors to the restrooms. Neither were being used. Sean unfolded the napkin and read a cell number he'd discretely scribbled onto it with his waitress's pen just minutes earlier: 518-0923. The last two digits had finally come to him.

It had occurred to Sean that Lisa may have changed numbers since they'd last talked, which might make sense with a new family and a new chapter in her life. But he was going to give it a try anyway. He slid some dimes and nickels into the closest phone and held his breath when he heard ringing through the receiver.

Memories of their first meeting flooded his mind. The same anxiety he'd felt back then now filled his stomach. Except this time, he wasn't showing up on her doorstep unannounced to tell her that her husband was dead. This time would probably serve as a reminder to her that he—Sean—was still alive.

"Hello?" her voice suddenly sounded in his ear. It was sharp; riddled with scrutiny as if she suspected the caller was a salesperson.

He said nothing for a moment, his throat dry. When he heard her sigh in annoyance, he spoke up. "Lisa?"

"Oh, yes," she answered. "Who's this?"

"It's me. It's, uh . . . it's Sean."

The phone fell silent. At least he thought it did. A lady's loud cackling from the casino behind him was all he could hear for a few seconds. "Hello?" he said.

"I'm here," she answered, her tone hard to read.

"Listen . . ." he began, swallowing and formulating his words carefully. "I know I'm probably the last person you expected to hear from tonight, but . . . ."

"You're here?" she said, more in a statement than a question. "In town."

His eyes widened, tightness constricting his chest from the thought that she'd spotted him cowering in the back seat of Dusty's car back at the school. "Yeah," he said. "How . . . did you know that?"

"Caller ID. Local area code."

"Oh," he said, releasing some air from his lungs. "Yeah. That makes sense."

"What are you doing here?" she quickly asked, her tone matter-of-fact.

"Yeah, well . . . I'm . . . I'm here in Vegas with a couple of buddies. One of them's getting married, and everything. And . . . well, the other one's Gary. He's here too. You remember him?"

"Your brother-in-law Gary?"

"Yeah. Yeah, that Gary."

"Are you guys getting along better now?"

"We are . . . We are," he said, nodding. "We've changed. Well, I've changed. He didn't really need to." He rubbed the palm of his sweaty hand down his face, lamenting how ridiculous he must have sounded.

"I saw you on television last year," she said.

Sean's hand fell from his face. "What?" he asked in confusion.

"That thing with the missile silo, where you were doing security. It was a short clip on the news. It took me a second to recognize you, even after I saw your name at the bottom of the screen. I'd never seen your hair that long before."

"Oh, yeah . . ." he said. "They told me that story went a bit national. I guess when an armed cult breaks into an old nuclear site, it's worth reporting . . . even outside of Colorado."

When Lisa said nothing, Sean continued.

"I'd have combed my hair, you know, if I'd known some guy was gonna stick a camera in my face like that."

"It was fine," she said after a moment, sounding as if she was swallowing her words. "How are you doing . . . health wise?"

"Health wise?"

"You know . . . with the . . . drinking. Are you still sober?"

"Yeah," he answered, squaring his jaw. He felt his eyes begin to moisten. "I had . . . I had a little relapse back . . . before the silo gig, but . . . I've been sober again for about, oh, four or five months now. And I'd gone a lot longer before that. I'm in a program now, and . . . It's going well. I feel . . . I feel better with it than I ever have."

"That's good," she said with a sniff and a tremble in her voice. "I'm glad you're doing well."

Sean wiped the beginnings of a tear from his eye, nodding his head. His emotions were swirling under his skin in a way they almost never did, and he wasn't sure where to take the conversation next.

"So, why did you call?" she asked softly.

"I . . . I'm not really—"

"I should tell you that I'm in a relationship now," she said with some hesitation.

"Yeah, I know."

"What?"

"I mean . . ." he began, weighing whether or not to bring up what he'd seen at the school. He quickly decided not to, worried she wouldn't buy his story for being there and instead mistake it for stalking. The last thing he wanted was to frighten her. "I just figured, by now, that you would be. That you would have found someone." He wasn't exactly lying. He never believed Lisa would have trouble finding someone else. She was a good person who many other suitors would be eager to try and make happy.

A few seconds of silence dragged by before she responded. "Then why did you call?" she pressed.

"Well, that's a good question," he said with a nervous chuckle. "And I hope I have a good answer . . ."

"Which is?"

"Part of the recovery program I'm in . . . part of what we learn, once we've gotten things back on track, is to make amends with those we've hurt."

"Oh," she said, digesting his words. "But you weren't really drinking when we were together. At least, I didn't see—"

"I know, but . . . I wasn't all there. I wasn't right in the head. I stopped drinking the wrong way—without the help I needed, and . . . well, I didn't . . . I didn't stop hurting people. And when we were told to make a list of those people . . . you were on it."

Some loud laugher broke out behind Sean—two men entering the restroom behind him. Sean gritted his teeth and held the phone tightly to his face, covering his ear with his other hand.

"You could have called me at any time, Sean," she said. "Why now?"

He released some air from his mouth. "I guess . . . I guess I wasn't ready to, and we're supposed to do it in person anyway— if we can, and ever since I got here . . ." He stopped himself, struggling with how much truth to drop on her all at once. After a few seconds, he decided to let the spigot flow. "Ever since I got here, everything I've seen and heard is like some billboard or a megaphone shouting at me that now is the time to see you."

He hated how clumsily the words had left his mouth, and agonized, as seconds of silence ticked by, over how they were being received.

"Billboards and megaphones," she finally answered, some unexpected levity in her tone. "That does sound pretty serious."

The corners of Sean's mouth curled. His chest began to loosen.

"There's just one problem though," she added. "I'm getting ready for a trip. Leaving tonight for a long weekend. I'm just finishing up some packing right now and I won't be back until Monday."

"Oh," Sean said, his head lowering to the top edge of the phone. "Okay. Yeah, we're heading back early Monday."

"I won't be back until Monday night."

Sean nodded and covered the receiver with his hand. "Figures," he whispered.

"I'll be here for another hour or so, though" she said. "Any chance—"

"I can't," Sean grunted. "We're getting ready to head into a show. Over at the Mirage. We have tickets to the *lions and tigers and bears* guys," he said with an eye roll.

"Oh my," she added, drawing a grin from Sean. He'd almost forgotten her humor. "Siegfried and Roy, huh? It's a great show, but I'm pretty sure there aren't any bears."

"No, probably not." He lifted his head, sighed, and turned toward the noise of the casino.

His eyes shot wide when he saw Dusty and Lumbergh standing just a few feet down the hallway, gazing back at him. Lumbergh wore a scowl of disappointment, his arms folded in front of his chest. He knew who Sean was talking to. Dusty did too, but his reaction was much different, an enormous smile decorating his round face. He held his thumb high in the air, expressing approval.

"Don't," mouthed Lumbergh, brows raised.

"Go to her," mouthed Dusty, enunciating each word carefully.

Sean covered the phone again, shaking his head. "I said I'd go to the show with you, and I'm keeping that promise. The tickets have been paid for, and . . ."

Dusty raised his hand, cutting short the statement. He approached Sean, his red boots scuffing along the carpet as he did. With each step forward, his eyes and smile grew wider, to the point where he looked like a caricature drawing of himself.

"What the hell are you doing?" asked Sean, sneering at the display.

Dusty reached forward, placing both of his hands over Sean's and the phone receiver.

"Jesus, come on," protested Sean, pulling the phone away. "Stop fucking around."

"Forget about the show, you silly bastard," Dusty said in a sultry thespian voice, his eyes trained on Sean. The line was probably from a movie, but Sean didn't recognize which one. "This is destiny, dammit. Go. To. Her."

Sean gazed back, eyes narrow. He glanced a Lumbergh who was still scowling, and then turned his back to both of them, tucking his chin low into the phone. With a tight stomach, he drew in a deep breath.

"Okay," he said. "What's your address?"

Chapter 7

Frank Sinatra's cover of "I Get a Kick Out of You" gently swayed out of a dust-lined Admiral clock radio at the back of a small, mostly dark office. A slice of light crept in through a narrowly opened door, but the only glare in the room came from a powerful desk lamp pointed at the center of the large wooden desk it sat on. Old metal file cabinets, each four drawers high, lined every wall. A couple of the drawers were open, each with a single folder tilted horizontally for special attention. A gray, shorthaired cat sat on top of one of the cabinets, licking its paw.

A fog of smoke hovered in the air above the desk, manipulated just a bit by a slow-moving ceiling fan. Below the cloud, an old man with sharp shoulders sat forward in a well-worn metal swivel chair. Half a cigarette dangled from his mouth. The man was quite thin and mostly bald with a freckled forehead. Through his bifocals he stared with a raised nose through a large magnifying glass on his desk.

The magnifying glass was held in place by a retractable arm, positioned at a near forty-five-degree angle. The man set down a precision knife and picked up a cotton swab with clear glue on its tip. He rubbed the swab in a circular motion on the left side of an open US passport under the lens. The page was colorful with varying shades of red, white, and blue. Printed on its right half was a conjured-up name and a local Las Vegas address. Once the glue was applied, he returned the swab to the table and grabbed the pair of tweezers next to it. His hand slightly trembling and his tongue tucked against the corner of his mouth, he used the tweezers to lift up a small, freshly cut photo of a middle-aged man with a thick beard. There was a semi-transparent imprint of wavy lines across the man's face.

A pair of footsteps came from outside the room. Rubber on linoleum. They picked up in speed as they grew closer.

"Hold on!" barked the man, nostrils flaring as he kept his eyes pinned to his work. "I need a minute!"

"Pops!" came another man's energized voice from the other side of the door.

"No. Not now, dammit!" warned the old man.

The door flew open, loudly banging against the open drawer of the file cabinet behind it. The cat on top of it sprang through the air, landing on the floor and scurrying off. A much younger man with dark hair—slicked back at the sides with sideburns that ended just above his earlobes—slid his body inside. He was out of breath, clad in a black, lightweight jacket over a T-shirt that stretched at his gut above his belt buckle.

"The fuck's wrong with you?" snarled the old man, his arms and cleft chin shaking. He quickly positioned the photo on the page, biting his lip as he pulled it into its place. "I swear to Christ, if this ends up crooked . . ."

"We've got a hit!" said the younger man, his brows arched.

The old man squinted at the photo a few more seconds before nodding his head, and laid his tools on the desk. "A hit? On what?"

"Kimble. Just now!"

The old man's eyes narrowed. He swiveled in his noisy chair to meet his son's gaze.

"You kidding me?"

"No," the son said. "I was in my office making a call when"

"Jesus," the father growled. "It's a cubicle." He wiped his hands with a rag and tossed it onto the corner of his desk. "You were in your *cubicle* making a call."

The son's face tightened. "Pops, what the hell does it matter?"

"Hey!" the father yelled, pointing a shaky finger at his son. "Don't you dare swear at me, boy."

"I'm sorry," the son said, raising his hands and lowering his head. "I'm sorry, Pops. It's just that—"

"You've got to *earn* an office here, and you haven't *earned* that yet. Until that happens, you're in a cubicle. You got that?"

"Yes. Yes, of course I got it, Pops. Gotta earn it . . . It's just that—"

The old man clenched his fist, again silencing his son. "Cause when you got an office, you can close your door . . . to work on something important—to work on something that requires a certain degree of concentration."

The son's eyes slid to the passport and tools on his father's desk.

The father continued, glaring at his son. "A closed door means *don't come in*. And when I say 'don't come in,' that *also* means *don't come in*."

"Point taken," said the son. "I mean, it was like an inch open, but point taken. I apologize. It's just that—"

"And the next time you swear at me, boy," the father added, "I'm gonna club you so hard your kids will be feeling it."

The son's face twisted in confusion. "I don't have kids."

"I know. It's a byproduct of never getting laid. I don't feel like explaining the meaning. I'm just sayin' that you don't get to swear at me."

"You swear at me all the time."

"You earn that right when you raise a wise ass . . . just like I earned my office by putting in the work."

"Okay. Okay. I said I was sorry. It's just that . . . I think we've got a sensitive time issue here."

The father crossed his arms in front of his chest. "Explain."

"When I was in my office—"

The father's teeth clenched.

"Sorry, cubicle. When I was in my cubicle, I heard a call come in to her on the tap. I know you said not to bother listening in, and just check the recordings first thing in the morning, but she's getting ready to leave town. *Going away for the weekend,* she said."

The father's head tilted to the side a bit, his mouth straightening. "In other words, you figured you wouldn't have to come in tomorrow if you hung out until she left."

"Well, yeah . . . maybe. But . . ."

The father grunted and shook his head. "Cubicle-level work," he mumbled before telling his son to get to what he'd heard.

"The guy who called her. His name is Sean. You know, *Sean* . . . from Colorado."

The father's eyes widened. He pulled off his bifocals and sat up straight.

"The old boyfriend? The guy with the account—"

"Yeah," the son interrupted. "That one. And get this. He's here in town—right now. They're going to meet in just a little while."

"Jesus," said the father, clenching the side of his desk. He slowly climbed to his feet. When the son moved in to help him, the father waved him off. "The timing. It's too much of a coincidence."

"I know," said the son, nodding.

"Why didn't you lead with the old boyfriend, dammit, instead of wasting my time with—"

"I tried, Pops. I—"

"Never mind. They're meeting *now*. You're sure?"

"Yes. Within an hour. At her house."

The father's gaze slid downwards, his eyes shifting from side to side. Multiple thoughts raced through his skull. "That's a hell of a short window."

The son nodded, eyes wide.

The father swallowed, then looked at his son soberly. "We've got to call him," he said in almost a whisper. He took a deep breath, removing his glasses and putting his other hand to his forehead.

The son's eyes narrowed. "Call who?"

"You know damn well who." The old man's voice shook.

The son gasped. "Jesus."

Chapter 8

Once Sean was a few blocks off the strip, the lights from casinos and traffic began to thin out. He was soon chugging along Interstate 215 in the Cruiser, headed southeast. The city of Henderson was farther from the school than Lisa used to live, but she said over the phone that it was just a twenty-minute drive. Maybe the new address belonged to her new guy.

His gut was twisted in knots, not just from the tight quarters of the front seat and the angst of what he'd say to Lisa, but also from the scowl of disappointment on Lumbergh's face as Sean left him and Dusty back at the Mirage. Sean couldn't push the image out of his mind. He worried that his brother-in-law was right—that meeting with Lisa would just open up wounds from the past at a time when he was making good progress in his life. At the same time, the Big Nudge seemed to be urging him forward, opening up traffic lanes and turning red lights green at opportune moments after exiting the Interstate.

Per Lisa's directions, he took a right off of North Green Valley Parkway and pulled into a neighborhood with a large, lit-up Nevada state flag riding a pole at its entrance. Behind the pole, along a brick wall, was a large white banner with bold red lettering that read, "New Homes Available!"

There wasn't much going on in the subdivision. Lit porch lights were scarce, and few people seemed to be home. Sean supposed it made sense for a Friday night, just a few miles away from the Entertainment Capital of the World. Every home looked virtually the same in the dark: adobe walls, clay tile roofing, and rock yards. The landscaping of palm trees, evergreens and assorted shrubbery helped distinguish the properties, but the foliage only hindered his view of the addresses printed above the garage doors.

The houses, nearly all two-stories, sat just feet from each other, separated by narrow side yards with tall fences and walls. It wasn't a bad neighborhood, but a definite downgrade from the sprawling, three-story house Lisa used to live in, or so he'd seen from pictures.

Sean entered a dark cul-de-sac. The only lights were on a house at the very end. The homes surrounding it were dark and their lawns were mostly dirt. They didn't appear to have been occupied yet. Sean spotted the number "29" under the two-door garage as he pulled up to the lit-up house. He swung the car along its narrow sidewalk and flipped off the headlamps. He let the engine run a few more seconds as he drew in a couple of deep breaths.

Squinting as he glanced in the rearview mirror, he saw little in the dimness other than a patch of his hair sticking up a bit in the back when he turned his head. He patted it down, and took quick inventory of his armpit with a quick sniff. *Good enough. It's not like we're still going out.*

The hinges of the car door groaned when he pushed it open. He grunted as he twisted his body and climbed out from behind the wheel. He stood up straight and tugged at the bottom of his shirt, gazing over the roof of the car. Beyond a partially lit up path of river rocks and a home security sign in the yard was the front door. It was open with a screen door closed in front of it. Inside, there was a short, lit-up hallway with a few framed pictures on the wall. There was a larger, brighter room behind it.

Sean closed the car door and shoved Dusty's keys in his pocket. He walked up the driveway at a consciously confident pace, losing sight of the front door behind the edge of the closed garage for a few seconds. A curved walkway brought the home's entrance back into view. That's when he saw a short, thin figure standing in the hallway, just behind the screen door.

"Hi Sean," came Lisa's voice, her tone timid but inviting.

"Hey," he greeted, feigning casualness as he raised a hand. *You can do this*, he told himself.

A sharp sputtering noise suddenly pulled his attention to an area of greenery between him and the garage wall.

"Oh, hurry!" Lisa said with urgency in her voice, suddenly standing alert. "There's a hole in the—"

Before Sean could process her warning, a narrow stream of water jetted out from the ground, taking direct aim at his pants—specifically his crotch.

"Gah," Sean groaned as he slogged forward.

Lisa quickly swung open the screen door, allowing him in to take cover from the punctured drip line.

"Oh God, I'm so sorry," she said, letting the door slam shut. "That damned thing. It's on a timer, and . . ." She stopped talking when she lifted her bright blue eyes to his and realized how close the two of them now stood in the small landing area. She took a subtle step back.

Lisa's hair was pulled back in a ponytail, just like the first time Sean had met her a little more than two years earlier. She wore a white, short-sleeved top tucked into jeans that ended just above her ankles. White running shoes over short socks covered her feet.

"It's okay," he said, his eyes fixed to hers longer than what felt appropriate. He caught his breath and pulled his gaze away, looking down at his pants and wincing at the sight of his wet, darkened lap. The water couldn't have hit Sean at a worse angle. He wondered if the Big Nudge had a previously unrecognized sense of humor.

"I can get you a towel," said Lisa.

"No, it's fine," said Sean. "You still run?" he asked, eager to change the subject. When her eyes narrowed, he added, "I just noticed your shoes, and—"

"Oh, yeah . . . Sometimes. Not as much as I used to." She glanced down. "Well, those are some fancy shoes *you've* got. I don't think I've ever seen you in dress shoes. Or even dress pants for that matter."

She said something else, but little of it registered with Sean as he nodded and focused his attention on the slightly raised tip of her nose. He remembered gliding his finger along it once, as they lay in bed on a crisp, autumn morning in Colorado. When her face tightened again, he realized she'd stopped talking.

"Listen, um . . . I won't take up too much of your time," he said. "I can just say my bit right here, and—"

"Don't be silly," she said. "Come on in. I'm not going to make you stand in the hallway."

Sean nodded and followed her down the short corridor. He noticed a security alarm keypad on the wall before his gaze shifted to the collage of pictures framed beside it. They included shots of Lisa with the man and the girl from the school. Some were taken at a playground. Others at a lake, and on a small boat. Their smiles carried from ear to ear.

"Got yourself a family now," Sean said matter-of-factly, trying to curl his lips upward. He nodded. "That's good. Good that you're . . ."

"Oh," she said, stopping and turning. She watched Sean as

he studied the pictures. "Yes, sort of. That's my boyfriend Greg . . . and his daughter."

"Oh, thank God," Sean gasped, his shoulders lowering. It took him just half a second to realize he'd shared the sentiment aloud.

"What?" asked Lisa, her mouth left dangling.

Sean shifted his focus to her. "I'm just . . . I'm sorry . . . I—"

Lisa's hands went to her hips. "What do you mean, 'Thank God'?"

"Listen . . ." Sean said, recalling what a leader in his recovery program often said about telling the truth. "I'm here for all the reasons I said on the phone. I swear I am. About my recovery. About making amends. All of that." He stood up straight and looked Lisa in the eye. "And part of that process is being honest with people . . . So, I'm just going to get it all out there, if that's okay with you."

"Okay," said Lisa, discretion in her voice. "Go ahead."

"When I came into town today . . . with Gary and the other guy . . . Well, the other guy was driving. His name is Dusty . . . And he took a wrong turn, and the idiot brought us right past your building of all places." Sean drew in a breath before continuing. "I mean, what are the chances, right?"

Lisa's face was riddled with confusion, but Sean continued.

"And that's when I saw you, and your boyfriend . . ." Sean hesitated. "That's really his name? Greg?"

Lisa's face soured. "Of course it's his name. What do you—"

"Sorry, that was a stupid question. Anyway, I saw you and *Greg*, and the little girl, and . . . there was this slow-ass crossing guard who was taking forever to help the kids across the street—"

"Wait . . . wait a second," she interrupted, shaking her head. "You were at my school today?"

"Not by choice. Honest to God, Lisa. I wasn't doing anything creepy . . . or stalking you, or anything like that."

Lisa cringed. "O-kay," she said in what sounded like a question.

Sean recognized that he was rambling and not making much sense, but all he could do at that point was let the rest of the sputtering air out of his deflating balloon of a proclamation. "I came here for Dusty's bachelor party. That's why I'm dressed like this." He lifted up his arms for a second to reveal more of his loud shirt. "But earlier I saw you kiss the guy—*Greg*, and then you kissed the girl . . . whose possible age was of some concern . . . And—" Sean stopped himself. "Well, we don't need to get into that."

Lisa glared at him with a dropped jaw. She was at a loss of words. After a few seconds, they finally came. "What do you mean her age was of concern?" Her eyes suddenly shot wide, having answered her own question. "Oh . . . Jesus," she said, her face loosening. "Oh God . . . Sean—"

"It's fine," he said, waving his hand. "Really. Lumbergh said I was an idiot to even think that, and he was right." He paused when his eyes—as unexpectedly to him as it probably was to Lisa—moistened. He lowered his gaze to the floor and swallowed. He turned his head to the side.

Lisa said nothing for a moment. She lowered her head in what looked like sympathy, her eyes glued to his face. "I'm sorry, Sean," she whispered. "I'm sorry you saw that, and thought that . . . " She raised her hand to touch his face but withdrew when his eyes met hers again.

"No. Don't be sorry," he said softly, a crackle in his voice. "You never need to be sorry, not when it comes to me. I mean . . . I knew that couldn't be the real story. You'd have let me know, and—"

"Yeah," she said, biting her lip before managing a grin. Her eyes revealed some glisten of their own. "I would have." She placed her hand on his shoulder.

Sean grinned and nodded back. "Phew." He chuckled, adding a little levity to the conversation. He stood up straight and turned back to the collage of pictures. "Anyway . . ." taking a second to rub his eye with the palm of his hand. "I'm glad you're happy and things are going well."

"They are," she said, nodding. Her grin remained. She arched her thin eyebrows and added, "I have to admit, this wasn't the conversation I'd envisioned us having."

Sean smiled. "Yeah, me neither. I guess getting sprayed in the crotch got me all emotional."

Lisa's eyes shot wide. She placed her hand on her hip and leaned back with a bubbling giggle that endeared itself to Sean the same way it used to. "Oh," she said, eyes suddenly bulging and her hand going to her mouth in a shushing motion.

"What?"

"It's okay," she said, waving off Sean's concern. "Hannah's sleeping in the other room. I just don't want to wake her. She pretty much sleeps through anything anyway, but—"

"Who's Hannah?"

Lisa smiled and nodded. "Reasonable question. She's Greg's daughter, the little girl you saw at the school."

"Oh . . ." he said, his gut contracting. "All of you live here . . . together then?"

"No," she answered. "Greg has a business dinner tonight. He works for a tech company. A lot of their clients are hotel and casino people, so in Vegas that means a lot of after-hours schmooze meetings. Hannah stays here sometimes. I'm just watching her tonight. Babysitting."

Sean's face hardened. "I thought you had a flight to catch."

Her eyes glanced off him for a moment. "I do, but I . . . well, I'm not as crunched for time as I pretended to be on the phone."

Sean's head tilted.

"I just . . . I wasn't sure how this was going to go," said Lisa. "After all this time. I guess . . . I guess I just wanted an out, in case . . ." The corners of her lips curled in apology. "I *am* leaving tonight. That's the truth. Just not for a few hours. Greg's coming back to get Hannah after his dinner thing. I'll be catching a red-eye to Traverse City. Found a great price on tickets if I left at a crazy hour."

"Traverse City . . . Michigan?" Sean asked. "Where we . . ."

She nodded. "Yeah, where you and I first met. I'm finally selling the cottage. Kyle's cottage. I haven't been out there since . . . right after the funeral, and there's just . . . well, too many memories, but I can't afford to keep the place anyway. Not on a teacher's salary. And now that the Moretti case is all wrapped up—"

"Sounds like a good move then."

"Yeah. I think so," she said, sliding her hands into her pockets. "You know, instead of us standing here in the hallway, why don't you come on in for a bit?"

Sean glanced down the hallway where part of a salsa-colored couch revealed itself over some lush, cream carpet. "You sure that's okay?" he asked.

"Yeah," she said, seemingly convincing herself with a nod. "Of course." She nudged her head toward the living room and led them down the hallway. "Would you like something to drink? I mean, like a pop or something?"

Sean chuckled. "No thanks. I'm good."

The room had a southwestern feel to it. Textured walls

below a vaulted ceiling bore a light, rustic gold. A couple of large paintings hung on either side of a wide window with closed, wooden blinds. One of the paintings was of a desert ravine; the other depicted a dark-skinned woman with long hair under a cowboy hat, leading a horse on foot. Vases with tall, artificial grass and prairie plants sat on end tables.

Sean's eyes traced the décor before floating over to the darkened kitchen area beyond it. He sat down in a cushioned chair, opposite the matching couch Lisa plopped herself on, in between some textured pillows.

A thick, square coffee table made of light-colored wood sat between them. On top of it rested some large, stacked picture books beside a clay vase with a Native American design. A multicolored rug sat under the table.

"This is nice," said Sean.

"Thanks," answered Lisa with a quick grin. "It's sort of a work in progress."

Sean noticed a large television at the back corner of the room. On a wooden stand beneath it lay a DVD set with some familiar television detectives on the cover.

"*NYPD Blue*," said Sean. "One of the best."

"I remember you saying once how much you liked it. Someone Greg works with let him borrow season one. You're right. It's good." She nodded at Sean, holding his gaze.

"You're not going to tell me that one of the characters reminds you of me, are you?" asked Sean with a hint of a grin.

She grinned a little back. "Okay, I won't tell you that."

Lisa's cell phone was sitting on the table between them, next to the vase. She caught Sean noticing it. "Whatever happened to that cell phone I bought you?" she asked.

Sean winced a little. "Well . . ."

"Oh, it's okay," she said. "I just thought it was odd that you called from a local number. You didn't have to keep the phone if you didn't want—"

"I washed it," said Sean.

"What?"

"In my jeans' pocket. I washed it. By accident."

"Oh," she said.

"So . . ." Sean began, taking a breath. He leaned forward with his elbows on his knees, looking Lisa in the eye. "Here we go . . . I know I was a pain in the ass back then. Hell, some would say I still am . . ."

Lisa watched him, eyes thinning with curiosity.

Sean continued. "But I'm in a good place now. Most of the time anyway. And when I look back over my life, I know there've been more screwups, and more people that I've hurt in some way—different ways—than I can even count." He lowered his gaze for just a second before returning it to her face. "I can't do anything to erase all of that, but what I can do is say I'm sorry."

Lisa nodded, her lips curling ever so lightly.

"In your case, Lisa, I'm sorry I wasn't the person you needed me to be at that point in your life. You know, the kind of person who has patience. The kind of person who listens, offers good advice . . . and gives you comfort and all that stuff. Kyle—he put you through a lot, and what happened with him . . . well, it was no easy thing for you. I mean, it wouldn't have been for anyone. I should have been more understanding of that, but I wasn't. And . . ." Sean squinted, his eyes moving on and off Lisa as he silently censured himself for his poor delivery. "I'm sorry. I've never been good with words."

"You're good with words right now," Lisa answered, drawing his gaze back to her. "And I think you're being a little hard on yourself."

Sean's eyes narrowed. He leaned back a bit.

"I had just lost Kyle," she said. "Your Uncle Zed had just been murdered."

It wasn't Sean's uncle who'd been murdered. Sean found out over a year later that Zed was his biological father. Lisa couldn't have known that, as she and Sean had parted ways before then, but Sean wasn't going to interrupt her at that moment to talk more about himself. Instead, he listened to her closely.

Lisa continued. "There were a lot of raw emotions there that hadn't been confronted. I think we both fended them off by turning to each other, and that kind of pressure wasn't healthy. It also wasn't fair, to either of us. We needed time to mourn, not jump right into a relationship."

Sean offered a subtle nod.

"That's not to say that I regret the time we spent together," she added. "I don't. Life's a journey, and it's all about experiences and learning and growing. And the fact of the matter is that on the day we met, you saved my life. And for that and for you, I'll always be grateful."

Sean's face loosened as he recalled showing up at that cottage that day to find one of Moretti's men working her over. The brutal thug was there for information on her husband, Kyle. He was armed, but so was Sean, and only one of them left the cottage alive.

Sean's gaze lowered to the floor when the weight of the appreciation in Lisa's eyes became too hard to hold. "Now, *you* were always good with words," he said.

Lisa's lips curled. "I'm glad things are coming together for you, Sean. I'm really glad you're sober, and I'll pray that you'll continue to be."

Sean nodded, eyes still averted. "Thank you."

Seconds of silence floated by, the awkwardness building in Sean's gut until he lifted his gaze back to Lisa. She was no longer looking at him, but rather toward the hallway they'd entered through minutes earlier. Sean followed her eyes to the glare of headlights that shone in through the screen door; they disappeared a second later.

"Is Greg here?" Sean asked.

She glanced at a clock on the wall. "He shouldn't be, unless the dinner fell through."

"Or he didn't like the idea of an old flame stopping by," Sean said. He would have felt the same way if the situation was reversed.

She shook her head, dismissing the notion. "He's not the jealous type." She climbed to her feet, eyes still forward.

"Probably a neighbor then," Sean suggested.

"I don't have any. Not yet, anyway." She walked to the hallway, placing her hand on her hip and staring through the door. Her eyes narrowed and she turned to Sean for a second, her face etched with suspicion.

"What?" he asked.

When she turned back to the door, her body jolted straight. "Oh God," she gasped, placing her hands to her mouth.

Sean sprang to his feet. His knee bounced off the table, knocking its vase to the side. "What is it?"

Just as her eyes darted back to him, the screen door swung open loudly. Lisa turned and ran to Sean. Her eyes were flush with terror.

"Guy with a mask!" she gasped in a deathly whisper. "He has a gun!"

Chapter 9

Sean's jaw clenched and he quickly pulled Lisa behind him. "Stay behind me." His hand went to his side, where he sometimes carried a gun when working a job. But he'd left his piece back in Colorado.

They heard the screen door swing open. Footsteps thundered down the hallway. Sean's eyes searched for something he could use as a weapon. The closest object was the vase lying on the table. He lunged for it, grabbing it by its neck. Tall grass fell from its lip.

When a figure dressed in black with a shiny handgun lurched out from behind the wall, Sean didn't waste a second. He snarled and threw the vase like a battle axe directly at the intruder's head. It collided with the man's covered face, exploding into pieces. The intruder crumbled backwards into the wall behind him, sending hallway pictures crashing to the floor along with his pistol. Lisa screamed.

"Get outside!" Sean yelled. He launched toward the disoriented man, lowering his shoulder. Barely catching a glimpse of the red and black mask, Sean caught the man just as he stumbled forward from the wall. He swung an uppercut directly under the man's jaw, snapping his head backwards. Sean quickly dropped to a knee and reached for the man's gun.

A gunshot rang out. Sean's arm jolted out from under him. He crashed to the floor on his side.

"No!" Lisa shouted.

With the burning in Sean's shoulder, he knew he'd been shot. The blast hadn't come from the dazed man on the floor. It had come from his left. Sean rolled to his chest, swinging his other arm toward the floored man's pistol. The gun was quickly stepped on by a second figure who'd entered the room from the same hallway. Also dressed in black, he swung his foot behind him, sending the gun a few feet backward, out of Sean's reach.

"Back up, goddammit!" commanded a gravelly, muffled voice. "Back up! And lady, you don't move an inch!"

Sean clenched his teeth, pain surging through his arm. His heart pounded against his chest. He moved his hand to his injured shoulder, doing so slowly and carefully; he didn't want the assailant to mistake the move for him reaching for a weapon. Where the bullet had struck him was warm blood. It ran along his fingers until he closed his knuckles together and applied pressure.

"I said back up," repeated the man standing above him, his voice more even and deliberate.

Sean propped himself up on the elbow of his good arm, cringing for a second from another flash of pain. He lifted his head to meet the man barking orders and saw a black, snub-nosed revolver pointed directly at him. It shook in the hand of the thin man holding it. Sean's eyes lifted to the man's face.

"What the fuck?" Sean muttered, confronted by the sight of another mask—this one resembling an alien from outer space. It was orange and white with buggy eyes and a long snout whose nostrils served as eye holes for the man behind it.

Made of cheap, Halloween-style plastic like his partner's, it was probably secured with an elastic string in the back.

The armed man, like his buddy who was slumped up against the wall and stirring a bit, wore black jeans and a dark lightweight jacket. He shook his head—a silent but unmistakable warning for Sean not to speak or do anything other than what he had just been instructed.

Sean slowly twisted his head back toward Lisa. The man switched his aim to her.

"Don't," Sean said.

His gun returned to Sean. The two men's eyes glared through each other's. It was then that Sean noticed the glimmer behind the armed man's eyeholes. He was wearing glasses, the mask's bulging snout providing the necessary room.

Lisa remained frozen by the coffee table, her chest pushing in and out as her eyes nervously shifted between the armed man and a door opposite the living room. It was open only a sliver. Sean suddenly realized why Lisa hadn't followed his instruction to try and get outside: Hannah, the one-year-old asleep in the other room. She wasn't going to leave her behind in the house.

Sean detected the odor of cigarettes as he slowly rose to his knees, backing up on them a step and a half before planting a foot and hoisting himself up to his feet.

"Well, you're a big boy," said the man with the gun. "Keep moving back."

Sean kept his hand over his wound as he stepped backward toward Lisa, moving in close to her. Lisa switched her head back and forth between the intruders and Sean's injured shoulder. Sean could feel her heavy breath against his neck.

"Good," said the man with the gun. "Let's everyone take a

second and just calm the fuck down, okay?" He stepped over his fallen partner's legs, shielding the man's face from Sean and Lisa. "Fix your fucking mask," he said matter-of-factly.

The armed man's hand continued to tremble as the man on the floor behind him groggily worked his hands across his damaged mask. Sean closed his eyes for a second and flushed the pain from his mind as best he could.

"Can I?" Lisa asked in a shaky voice, nudging her head at Sean's shoulder.

The armed man stared for a moment, then nodded.

Lisa carefully pried at Sean's fingers to take a closer look at the wound, gently lifting up his bloodstained shirt. As she did, Sean studied the frame and posture of the armed man's body. He was thinner and frailer than Sean had originally thought, though his jacket stretched a bit at his chest. He was also older, with a hunch to his shoulders, and a mostly bald head with some gray hair sticking out from the edge of the mask. Sean wondered if the man's shaking hand was more a sign of his age than it was nervousness.

"What the hell is this?" asked Sean, glaring at the intruders. "What do you want? Money?"

The man glared back through the alien's nostrils for a few seconds before answering. "Give us a minute."

The younger man on the floor grunted in frustration as his elbows bobbed up and down. "It's broken," he finally said, his voice cracking. "He snapped the whole damn thing in half."

"Oh . . . Oh, that's fucking great," said the man with the gun, his voice oozing with irritation. His eyes rolled behind the alien's nose holes. "Some fucking surprise. A fucking $5 mask."

"We were in a hurry," the man on the floor bemoaned.

"Shut up!" the older man snarled. He took a breath. "You

don't need to be saying anything!" He shook his head. "Wearing children's masks to a shakedown . . . Stupid."

A shakedown? Sean thought. He turned his head to Lisa, who was still examining his shoulder.

"Is there one hole or two?" he asked calmly, trying to ease her nerves.

"I don't know," she said, her voice quivering. She twisted her head around to the back of the shoulder. "I just see one."

"Shit." He covered the wound back up with his hand. He felt a bump just under the skin. He hoped that meant the bullet hadn't gone very deep.

"I just need some tape or something," said the man on the floor, still trying to salvage his mask.

"Jesus Christ," grumbled his armed partner.

"Please," said Lisa, turning to them. "Please, just take whatever you want and leave. I have some cash in my purse, and—"

"Right now, we just need tape," said the man with the gun. "That's all. Just some fucking tape. Then we can have a nice little, constructive talk."

Sean's face recoiled at the bizarreness of the exchange, controlling his breathing as he more closely examined the intruders. Neither appeared to have brought anything with them other than their disguises and firearms. No bags to shove valuables into. No tools for a break-in. The seated man's offhanded remark that their actions were hurried seemed to check out.

Because their masks only covered their faces and not the backs of their heads, Sean could make out dark hair on the younger man. When he turned his head a little, he saw long sideburns down his jawline.

"There's some tape in a drawer," said Lisa nervously. "In the kitchen behind you."

The armed man nodded, cocking his head back a couple of inches. "Get up and get it," he said to the man on the floor. "Cover your face. And first, pick your damned gun up off the floor! Jesus."

The man behind him worked to pull himself upright, awkwardly holding a gloved hand over his face. In his other hand, he held the two pieces of his broken mask. Sean couldn't make out much more of his appearance other than that he was white and had a gut. His movements were quick enough to suggest that he was in his thirties or maybe forties.

"We're doing this for your own good," the older man said to Sean and Lisa. "If you don't know who we are, it's much better for you."

"Well, gee," said Sean. "I guess we should be grateful."

"Sean," Lisa muttered, urging caution.

The younger man, with his hand over his face, walked on unbalanced footing over to where his partner had kicked the gun. He kept his back to the two in the living room, lowering to a knee and gathering the weapon from the floor. The pistol had a chrome finish and was relatively small. It looked to Sean like a Raven MP-25. The intruder clumsily held it in the same hand as the halves of his mask. Sean shook his head at the farce.

"I'm gonna have a black eye," said the younger man to his partner as he climbed back up to his feet. "It's all swollen. I can feel it."

"Yeah, well maybe that will teach you a lesson. Coming in here like Charles Bronson. Now fix your stupid Star Trek mask."

"Star Wars," said the man as he passed behind his partner.

"What?"

"It's Star Wars, Not Star Trek. Mine's Darth Maul. Yours is—"

"Just shut up and start taping."

"You're Jar Jar . . . "

"I'm what?"

"You're—"

"Just . . . You know what? Shut up. Fix the mask. We don't have all night."

Sean could feel his own blood boil. The more the men talked, the more apparent was their buffoonery. Yet, they were in control. They had gotten the drop on him, incapacitated him, and now they held all the cards. Armed, and therefore dangerous . . . and in charge. And there was nothing, for the moment, that Sean could do about it.

The younger man disappeared into the darkened kitchen. The sound of drawers opening and closing soon followed.

"The drawer by the fridge," said Lisa.

Another drawer slid open. Snaps of vinyl followed. A half minute ticked by before the man reappeared from the kitchen, his red and black mask now held together by mangled mounds of black electrical tape.

"There was . . . " Lisa began, catching herself. "Never mind."

"What?" said the older man.

"There was regular tape in there too," she answered. "Masking . . . Scotch . . . "

The older man turned to his partner, gazing at his mask. "Jesus . . . Can't do anything the easy way, can you?" He shook his head in disgust.

"I didn't think the other stuff would be strong enough, Pops!"

"Jesus, shut up!" the older man said sharply.

The younger man seemed to have just revealed that they were a father and son team, and everyone in the room had noticed.

Shoulders deflated, the younger man raised his gun at Sean and Lisa. The older man then lowered his weapon to his side, giving him a chance to rotate his shoulders and neck to seemingly address some physical wear. He grumbled something under his breath.

He took a moment before speaking again. "We know who you are," he finally said. "You're Lisa Kimble. School teacher. Formerly married to Kyle Kimble, before he went and offed himself."

Lisa's face tightened. She opened her mouth to speak but was cut off.

"And you're Sean Coleman," the older man added, twisting his head to Sean.

Sean's eyes widened. He wasn't expecting the men to know a thing about him.

"Security guard from Colorado," the man continued. "You have a bit of a history here with the lovely Lisa. With her dead husband too."

Sean's visit with Lisa had been spur of the moment. There were only two ways the men could have known he'd be there: if Lisa had told them, which made no sense, or if they'd been listening in on their earlier phone conversation. *A wire tap.*

"You guys are feds?" Sean blurted out.

The older man cocked his head to the side. "Do we look like feds to you?"

"No, you look like an aisle at Toys "R" Us. But you've got her phone tapped, and Kyle Kimble was part of a federal case."

The man scoffed, shaking his head. "It doesn't matter who

we are. What matters is that we know what you did, and we're pretty sure we know what you're doing right now."

"Bleeding?" said Sean, glancing down at his shoulder.

"Don't play stupid," said the older man, returning his gaze to Sean.

Sean could feel Lisa's eyes switch to him, questioning what she was hearing. The pressure from her hand on his shoulder eased a bit. Sean shook his head, the man's words lost on him. It didn't seem feasible that the intruders could know or care about the details of his recovery program—his actual reason for being there. The men were clearly working under a very different assumption.

"I don't know what this is about," said Sean. "But if you want to clue me in, I'm all ears."

"Quit jerkin' us around," the older man sneered. "Your arrival in Vegas isn't just a case of convenient timing. We both know that. What I don't know is whether or not *she* knows what's going on."

Sean turned to Lisa, her eyes wide and prying. He couldn't fathom how he'd brought this situation on her. He shook his head and focused back on the intruders. "What the fuck are you fucking idiots talking about?" he shouted, causing everyone in the room to jump. "What do you think I'm doing? Just spill it!"

The tense silence that followed heightened with the whine of what sounded like hinges. Everyone's attention turned to the door opposite the living room. The armed men's pistols swung toward it. There, just a couple of feet off the floor, a tiny, delicate hand pulled the door open wider.

Sean's heart fell to his stomach.

"No," gasped Lisa. "No, Hannah. You stay there, honey."

The little girl, with frazzled hair and her fist rubbing her eye, waddled out into the living room. She wore pink, one-piece fleece pajamas that covered her from neck to foot. A cartoon cat's face was embroidered across her chest.

"Grab the kid," the older man said to his partner. He raised his gun back up to Sean and Lisa.

"You serious?" asked the other man.

"Don't you dare!" Lisa shouted. She turned to the toddler, her hands cautioning the child's approach. "Hannah, honey . . . No, no."

The girl crept her way toward Lisa, ignoring the others. Her arms were raised. She wanted to be held.

"Let her hold the girl!" said Sean to the men. "You don't need to do this. I'll tell you whatever you want. Just leave them alone."

"No," the older man said snidely. "You wanted to play games? Let's play games." He nudged his head to his partner, doubling down on his order. The younger man quickly circled around him toward the girl.

Sean turned to Lisa. "Take her and lock yourselves in the bedroom," he said, aware the men could hear him. "Now."

Sean stepped forward, placing his body between the intruders and Lisa. He spread out his good arm, walking sideways to give Lisa cover as she went for Hannah. "Leave them out of this. She doesn't know anything. I told you I'd cooperate."

"Out of the way," said the younger man, pointing his gun at Sean as he approached.

Sean knew that if he went for the man's gun, his partner would fire off another round. This time, he'd likely end up with something worse than a shoulder wound. And he wouldn't do any good to Lisa and the girl if he were dead. Still, they had come for him and it seemed that they preferred him alive, at least for now. He bet on that fact earning him some leverage.

Sean kept himself in front of Lisa as she scooped up the child in her arms and darted into the bedroom. Sean stayed out, shielding them until the door slammed shut. The lock snapped. The younger man stopped, keeping his gun aimed at Sean's chest and glancing at his partner for instructions on what to do next. Sean's wager had paid off.

"Come on, let's talk," Sean said calmly, closing his arm and placing his hand back to his bloody shoulder. "They're not going anywhere. They're no threat to you. Tell me what you want from me and we'll finish this up right now."

"She could be in there calling the police!" shouted the younger man at his partner.

The older man, surprisingly calm in his demeanor, shook his head. "Do you remember tapping a phone in there?" he said. "You don't. Because there isn't one, and her cell's right there on the coffee table."

A buzzing sound from the older man's pants drew his hand to his front pocket.

"She could have a gun in there," said the younger man, unfazed by the buzzing, perhaps not hearing it.

"She hates guns," said Sean matter-of-factly.

The older man nodded. "She wouldn't keep one in the kid's room, numb-nuts." He turned toward the door, raising his voice. "If we hear anything from you in there—and I mean *anything*— a window opening, furniture moving, you calling out for help . . . we'll kill him. Do you understand?"

A few seconds slogged by before Lisa answered in a shaky voice. "I understand."

The older man had some difficulty sinking his gloved fingers into his pocket. He finally dragged out a black cell phone with a small antenna. It buzzed louder.

"Is it him?" asked the younger man, appearing tense.

"Yeah," said the older man. He took a deep breath, then tapped a button and held the phone to his ear.

"I'm here," he said into the receiver. After a few seconds, he added, "Yeah. We're there now."

Sean couldn't make out what the voice on the other end of the phone was saying, only that it was deep enough to belong to a man.

"Nothing we couldn't handle," said the older man. "How far out are you?"

Sean now understood that the "shakedown" was being orchestrated by more than just the two men. They'd soon have company. If the masked men weren't feds, they were likely mobbed up . . . like Lisa's late husband. Though they currently had control of the situation, the men were heavy-handed and clownish. Not professionals and not *serious men*. The same might not be true of whomever would join them, whether it be one person or ten. Regardless of the number, the men who stood there now clearly feared the person on the other end.

Sean agonized over what to do. The new circumstances called for a decisive plan, and he wasn't convinced he had time to come up with one. For now, there was at least a physical barrier between the intruders and Lisa. It was a small advantage, but it was something. Right then and there would probably be his best and maybe last opportunity to try something.

"We'll be here," the older man finished up. He pushed a button, ending the call.

Sean decided he'd strike as the man shoved the phone back in his pocket. He was the slower of the two. Sean would grab his gun, shoot the younger man first, then take out the older.

Sean hoped to God he could pull it all off with only one good
arm.

But just as the older man was about to holster his phone,
the piercing cry of the house alarm suddenly blared through
the home. Both intruders snapped to attention, the cell phone
falling to the floor. Their guns both rose to Sean's head.

Sean's mouth gaped open, his heart pounding. The
intruders shouted over each other for him to freeze. He hadn't
moved an inch, but they were panicked and seemed to think
he was somehow responsible.

"Get down on the floor!" the old man shouted, looking over
his shoulder toward the front door. He turned to his partner.
"Get her out here now!"

Sean remained still. The men were so on edge now that any
quick movement on his part would send them to the next level.
It had to have been Lisa who'd tripped the alarm. He didn't
know how but no other explanation made sense.

"On the floor!" the old man shouted again over the wailing
alarm. His gun, pointed at Sean's face, was shaking so hard
Sean worried it would go off on its own.

"Open the door!" the younger man demanded. He yanked
at the doorknob before taking a step back and planting a hard
foot just below it. The wood cracked but the door remained
shut and locked. He quickly twisted his body and turned his
gun toward Sean again before refocusing on the door. "Open
it now!"

She had to have gotten out a window with the kid, Sean thought.
That's what set off the alarm. He pictured Lisa running down the
street to the nearest neighbor, the little girl in her arms. *Good,*
he thought.

"Get down!" the old man shouted at Sean again.

Sean finally complied, lowering himself to his knees. He

wasn't willing to go any lower until he was certain Lisa had really escaped. In a stolen glance, he noticed the older man's phone lying on the carpet just a few feet in front of him.

"If you're not out here in three seconds, he's dead!" shouted the older man as his partner stepped back to plant another kick into the door.

Sean prayed that the room was empty.

"One . . ."

When the high-pitched scream of a child filtered through the noise of the pulsing alarm, Sean closed his eyes. His gut clenched. *They hadn't made it out.*

"Okay!" screamed Lisa. "Don't hurt him! We're coming!"

"No, Lisa!" shouted Sean.

"Two!" shouted the older man.

She must have unlocked the door, because a second later the younger man was able to shove it open freely. Around the side of his body, Sean saw Lisa, her face pale and tight with fear as she held the crying girl in her arms.

"Get out here!" snarled the man.

"I don't know what happened!" she insisted, her voice muffled by the alarm. "I don't know why it's going off."

The younger man held her between his crosshairs, walking backwards and guiding her into the living room. Hannah cried loudly, the little girl's face turning red as she held her breath.

"Turn it off!" the younger man roared, grabbing her by the shoulder.

"Don't touch her, you son of a bitch!" Sean wailed.

"Shut up!" the older man warned him.

Lisa, Hannah, and their captor disappeared around the corner, making their way toward the security panel Sean had seen on his way in. Sean could hear the man yelling at Lisa to punch in the alarm code, but the deafening siren continued on. After some swearing, he pulled her back into the living room, the two of them stepping over broken picture frames. Hannah continued to cry.

"It's not turning off!" the younger man yelled.

"It's not taking the code!" yelled Lisa, the veins in her neck showing. "I don't know why!"

"Dammit!" the older man shouted. "The security company's gonna call and verify things. What number will they call?"

With the man's focus on Lisa, Sean was tempted to steal the cell phone from the floor, but his attention was back on Sean in no time.

"I don't know!" said Lisa, a tear streaming down her face. "We just installed it. It might be under my boyfriend's number! I don't know!"

"Oh, for God's sake!" shouted the older man. He backed up toward them. "This is no good. We can't stay here."

The man seemed to know, as Sean did, that without confirmation of a false alarm by the homeowner, the security provider would call the police.

"Take them out to the van!" the older man shouted at his partner, who again grabbed Lisa by the arm.

"No!" pled Sean.

"Don't worry, asshole," shouted the older man. "You're coming too. Get over here!"

Lisa and Hannah were now out of sight, being rushed down the hallway to the front door. Sean needed to stay close to her. He started forward, but when his captor glanced at the floor, eying his fallen cell phone, Sean saw an opportunity to buy them some time. He brought his foot down hard on the device, the resulting crunch audible even over the alarm.

"Fuck!" the older man yelled, his glare bouncing between his phone and Sean.

Sean forced a confused expression across his face, raising an eyebrow and lowering his focus to the floor as if he hadn't realized what he had just done. When he stepped off the phone, its mutilated face and snapped-off antenna laid beside each other. It looked inoperable, its severely cracked display dim.

"Move, dammit!" the older man ordered, his gun glued to Sean's face. He motioned Sean to the hallway, taking a couple of steps back.

Sean walked forward, subtly glancing backward as he made his way toward the hallway. He watched his captor hunch down to a knee, keeping his gun raised as he picked up the pieces of his phone with his free hand. The alarm still blaring, Sean hoped the man wouldn't be clear-headed enough to take Lisa's cell phone from the coffee table as a replacement. Sean picked up his pace to ensure so, briskly rounding the corner and loudly stepping on broken plastic and glass as he made his way down the hallway. He knew the older man wouldn't want him out of his sight, even for a second. Sure enough, the man was behind him in no time, shoving pieces of the phone into his pants.

Unless the men had another phone between them, they'd have to stop somewhere to sync up with whoever was calling the shots.

Chapter 10

"Ow!" Dusty shouted when he took an elbow to his head from a man trying to signal someone's attention. Dusty fumbled to straighten his hat, in turn elbowing Lumbergh in his head.

"Dammit," Lumbergh growled. "Just . . . keep walking. Everybody keep walking," he shouted as if he were taking a lead on clearing a crime scene.

A long-haired woman with heavy makeup and a thin face shouted something over people's heads, her voice echoing across the boisterous auditorium. Some people sobbed. Others exchanged confused glares as they were led out, by the hundreds, through the theater's hastily opened doors. The crowd funneled out onto the dazzling red carpet in the lobby, their shoulders pinned together like livestock. Shaken hotel employees with wide eyes did their best to guide the eclectic herd toward the casino.

"Jesus," said Dusty, his face drained of color. "Did that really . . . just happen?" He was out of breath.

"Roy got eaten!" a large woman with permed hair and flared nostrils shouted into her cell phone.

"Bitten, not eaten," clarified the middle-aged bald man behind her, presumably her husband. He straightened his jarred glasses and gazed across the top of others' heads.

"Bitten!" revised the woman. "By a lion!"

"Tiger," corrected the husband.

Two security guards in black, one with a radio in his hand, and the other shouting, "Move it!" pushed their way through the crowd in the opposite direction, trying to get inside.

"This is terrible," said Dusty, swallowing hard. "Do you think . . . ? You don't think Roy's dead, do you?"

"No," answered Lumbergh, not wanting to deal with a potential nervous breakdown from Dusty if he was. He eyed a gap in the crowd and angled his body to make his way toward it.

It had been a horrific scene onstage. In what was clearly an unscripted moment, one of the tigers had knocked one half of the performing duo to his back, then proceeded to drag him offstage in his mouth. Desperate stunt handlers and stage hands chased after them, shouting and screaming before disappearing behind a curtain. The show abruptly ended and attendees were instructed on the loudspeaker to vacate the auditorium.

"Shouldn't you be helping on stage or something?" Dusty asked, sticking close to Lumbergh. "Being a police chief and all?"

"What do you want me to do, arrest the tiger?" said Lumbergh. "Roy needs EMTs, not me."

As if on cue, a siren blared from somewhere behind them. A stage door might have been opened to let in a fire or ambulance crew from a rear parking lot.

"See?" Lumbergh said, turning back to Dusty. "He's getting the help he needs."

When Lumbergh noticed Dusty's glazed eyes and puckered lips, he grabbed him by the arm and picked up their pace. He led Dusty through the sea of tourists until they reached an adjacent walkway just short of the casino area. He pulled Dusty around the corner, telling him to lean back against the wall and take in some deep breaths. Dusty complied, but when he tilted forward to place his hands on his knees—his eyes wide and his lips clamped tight—Lumbergh knew he was about to vomit.

With no bathroom nor trashcan in sight, Lumbergh's orderly instincts compelled him to spare the hotel carpet. He snatched the hat from Dusty's head and held it upside down under his chin, just as the puke discharged from the broad man's mouth. Lumbergh held the hat there, collecting the foul clump of buffet food from earlier. He patted Dusty's back with his other hand.

"It's okay," said Lumbergh like a parent to a sick child. "You'll feel better now."

Dusty coughed and belched, opening his eyes. "God!" he suddenly shouted, realizing how Lumbergh had used his hat. He took a quick step backward, wiping his lower lip with the back of his red sleeve. He glared into the abyss of the hat's crown, eyes narrowing with sadness. His head slowly rose to meet Lumbergh's gaze. "Why?" he whispered, the tremble in his voice echoing a sense of betrayal.

"This is the house that Roy built," Lumbergh forced out. "He and Siegfried. It deserves our respect, especially now."

Lumbergh bit the inside of his own cheek to keep his face straight. One thing the police chief had learned from his career in law enforcement—much of his experience coming from his days in Chicago—was the ability to read people. When it came to perps, that sometimes meant manipulating them into a preferred line of thinking to get a confession. Dusty was no perp and Lumbergh wasn't after an admission of any kind, but over their long road trip from Colorado to Las Vegas, he'd come to learn and accept Dusty's dedication to performance art. As bizarre as it was, it was also entirely sincere. By talking

Dusty's language, Lumbergh hoped to diffuse the situation as best he could.

Sure enough, Dusty straightened his chins and nodded. He took back his hat and gave it another once-over. "Maybe a dry cleaner can—"

"No. It's a goner. It's going in the next trash can." When Dusty groaned, he added, "I'm sure we can find you something similar. This is Vegas, after all."

Curious gamblers pushed back against the crowd exiting the auditorium, trying to make sense of all the buzz as a mustached fireman in full gear now stood in the walkway. He spoke something into his radio.

"This is going to be a zoo," said Lumbergh mostly to himself. "Reporters, fire trucks, traffic hell outside."

"What do you want to do?" asked Dusty.

"Well, it's *your* night. What do *you* want to do? We have some extra time on our hands now."

Dusty placed his hand to his chins and tilted his eyes. "I wouldn't mind going back to Fremont Street, by our hotel. They have that overhead light show that's supposed to be amazing. Every hour on the hour. But Sean has the car, so we'd better . . ."

Lumbergh sighed. "That's going to turn out to be a big mistake. I know it."

"It was meant to be," quipped Dusty.

"No, it wasn't," Lumbergh shook his head. "Sean went through a lot of shit, and he's finally back on the right track. He didn't need this to fog things up for him."

Dusty's eyes lowered, drawing some guilt from Lumbergh.

"I don't mean to make you feel bad," said Lumbergh. "I just . . . Listen, Sean's supposed to meet us at the front of the building. We can gamble or something until he gets back. Then we can all drive back to Freemont."

"Why don't we just call him and sync up?" asked Dusty. "We can take a cab downtown if he's not going to be back for a while."

Lumbergh squinted. "He doesn't have a phone."

"Lisa does. 518-0923."

"That's her number?"

Dusty nodded, a self-satisfied grin developing.

"How do you know that?"

"I saw Sean write it down on a napkin at dinner, right before he took off to call her."

"And you remembered it?"

"Of course! Nine twenty-three. That's an easy one."

"It is? Why? Is it your birthday or something?"

"No, silly. It's Ray Charles's birthday. Only one of the greatest American entertainers of all time!"

Lumbergh glared at Dusty in disbelief. He finally shook his head and said, "Okay, but let's get rid of the hat first. And maybe get you some gum . . . or a mint."

Dusty nodded, and the two made their way through the converging crowd to the casino. There, Dusty forced his hat into an overflowing receptacle. The two returned to the restrooms Sean had called Lisa from. The phones were all occupied.

"Just use mine," Dusty said, quickly reaching into his pocket to pull out a small cell phone.

"Didn't know you had one," said Lumbergh, taking it. He noticed a yellow balloon sticker on its backside. There was a phone number with an "843" area code written in pen on the sticker. "Whose number is this?"

"Mine."

"You have your own number written on your phone?"

"Of course."

"Why?"

"Since I never call myself, I have trouble remembering it."

"You can remember a phone number you saw for a second on a napkin, but you can't—"

"Ray Charles . . ." Dusty reiterated.

"Okay, fine."

"Just don't talk too long, okay?" said Dusty. "I don't have a lot of minutes and I want to call my mom and tell her about Roy." He repeated Lisa's number to Lumbergh and then retreated to the bathroom to rinse out his mouth.

Lumbergh dialed the digits and waited as the phone rang for what seemed like an eternity. When he heard a couple of clicks, Lumbergh struggled with whether to leave a message. But it wasn't an answering machine or voicemail that had picked up. It was a person, and it wasn't Lisa.

"Who's this?" a man asked abruptly. He had an unusually deep voice.

Lumbergh squinted. "Hi. Is this Lisa Kimble's number?"

"It is," the man answered. "Who am I speaking to?"

There was a rich steadiness in his tone, almost as if he were speaking into a microphone in a recording studio. Lumbergh couldn't tell if what he was hearing was the man's natural voice or if there was something off about their connection. Either way, Lumbergh was taken aback by what quickly felt like an interrogation.

"An old friend," Lumbergh answered. "Can I speak to her?"

A few seconds ticked by before the man answered. "She's . . . unavailable at the moment. I'd be happy to take a message."

Unavailable? Lumbergh thought.

Out of the corner of his eye, Lumbergh watched Dusty return to his side from the restroom. The second he opened his mouth, Lumbergh held up his index figure to fend off questions. Dusty nodded and slid his fingers along his mouth to indicate that he was *zipping his lip*.

"Well . . ." said Lumbergh, turning away from Dusty. "I'm really trying to get ahold of Sean Coleman. He's supposed to be with her."

As the words left Lumbergh's mouth, he began to wonder if he was speaking to the man he'd seen with Lisa in front of the school earlier—her boyfriend or maybe he was her husband. But the voice didn't seem to match the man's build. Having questioned a lot of people over the years, Lumbergh had a good sense of such things. The person he was talking to was likely much larger in size. Older too. There was also a hint of a Spanish accent that didn't seem to fit what he saw of the man from the school.

"Ah yes, Sean," said the man, suddenly sounding more relaxed. "They stepped out for a moment. I expect them back soon."

"Okay," Lumbergh muttered, unsure of why they would have left Lisa's home.

"Is that Sean?" Dusty whispered, unable to stay silent any longer. He grinned widely and held up a thumb.

Lumbergh ignored him.

"Do you want to leave a message?" asked the man.

Lumbergh thought about it for a moment, deciding it was probably the best option given the circumstances. "Okay. We were set to meet up with him later to go out, but there's been a change of plans. We want to meet him downtown instead. In front of our hotel."

Lumbergh turned to Dusty. "Nine thirty sound good?"

"Give him until nine forty-five," said Dusty. "Just in case he's getting lucky." He added a wink, the sight drawing a wince from Lumbergh.

"Let's say nine forty-five, in front of the Dusty Nickel," Lumbergh said into the phone.

"Nine forty-five," said the man. "And who are you?" What sounded like a distant police siren made its way through the receiver.

"Gary Lumbergh. Sean's brother-in-law."

There was silence on the other end.

"Hello?" said Lumbergh over the casino ruckus. He thought for a second that he'd been disconnected, but the persistent sound of the siren hadn't gone away; in fact, it had grown louder. Dusty tapped him on the shoulder but Lumbergh quickly shrugged him off.

"Gary Lumbergh," the man finally confirmed, his voice suddenly more serious.

"Yes."

"I'll let him know. And you mentioned 'we.' Who's there with you?"

Lumbergh squinted, not understanding the relevance. "Friend of ours."

"Very good. Enjoy your night." There was a quick but subtle whack in the background, as if a screen door had just been closed. The siren was even louder.

Before Lumbergh could say another word, the phone went dead.

"Okay then," muttered Lumbergh, hitting the "End" button.

As he handed the phone back to Dusty, Lumbergh couldn't

help but think there was something oddly familiar about the way the man spoke, not just his dialect, but also the even, bottomless tone. It reminded him of someone, though he couldn't place who.

Chapter 11

"Where are you taking us?" Lisa asked with a crack in her voice. She sat on the thinly carpeted floor of the cargo van, her legs coiled under her and her back against the wall opposite of the side door. She returned to shushing Hannah, holding the girl against her chest.

"That's a good question, Pops," said the younger man. He sat behind the wheel, leaning forward with his head bouncing nervously between the side mirrors. He no longer wore his mask but had pulled the rearview mirror downward so those behind him couldn't see his face.

"Why don't you say it again, just in case they're complete morons and haven't figured it out yet?" growled the older man. He sat against the side door on the right side of the van, legs spread out and staring through his mask at Lisa. He held his gun with both hands due to the bumpy ride, keeping it aimed at Sean in the back.

"What?" said the driver, the van rattling after catching a rough part of road. The older man's inference was lost on him.

"Why don't you call me Pops one more time?" he said, shaking his head. "Go ahead, do it. Five more times even. Why not?"

The driver turned his head away, toward his side window, in apparent shame. "It's a nickname in some cases," he muttered.

"What's that?" the older man snarled.

"Nothing."

"No, speak up!" he pressed, leaning forward and twisting his head around the edge of the passenger seat, toward the driver. "Because unless you want to go on Maury Povich and announce a DNA test, I don't think you could make it any clearer."

"I . . . I didn't—"

"No, let's just roll with it. Call me 'Pops.' I want you to. I want you to, because if you can't call me that, you might accidentally call me by my full name, or maybe blurt out my address or social security number!"

"Come on, Pops—"

"Now you got it!" the older man shouted, slapping his own thigh before returning both hands to his weapon. "Perfect! So, I'll be Pops and you'll be Asshole. How does that sound? We on the same page?"

"I didn't mean to—"

"Great! We're in agreement. Asshole it is!"

Hannah began crying again, frightened by the yelling. Lisa attended to her as the father shook his head in irritation.

Sean had watched the family squabble from the back corner of the van, not saying a word. His teeth were clenched as he strained to twist his wrists, now bound behind his back with duct tape. The son had done about five laps with a roll from the glovebox, just a few blocks from Lisa's house. He'd done the same with Sean's shoulder and under his armpit, fastening some wadded-up handkerchiefs to his skin and over the bullet wound. His sleeve back down, Sean added more pressure to the wound by leaning up against the wall of the van. The bleeding seemed to have stopped, but the pain hadn't gotten any better.

As his captors argued, Sean became convinced there had

indeed been only one cell phone between them—the one Sean had destroyed back at the house. He'd bought himself and Lisa the time he'd hoped for, but he hadn't expected the restraints. They would make a successful escape much harder . . . at least for him.

Whenever a streetlight shone through the passenger window, Sean observed his surroundings carefully, looking for something he could use to help Lisa and Hannah get away. He also paid attention to the details of the automobile in case he somehow was able to escape and had to identify it later. As he was being pushed inside earlier through its rear doors, he made the van out to be a GMC Savana, dark blue or black in color. It looked at least five years old and was in decent shape. In the dark, aided only for a second by the dome light, he caught the last two letters of the Nevada license plate: "GZ." The rest was concealed by a trailer hitch that clocked his knee hard as he was shoved forward.

There wasn't much inside the vehicle. It was likely used for some type of work, being that the only seats were the two in front. A couple of thick cardboard boxes, each probably three feet in length, sat behind the driver's seat. There must have been something heavy inside them, because they didn't budge when the driver took corners hard. He even thought he'd heard a metal clank inside one of them when the vehicle bounced over a pothole. The interior of the van smelled like cigarettes.

The only windows were up front and in the very back, but the rear ones were covered with louvers that didn't look factory. They would make it hard to get the attention of a driver behind them.

"Really, Pops, where are we going?" asked the driver.

It was hard to tell from under the mask and in the dark, but the older man seemed to be dwelling on the question himself. Whatever hurried plan they'd had back at Lisa's house had fallen completely apart because of the alarm. It was clear there had been no Plan B. The only thing certain was that they needed to get ahold of whoever was supposed to meet them at the house.

Though Sean was separated by Lisa by little more than a wheel well, she felt a mile away at that very moment, her eyes trained on Hannah who was starting to calm back down in her arms. Lisa hadn't glanced back at him once since the van sped off from her home, and he wondered if she blamed him for what was happening. He could understand if she did. They'd come for him, after all, for a reason Sean still didn't understand. All he knew from what the men had said earlier was that if he had never turned up on her doorstep, they wouldn't have either.

The men hadn't brought the issue back up since leaving the house. Sean wasn't going to either. For now, the two were off balance and unsure of themselves. Sean figured that had to play to his advantage. He soon discovered that Lisa saw things differently.

"Listen," she said, commanding the father's attention. "I don't know who you are, but I can't imagine I've done anything to harm you. Why don't you just tell us what you want? You were about to before. Maybe we can help and then you can just let us go."

The man held up his index finger, turning to his son. "Get us onto 95 heading south."

"95?" said the son. "There's nothing there. Just desert."

"Yeah. That's the point."

"Oh God," Lisa gasped. "We can talk about this!"

The father shook his head. "Relax. Right now we don't

have a reason to kill you. Don't give us one. We just need to regroup."

"In the desert?" Sean asked, bringing all eyes to him.

"Yeah," said the father. "We need some privacy."

"It's private here in the van," said Sean.

"Yeah, well, it was private inside her house too, but someone had to go ahead and set off the alarm," he said in a raised voice, his eyes turning to Lisa.

"I had nothing to do with it," she insisted. Her tone sounded so sincere that Sean half believed her.

The father ignored her, turning back to his son. "There's a solar farm about ten miles down. On the right. It's got a parking lot for day workers. There'll be no one there now. There's a payphone in that lot. We'll let him know where we're at."

The son nodded, looking into his side mirror before making a sudden turn and forcing everyone to lean to the left.

"You'll let who know where we're at?" asked Sean. "Who are you taking your marching orders from?"

The father turned back to Sean, glaring at him through his mask. His tone dry, he answered, "You don't want to know."

Chapter 12

The Dusty Nickel Hotel & Casino was a throwback to another era. Positioned a couple of blocks southeast of Fremont, the local businessmen who built it in the early 1970s believed it would help revitalize the area to better compete with the rapidly expanding Las Vegas Strip. They took a property that was once part of Vegas's first train station dating back to the early 1900s and turned it into an eighteen-floor luxury casino with close to eight hundred rooms. But twenty years later, the Strip commanded over 80 percent of the city's casino market, and hotels like the Dusty Nickel had faded into the background of the nostalgia surrounding the downtown area's main drag of neon signs and blinding exteriors.

Though the business was still in operation, its luster and charm had long since vanished. The concrete walls outside were remarkably weathered, burnt-out bulbs weren't replaced all that quickly, and the walls inside probably hadn't been touched with a brush in ten years. It was a slowly dying venture propped up by first-time tourists with tight budgets. Still, Lumbergh found himself mesmerized by the vertical light show that ran up and down the four tall columns that made up the building's façade. They were coordinated with digital music and went all the way up to the building's roof and lit-up marquee sign. The dot of the *I* in the word "Nickel" was in the shape of an actual nickel—something Lumbergh hadn't noticed in the daytime when they checked in.

"What time do you have?" asked Dusty, yawning a little as he leaned up against the wall next to a set of revolving doors. The bright veranda above revealed some grime on his outfit from the cab ride over.

Lumbergh glanced at his watch. "A little past nine thirty. He should be here soon." He lowered his arm. "I'm half surprised he didn't beat us here with all that traffic."

The two had gotten there just five minutes earlier. Las Vegas Boulevard was a swamp. Lumbergh didn't know if it was because of what happened back at the Mirage, or if it was typical of a Friday night. Either way, Sean wouldn't have had to contend with the gridlock returning from Henderson.

Lumbergh watched as two cabs pulled up the circular driveway, almost bumper to bumper. There was only one doorman on duty, an older fellow with a bald head, portly build, and a dark suit who shuffled his way over to the first cab to open the passenger door.

When Dusty's phone rang, Lumbergh swore under his breath. He was sure it was Sean calling with an excuse for why he wouldn't be rejoining them that night. Dusty peeled himself off the wall and dug into his pocket. When he pulled out the phone, Lumbergh snatched it from his hand.

"Hey!" Dusty protested.

Lumbergh tapped a button and held the phone to his ear. "You're ditching us, aren't you?" he said sharply. "Your own friend's bachelor party—"

"What have you done with her?" a panicked, desperate voice rang out. It belonged to a man. "Please don't hurt her. I have money!"

"Sean?" Lumbergh asked, though the voice didn't sound

like his brother-in-law's. He glanced at Dusty and held the phone tighter against his face.

"I'll give you whatever you want," continued the man. "Please . . . please just don't hurt her!" There was a loud crumpling noise in the background, as if the man was outside in the wind.

"I'm sorry," said Lumbergh, his heart ticking up. "I don't understand. Who is this?"

"Greg," he quickly answered. "Greg Wendice. I'm the girl's father." A horn blared through the phone. The man had to have been driving.

"What girl?" Lumbergh shouted.

Lumbergh's bark drew the attention of the doorman and a middle-aged woman with red hair who'd stepped out of the second cab; she was flanked by a couple of young teenagers with colorful shirts and small suitcases, probably her sons.

Wendice shouted back, "Are you with them or not—the men who took them?" Another horn blasted.

Lumbergh was at his wits' end trying to decipher what Wendice was saying. "Listen, my name is Gary Lumbergh," he told him. "I'm a police officer. I don't know what you're talking about, but if you need help, I can get it to you."

Dusty glared at Lumbergh with wide eyes. "What the hell's going on?" he asked, his face uncharacteristically serious.

"Police?" the man said, confused. The reception cut out for a second before returning. "You were talking to him—the big man with the gun. From your phone!"

Lumbergh squinted. "About twenty minutes ago?"

"Yes!"

"Okay," Lumbergh said, trying to calm himself. He took in a breath, working to clear his head. "Who was taken?" He snapped his fingers at Dusty. "I need something to write on."

Dusty nodded, searching his pockets. Coming up with nothing, he jogged over to the doorman.

"Hannah, my daughter," stressed Wendice. "And Lisa!"

"Lisa?" said Lumbergh.

"And some big guy she was with. I don't know him, but they looked like friends."

Lumbergh's jaw dropped. The man had to be referring to Sean. "Okay, where did this happen?" he asked, steadying himself.

"At Lisa's house."

"Were you there? Where are you now?"

"No! I was across town. I'm on my way there now. I saw it . . . I saw it from a camera—a security camera, as it was happening." The man paused to take a breath. "Two guys broke in through the front door, and they were threatening them. And they had guns. I think they shot Lisa's friend."

"They shot him?" Lumbergh shouted, his heart dropping to his gut.

"Yeah, I think in the arm. He got up afterwards. I saw it happening and I set off her house alarm remotely. I thought it would scare the men off, but they took all three of them and then they left! God help me, I don't think I should have done that."

"Okay, just calm down," said Lumbergh, taking some hotel stationary and a short pencil from Dusty.

An older man with oiled hair, gold glasses, and a pinstripe suit had emerged from a revolving door at the front of the hotel. Behind him came a skinny blonde woman in her twenties wearing a miniskirt and a small purse. She leaned on the man's shoulder while reaching down to adjust the strap on one of her high-heeled shoes. Lumbergh's raised voice and seriousness drew their attention as the man pulled a pack of cigarettes from his pocket. The family by the cab also looked on curiously.

Wendice continued. "Just like a minute after they left, some other guy shows up. Big, freaky looking dude with a big-ass gun. He beat the hell out of the alarm console. No way he's a cop. I saw him pick up Lisa's phone and talk into it. I tried calling it after that and no one picked up. So . . . so I did a remote lookup on the last caller and that's how I got you!"

Pinning the phone between his shoulder and ear, Lumbergh scribbled down Wendice's name and other bits of information. "Could you hear what they were saying?"

"Who?"

"The first men. The ones who took Sean and the others."

"No, there aren't any microphones inside. Just the camera."

"Okay, did you see what kind of vehicle they left in?"

"No, the camera's inside. There aren't any outside."

Lumbergh's eyes narrowed. "There's a security camera inside her house, but not outside?"

The man went silent for a few seconds. "It's a long story, okay? But please, my daughter!"

"Okay, listen," Lumbergh said, holding the phone away from his face for a moment and glancing at the display screen. "I've got your number. You need to call 9-1-1 immediately and tell them everything you've told me. I'm not with the local PD."

"I already did!" the man shouted. "The cops are probably there now, at Lisa's. That's where I'm headed!"

"What is happening?" Dusty demanded, throwing his arms up in frustration. He seemed to speak for the onlookers as well.

Lumbergh turned to him, placing his hand over the phone. "I'll explain later. Right now, we need that cab." He motioned toward the vehicle; its driver had just gotten back behind the wheel. "Keep it here. My gun's in the safe up in my room. I need to get it."

"But—"

"Please, Dusty! No bullshit! Just do it!"

Dusty nodded. "Okay, okay." He jogged over to the cab, waving his arms to get the departing driver's attention. The doorman, who was returning to the podium just outside the hotel entrance, twisted his head, glaring confusedly at Dusty.

Lumbergh pressed the phone back up against his face. "Okay. When you get there, tell the police on the scene to track Lisa's cell phone. Even though no one's picking up, the man you saw may still have it on him. And give me Lisa's address. I'll meet you there."

Wendice provided the address and Lumbergh quickly wrote it down.

The screech of a pair of tires grabbed Lumbergh's attention for a moment. A late-eighties black Suburban with darkened windows had pulled up along the driveway. The doorman made his way over to the dust-covered vehicle, extending his hand to open the passenger door.

"Thank you," said Wendice, drawing Lumbergh's focus back.

"Okay," answered Lumbergh. "I'll see you soon. We'll figure this out." He ended the call and shoved the phone in his pocket.

Taking a moment to collect himself, Lumbergh leaned forward, placing his hands on his knees and gazing down at the sidewalk. "Jesus Christ . . ." he muttered, the reality of the situation washing over him.

A sudden commotion drew Lumbergh's attention back to the driveway. The passenger door of the Suburban had swung open hard, toppling the doorman down. Out hopped a bald, brown-skinned man with a red bandana covering the lower half of his face. In jeans and a gray T-shirt, he made a beeline for Lumbergh. When he raised his hand, Lumbergh saw the muzzle of a silver revolver. The man pointed it right at the police chief.

Lumbergh gasped, frozen. There was nowhere to take cover and he had no weapon. The red-haired woman screamed, her sons bolting off without her. The doorman scrambled away on his knees and elbows, eyes bulging out of his head. Rapid footsteps fled in multiple directions.

"*Ven aca!*" the man yelled. "Lumbergh!"

The back seat door of the Suburban swung open. Inside was another man. He was thin with long, dark hair. He, too, wore a bandana and jeans. In his hand was what looked like a Glock.

But just as the man approaching Lumbergh began to shout again, something big and red slammed into the side of his body, snapping the man's head sideways and dropping him to the pavement. It was Dusty. He went down hard with the man, landing on top of him.

Lumbergh didn't waste a second. He lunged forward, going horizontal and grabbing for the man's revolver as Dusty did his best to keep him pinned.

The red-haired woman lowered her head as she dashed toward the revolving doors, knocking the man with the cigarette over on her way. The blonde in the miniskirt had already fled. The cab sped off, peeling rubber as it did.

When Lumbergh grabbed the bulldozed man's wrist with both hands, the gun went off. A glass pane on the building shattered behind them. A woman screamed. The man in the back of the Suburban leaped from the vehicle. He shouted something in Spanish, his voice high like a teenager's. His partner on the ground floundered underneath Dusty, kicking his legs and shoving his empty hand against Dusty's chin. Lumbergh cocked his arm and drove his elbow into the man's armpit. The man yelled in pain, his grip on the pistol loosening and his other hand falling from Dusty's face. Lumbergh pried his fingers from the weapon, the man protesting with loud snarls and grunts.

The other man stood on confused footing, looking back and forth from the unseen driver to the entanglement of bodies on the pavement. He hollered again, pointing his gun, but didn't seem prepared to shoot with his partner in the line of fire. The driver yelled something in Spanish, drawing the standing man's focus to the doorman who'd been lying flat on his chest and covering his ears since the shot had rung out. The man jogged to the doorman, reaching down and grabbing him by the back of his collar.

Lumbergh's hands were wrapped around most of the pistol. He had just about gotten it free when Dusty arched his neck and swung his head forward, opening his mouth and sinking his teeth directly into their adversary's neck. The man howled, his eyes bulging as he took the same punishment that Roy did earlier.

Lumbergh clenched his teeth and yanked the gun free. He spun to his knees, just as the other man was pulling the doorman to his feet. Lumbergh watched him slide his Glock up against his hostage's temple. If given another couple of seconds, the doorman would become a human shield. Steadying his aim and closing an eye, Lumbergh fired. A pop echoed off the building. The man's body buckled forward, the gun and doorman falling from his grip before he staggered backwards.

His eyes were scared and his body shook. His hands went to his abdomen.

"Freeze!" Lumbergh yelled, still pointing the gun as he struggled for breath.

The driver shouted something, and the injured man turned and stumbled backed toward the Suburban.

"*Alto!*" Lumbergh yelled, his eyes swinging from the man to the still concealed driver. Through the corner of his eye, he saw the downed man still fighting with Dusty, kicking and doing his best to squirm out from under him. The bandana had been pulled from his face, revealing a black goatee and piercings on his ears and nose.

The man with the bullet in his gut made it to the Suburban and threw himself inside, collapsing onto the floorboard. He cried out. The driver took off. The door swung shut as the vehicle hopped over a median and took out some hedges before speeding back toward the street. Lumbergh looked for a license plate, but there wasn't one.

"Chief!" Dusty shouted.

Lumbergh turned to see Dusty barely hanging onto the other man, his arms wrapped around the man's ankles. From his rear end, the man pulled one leg free and sent a hard stomp square into Dusty's face, breaking his hold. As the man scrambled to his feet, Lumbergh moved in.

"Freeze!" Lumbergh yelled again, standing just a few feet away. Lumbergh held the pistol firm with both hands, lining up the sights.

The man stayed put, glaring back as he slowly stood up. His chest heaved in and out and blood ran down his neck. His eyes shifted nervously between Lumbergh and his surroundings. Seeing his partner shot in the stomach had likely given him second thoughts about making any sudden moves. On the ground, Dusty lay on his side with his hands covering his face.

"*Now* can you tell me what's happening?" Dusty groaned, his voice muffled from his fingers.

"I've called the police!" a man shouted from somewhere behind them, causing Lumbergh to jump. It was probably a hotel worker.

Lumbergh nodded. "Get down on your chest!" he told the assailant.

The assailant stared at him, not moving. His eyes suddenly burned with what looked like hatred. Deep breaths swept in and out of his body.

"I said . . . get down on your chest," yelled Lumbergh.

Lumbergh watched his attacker's jaw square. When Dusty pulled himself to his knees, the man's focus switched to him. His eyes widened at the sight of his bandana clenched in Dusty's hand. It was clear he hadn't realized until just then that his face was fully exposed . . . and with it, his identity.

"Don't make me shoot you!" said Lumbergh. "*Bajar!*" he shouted, hoping he was getting the Spanish right.

The man stayed put, his face slowly twisting into a sharp scowl. It was aimed directly at Lumbergh. His body tensed up, his arms and shoulders trembling.

"Dusty," Lumbergh said carefully. "Get up and get behind me." His years of law enforcement told him that the man now had no intention of going quietly.

The man didn't flinch with Dusty's footsteps or the sound of a police siren that echoed in the distance.

"You don't want this," Lumbergh said, his eyes on the man as Dusty took cover behind him, holding his bloody nose.

Lumbergh held the gun steady. "Whatever's going down isn't worth dying for."

The man's entire body was now trembling. Having not frisked him, Lumbergh knew he may have had another weapon on him somewhere.

"Lumbergh," the man sneered in disgust, his nostrils flaring. He spit on the pavement between them. His tone was unmistakably personal. Lumbergh didn't understand why.

The man dropped to a knee and reached for his left ankle. Lumbergh fired. Three shots lit up the driveway like a Vegas marquee.

Silence filled Lumbergh's ears though he was sure things weren't silent around him. A shadow crossed behind him. Headlights shone through the corner of his eye. And the man before him now lay still on cracked pavement.

Lumbergh forced some breaths from between his lips and carefully moved in close, gun aimed at the man's punctured chest. He carefully lowered to a knee beside him, taking a hand off the gun to slide it along the man's ankle. He felt nothing other than a grimy sock. The same was true of the other leg. The man had only pretended to go for a weapon.

Lumbergh placed a couple of fingers over the man's bloody throat and checked for a pulse. There was none. When Lumbergh turned to check on Dusty, he found him sitting on the edge of the sidewalk, his head low with his hands over his face.

"You okay?" he asked, climbing to his feet.

Dusty nodded, but kept his hands put. Blood from his nose dripped down his fingers to his pants. He wasn't in character, as Lumbergh had so often seen him. He wasn't putting on a front. He was quickly coming to terms with the realness of what had just happened. Lumbergh walked over to him and placed his hand on his shoulder.

"Thank you," said Lumbergh, taking a breath. "Now, let's figure out what the hell is going on."

Chapter 13

The crackle of gravel under the tires echoed up through the van when the son took a hard right turn.

"You see it, Asshole?" asked the father, his eyes on Sean.

"Yeah," answered his son, shaking his head at his new nickname. "On the other side of the lot, past the work trailer."

The father nodded. "You know, I'm half surprised you haven't offered us any money," he said, his statement directed at Sean.

Sean scoffed. "Money for what? Gas?"

"He means to let us go," said Lisa, irritated.

Her sharp glance and tone brought back memories of how they talked toward the end of their relationship.

"I know what he meant," said Sean, his voice even and his eyes shifting back to the father. "But something tells me these two aren't exactly in the *highest bidder* businesses. And if they are, they suck at it."

"Excuse me?" said the father as the van began to slow.

"Is a recap really needed?" said Sean. "Or can we just agree that if this were all about money, you would have targeted people who actually had some."

The son shook his head. "You've got *some* balls," he said, bringing the van to a stop. An overhead lamp, probably above the payphone, lit up the cab a bit as he carefully pulled his mask back over his face.

"Common sense doesn't take balls," said Sean. "She's a teacher. I'm a security guard. How much you think each of us are pulling down a year?"

The father chuckled, shaking his head. "Yeah, it's not your official take-home pay we're after, pal." He reached behind him and opened the side door.

The son killed the engine and twisted in his seat to face the back of the vehicle. He leveled his pistol as his father crawled out of the van, stretched his back under the dome light, and slammed the door shut behind him. Hannah's head shot up straight, her head bobbing before she lifted it to Lisa. Everyone listened to the old man walk across the gravel until his footsteps faded.

"Your father brought up my late husband back at the house," said Lisa, turning to the son. "He did it a couple of times. You say this is about Sean, but it clearly has something to do with Kyle as well. Why don't you just come out and say what it is?"

Sean understood what Lisa was doing. The father had some wits about him. The son, not so much. If anyone was going to be manipulated into giving up information, it would be him . . . when his father was out of earshot.

The son glared at Lisa before switching to Sean. "Why don't *you* tell her?"

Lisa's head switched to Sean.

Sean grunted. "Tell her what? I'd never even met Kyle Kimble."

"Oh, is that a fact?" said the son.

"Yeah," answered Sean. "That's a fact. I saw him exactly once—from a distance—a minute before he put a bullet through his own head. We never said a word to each other. Hell, he didn't even know I was there watching him." Sean lowered his head. "I was just a random guy who saw a stranger off himself. Some desperate son of bitch who thought his life was over because . . ." Sean hesitated, his head lifting. A moment of clarity washed over him. He looked at Lisa and then turned his attention back to the son. Leaning forward he said, "Because of Vincenzo Moretti . . ."

The son said nothing, seemingly waiting on Sean to say more.

Kyle Kimble had chosen suicide over a far more painful end. Moretti had tortured and murdered his own wife over the affair she'd had with Kyle. Kyle had narrowly escaped the night before, but the crime lord's men were quickly closing in. He feared that if he didn't take his own life, painlessly and on his own terms, they'd keep him alive just long enough to force him to watch Lisa tortured and murdered as well.

"This is about him, isn't it?" Sean added.

"Moretti?" said Lisa.

"It's the only thing that makes any sense," said Sean, his eyes on the son. "Is this some kind of revenge bullshit because Moretti's stuck in a federal prison? Is he who you assholes work for? How about the guy your *pops* is chatting with? Does he work for Moretti too?"

The son said nothing, glaring through the mask. Perhaps he was worried he'd already given away too much information. Or maybe Sean was so far off that the man hadn't a clue what he was talking about. Something told Sean it was the former.

"Jesus, if it's revenge you're after," said Sean, "take it out on me. Lisa and the girl have nothing to do with this."

"I'm . . ." stammered the son. "I'm not saying nothin' else."

There was enough light coming in through the windshield to trace the lines of Lisa's softened face. She was looking at Sean, no longer in irritation. The truth was that both she and Sean were instrumental in putting Moretti behind bars. Lisa had spotted Moretti at the airport in Denver where he was attempting to leave the country, and Sean had knocked him out cold as he tried to escape security. But Sean was now re-writing history for Lisa's benefit.

"Jesus, fuck!" The words carried in from outside the van.

Gravel snapped with hastened footsteps. A second later, the side door swung open and the dome light popped back on. The father leaned in, his thin shoulders trembling as his masked faced nervously pivoted between Sean, Lisa, and his son. Heavy breathing poured from behind the plastic.

"What's wrong?" asked the son.

The father placed his hand to the side of his head, again surveying the van's occupants before settling on his son. "Something . . . happened," he said, uncertainty in his voice.

"What? What happened?" asked the son.

"Just . . ." said the father. "Just let me think." His gun was still in hand but it now was lowered to the ground.

Sean and Lisa looked at each other. Hannah twisted in Lisa's arms.

"God, this is so fucked up!" the father shouted, slamming a fist up against the side of the van. He moaned afterward, curling forward with his hand under his chest, as if he'd hurt it. "This was supposed to be fucking business!"

"Pops?"

"Shut up!" he lashed out at his son. He quickly raised his gun at Sean.

"Whoa, take it easy," said Sean, pushing himself back against the rear doors.

Whatever the father had just heard over the phone was tearing him apart at the seams. He was desperate, erratic, and even scared.

"Your time is running out fast, hotshot!" the father snarled at Sean. "Do you hear me? We've entered a whole new level now—a whole other dimension. You got that? So no more bullshit!" The reflection from the dome light bounced off his glasses as he spoke.

"How many times do I have to tell—" Sean began.

"The two-hundred large that showed up in your bank account less than a week ago!" the father blurted out. "We know where it came from."

Hannah wailed, the sharp, loud voices frightening her.

Sean yelled back over the child, his eyes bulging. "My fucking bank account? That's what this is about?" He didn't know how the men were privy to his personal finances, but the revelation didn't explain their actions. The deposit the old man spoke of was related to security work he'd done months earlier, back in Colorado. The men's rabid interest made no sense. "No way this is about just $200K! You broke into a home and kidnapped people! What's your real game here?"

"It's not a game!" the father yelled, as Hannah's screaming only added to the overflowing tension. "Jesus, shut her up!" he screamed at Lisa.

"She's screaming because you are!" Lisa snapped back. "She'd be asleep in her bed right now if you two—"

"Asshole!" the father barked, turning to his son. "Get them out of the van! I can't fucking think with that kid screaming!"

"Don't you hurt them," Sean warned as the son exited the van.

"Shut up!" yelled the father, taking a step back and motioning Lisa forward with his gun.

She glanced at Sean with wide, unblinking eyes before crawling toward the door and hopping out, Hannah screaming as she did.

"That motion sickness stuff," said the father to his son. "Dramamine! You still got that in the glovebox?"

The son nodded.

"Have her give the kid some. It'll put her to sleep. I've had it with the crying. Best the kid's not awake for this shit anyway."

The son leaned over and popped open the glove compartment, following his father's orders. He got out and circled over to the open door of the van. "Come on!" he said to Lisa.

His father climbed all the way inside the van, kneeling as he brought his gun back to Sean. The crying and bickering between Lisa and the son grew further away along with their footsteps.

The father glared at Sean, his chest moving in and out. His breath filtered audibly through his mask. His raised his empty hand to the plastic and then peeled it from his face, the elastic string snapping as he did. Beyond the round rim of glasses with thin frames, the light revealed a mostly bald, freckled forehead . . . and the sunken, wrinkled face of an elderly man who wouldn't have looked remotely threatening under any other circumstance.

"You know what this means?" said the man, his narrow eyes pinned to Sean. His tone was dead serious. "It means you'll soon be dead. But the dame and the girl don't have to be—not if you tell us where the rest of the money is . . . right now. If you do, we'll let them go. I promise you. And for all my flaws— of which I admit there are many—I'm a man who keeps his promises."

Sean stared back, saying nothing. His mind raced as he absorbed the sobering words.

"We have ten minutes tops until he's here," the father continued. "And then it will be too late. He might just kill them for the fun of it—for the reckoning . . . because that's what he does. Do you understand me? That's who he is."

Sean glared back, the hair on the back of his neck raised as he tried to make sense of what the man was saying. He didn't know what other money the father could be referring to; there wasn't any. But Sean was certain that the father believed otherwise. Removing his mask and the weight with which he spoke all but ensured it. No one could be that good of an actor.

"Who's coming?" asked Sean, his voice steady and direct.

The father's face tightened, his upper lip disappearing in what almost looked, for a second, like sympathy.

When Sean heard the name, his breath left him, and his heart sank to his stomach. He needed no further convincing of the soullessness of the individual he would soon meet. He knew well of the many dead bodies the man had left behind in Mexico, and every day felt the deep, torturous loss of what the man's family had done to his own.

Lautaro Montoya, the Mexican crime lord. His brother Alvar had murdered Sean's father.

Chapter 14

The Montoya brothers were once described as a "two-man criminal plague" in a Chihuahua, Mexico newspaper. Less than twenty-four hours later, the author of the piece was found dead in a salvage yard in the southern part of the city. His decapitated head had been impaled on the hood ornament of a junked Studebaker, a copy of the article shoved in his mouth. The rest of his body was left neatly in the vehicle's bed, minus the eight fingers and two thumbs he'd used to type the piece; those were never recovered.

Lautaro and Alvar had terrorized their territory south of the border for years, keeping the local law enforcement at bay through intimidation that went well beyond idle threats. Both well above six feet tall, the imposing drug lords demonstrated a wiliness and shocking indifference to torturing and killing not only rival dealers and other perceived adversaries, but also members of their families. By the 1990s, surviving witnesses didn't dare speak of what they saw, especially after they brazenly gunned down a traffic officer in broad daylight outside a restaurant, whose death stemmed from the unfortunate luck of him being married to a small-time dealer's sister.

But it was the murder of the journalist in Chihuahua that ultimately led to the end of the crime ring. It turned out that the reporter's family had close connections to a high-ranking official in the country's Department of Security and Civil Protection. A week later, in an early-morning synchronized operation, two teams of heavily armed Federales separately stormed the brothers' homes.

Lautaro, the older of the two, went down relatively easy and ended up in prison. An ill-fated decision to load up on methamphetamines and hookers just a few hours earlier left him easy prey for a stun grenade and the half dozen masked men in swat gear who'd kicked open his villa door.

Alvar was a different story. He managed to escape in a hail of gunfire, sending two officers to the emergency room that night with multiple bullet wounds. They survived. The same couldn't be said of the two US border agents who are presumed to have recognized Alvar at their remote checkpoint in Texas the next day.

Once in America, Alvar managed to evade authorities. He fell off the radar for a couple of years, changing his appearance and name, and eventually going to work for Vincenzo Moretti out of Vegas. He served as private muscle for Moretti, as well as a go-between guy for trafficking meth. That's what ultimately brought him into Lisa and Sean's life.

Lisa always knew her late husband Kyle was an accountant. What she didn't know was that he was *Moretti's* accountant. He'd successfully kept that detail hidden from her for years. Kyle crunched numbers and funneled money for Moretti. He was intimately familiar with the financial details of nearly all of Moretti's business dealings . . . including the illegal ones.

In the summer of 2001, Kyle accompanied Moretti and the rest of his inner circle on a business trip to the Colorado mountains. A legalized gambling measure to revive some local economies in the state's high country had opened up an opportunity for Moretti to expand his casino empire outside of

Nevada. Unfortunately, that's where Moretti discovered that Kyle had been having an affair with his young immigrant wife.

Moretti killed her that night, and the next morning Kyle killed himself on a bridge just outside of Winston. Sean was a hapless witness to the event. Unfortunately, the killing didn't end there.

Kyle's final living act, prior to putting a bullet through his own skull, was to mail Moretti's financial ledger to the Las Vegas branch of the FBI. It was a move Moretti hadn't seen coming. He'd figured out early on that Kyle had taken the ledger, but when news quickly came of the man's suicide, Moretti's top priority switched to tracking down where he'd stashed the financials. And the only lead he had to go on was the report of Sean having witnessed Kyle's final seconds.

When Alvar came to Sean's home looking for answers, he didn't find Sean. Instead, he found Sean's father, Zed. A violent confrontation resulted in Zed's death. A day later, Alvar Montoya's reign of terror came to an end when he lost his own life in a shootout with Lumbergh at a remote property a few miles north of Winston.

The incident made national news, and even turned Lumbergh into somewhat of a folk hero back in Chihuahua and other areas in Mexico as *the man who slayed Alvar Montoya.*

Months later, Lautaro escaped from a maximum-security prison in Mexico. Lumbergh and others were concerned at the time that he may come looking for revenge for his brother's death. But some anonymous threats Lumbergh received turned out to be a hoax, and though Lautaro was never recaptured, he also, for whatever reason, never came knocking.

There was speculation from the feds that the Montoya brothers had had a falling out, prior to the raids in Mexico. There was even a theory that Lautaro believed Alvar had set him up to take the fall for their crimes south of the border, and that he had planned to flee north all along—to lower his profile and scale back operations. If so, it could have explained Lautaro's disinterest in avenging his brother after his escape.

There had been a couple of alleged sightings in the US over the months—one in Texas and one in California. Neither were confirmed, though there was a sense that Lautaro had likely fallen into his brother's American footsteps, acting as a liaison or independent contractor smuggling drugs up from connections in Mexico. Being a certified pilot, he had an edge his brother hadn't. But it was all speculation about a man who'd become a virtual ghost.

That was about to change. In minutes, Sean would come face to face with the man. And as he sat in a van with a bullet in his shoulder and his hands still tied behind him, he pled with the old man who'd brought him to the desert somewhere south of Vegas.

"You need to get them out of here right now!" he yelled. "Both of them!"

"That's entirely up to you, pal!" the old man growled. "Where's the rest of the money?"

"Jesus, I swear to God I don't know what you're talking about!" yelled Sean, a vein protruding at the center of his reddened forehead. "All I have to my name is that $200K—that and another hundred or so in my wallet. You can have it all! I don't give a shit! But that's all there is."

"You know what Montoya's capable of," the father shouted, "so don't—"

"You're damn right I do!" Sean yelled over him. "That's why I'm telling you to get the others out of here, right now, before it's too late. You really want their deaths on your hands? A woman and a little girl?"

The old man's mouth closed. He seemed to be thinking, and his eyes shifted between Sean and the open van door.

"I'll stay here with you, outside in the parking lot," Sean said, his gaze leveled at the father. "I'll answer for whatever needs to be answered for. Just tell your son to get the others back in here and drive them somewhere else—and fast!"

The father glared blankly through his glasses at Sean.

"Please!" Sean added.

The father's jaw grew so tight that he looked like his teeth were about to crack. "You don't understand," he said. "That may have worked before, but for him, this is no longer about the money. Everything's changed. Everything's fucked!"

"What's fucked?" Sean asked. "What are you saying?"

The old man opened his mouth to reply, but a cough came out instead. He cursed his way through it, holding his fist to his mouth. "Vincenzo Moretti!" he belted out. "You know who that is."

Sean nodded. "This *is* about revenge then."

"It *wasn't*," the father said. "It was about the shitload of money that Kyle Kimble embezzled from him."

Sean's face recoiled. "What?"

"Dammit, I'm talking about the millions that . . . ." he began, before pausing and honing in on Sean's confused eyes.

"Listen," Sean broke back in. "I don't know what you think happened, but I've never taken a cent from Kimble, or Moretti, or Montoya, or any of those assholes. I came out here to Vegas, on vacation, for exactly one reason: my buddy's bachelor party. I visited Lisa because she happens to live here."

The father blinked, his eyes narrowing. They suddenly widened in what looked like a moment of realization. "Oh Jesus," he growled, placing his hand to his head. "Ah, fuck!"

"What?"

"*Lumbergh . . .*" said the father, shaking his head. His shoulders deflated. "God, I knew that name sounded familiar. He's the guy who killed Montoya's brother, isn't he? The lawman from Colorado. *That's* who you came out here with?"

Sean's gut tightened. He didn't answer. The utterance of his brother-in-law's name was the last thing he was expecting to hear. He didn't want to put Lumbergh in danger by acknowledging his whereabouts.

The father lowered his head, his gun lowering a little with it. "Jesus. This wasn't about settling up with the dame, was it? Just a goddamn booty call. Fuck. It's Nevada . . . You couldn't just pay for one like everyone else? Maybe with some of that $200K?"

Sean squinted. "What?"

The father shouted back. "*Three weeks ago*, the federal case into Moretti officially ended! *One week ago,* you came into a big chunk of money—the kind of money a self-employed security guard from Colorado can't make in ten years! *One hour ago,* you show up on Kimble's wife's doorstep, two states away! And in some strange, fucked up way, it was all one big coincidence?" He shook his head, wiping his nose with the back of his hand. A snort fell from it. "Who are you, the unluckiest son of a bitch on the planet?"

Sean shrugged his shoulders. "Pretty much. Now can you get Lisa and the girl the hell out of here?"

"Like I said, pal, it ain't that simple."

A gunshot suddenly rang out. The old man jumped, his head spinning toward the open door. Sean's body jackknifed forward, pain shooting up his shoulder as his breath left his lungs. Hannah bellowed.

"Jesus," Sean gasped.

"The hell?" the father snarled, turning and sliding out of

the vehicle, his gun raised. He glanced back at Sean before disappearing outside.

Heart racing, Sean turned his hips and pulled himself to his knees with a grunt. He climbed forward, digging his knees into the carpet. Pain surged through his shoulder with every bump forward. When he reached the open door, he nearly fell straight through it, but managed to hook the edge of the side wall with his good shoulder.

"Stop where you are!" Lisa yelled from somewhere in the dark.

Sean couldn't see her, but the old man was still visible a few feet in front of him. His arm was raised, his gun pointing toward something. Sean lurched forward, unfolding a leg and planting his foot on the gravel. He lunged toward the man, lowering his shoulder and sending it hard between his shoulder blades. Sean cried out from the pain of the lodged bullet, but he'd made the contact he needed to. The father's body buckled and he tumbled forward to the gravel. Sean fell to a knee behind him, his heart pounding.

"Lisa!" Sean yelled, dust in his mouth.

Another shot went off, this time lighting up the darkness. It was enough for Sean to see Lisa, for a split second, standing below it. Her arms were raised high, her hands pointing a pistol at the sky. The son was curled up on the ground just a few feet from her.

Sean couldn't see Hannah, but her screaming pierced the air like a tornado siren.

"Get his gun, Sean!" Lisa yelled.

Sean's eyes went to the old man. He was crawling along the ground, his left arm reaching out in front of him. The gun must have been knocked the from his hand. Sean slogged his way around him, spotting an object just inches away that reflected some light. With his arms still bound behind his back, the best he could do was kick the weapon. If he'd aimed for Lisa, it might end up in the hands of the fallen son instead. Sean twisted his hips and booted the pistol past the front of the van. It skipped off the ground a couple of times before rattling the bottom of a tall chain-link fence about thirty feet away.

"Get over by your dad!" ordered Lisa. "Now!"

Sean squinted, his eyes struggling in the dark as he spun his head, trying to pinpoint the direction of Hannah's wailing.

"Is she okay?" he asked, some spray shooting out of his mouth.

"Yes, I set her down. I'll get her. Take my gun!"

"My hands are still tied," Sean said.

"Dammit," Lisa whispered. "Okay . . ." she said to the father. "You stay on your chest and don't move. Son on the ground, you untie Sean."

Sean was taken aback by her take-charge attitude. He'd never seen that side of her. But the accolades would have to wait for another time.

"This won't save you," the father warned, leaning up on his elbows. His glasses had been knocked from his face.

"Shut up!" Sean said as he struggled to his feet, wincing with the pain of movement. He walked over to the son, taking brief notice of the tall, metal street lamp whose light he'd seen through the windshield. The lamp stood just a few feet inside of the fence. Well beyond the fence were tall, v-shaped pylons, high electric wires connecting them. They were lit up by faraway spotlights. Below the street lamp was the payphone, some graffiti written over its dented box cover.

The phone would be Sean's first stop once his hands were free.

"Get up and get your fingers working on my wrists," he said to the son, sending his boot up under his ribs to turn him over.

The son grunted and crawled to his knees, still hunched over. He no longer wore his mask. It had either fallen or broken off.

"She got you in the nuts, didn't she?" the father asked of his son, his tone deflated with disappointment.

"She stabbed me!" he cried, his hand going to his shoulder.

Sean's head turned to Lisa, his eyes confused.

"In the shoulder . . . with a letter opener," she explained. "Grabbed it from the guest room, when Hannah and I were locked in there. But yeah . . . then I got him in the nuts."

"Jesus, what have I always told you?" the father said to his son. "Always watch your nuts around dames. Men got a code not to go there, but dames—"

Before the father could get out another word, the son yanked himself to his feet. He clumsily stumbled forward and planted his leg toward the chain-link fence. Sean was unable to process what the son was doing before he hurled something from his hand through the air as if he were throwing a touchdown pass. There was a faint jingle, barely detectable over Hannah's crying. Lisa swung her gun toward him.

"What was that?" she demanded.

The son lowered his arms and turned back toward the others, still hunched over a bit. Even in the darkness, Sean could make out his inflated cheeks. They oozed with self-satisfaction.

Sean's gaze lowered to the dense scrub on the other side of the fence. Cacti, yucca, and tall weeds were partially lit up by the street lamp. For the first time, he noticed barbed wire lining the top of the fence, curved outward.

"Did you throw the van keys over that fence?" Sean asked.

The son snorted. "You're damn right I did. You aren't going any—"

Sean snarled and lunged forward, slamming his knee directly into the son's crotch. The son's body snapped forward, the jolt lifting him off the ground before he came crumbling back down to the gravel. He sucked wind, rolling to his side.

Sean turned toward the father, nostrils flaring.

"A man with no code," the father grumbled, shaking his head.

"Sean, look!" Lisa shouted. "A car is coming!"

Sean spun toward the road they'd come in on. To the north he watched a lone pair of headlights slice their way toward them through the dark. A second later, the faint sound of the vehicle's engine could be heard.

"We can get the road and flag them down," Lisa said.

Sean turned to the father, who was still on the ground, his head propped up toward Sean. He said nothing.

"No," Sean said, watching the vehicle's speed. It had to be going at least ninety miles per hour. "We're too late."

"What?" Lisa shouted.

"We need to get out of here. Right now. On foot."

Sean's head swung along the landscape to the west, away from the road. Small, evenly spaced, red and white control lights traced the plain. Sean remembered the father describing the area as a "solar farm." The lights had to belong to large rows of solar panels. The fencing didn't extend in front of the area.

"Let me untie you," Lisa said.

"No time. Grab Hannah."

"We can use the phone. We can call 9-1-1!"

"Forget it! We'd be dead before we could get three words out!"

"He's going to get you either way," said the father as Lisa turned and went for Hannah. "You think you're going to make it out of this?"

Sean ignored his question, but posed some of his own. "How did Montoya know Lumbergh was here?" he asked, out of breath. "What changed the second time you talked to him? How did this go from a *business deal* to total shit?"

The father shook his head, lowering it toward ground.

"Tell me, or we'll take the time to kneecap your boy!" Sean yelled.

"Yeah, right" the father grumbled, lifting his head back to Sean. "But what the hell, I'll tell you how fucked you are. Something went down a little while ago. Your brother-in-law shot Lautaro's son."

"What?" Sean barked. "How?"

"Don't know, don't care. But the kid's in bad shape. And when Montoya's after blood, he gets it!"

Sean heard Lisa race up behind him, Hannah sniveling in her arms. The headlights were moving even faster. The vehicle would reach the turnoff in seconds.

"Let's go," Sean said, turning back toward the panels.

Chapter 15

"That ain't right what he did to you, Pops," said the son, hunched over on his knees, breathing hard. One hand was folded over his crotch, and the other over his shoulder. The approaching headlights lit up his face, casting a long shadow behind him.

The father returned to his son's side after retrieving his gun from near the fence. In the seconds it had taken him to find it, the night had swallowed up their former captives. The father watched the incoming vehicle, adjusting his glasses. His eyes narrowed as the headlamps drew in closer.

"What do you mean, *ain't right?*" he asked, belatedly responding to his son's statement.

"The way he knocked you down to the ground like that. That's elder abuse."

The father rolled his eyes, letting out a cough before tucking his pistol into the back waistline of his pants.

A bar of light suddenly lit up above the approaching vehicle's cab. It appeared to be an SUV. The glare nearly blinded the two, the son lifting his arm up in front of his face. The father's heart was pounding; he drew in a deep breath to try and ease his nerves.

"Get up and let me do the talking," the father said, his voice stern but shaky. "I mean it," he added as the son pulled himself up off the ground, slapping dust from his pants. "Don't say one fucking thing. You don't fuck around with a guy like this."

The son nodded. "Okay, Pops."

The father prayed his son would take his words to heart. He raised his hand high, motioning the vehicle forward in hastened fashion. He knew the driver needed no further guidance, but expressing some urgency was the smart play. *The escapees haven't gone far. Coleman is injured. They have just one gun among them, with only a few bullets.* It was the outline he'd present to Montoya and his crew, hopefully compelling them to look past his and his son's incompetence, to focus on an easy recapture. He and Montoya had had successful business dealings in the past. He hoped that counted for something.

Then again, Montoya's son had been shot. He very well wasn't thinking rationally.

The vehicle skidded to a halt about fifteen feet in front of them, its engine still rumbling. It was an 80s Ford Bronco, white in color and no plate below the grill. The bright lights and tinted windows concealed its occupants. The father could make out some movement and some shuffling from inside the cab, but not much else. The driver's side door suddenly swung open, causing both men to jump.

A man of average height and weight plopped out. He had short hair and was wearing some type of jean jacket. The rest of him was hard to make out behind the glare. Another man squeezed out of the Bronco behind him. He looked a little taller and had a ponytail and a snug, white T-shirt.

A voice came from inside the Bronco—what sounded like half a phone conversation muffled by the engine. It was in Spanish. The voice was deep and the tone was angry. The father recognized it. It belonged to Lautaro Montoya.

"They in the van?" the driver asked in a Spanish accent. He reached behind him and pulled out a handgun, quickly checking its action.

The other man whipped out a pistol as well. It looked like a revolver. He held it at his side.

"No!" the father answered, his voice cracking. He swallowed.

The driver looked up, puzzled.

"Listen . . . Coleman blindsided us! He stabbed my son and grabbed his gun! I shot him . . . in the shoulder. He's injured and he's almost out of bullets. They ran off in that direction, just now." He swung his arm toward the solar field. "You can catch them if you move quickly!"

The driver glanced back at his ponytailed partner, quickly saying something to him. He then raised his gun toward the van as the partner cautiously jogged over to it, his arms horizontal with his revolver in front of him.

"There's no one in there," the father said, his eyes shifting back to the passenger side of the Bronco where the conversation continued without pause.

The men ignored him. When the man with the ponytail reached the open door of the van, he dropped to a knee and swung his arms inside, covering the vehicle's rear. He checked out the seats in front next, then lowered to his knees to check the undercarriage. He yelled something in Spanish to the driver, who turned to the inside of the Bronco. He appeared eager to speak but didn't want to interrupt Montoya.

The man with the ponytail directed his gaze across the area, peering through the fence and then toward the solar field.

"They went that way!" the father said, pointing again.

"This way here!" the son shouted out, his finger tracing the same direction. The comment earned a disapproving glare from his father.

The ponytailed man ignored them. He may not have understood English.

Montoya's voice suddenly shot up in volume, drawing everyone's attention to the Bronco. He shouted a three-word sentence before going silent. The driver looked nervous, his focus shifting between the vehicle's cab and the direction the father had pointed him in. He finally spoke to Montoya, his muffled words appearing to leave his mouth carefully.

A chill slid up the father's spine. He turned to his son who glanced back. "Remember," he whispered. "Don't say shit."

Montoya must have given an order, because the driver quickly turned to his partner and brought him back to the vehicle with the swing of his head. The driver leaned into the cab behind his seat and pulled out a rifle, handing it to the ponytailed man. It was some kind of semiautomatic with a scope up top. The partner took it, pulled out its magazine, then checked it over before snapping it back into place. The driver pulled out a similar rifle and went through the same motions.

"Got an extra one of us?" the father asked, trying his best to sound assertive. "We'll cover you."

"No," the driver said. "You stay here. He wants to talk to you."

The father swallowed.

The driver reached back inside the vehicle and pulled out a long flashlight. He flipped it on and off, nodded inside, and then slammed the door shut. He said something to his partner and the two took off on foot, jogging past the father and son without further acknowledgement.

The father turned and watched them make their way toward the solar field. The metallic cry of hinges pulled his focus back to the Bronco.

"Pops," said the son, nudging his shoulder against his father's.

"Be cool," the father whispered.

From behind the open passenger door emerged the tall, thick frame of Lautaro Montoya. His faced was cloaked by darkness. When he left the vehicle, the top of his head rising high above the window, the vehicle lifted a good inch or two from the release of weight.

"Mr. Montoya," the father blurted out. "Your son. Is he getting the proper treatment? I know people—doctors who can help him, and they'll do it off the books."

Montoya didn't respond. He slowly and steadily made his way around the door, his gaze directed toward the father and son as the hard soles of what sounded like cowboy boots dug into gravel. He stopped in front of the grill of the Bronco, standing between the headlights, his fists clenched at his sides, with no weapon in either of them.

"Your men," the father said. "They'll have him soon. There's nothing to worry a . . ."

He stopped when Montoya raised his arm, appearing to hold his index finger in front of his mouth. With the father's silence, Montoya's arm lowered back to his side.

"Nothing you couldn't handle," Montoya said, the depth in his voice pressing against the father's body like a gust of wind.

"What?" the father said, his tone timid.

"That's what you said on the phone, at the bitch's house. *Nothing you couldn't handle.*"

The father felt his son's eyes on him, prying for some sort of direction. He had none to offer.

"Listen," said the father, taking a second to clear his throat. "I'm sorry. We had them. Everything was fine, and then the goddamn house alarm went off and it wouldn't shut off—"

"And this is of my concern?" Montoya interjected, his delivery monotone.

"No," the father said, his eyes lowering to the ground. "Of course not."

"But it's okay," the son broke in. "Your guys will have them any minute now."

The father's heart nearly stopped as his son spoke out. "But that's no excuse," the father quickly added, pulling the focus back to him. "You're absolutely right. We dropped the ball and we want to make things right. So . . . That finder's fee . . . Don't worry about it. Keep it."

Montoya said nothing. As seconds that felt like minutes ticked by without another word spoken by either party, the father's body tensed up. In his mind, he rehearsed sliding his hand to his backside, pulling out the pistol, and unloading it into Montoya. His reflexes far from what they were as a young man, he prayed he wouldn't have to commit to the action.

When Montoya eventually leaned his rear up against the grill of the Bronco and crossed his arms in front of his chest, the father let some breath escape his lungs.

"Keep it?" said Montoya. "After all those hours of listening to phone calls and tracking financials."

"Yeah," the father said, glancing at his son whose puzzled eyes he could read even in the dark. "We'll call it even."

"Even?" said Montoya.

"Sure. Yeah."

Montoya nodded. "I suppose that's fair," he added after a few seconds.

The son's head bobbled between the father and Montoya. He clearly didn't agree with the terms. "Pops?" he whispered.

"Shut up," the father whispered back, under his breath.

"Shake on it?" said Montoya.

"What?" said the father.

Montoya shrugged his shoulders. "A gentleman's handshake. To seal the deal. You're from a time when a man's handshake was his oath, are you not?"

The father glanced at his son again. "Yeah," he said. "I'm from that era."

"Come on, Pops," the son muttered.

"I said shut up," the father hissed through his teeth.

Though the front of Montoya's face was still hidden in the dark, the glow of the headlights traced the contour of his head and wiry hair. The swelling of his cheeks suggested a large grin had formed across his face. He unfolded his arms and began walking toward the two.

The son's shoulders slumped. "This ain't right, Pops."

Montoya extended his hand toward the son, keeping his gaze on the father. The son swallowed to say something, but before he could get out a word, something flashed from Montoya's sleeve. Two loud pops rang out. The son's body toppled violently backwards.

"No!" the father yelled. His eyes bulged through his skull as he watched his son's body fall flat to the gravel.

Dust floated in the glare of the headlights as the father dropped to his knees. He crawled quickly to his son, his glasses falling from his face as he reached for his boy's chest. What looked like steam rose from his jacket. It was warm and wet to the father's touch.

"No, no, no," the father said as his son gasped for air.

The father peeled off his son's jacket at the zipper. His vision was blurred from his missing glasses, but the flow of blood down his shirt led him to an entry wound. He covered it with his hand, applying pressure and gritting his teeth as he tried to figure out where the second bullet had entered. His son's pulse pressed against his father's hand, weakening by the second.

"You son of a bitch," the father growled, sweat pouring down the side of his face and his eyes welling up. "I'm gonna kill you. I swear to God."

Montoya's long shadow moved over the son's body, further impairing the father's vision. "What's that?" he asked, unimpressed.

The heartbeat under the father's hand suddenly stopped. A wheezing sound poured from the son's mouth. The father removed his hand and crawled closer to his son's face, lifting his head. He couldn't see his boy's eyes. Montoya's shadow was preventing it.

"Victor," the father said, tears dropping onto his son's chin. "My boy . . ." His nostrils flared as the fear in his gut quickly boiled over into anger. "I said," he repeated, "I'm gonna kill you, you soulless fuck."

With a grunt, the father snatched the pistol from his pants. He spun to face Montoya.

Two more shots rang out.

Chapter 16

Lumbergh's mind was sprinting circles as he sat in the passenger seat of a dark Ford Crown Victoria, waiting for the traffic light in front of him to turn green.

"Are we almost there?" he asked, turning to the driver.

"About five minutes out," answered Las Vegas Metro detective, Kim Holman. Mild irritation accompanied her voice, having been asked the same question five minutes earlier.

Holman was an attractive woman in her thirties, thin with dark eyes, long dark hair, and a chiseled face. She appeared of Hispanic decent, though her name didn't reflect it. She was the first detective at the Dusty Nickel and had quickly taken charge of the crime scene, directing officers to rope off the area to keep the press and onlookers away. She'd rifled through the dead man's pockets, as Lumbergh had secretly done before she arrived, discovering as he had that there was no wallet or ID.

Her partner was a man in his fifties with thick, silver hair, a darker mustache, and whose name Lumbergh had already forgotten. He had shown up a few minutes later. He was a rough, old-school-looking detective, but seemed to take his lead from Holman. He had stayed behind to take pictures, fingerprint the dead man, and canvas the area for additional witnesses. Dusty remained behind too, Lumbergh having told him that Sean may try to reach them at the hotel. Lumbergh didn't believe that would likely happen, but he knew Dusty would otherwise get in the way and slow things down if he accompanied them to Lisa's house. To seal the deal, Lumbergh suggested he "assist" Holman's partner, an elevation of stature he knew that Dusty couldn't resist.

The light turned green and Holman stepped on the gas. She leaned forward in a dark, casual suit, and tapped some buttons on the dashboard GPS before glancing in the rearview mirror and switching lanes. Her police radio buzzed from activity related to the Roy Horn incident—traffic issues, crowd control, and some looting in a Mirage gift shop. She turned the volume down.

Lumbergh had yet to get a good read on Holman, but she was direct and to the point. He appreciated that.

"I've got to be honest with you, Chief," said Holman. "I think your Vincenzo Moretti theory's a stretch." She shoved a hand into her black dress pants, digging for something.

"So do I," Lumbergh conceded, drawing a quick glance from Holman. "But it's all I've got right now. You had to have seen the look in that man's eyes. This was personal somehow. He knew exactly who I was when he walked up to me."

"Well, you *are* kind of a celebrity," said Holman, her eyes shifting back to him with only a hint of a grin.

Lumbergh scoffed. "Maybe with attendees at Las Vegas's Chiefs of Police Conference. My point is that they came after Sean and me. They grabbed him and I think they were trying to grab me. The only tie we have to this city is Moretti. Associates of his would make sense."

"Stick of gum?" she offered, drawing an open pack from her pocket.

Lumbergh's eyebrows arched. "Yeah," he said, reaching over and prying one out.

She did the same and returned the pack to her pocket. They both worked the wrappers off.

"Here's my problem with the theory," she said after sliding the gum into her mouth. "Kingpins like Moretti aren't the type of people that others avenge. They don't have real friends or personal loyalty. Their associates exist for exactly one reason: money. That's it."

"And when that money suddenly goes away, like it did for Moretti? You don't think some people were pretty pissed off?"

"I'm sure they were," she said, a streetlamp momentarily exposing a light blue, button-down shirt under her jacket. "But this is Vegas. There's money to be made everywhere. Some of it's legal. Some of it's not. Either way, people with thick roots in this town don't wallow in self-pity and resentment when they lose, like some weekend 'Vegas, baby!' tourist who blows all of his Christmas bonus at a craps table. They adapt. They find other ways."

Lumbergh nodded, his eyes fixed on the road. "You said Greg Wendice has three men on tape. And he's got the recording on him?"

"That's my understanding."

"He said it's from a security camera. Hopefully the quality is good enough to get an ID on at least one of them. I have some questions I want to ask him. You okay with that?"

Holman tapped her turn signal and quickly pulled into a neighborhood separated from the street by a tall brick wall. Her wheels screeched as she took the corner. "I am," she replied, "as long as we both understand who's leading this investigation."

"I respect your jurisdiction, detective, and I appreciate your courtesy."

"Anything for a celebrity," she quipped, her lips curling subtly again.

After a few turns down side streets, the flashing lights of police cruisers at the end of a cul-de-sac guided them to the front of Lisa's house. Dusty's car that Sean had borrowed was parked out front.

Holman parked off to the side. The two left the vehicle, whisking their way past uniformed officers, some of whom Holman acknowledged with a nod. Lumbergh's Glock from his hotel room was now holstered at his side. A black Beretta hugged Holman's hip. Her loud footsteps on the wet sidewalk, along with a raised badge from a chain around her neck, caught the attention of a short officer with a crew cut. He stepped aside to let them through the front door. Lumbergh noticed the officer checking out Holman's backside as she entered, drawing his scowl.

The hallway was covered with broken glass and wood from destroyed picture frames. There appeared to be a shattered vase in the mix too. A plain-clothed, clean-cut man of Asian descent, with his legs spread out wide to avoid stepping on debris, was taking pictures of something on the floor. Lumbergh peered over his shoulder to see some trace amounts of blood.

As Holman asked an officer for Wendice's whereabouts, Lumbergh gazed across the adjoining living area where he spotted more splotches of blood on the carpet, flanked by strips of tape put down from someone in forensics. He knew from Wendice's account that Sean had been shot in the arm and that the blood was assuredly his. There wasn't enough of it to suggest Sean was in danger of bleeding out, but the revelation didn't bring Lumbergh much comfort. His brother-in-law wasn't in any less danger.

"Did someone take blood samples from each marking on the floor?" Lumbergh asked the man with the camera. "Both here and here?" he added, pointing to the hallway and then the living area.

"Yes," the man answered, looking up from his camera and glancing between Lumbergh and his colleagues. "I did."

"And you're going to test them all to see if they match anything you have on record? They might not all be from Sean Coleman."

"I'm sorry," the man said, blinking. "Who are you?"

"Chief," Holman interrupted from the hallway. "Wendice is upstairs."

Lumbergh nodded and took another quick scan of the living area, this time lifting his gaze and searching for the security camera Wendice had described on the phone. All he saw mounted was artwork and other wall décor.

The two twisted their way around more glass and walked up a carpeted staircase with a couple of plaques on the wall to the second story. There they found a young, red-haired officer with a freckled face stationed outside a bedroom doorway.

"He's pretty shaken up, with his daughter and all," the officer said, approaching them with his hands on his belt.

"Has he given you anything else?" asked Holman.

The officer opened his mouth to answer but was cut off by the word "Fuck!" yelled sharply from the next room.

"He's having some kind of problem with his computer, trying to pull up the video," explained the officer. "Something to do with file . . . formats. I don't know." The officer shook his head.

"Okay, we'll take it from here," said Holman.

"Wait, wait!" came Wendice's voice again. "There we go, there we go!"

"Sounds like a breakthrough," said Holman, raising her thin brows. She turned and entered the room.

The bedroom, which appeared to be the master, was relatively small in size with few pictures on the walls. A queen bed with a light blue comforter and pillows took up most of the space. Across a beige carpet, against the opposite wall, was a short wooden dresser. Wendice was kneeling in front of it with his back to them, tapping a key on an open laptop computer. Multiple cords from its back dangled off the side of the dresser and disappeared behind it. Across the screen was what looked like a large status bar.

Wendice was dressed in a plaid, two-piece suit. Dark blue and made of a material that reflected light from the ceiling fan above, it appeared expensive. His hair was a disheveled mess and his face in the mirror behind the dresser was taut and pale. It was a stark difference from how he looked earlier that day in front of the school. His eyes were glued to the computer screen like a surgeon examining x-rays.

"Mr. Wendice . . ." said Holman, the two walking up behind him.

"Almost got it," he said, out of breath. "A co-worker had to zip the files to email them to me, but I didn't have the right software installed to play them."

Holman nodded.

"But that should change in just a couple of seconds . . ." said Wendice.

The status bar disappeared, and with a few clicks he opened a window with the image of the living room Lumbergh and Holman had just left. The point of view was from somewhere along the upper wall, opposite the main hallway.

"Where's that camera?" Lumbergh asked as Wendice began fiddling with a slider bar at the bottom of the window. "I didn't see one out there."

Wendice quickly spun toward him, a white shirt and shiny

pink tie now visible. "You're Lumbergh?" he asked. "The policeman I spoke with on the phone?"

Lumbergh nodded.

Wendice's focus went back to the screen. "The valance, above the window to the backyard," he answered. "There's two pieces to it. The camera is between them. It's pretty small . . . the camera, I mean." He used his laptop's touchpad to carefully drag the slider bar to the right, speeding up the video.

"It's a *hidden* camera?" said Lumbergh, drawing a glance from Holman. Wendice didn't respond.

Lisa's image appeared in fast motion on the screen, speaking into a phone, and pacing back and forth in the living room. She wore an oversized shirt and some sweats, and held the girl in her other arm. Wendice tilted his head away from the laptop for a second, his lips tight and his eyes receding. The image of his daughter was pulling at his emotions, but she soon disappeared from the shot, along with Lisa. Lisa returned without her, now wearing jeans and a tighter-fitting, light-colored shirt. Her hair was pulled back in a ponytail. She left the room a second time.

"Okay, where does Sean come in?" asked Lumbergh.

"So that *is* Sean?" asked Wendice, more in the form of a statement than a question. He glanced back. "The ex?"

Lumbergh saw what looked like resentment in his eyes, or perhaps it was just the stress of the situation. "Yeah."

"It has to be any second now," said Wendice, eyes back on the screen. "I didn't see this first part before, but . . ."

Lisa reentered the room, this time with Sean.

"Okay, there!" Lumbergh shouted.

Wendice removed his hand from the laptop and the three leaned in for a closer look. The picture was relatively clear, but Lisa and Sean were at the far end of it. They talked for a

while and then sat in the living room and talked some more.
Wendice returned his finger to the touchpad to speed the video
up some more. He removed it when Lisa got to her feet. She
walked toward the hallway. When her body suddenly jolted,
and Sean jumped to his feet, the three gasped.

"Here it comes," warned Wendice.

Chapter 17

"**D**o they see us?" Lisa gasped, her fingers taking a break from the tape around Sean's wrists. The echo of gunfire still rumbled off the land.

"No," Sean whispered. "It's not us they're shooting at."

"At what then?" asked Lisa.

"Pops and Asshole."

Sean was sitting on the dirt with Hannah on his lap, her little hands trying to latch onto Lisa's familiar voice in the dark. His good shoulder was propped up against the base of a large, angled solar panel. They'd put at least a couple hundred yards and dozens of rows of paneling between them and the parking lot, under the faint light of the crescent moon above.

The solar farm was far larger than Sean could have imagined. It seemed to go on forever. The panels were organized in a giant grid with each square *cell* consisting of probably twenty-five rows. Each row looked around three hundred feet long and the cells were separated by dirt walks and—in some cases—narrow gravel roads for work vehicles.

Lisa swallowed. "Why shoot them?" Her hands returned to the duct tape as a gust of wind pressed against them. Sean could feel her fingers trembling. The air outside was still warm, but the tension was causing a cooling effect.

Sean pulled at his wrists, giving her as much room as he could. "Pissed off we escaped. Tying up loose ends. Maybe greed. Hard to say." He grunted at the strain he was putting on his wound.

"Greed over what?" she pressed, digging her nails into the tape.

"Money. They think your ex took a bunch from Moretti before he died. It's what they're after. Or *were* after, anyway."

"What do you mean?"

"Don't you have a letter opener?" Sean asked, getting back to the matter at hand. "To cut the tape? You used it on the son."

"I dropped it when I grabbed his gun. It's back in the parking lot."

Sean grunted. "I've got some car keys in my pocket. Maybe those will work. Take the girl and I'll lean back."

Lisa did, lifting Hannah into her arms. Sean lowered himself horizontal, wincing from the movement.

"They're in my right front pocket. I'm sorry, but you'll have to be the one to pull them out."

Lisa drew in a breath.

"I promise this isn't a trick," Sean quipped.

"Ugh. I know that. Give me some credit." With her other arm still around Hannah, she shoved her left hand, fingers together, into Sean's pocket. "How do you play into this?"

"What?"

"They came for you. They think you know something about this money." She found the key ring, hooked it with her fingers, and grunted as she pried it from Sean's pocket.

"Yeah. They think I have it," he answered, rolling to his side and lifting his wrists.

"And why is that?" she pressed, some irritation in her tone at the brevity of Sean's response.

"Because they're presumptive assholes who drew a conspiracy theory out of some coincidental timing and a spike in my bank account. Now let's get me free so we can get the hell out of here. They'll be coming for us."

Lisa hesitated, but just as Sean was about to question her about it, he felt her pressure on his binds again. She worked the teeth of one of the keys across the tape. The corners of Sean's mouth curled when he heard a tear.

"Two hundred thousand," she mumbled. "That's what the old man said." A few seconds ticked by. "Where'd you get that from?"

"It's from a security job I did. It's a long story, but believe me it's on the up and up."

Lisa scoffed. "Still, this can't be about two—"

"They think there's a lot more," interrupted Sean. "Millions." When he heard the tape tear again, he flexed his arms as best as his shoulder would allow him. What was left of his binds snapped.

Lisa backed away from him as he turned to his knees, facing her.

"Good," he said. "Thank you." He rubbed his wrists, restoring some circulation before peeling off the remaining tape. It took some arm hair with it.

He shifted his eyes between Lisa's darkened face and some grumbling from Hannah. When he carefully pressed his opposite hand against his injured shoulder, he winced from the rush of pain it brought. It felt swollen, but it was hard to tell for sure underneath the layers of tape. The dryness of the tape, however, indicated that he wasn't actively bleeding.

"It can't be good, having this bullet in here," Sean said, relaying his thoughts out loud.

"Are you thinking we should try getting it out?"

"Not unless you're hiding some pliers somewhere. Let's just get out of this alive first."

She nodded. "You'd better take this," she said, reaching behind her and bringing the pistol forward.

It was small in his hand, but he didn't believe he'd have any trouble firing it. Rubbing a finger along its barrel and what felt like a pearl grip, he was sure his initial assessment of it being a Raven MP-25 was correct. An old-school Saturday night special that held seven rounds max. He released the clip, running a thumb along its side. He made out four bullets in the magazine. The weapon wasn't much, but it was something.

"I know this is a lot to swallow," said Sean. "It is for me too. But the man who's now after us makes Pops and Asshole look like Mouseketeers. And he's after blood, not just money."

"What?" Lisa gasped.

Sean cleared his throat. "I don't know how it came about, but Gary somehow shot the guy's son tonight. And . . ." Sean stopped when he heard something. It sounded like something brushing along metal. It persisted, but after a few seconds, he dismissed it as a tumbleweed stuck up against one of the panel bases.

"And what?" Lisa whispered.

"And . . . he's Alvar Montoya's brother."

Lisa said nothing at first. All Sean could hear and feel was an uptick in her breathing. He knew she understood the stakes.

"Who Gary killed," she finally said.

"Right."

Lisa pulled Hannah closer to her chest. "Safe to say we can't talk our way out of this."

"Nope."

The second the word left his mouth, a beam of light bounced off the ground a few hundred feet away in front of them.

"Jesus," Lisa whispered, propping up her body.

The light quickly disappeared.

"Don't move," Sean whispered to Lisa, raising his pistol.

The area where the light had shone was down a gradual hill from them. At least a couple of cells separated them from their pursuer. Due to the hill and the outward angle of the panels, Sean and Lisa had good visual cover . . . for now. The light looked like it was along the same route they'd ascended. It was then that Sean realized their footprints were likely in the loose sand below, and had given their pursuers something to hone in on.

Whether it was Montoya or one of his men, whoever it was must have known that Sean was armed. Keeping the flashlight on for only a second had been done to prevent him from lining up a shot.

Sean glanced over his shoulder. Behind him, a vague outline of rows and rows of panels stretched up the terrain like seats at an amphitheater. It seemed that they were in a valley. If the terrain was anything like he'd seen on the drive in that afternoon with Lumbergh and Dusty, they were likely at the base of a mountain range.

"Which way should we go?" Lisa whispered.

"Up," Sean whispered back. "And do it quietly."

"Won't that take us farther from the road? Shouldn't we work our way back, and try waving down someone?"

Sean shook his head. "The only car on that road since we got here has been Montoya's. And there's barely any cover between here and there. No buildings. Probably no trees. At best some short scrub. Our best shot is up. They can't shoot through these panels, and they'll be good for hiding behind. We'll also have the high ground and have an easier time seeing them coming."

"The panels won't go on forever," Lisa whispered. "They'll end when this hill gets too steep."

"I know," Sean answered. "We'll deal with that when it happens."

The two climbed to their feet, keeping their heads low. Lisa hiked up Hannah against her chest, supporting the girl's bottom with her arm. Sean winced from the tension on his wound. The three jogged west toward the end of their cell, Lisa leading the way while Sean kept his focus down the hill. His height let him peer over the top of the paneling. He kept watch for another flicker or other movements.

When Hannah suddenly let out a loud babbling noise, Sean's pulse shot up. Lisa quickly tamped it down with some shushing.

"Did you give her that medicine?" Sean asked in a whisper. "From the van—the drowsy stuff?"

"Yeah, but it takes a little while to kick in. At least she's not crying."

When they reached the end of the cell, Sean made his way in front of Lisa, putting his body between her and the dirt path up.

"Go across," he whispered, his gun pointed down the hill.

She did, and Sean followed behind her to the next cell.

"We'll head up two or three when we get to the end of this one," Sean whispered. He had to repeat himself because an uptick in the wind muffled part of his instructions.

The wind was a double-edged sword. It may well have been keeping their pursuers from hearing them move across the dirt, but also kept Sean and Lisa from hearing the same from them. Sean would have to rely on his sight and his instincts. He had pretty good vision. His instincts were less reliable. Any assistance from the Big Nudge would have been more than welcome.

When the gust tapered off, a new humming sound emerged. It was steady, sounding like machinery.

"What is that?" whispered Lisa, twisting her head back toward Sean as the sound grew louder.

"A car engine," Sean answered, popping his head over the panels again. "We've got to move faster."

They reached the end of the cell. Sean stepped in front of Lisa again, his eyes trained down the hill. "Go up three rows, then go left," he said.

She darted up the hill along the pathway, Hannah making some noises as she did. Sean went up after her, keeping his eyes and aim behind them. A bright light suddenly flipped on down the hill, spreading out along a lower cell like a searchlight. The wide beam wasn't aimed at Sean and Lisa, but it exposed a good amount of ground and paneling beneath them. It had to be coming from Montoya's vehicle.

When a thin shadow appeared on the gravel, its movements matching a person running, Sean gasped.

"Go right, go right!" he directed in a strong whisper, changing the plan.

Lisa followed his words, quickly switching directions and sliding back inside the cell they'd just left. Sean was close behind her.

"Wait," he said when he was sure they were out of sight.

Lisa stopped and spun around. Sean lowered himself to a knee, peering under the panel with his gun pointed forward. He watched the figure of a man dart, unfazed, across the pathway to the other side.

"Did they see us?" asked Lisa.

"I don't think so," he replied. He turned to her. "There's at least two of them. Probably more."

The engine below loudened, stealing back Sean's gaze. The light moved along a pathway below, too bright to have come from just headlamps alone. The vehicle must have had a row of spotlights up top, suggesting an SUV. If so, that meant a four-wheel drive, and a vehicle well-equipped for the terrain. The only problem for the driver would be the width of the pathways leading up the hill. They couldn't have been much more than six feet. The perpendicular paths that pointed east and west were wider, specifically designed for automobiles. To get any higher up the hill, an SUV would first have to drive all the way to the edge of the farm. It wouldn't, however, stop someone on foot from catching up to them. That was Sean's primary concern.

"We've got to go up one row at a time," he told Lisa. "Quickly onto the path and then back inside. Any longer would leave us exposed."

"Can't we just work our way up *under* the panels?" she asked. "Around the supports, and stay off the path all together?"

"They're too low," Sean said, shaking his head. "We'd have to crawl, and we don't have that kind of time. Listen, I'll be right behind you. They'll never get a clean shot at you and the kid."

"Sean—"

"There's no more time to argue. If something happens to me, just keep going up. We're at the bottom of a mountain. There'll be places to hide above. Rocks. Maybe some trees. Keep heading north. That'll be the way back to town."

Sean took Lisa's silence as her understanding his words. "Okay," she finally said.

"Good. Let's go."

Lisa hurried around the edge of the paneling with Sean close behind her. He kept one eye on the path as they darted back inside. They waited a moment before repeating the drill. Each time, they took a few extra seconds before moving on.

They'd made it another four hundred feet or so when a thin light appeared along the roadway above them, about a hundred feet to their right. Sean's eyes shot wide. He lunged ahead of Lisa, grabbing her arm and pulling her down the preceding row. Hannah chuckled from the excitement, sending a chill up Sean's spine. The light drew in closer a couple of feet before disappearing.

Sean guided Lisa in close behind him, tugging down on her arm as he lowered himself to his knees. She went down with him, holding Hannah closer to her chest. Sean hoped the girl hadn't been heard. He aimed his gun under the panel, crunching his body forward.

The beam had been too small and short to have come from a vehicle. It must have been from a flashlight. Because it had come from the east, Sean knew it wasn't the man he saw running before. There were at least three pursuers.

Sean's chest throbbed as a stream of sweat slid down his face. He squinted, trying to make out any kind of movement in the dark. The wind flared up again, sweeping through the area.

Sean turned his head and pressed his nose against Lisa's ear just long enough to tell her to scoot under the panel behind them and stay low. Hannah latched onto Sean's nose for a second with her little hand. Lisa pulled it away and slid to her side on the dirt, lowering Hannah beside her. Sean lowered himself in front of them, his gun still pointing forward.

Between Lisa's bright white top and Sean's loud aloha shirt, they weren't well camouflaged. The night and the slope were their only cloaks.

When the wind died down, the crackle of shoes on gravel

kept Sean perfectly still. It sounded like it was coming from directly across from them, maybe ten feet away, separated only by the metal stilts of a single row of paneling. Sean's eyes strained in the dark to find a target, any kind of displacement. He would only shoot if he was certain he could put down the individual. He didn't have enough ammo, nor cover, for a sustained firefight. The best-case scenario was the person walking right on by, none the wiser that they were there, almost flat against the dirt. Then they'd cut back to the east, away from the activity of the last few minutes, and continue their ascent.

Sean finally spotted the outline of something moving on the other side of the panel. A pair of legs, their motion lining up with the footsteps. Sean lined up a shot, hoping he wouldn't have to take it. The individual's movements were calm and deliberate, unlike the other who'd flown by down below. Montoya and his people must have been working to cover the perimeters before pushing in toward the center and flushing out their prey.

The roar of the vehicle's engine rose above the wind again somewhere below. Sean could feel Lisa's shoulder trembling against his leg. When the flashlight flipped back on, she pressed herself tighter against him. The beam spread out away from them, up the hill across the cell to the north. Sean drew in a breath but kept his aim steady.

The light then swung to the south, under the panel toward the path they'd just left. Sean tried to *will* the beam to stay there, but to his dread, it slowly crept across the dirt toward them. He didn't move, his pistol locked just above the light.

It came within just a few feet when a man's voice suddenly spread out across the valley, shouting something in Spanish. It was crosstalk, likely between the driver of the vehicle and the other man on foot. It came from somewhere below. The light went off. The man who held it began walking away, his attention pulled on by the exchange.

A rush of ease washed over Sean. He swallowed, still following the footsteps with his gun. It was then that Hannah, for some reason, shouted out in apparent glee. Sean's eyes popped wide. His heart stopped. The light flipped back on. Its beam shot across the land toward them. A half a second before it landed squarely on their faces, Sean pulled the trigger.

With two loud pops and quick flashes of light, a man's voice howled in the dark. The flashlight fell to the ground. A hard thud followed it.

"Hector!" the fallen man cried.

"Stay here!" Sean said as he scrambled to his feet. "Freeze, asshole!" he yelled, not knowing the man's condition. He darted toward the flashlight, pistol leveled.

Hannah was crying again, frightened by the gunfire. When Sean crossed onto the upward trail, he saw a man's shoulder lit up from the light. The man was lying on his back, blood decorating his white shirt.

"Don't move!" Sean ordered.

The man rolled to his side just as Sean reached him. His arm went for something to his left, but Sean lunged forward, landing across his body and forcing him onto his stomach. The man cried out as Sean dug a knee into the swell of his back. Sean pressed the muzzle of his pistol against his head, just above a long, dark ponytail. With his other hand, he managed to pull the flashlight and spread its beam across the ground beside him. There he found a hunting rifle with a scope and wood stock. It looked like a Browning BAR, but he didn't have time for closer inspection.

"Lisa!" he shouted over Hannah's crying. "I got him, but I need you!" He bit his lip from the surge of pain in his shoulder.

Within seconds, he heard her approaching. Hannah wailed as they emerged around the corner. Suddenly, their bodies were silhouetted from large, bright lights below.

"Fuck!" Sean shouted, the glare nearly blinding him. "This way, fast!"

The man underneath Sean was barely moving, a wheezing noise coming from his mouth. Sean's knee was wet and warm from his blood. He hoped the man was no longer a threat. Sean chose the rifle over the flashlight, reaching over and grabbing it from the ground while he kept hold of his pistol.

The screech and crashing of metal tore through the air down below. Sparks flew as Montoya's vehicle sped up the hill toward them, its side mirrors smashing against metal edges of solar panels.

"Down here!" Sean directed Lisa, pointing east with the rifle. His body was completely lit up by the headlights.

She rounded the corner, Hannah's chin bumping against her shoulder. The second they were out of his way, Sean unloaded his pistol into the driver's windshield, squeezing the trigger until the weapon was out. Glass crunched with each shot, but the vehicle roared toward him without pause. Sean dropped the pistol and took off after Lisa, fumbling in the dark for the rifle's safety. When he turned back, the still lit flashlight exposed the man with the ponytail on the ground, rolling to his side and reaching toward the front of his waist.

"Go! Go! Go!" Sean yelled forward at Lisa, worried he had a handgun stashed there.

When Sean spun back around, the man was now propped up on an elbow, his arm level and pointed toward them. Before Sean could shout for Lisa to get down, the front bumper of a white Bronco smashed into the man's head. The rest of his body was dragged underneath the vehicle before its grill crashed into the next row of paneling.

"Go left!" Sean shouted at Lisa, wincing.

At the next walkway, Lisa went left. Sean followed. They jogged up the new path, which quickly grew steeper, Sean's tight dress shoes almost causing him to trip. He wondered for a second if he'd shot the driver after all, and perhaps his foot had stuck to the gas pedal. But the slam of a car door signaled otherwise. More likely, the driver hadn't seen his partner lying mostly flat on the hill until it was too late. Either way, the collision had slowed things.

But it didn't last long. Within seconds, the engine was roaring again. Metal cried and the headlights below switched directions. In no time, the driver was speeding east along the roadway to get to the bottom of the path Sean and Lisa were slogging up.

"Cut in left!" Sean shouted over Hannah's wails; he knew they'd soon be in the driver's sight.

When she did, Sean swung in behind her and immediately dropped to a knee. Out of breath and taking partial cover behind a panel, he brought up the rifle and began lining up a shot through the scope. The Bronco was skidding in the dirt and gravel to a stop a couple hundred feet down the hill. Sean took a breath, doing his best to ignore the biting pain in his shoulder. The second a flashlight extended from the window toward his perch, he took the shot. Then another. Sparks flew off the vehicle's roof and one of the bar lights exploded.

The flashlight dropped from the window. It hadn't even reached the ground before a hail of gunfire was returned, lighting up the night. Sean dove to his right, landing on his chest as metal and silicon were shredded to pieces around him.

The rapid fire echoed across the valley as Sean crawled along the gravel. The driver had to have a military rifle of some kind. Perhaps even a fully automatic. Sean raised his head to tell Lisa to run but found that she'd never stopped. He couldn't see her, but when the shooting tapered off, he could hear Hannah's crying.

Sean scrambled to his feet and ran across the gravel, rifle in hand, toward the child's voice. The engine below rose again.

"Lisa!" Sean shouted, grunting as he jogged forward.

The crying grew louder as Sean reached the end of the cell. Tracing the noise, he veered around the corner, calling out Lisa's name again so she'd know it was he who was approaching. Below, the Bronco sped off, headed toward the east end of the farm . . . probably to try and cut them off up top.

Sean could barely see beyond the next couple of rows, but Hannah's voice was like a homing beacon. With the engine fading in the distance, he worried the man on foot would hear the child too. He called for Lisa again, this time in a softer voice. He couldn't understand why she wasn't answering.

Hannah sounded just a few feet ahead, her cries low to the ground. Sean suddenly spotted movement, the child squirming around on the ground. Beside her, he made out the outline of Lisa's body, lying facedown on the gravel.

Chapter 18

"I knew that guy was trouble," said Wendice, his hands on his face and his arms trembling. The video had just shown the two masked men with guns exiting the house with their captives. "I worried what would happen if he ever showed up, looking for her. Oh God." His voice waned.

Lumbergh and Holman shot glares at each other.

"Wait, you know who one of these guys is?" Lumbergh asked, moving around the side of the dresser.

Wendice growled in frustration. "No, not the guys with the masks!" His head spun to Lumbergh, red eyes glistening. "Sean!" he shouted. "She told me about him. She told me his story . . . and their past. The guy's a fucking loser. And then he shows up here out of the blue tonight, and suddenly people with guns are breaking in through the front door?"

"You're blaming *him*?" Lumbergh snapped back angrily, leaning forward. He glared daggers at Wendice.

"Chief," Holman cautioned, raising her arm between them. "Let's take it back a notch."

"They have my daughter!" Wendice yelled. "Don't you idiots understand that?"

An officer poked his head in from the hallway. Holman waved him off, signaling that the situation was under control. Lumbergh drew in a deep breath, taking a step back.

"Mr. Wendice," Holman calmly said, placing her hand on

the kneeling man's shoulder. "We absolutely understand that, and right now, everything that *can* be done *is* being done. But we need to figure out everything we can about the men in your video, in order to get your daughter back quickly and safely. Sean is Chief Lumbergh's family, so he's every bit as invested as you are in locating these men."

Wendice lowered his head and covered his face with his hands again. "Okay. God. I'm sorry, I didn't . . . I'm just . . ." His hands went to his pink tie, loosening, pulling, and stretching it until it slipped over his head. He threw it to the floor in frustration.

"It's okay," said Lumbergh. He glanced at Holman before continuing. "I need to ask you a question, though. First, let me be clear that no one's accusing you of anything. We're just trying to get a full picture of things."

Wendice's face, contorted in confusion, returned to Lumbergh.

"Why is there a hidden camera in Lisa's living room? And why do you have access to its feed? As I understand, you don't live here."

Wendice's eyes widened. "You think . . . you think I have something to do with this? I'm the one who—"

"No, I don't," Lumbergh interrupted, just as Holman flipped him a stern glare. "But residential security cameras are usually on the outside of homes. And homeowners who use them inside don't typically hide them. What would be the point? If there was some unique security concern in Lisa's case, it's best that we know about it."

Wendice's eyes shifted nervously between Lumbergh and Holman. He opened his mouth to speak when some motion on the computer screen drew the attention of all three back to the video. A tall, broad-shouldered man at the far end of the shot was savagely slamming the stock of a large rifle against the security console on the wall.

"This is the last guy, the one I told you about," said Wendice, swallowing. "He didn't wear a mask."

All three leaned in close to the screen, but the man was standing too far away to get a detailed look at his face. He appeared to have relatively short hair. It was wiry and looked salt and pepper in color, but it was hard to say with the black-and-white picture. He had a dark complexion and wore a lightweight jacket and jeans. His shoes appeared to be cowboy boots. The stranger surveilled the inside of the house, disappearing from view a few times as he searched through the kitchen and presumably the second level. And at one point he appeared to shout out at someone who was either at the other end of the hallway or outside. He wasn't alone.

"He's not touching anything," Lumbergh noticed.

Holman shook her head. "Yeah. They'll dust the front door for prints. The knobs upstairs too. Maybe we'll get lucky." She turned to Wendice. "Does he get any closer to the camera?"

"Yes," Wendice answered, his eyes glued to the screen.

The intruder's attention suddenly turned toward the living room. He walked toward the coffee table at its center, hesitating a moment before leaning forward and picking up a small object from it.

"That's Lisa's phone," said Wendice.

"That's me talking to him on the other end," added Lumbergh.

The stranger looked at the phone for a couple of seconds before bringing it to the side of his face. When he did, his head was tilted upward.

"Pause it!" said Lumbergh. "Can you pause it?"

Wendice nodded. With a click, the video froze. The man's

face was unobscured but it was still distant enough to preclude distinguishing features.

"Can we zoom in on that?" asked Holman. "Zoom in and get a screen shot?"

"I'll try," said Wendice, working the touchpad again. "The resolution isn't optimal. Maybe with some better imaging software . . ."

The dimensions of the video window were maximized, and Wendice clicked a couple times on a 'plus' button. The picture became too large, transfixed on one of the man's eyes.

"Ugh," Wendice grumbled. He slid the pointer to a button with a minus sign, but Lumbergh reached forward and held his wrist.

"Wait," he said, his eyes narrowing.

"What is it?" asked Holman.

Lumbergh said nothing, staring directly at the man's cold, dark eye. Despite some blear, the callousness he read behind it was chillingly familiar. After a few seconds, he felt the confused gazes of the room's other occupants bearing down on him.

"Okay, zoom out," he said, shaking his head.

A click filled up the screen with the man's face, now entirely visible but hazy with some continued blurring from pixilation. The spell behind the man's eyes, however, persisted. It drove up Lumbergh's pulse. He'd seen the man before, looking different in some manner. Time and misplacement couldn't close the book on the story told by those eyes.

Lumbergh finally realized where he'd seen the man. It was on another computer screen almost two years earlier. Those photos had been grainy too, illustrating the man and his aura at a younger age. Lumbergh stepped back from the laptop. Springs from the bed behind him groaned as he unconsciously sat down. His gaze floated to Holman. She was staring at him, her face tight with concern.

"Montoya," he said, his chest tightening as the word left his mouth. "Lautaro . . . Montoya."

Chapter 19

Sean gasped and lunged forward, dropping to his knees in the dirt beside Lisa. His heart pumped with panic through his body.

"Jesus! Lisa!" Sean dropped the rifle. He placed his hands carefully on Lisa's shoulders. When he felt her recoil from his touch, he knew she was still alive. "Are you shot?" he quickly asked.

Her hand slid up from under her and went to the side of her head. "No," she said in disorientation. "Hit my head."

Air rushed from Sean's lungs. He gently rolled her onto her side and then her back, his eyes taking notice of a metal, horizontal support that protruded out from the solar panel beside them.

"Hannah," Lisa muttered, her head confusedly shifting from side to side.

"She's here, next to you," Sean said, pressing his hand against Lisa's forehead and feeling warm blood. It wasn't coming out fast—probably a minor cut. She'd likely just had her bell rung. "Baby, we've got to go. They'll be back on us any second."

He hadn't called Lisa "baby" since the final days of their relationship. If the word had come out under any other circumstance, he would have scolded himself for the slip. But at that moment, it was the least of his worries.

"Can you walk?" he asked, reaching over her body and scooping the toddler into his arms. He grunted from the pain shooting up his shoulder.

"Yeah," she said unconvincingly.

She groggily propped herself up on her elbows, her hand favoring her head again. She turned over and used Sean's good shoulder to slowly lift herself upright. Sean shushed Hannah as he'd seen Lisa do earlier, but he wasn't having the same luck. She continued fussing.

Their pursuers would surely hear her, even with the wind still running some cover. Sean worried Lisa was still too wobbly to carry Hannah, so he kept the child propped up in his large arm and pinned against his chest. He asked Lisa to hand him the rifle, but quickly realized the difficulty of trying to carry both the weapon and baby with a bullet wedged in his shoulder.

"Can you carry the gun?" he asked. "It's not super heavy."

She grunted an *uh-huh*, and he returned it to her. They continued up the hill. Lisa was a step behind Sean with a fistful of the back of his shirt to keep herself close and steady. Sean's eyes panned their surroundings. He searched for light or any kind of movement as he worked again to quiet Hannah, bobbing her up and down like he did his niece on occasion.

He felt warm blood trickle down his left arm, and knew he'd reopened his wound. It had to have happened during the shootout, when he'd thrown himself to the ground. He hoped time and the tape still wrapped around it would let it clot again.

"I don't suppose you ever learned how to shoot?" Sean asked, his voice low.

"Huh-uh," Lisa answered. "Shooting in the air down there . . . It was the first time I've fired a gun since . . ."

"It's okay," Sean said.

He knew she was referring to the time he'd talked her into

shooting at some bottles he'd set up behind his Colorado home, back when they were together. She wasn't comfortable with it, which didn't bother him at the time. Part of him liked how averse she was to violence. It enforced his role as her defender; at least that's how he saw things back then. In their current situation, however, it was proving a liability.

"If something happens, we'll trade," said Sean. "We've got to head west. Keep going up, but in tighter with the slope. It'll make things harder for the driver."

"What about the other guy—the one who was running?" Lisa asked. "Won't that put us closer to him?"

"Yeah, but I'm counting on him having less firepower than the asshole in the Bronco."

The man behind the wheel had to be Montoya. Sean was sure of it. From the reports down south, he was a tall, large man like his late brother; assuredly not the spry individual who'd run by below, nor the man who'd ended up underneath the Bronco.

Hannah was finally quieting back down. It was probably from a combination of the rocking, Lisa's voice beside her, and the drug finally kicking in. Her head rested against Sean's shoulder as they made their way west. He could feel her breath on his ear and her drool through his shirt. Before long, he made out some light snoring.

Lisa had gathered her wits and was probably well enough to hand Hannah back to her, but Sean worried an exchange might wake the child back up. That could lead to more crying from the exhausted toddler, and that was something none of them could afford.

They crossed down every third or fourth row, moving diagonally toward the farm's northwest corner. A couple of times they heard the Bronco's engine in the distance, and saw headlights bounce above some panels far to the east. Montoya probably figured they'd cut back toward the road, the closest path back to civilization.

The slope grew sharper and the wind had died down for the time being . . . perhaps from the mountainside giving them some cover. The air, however, had grown cooler.

Sean knew it wouldn't be long before they reached the edge of the farm. They slowed their movements, listening and watching for any signs of the man. When the thin moon above revealed nothing but a rocky hillside beyond the next stretch of paneling, Sean understood that they'd reached the end. Somewhere in the dark, the man was waiting for them to emerge.

Sean shot a look behind them, then held Lisa's wrist and pulled her just under the panel. He lowered to his knee and she went down with him.

"I need the rifle," he whispered in her ear. "Will she wake up and start screaming and shit if I switch her back to you?"

Lisa leaned in close to Hannah's face, pressing her ear close to the child's mouth. "I don't think so." She lowered the rifle to the ground.

Sean leaned forward, letting Lisa pry Hannah off his chest. The toddler squirmed and mumbled at first, but then rested comfortably against Lisa's body. Sean grabbed the rifle. He was weary of checking its clip. It was dark, he was unfamiliar with the weapon, and he was worried he'd make too much noise. Worse, it could jam. What he did know is that a Browning BAR held between four and five rounds, depending on if there was one in the chamber. Assuming it had been full prior to Sean's two shots at Montoya, he had two or three remaining. That wasn't much.

He pulled himself upright, his feet aching from his shoes as he did. He stayed low, motioning to Lisa who swung in behind him. They kept tight to the paneling, knowing it would be their only cover if bullets started flying.

There were two logical tactical positions that Sean could think of from the man. He'd either be tucked in low under a panel, along the edge of the farm . . . or hiding somewhere along the hill, perhaps behind some rocks. Either way, the man would have a broad view of the area. Sean believed his best chance was to draw the man into the open, or at least get him to give away his position. The question was *how*.

He wished it were as simple as it was on old television Westerns like *Bonanza*, where he could just toss a rock off to the side and wait for the hair-trigger *bad guy* to take a shot at it. But this was reality, where Sean was no Adam Cartwright and the men after them weren't character actors. It was a shame, because there were plenty of rocks littering the ground.

The closer they got to the end of the panel, the slower and more cautious Sean's movements grew. About a hundred feet to the west were large rocks along the hill, at least a dozen. More were surely scattered out beyond them, cloaked in darkness. The close ones looked five to six feet in diameter—boulders that had broken loose from above and long ago rolled down. If they could make it to the rocks, they wouldn't be as vulnerable. Montoya's vehicle couldn't reach them, and a clear shot from below would be difficult to land—especially in the dark. They'd have plenty of hiding spots as they made their way north.

Montoya's man surely knew these things as well, which made the chances he was hiding behind one of the rocks even stronger. If he was, the three of them would be easy pickings in a matter of seconds, once they made their way out into the open.

Sean stopped, with Lisa nearly running into him. His eyes

shifted from side to side before he turned to her, motioning her under the panel. He quickly joined her.

"We need to know where this guy is," he whispered. "Otherwise, we'll find out the hard way."

"What do you want to do?" she asked.

"You stay here. Keep low. Be ready to run for those rocks when I say to." He pointed at some of the closer boulders.

"Okay," she said after a moment.

"And if something happens to me . . ." he said. "Just stay alive. You and Hannah. Okay? Stay hidden if you need to. Travel north when you can. But hang in there."

She said nothing. Sean could only imagine how tightly her gut was knotted from hearing his words. He placed his hand on Lisa's shoulder and nodded, unable to think of what else needed to be said.

He moved across the walkway to the next panel up the hill, lowering himself to his hands and knees, before going lower to his chest to crawl under it. With his hand wrapped around the rifle, he continued along the dirt and gravel of the next walkway's shoulder, fighting through the pain in his shoulder until he made it to the end of the panel. There, he pulled the rifle in front of him, resting on his right side. His eyes focused on the dirt road that marked the farm's border.

Downhill, the man was nowhere to be seen. Sean's head panned slowly across the terrain. He watched for movement beyond the grass and scrub that rustled in the breeze. He held his gaze on the rocks, even using the scope on his rifle for a closer look, before turning his attention uphill.

There was no sign of the man, yet he had to be there . . . somewhere. He hadn't come running when his shot-up partner cried out his name. He'd stayed put when Montoya was firing from his vehicle. He must have had strict instructions to stay where he was until he heard otherwise.

His name, Sean suddenly thought. When the man who'd been run over first fell to the ground, he'd called for his partner by name. Sean struggled to remember what that name was. Seconds that felt like minutes agonized by before it came to him.

Sean bit his lip. He took a breath and then cupped his hand to his mouth, whispering as loudly as he could in a forced Spanish accent. "Hector!"

His hand quickly went back to the forearm of his rifle. His other hand wrapped around the weapon's grip and trigger. He pressed his body as low to the ground as he could, remaining perfectly still. Only his eyes moved, bouncing up and down the hill. He was banking on Hector not knowing of his buddy's fate. It made sense that he wouldn't, being that Montoya had taken off in the opposite direction immediately following the incident. Unless the two were in touch by cell phones, they had yet to sync up.

Sean's summons, however, went unanswered. He again called out Hector's name, counting on his strong whisper disguising his voice. He felt like a theater understudy feeding a forgotten line to an actor on stage. He waited, the thought soon occurring to him that Lisa might not understand what he was doing, or even mistake his voice for one of their pursuers. He hoped she was staying put.

He was about to try for a third time when an answer finally came.

"Miguel?"

He heard it from somewhere down the hill. The voice couldn't have been more than three rows away. The discreet tone mirrored his own.

Sean's pulse jumped. He stretched his neck forward and pointed his rifle in the direction of the voice. His finger rested on the trigger. "*Sí!*" he answered back, exhausting what little Spanish he knew.

He saw some movement down the hill, a figure slithering out from under a panel before standing up with a rifle in hand. Sean used the scope to line up a shot as the man cautiously approached him, uttering something in Spanish that sounded like a question. Sean hadn't a clue what he was saying.

Even under the circumstances, Sean's conscience nagged at him. He didn't want to kill the man. He didn't want to take *anyone's* life. He'd had to before, and the memories still haunted him. But Montoya and his people were killers, and all that mattered at the moment was protecting Lisa and the child.

He pulled the trigger. Nothing happened.

Sean's eyes shot wide. Sweat dripped from his forehead. He pulled the trigger a second time, then a third. All that came were empty clicks. He was either out of ammo or the gun had malfunctioned. Either way, there was no time to fix things. Hector was just a few yards out, his posture tightening with suspicion. It didn't seem he'd heard the misfires, but the silence and reluctance of his alleged partner to reveal himself was drawing Hector's lowered rifle a bit higher.

"Miguel?" Hector whispered, stepping between the row of panels just below Sean's.

A metal clunk suddenly drew Hector's attention down the row beside him. Lisa must have bumped against something. Hector spun toward the noise, raising his rifle, and aiming it down the pathway.

"Show yourself!" Hector shouted in a thick accent.

When he took two steps forward between the panels, Sean rolled out from under his refuge. He clenched his rifle by its stock and barrel, and rose to his backside before carefully sliding to a knee and pulling himself upright. He quietly followed Hector, keeping as light on his feet as he could. The crackle of gravel below his shoes suddenly alerted the gunman to his whereabouts.

Hector spun around, his rifle raising horizontal just as Sean slammed the stock of the Browning into the side of his head. Hector's gun went off and he stumbled backwards. Sean stayed on him, lunging forward and wedging the forearm of his weapon under Hector's chin. Hector toppled backwards with Sean landing on top of him, the impact causing both rifles to bounce by the wayside. Sean switched to his fists. He sent a right cross into Hector's head and quickly delivered another one. Hector bucked beneath him like a bronco, legs kicking and arms flailing.

"Go, Lisa!" Sean shouted.

Hector latched onto Sean's forearm after a third shot to the face. He planted a foot and twisted his body to the side, trying to leverage Sean off him. His other hand pressed against the bottom of Sean's chin, forcing his head back. Both men grunted and snarled as Sean worked to keep Hector pinned.

Out of the corner of his eye, Sean saw Lisa whisk past them with Hannah toward the rocks. She hesitated for a moment, taking notice of the rifles laying on the ground.

"No, just go!" Sean yelled.

Lisa had her hands full with the child, and Montoya had likely heard the shot and would be there soon. There wasn't a second to spare, and one of the rifles was inoperable anyway. Still, Lisa faltered.

"Go!" he yelled again, grabbing Hector's neck with his left hand and squeezing his throat.

She growled in frustration but heeded his words, taking off

toward the rocks. Her quick footsteps disappeared the second that burning pain shot up through Sean's shoulder. Hector's hand had slid from Sean's chin to his injured shoulder. He squeezed it the way Sean was squeezing his neck. Sean snorted in pain, his nostrils flaring as he kept up the pressure around Hector's throat.

Beams of light shot across the sky above them. Montoya was coming.

A sick, gagging noise poured from Hector's mouth. His hand fell from Sean's shoulder, moving to his own belt. He must have had another weapon stashed on him, just like his partner. He was going for it.

Sean snapped his right arm free of Hector's grip and rocked him with another fist to the head. He then slid his hands to the man's belt. There, he found what felt like a holster and the textured grip of a pistol. Sean yanked the weapon free just as a handful of dirt and gravel was tossed in his face by Hector. Hector bucked and turned to his side, knocking Sean off balance. Sean felt Hector slide out from under him, feet kicking at his chest as a car door slammed somewhere above.

Sean's eyes stung from the dirt, shifting between a shadow moving across the top of a panel, and Hector rolling underneath it for cover.

"*Señor Montoya!*" Hector screamed. "*Aquí! Aquí!*"

Sean stumbled backwards, wiping his eyes with his forearm. Squinting, he swung his gun in front of him. Hector shouted in Spanish. Montoya answered back, his deep voice echoing across the landscape. Sean didn't know what they were saying, but Montoya's voice had hailed from the northeast. That meant Sean had a clear path to Lisa. The only other option was another fire fight with Montoya, whose hellfire weapon Sean knew he couldn't contend with.

Sean took off down the walkway toward the rocks, shoving his new pistol in his pants and quickly scooping up Hector's rifle.

Hector continued shouting to Montoya, keeping his boss apprised of the situation. Sean immediately regretted not silencing the snitch when he had the chance. Even with dirt biting at his eyes, he could have fired a couple of shots at the thug as he scurried way, and probably gotten him. But Hector was no longer armed, and in Sean's initial thinking, no longer a threat. He wouldn't be as charitable next time.

Sean huffed and puffed, his lungs burning as he shot past the edge of the cell. He veered right toward the boulders just as gunfire erupted from somewhere behind him. Bullets tore into metal. Sparks and flashes of light from Montoya's gun lit up the terrain like a strobe lamp. Sean's angle kept him just out of reach of the lead whizzing past him. He knew the cover would only last as long as it would take Montoya to reach the end of the cell.

The ground went from dirt to gravel and shale. His shoes dug into the rubble, sliding as he fought for traction. He worked his way up the incline toward the boulders, teeth gritting and hair wet from sweat. When he stole a quick glance behind him, he saw nothing in the dark but the outlines of panels. He worried one of the men was lining up a night-scope between his shoulder blades.

"Lisa!" Sean grunted as he stumbled forward. He moved his right fist to steady himself as he climbed over rocks that grew larger in size as he got higher. "Lisa!" He received no reply.

Dirt and rock crumbled beneath his feet, filling the sides of his shoes as he struggled to pull himself between a couple of two-foot-wide boulders.

Bright lights suddenly flipped on from somewhere below, casting a long, horrifying shadow forward from Sean's body. They were the lamps from Montoya's vehicle.

Sean was a sitting duck.

Chapter 20

Sean gasped and lunged forward, twisting his body and rolling on his side over the small boulders. He dropped down behind them, flattening himself as best he could. His mouth gaped open from the pain the move brought to his bleeding shoulder.

Over his heartbeat, he could hear rocks and earth from his wake still tumbling down the hillside. He held his rifle flat against his chest, laying perfectly still. He prayed he hadn't been seen from the vehicle. If he'd made it higher than the view through its windshield, there was hope. Still, Montoya and Hector knew he'd gone up, and that he couldn't have gotten so high that he was out of reach.

Tasting dirt in his mouth, Sean carefully turned his head uphill. Though the vehicle's beams were aimed somewhere below him, enough of the hillside was lit up to provide Sean with a better look at the terrain. Somewhere among the slabs of rock above were Lisa and the child, hiding and wondering—as Sean was—about their pursuers' next move.

The beams began to shift and bobble. Soon came the rumble of the vehicle's engine again. The Bronco was moving closer to the bottom of the hill, doing so slowly. A squeal of brakes brought a chill to Sean's spine. He squirmed slowly on his back, turning his head to try and peer around one of the boulders that was keeping him from the men's view.

If the men inside had seen him, they'd have jumped out and fired. Instead, they were being cautious. A cry of dry hinges was followed by an amplified clunk.

"Amigos," came Montoya's deep, eerie voice. He had a PA system of some kind on his Bronco. "Why delay the inevitable? We all know how this will end."

Sean lowered the side of his face flat against the ground where a small gap of light slid in between the boulders. With his finger on the trigger of his rifle, he squinted and followed the light to the front of the Bronco. The vehicle's doors were wide open, a man standing behind each of them for tentative cover. They likely didn't know Sean's precise whereabouts and they seemed weary of setting themselves up for hidden sniper fire. Little did they know that Sean couldn't get a clean shot off from his position if he tried.

"Sean Coleman . . ." Montoya continued, "I won't lie to you by telling you that you can get out of this alive. I'm guessing the old man explained to you why. This is about *familia*. An eye for an eye, as they say. But I'll take more than an eye. A lot more."

Sean held still, watching and listening. It was all he could do for the time being.

"Still . . ." said Montoya. "I do place some blame on myself."

Sean watched the shorter man on the passenger side of the Bronco turn his head to his boss.

Montoya continued. "I should have killed Lumbergh some time ago. I should have walked up to his quaint little doorstep and bright red door in Winston, Colorado. I should have kept his tall, skinny wife and cute little daughter company until he got home from work one night. And then I should have made him watch what I did to them . . . before slicing his throat and cutting off the hand that pulled the trigger on my brother."

His words stole Sean's breath. Montoya knew exactly what Lumbergh's home looked like. He knew the details of his family—Sean's sister and niece.

"But I didn't," Montoya went on. "I thought time was on my side. I waited. And now my son . . ." He didn't finish his sentence, instead taking in a breath. "For my oversight, I accept some blame for what happened downtown. Some. And for that, I'm willing to cut you a small break."

Sean squinted.

Montoya continued. "I'm going to give you to the count of ten to toss your weapons and start making your way back down here. If you do, I'll only kill you. Well, you and your brother-in-law when I get my hands on him. I'll let the woman and child go. They mean nothing to me beyond the restitution I'm owed by Vincenzo Moretti."

It was essentially the same deal Sean had tried to negotiate with the old man earlier. But the situation had changed. Sean didn't believe for a second that Montoya would honor the terms. The Montoyas were notorious down south for going after the family and associates of their enemies—real and perceived. Lautaro had just threatened as much with Lumbergh's wife and daughter. He'd have no qualms at all with killing Lisa and even Hannah. None. Their best chance of making it through the night was Sean staying alive.

"The choice is yours, *amigo*." Montoya said, clearing his throat afterwards. "*Uno* . . ."

Sean closed his eyes and drew in a deep breath. He wasn't going anywhere, but he needed a plan for when Montoya reached ten, and he and Hector began their way up the hill.

It didn't seem that either of the men below had a flashlight, otherwise it would have been used to light up the higher parts of the hill. Miguel had one when Montoya ran over him, and

Montoya had dropped his from the window of his vehicle during the shootout with Sean. Those must have been the only two the group had. That was at least one advantage Sean had going for him, but the lights on the Bronco were plenty bright enough to make any move from his position dangerous. He could try shooting them out, but he didn't have enough wiggle room to pull it off without exposing most of his body to the gunmen.

When Montoya reached *quatro*, Sean heard something skip lightly across the rocks above him. He twisted his head uphill but saw nothing. After *cinco*, he heard it again, this time seeing a small, pea-sized rock hop its way down the hill until it bounced off his forehead. He squinted, averting his eyes and following the direction of where it had come.

"*Seis!*" Montoya shouted, aggravation building in his voice. It didn't seem he'd seen the rock.

Sean homed in on a staggered row of large boulders. His brows arched when he saw movement behind one of them, an arm waving. It was Lisa, trying to get his attention out of view of the others. She was maybe eighty or ninety feet above him and to the right. Unlike him, she had solid cover.

Sean nodded, but doubted she could make out the subtle gesture from that distance. She started doing something different with her arm, cocking it back and then arching it forward as if she were throwing a football. She was trying to tell him something, but he didn't understand what.

Montoya inhaled audibly as he was about to say *nueve*. The loud crack of rock on rock, somewhere south of where Sean lay, broke the count. A crack of pistol fire rang out from below; it lasted only a second. Something was shouted in Spanish, followed by the slam of a car door. The Bronco's engine rumbled just long enough for the lights to shift southward and the brakes to squeal again.

Lisa had pulled off a *Bonanza*, throwing a rock as a momentary distraction. Sean could barely believe it, but the interference wouldn't last long. Still, with less light in his direction, he knew he couldn't waste the opportunity. Sean sat up from his position, turned, and draped the barrel of his rifle between the boulders. Montoya was in the driver's seat and Hector was circling on foot to the driver's side of the vehicle. Neither man was a clean target, so Sean went lower. Using the scope, he aimed for the right headlight. He fired, sending sparks off the grill of the Bronco. He quickly took a second shot, this time shattering the headlight. Part of the hill went darker.

Hector dove to the ground, taking cover. The Bronco shook hard as Montoya pulled himself out of the vehicle, swinging around beside Hector. Sean knew he was on borrowed time, but he had to try for a tire. There were too many lights and too few bullets to take all of them out, but if he could disable the vehicle, at least those lights couldn't follow. Steadying his rifle, he fired at the right front tire. He didn't hear contact so he took a second shot. This time, he didn't waste time assessing the damage. He quickly crawled to his feet and pumped his legs up the hill toward Lisa.

Hector shouted wildly below. Even in the dark, Sean had been spotted. His jaw square and nostrils wide, he climbed up the hill perpendicularly, legs driving forward. He struggled to hold onto the rifle as he kept planting his fist on higher ground to keep himself upright. He grunted with each lurch upward.

"Sean!" Lisa warned.

He knew what was coming next and immediately changed direction, stumbling horizontally along the hill as a flood of gunfire blasted below. Rock and earth exploded around him. He threw himself flat, dust and rubble bouncing off his face. The line of fire continued past him along the hill.

Montoya must have just seen his movement and fired in his general direction. They didn't have him pinpointed. Sean tilted is head up toward Lisa's boulder. He could barely see it now, but made out its outline after wiping some dirt from his eyes. The gunfire momentarily halted. Sean twisted his head down the hill.

Shadows crossed in front of the vehicle's remaining lights. The men were repositioning. Whether or not they were coming up after him, their mobility meant a less steady shot from below. Sean yanked himself up and beelined for the boulder, aggressively climbing toward it from the opposite side.

A loud gasp greeted him when he swung his body around the rock and collapsed onto the rubble.

"Oh, thank God!" Lisa whispered, relief in her voice as she lunged forward and swung her arm around his waist.

Sean felt Hannah's small, sleeping body between them as they hugged. His shoulder burned and he could barely catch his breath, but Lisa's embrace instantly brought him some comfort—some warmth . . .the way his seemed to bring to her.

"I thought they got you," she whispered, sniffing. "I saw you go down . . . and . . . I thought they got you . . ." She backed away from him when her arm slid across his shoulder. "You're bleeding?"

"From the old bullet. I don't think I'm wearing any new ones." He took a breath and a step back. "We've gotta go. Keep moving." He turned his focus to the row of large rocks that decorated the hillside. "They'll be more cautious now. Slower, because we have better cover and better visual. But they'll be coming, and we don't have enough ammo to take much of a stand. No extra clips. Just a few shots left.

"Okay."

"You still okay carrying her?"

"Uh-huh," she said, breathing almost as heavily as Sean.

"We're going to get through this," said Sean, placing his hand on her arm. "You hear me?"

She nodded.

He nodded back, hoping what he'd just said was the truth. "Okay," he said, swallowing. "Let's go."

Chapter 21

"Montoya wasn't on Metro's radar at all?" Lumbergh pressed, his teeth punishing a second stick of gum as he watched brake lights flare up ahead of Holman's car. "Did you even know he was in the state?"

"No," said Holman, her hands clenching the steering wheel as she pressed down on the brakes. "Damn this traffic." Her gaze shifted to Lumbergh for a few seconds before returning to the road. She looked as if she wanted to say something else.

Her hesitation wasn't lost on Lumbergh. "What is it?"

Holman shook her head, sighing. "About a month ago, a police dispatcher got an anonymous call. Some guy with a thick Spanish accent insisting he saw Lautaro Montoya outside a gas station on the north side of town."

Lumbergh twisted in his seat. "And you're just now telling me this? You know my history with this guy's family!"

"Oh, cut me a break, Chief," said Holman, checking her mirror and switching lanes. "It was *one* phone call. Anonymous. An officer was sent out; he looked around and asked around. The employee on duty saw nothing, and the only security camera at the scene wasn't operational. We came away with nothing. It might as well have been an Elvis sighting."

"But it was big enough of a deal for you to hear about it—to know about it."

"Only in passing. Water cooler talk. Metro hasn't heard a peep on him ever since."

"Until tonight."

"Yes, until tonight," Holman ceded, tilting her head. "And now that we have actual proof, and not just unsourced gossip that he *is* here, let's focus on finding him so we can find the others."

Lumbergh knew Holman was right. There wasn't a reasonable line of thought that would have connected Montoya to the transpiring events, prior to Wendice's video. The top priority now was tracking Montoya down. Unfortunately, that road was already leading to dead ends.

There was hope at first that Lisa's cell phone could be pinged through her service provider to reveal its general location, or at least the direction in which it was headed. Montoya, as shown in the video, had left the home with the phone in his hand. The lead dried out, however, when the phone was discovered by an officer in a dirt yard a couple of lots down the cul-de-sac. It had likely been tossed from a window.

Canvasing the neighborhood also went nowhere. Lisa lived in a new construction area, and her closest neighbors were several doors down. The only people home were an elderly couple watching television, who hadn't seen or heard a thing.

The APB on the Suburban from back at the hotel had yet to turn up anything, and there hadn't yet been any reports of gunshot injuries from area hospitals or clinics. If any came in, Holman would be among the first notified.

Their best hope for the moment was identifying the man Lumbergh had shot. He was one of Montoya's people. If they could search his home and talk to his friends and family, they might get some useful information that could lead them back to his boss.

For now, the plan was to regroup back at the station and pull in some resources.

"What do you think about getting the feds involved?" asked Holman, her eyes sliding to Lumbergh. "Maybe they've got a line on Montoya—some lead we don't know about."

"I very much doubt that," said Lumbergh. "If they had something, they'd have already moved on it. They get how dangerous this guy is. Agents would be all over his ass if they had an idea of where he was. Plus, the bureau is supposed to give me a heads-up if they hear anything on him. I haven't gotten a call in probably eight months, and the last one was mistaken identity." He shook his head. "No, FBI bureaucracy would just slow this thing down."

Holman nodded. "Good, I'm glad we're in agreement."

"I'm surprised you even brought them up. You'd have been the first detective I'd met who thought of federal intervention as a good thing."

"Not me," she said. "Just wanted everything on the table. With a little girl among the kidnapped, it may become inevitable."

"Understood," said Lumbergh. "As long as we have access to their fingerprint database . . ."

"We do," said Holman. "My people are running your guy's prints both locally and nationally. He's got to be in the system . . . somewhere."

"Unless he's fresh up from Mexico."

Lumbergh gazed through the windshield, his eyes floating over staggered streetlamps that lit up sections of the highway. There was something from back at Lisa's house that was still nagging him.

"What did you make of Wendice's story back there, about the camera?"

"The *nanny cam* explanation?" she answered.

Just before leaving the house, Lumbergh had pivoted back to his concern about Wendice placing a hidden camera in Lisa's living room. Wendice was reluctant to address it, and once he did, it was apparent why. He explained that he had serious trust issues stemming from his ex-wife. She'd had a history of depression and substance abuse problems, and had left him and his daughter shortly after she was born. It was a very rough time, according to Wendice. He was suddenly a single parent, raising an infant on his own. He had a good, high-paying job in security and surveillance technology, but was overwhelmed, and his daughter was growing up without a mother.

He'd had a nanny for a while—a college student with a flexible schedule who stayed at his home most days to take care of Hannah. But after losing track of some security inventory he kept at his home for trade shows and presentations, he set up one of his company's hidden cameras that not only captured the student stealing merchandise, but also her negligent treatment of Hannah: rough handling and letting the baby cry in soiled diapers while she sat out on the back patio and talked to friends on the phone. He terminated the relationship.

It felt like extraneous information until Wendice got to the point. When Lisa came into his life, and the two's relationship grew more serious, Lisa would offer to watch Hannah from time to time, often at her own house. Greg wanted to trust her with his daughter, but having been burned twice by the only maternal figures Hannah had ever known, his paranoia had gotten the better of him. He understood that by admitting to the police that he had surveilled Lisa without her knowledge, he was confessing to breaking the law. He told Lumbergh and Holman that he was prepared to accept the legal consequences for it, once his daughter was back.

Still, the confession wasn't sitting well with Lumbergh.

"Were you buying what he was selling with that?" asked Lumbergh.

Holman shrugged. "It was certainly strange, but it didn't strike me as too terribly hard to believe. There are a lot of insecure guys out there. Control freaks. There are probably more here in Vegas than most places. I know a number of them personally," she added with a chuckle. "If Wendice was going to make up a story, why would he implicate himself of a crime?"

Lumbergh's eyes narrowed. "He might if the *real* story is even worse."

"What are you saying?"

"I don't know," said Lumbergh, shaking his head. "He probably told us the truth. It's just that . . . If you were that worried about the safety of your child, to the point where you set up a video camera in someone's home to record things when you weren't around, wouldn't you put that camera in the room where your child is sleeping and spending most of her time? The kid's bed was in the side room."

"Well," said Holman. "I don't have kids, but if the concern is with what the adult's doing, and not what the child's doing, the living room makes more sense. That's where an adult would spend most of her time at home."

Lumbergh nodded. "I guess. I'm just trying to apply this to how my home works, and my own daughter, and—"

"And that right there is your problem. I'm guessing you trust your wife."

"I do," he said, his lips curling.

"That's why it's so confusing to you. You have a healthy family life. That's a good thing."

Lumbergh nodded.

"Speaking of your family . . ." said Holman after a few

seconds. "Back at the hotel, you said you hadn't called home yet. And you've been with me ever since. Don't you think you should check in? Your wife is Sean's sister, after all. She should know."

"Yeah," Lumbergh said with a nod. "I was hoping to have better news before I called her, and Dusty's cell phone is almost out of charge, so . . . And now she and Ashley are surely asleep."

"You should call her anyway," said Holman, leaning forward and reaching into her car console. She pulled out a cell phone.

Lumbergh took it. "Thanks." He drew in a deep breath, readying himself before dialing the number. He stopped a digit short when the phone began ringing and vibrating in his hand. "You've got an incoming."

"Sorry," said Holman, taking the phone back. She glanced at the display before answering. "Holman."

Lumbergh couldn't hear the voice on the other end, but by Holman's straight tone and demeanor, it appeared to be a work call.

"Okay," she said. "Are you telling me this because you got a print off it?"

Lumbergh's eyes narrowed. "A print off what?" he asked.

Holman ignored him, listening intently. "Okay," she said into the phone. "How many Vespers are there in the area?" After a pause, she said, "Two?"

"What the hell's a Vesper?" Lumbergh persisted.

"Hold on," she whispered to Lumbergh before turning her attention back to her phone. "Okay, Corbett is already downtown. Tell him to check out the one on Sunrise. I'll take the Pecos store. If we're lucky, they were in tonight." She finished and hung up, dropping the phone back to the console.

"What's happening? Something on the dead guy?"

"No, that was an officer back at Kimble's house," said

Holman, checking her mirrors and flipping on her blinker. "Remember what you said when those guys with the masks showed up in his video?"

"Yeah, that they didn't know what the hell they were doing. If you're covering your face for a crime, you don't use a flimsy Halloween mask. Too hard to see through for the wearer, and too easily pulled off . . . or destroyed, which Sean looked to have done with the younger guy."

Lumbergh and Holman had agreed from the video that there was a significant age discrepancy between the two masked men. The one who'd stayed on his feet throughout was quite a bit older, judging by his movements. His hair also looked gray in the closing shot as they left the home.

"You also said they were rushed," added Holman. "Otherwise, they would have come in better prepared."

"I did. Are you going to tell me what I've won?" Lumbergh asked impatiently.

Holman quickly pulled north onto a side street, drawing a honk from another car. "They found a red sliver of plastic in the kitchen. It looks like it came off one of the masks."

"The guy who Sean floored as he was coming in. Did they get a print off the plastic?"

"No, not a print. A price tag . . . or at least a partial one, stuck to the inside. Not enough to tell us how much it cost, but enough to tell us where it was purchased. If they were as unprepared and in as much of a hurry as you think . . ."

"Then they might have bought those things tonight," said Lumbergh, completing her sentence.

She nodded. "Vesper is a drug store. There are only two of them here in Vegas. One downtown and one just west of Henderson. My partner will check out the downtown location. We'll check the other."

"Hell, if we can get a description of those two, or of their car . . ."

"Then we'd be one step closer to finding the others."

Chapter 22

The terrain was rough and the night made things harder. Lisa led the way, hiking Hannah up in her arms as she shuffled around the inside of the next boulder. Sean was close behind, keeping his head low, with rifle in hand as they carefully moved from one large mass to another. Both used their hands for balance as they proceeded along the ridge.

When they reached a ten-foot gap in the rocks, Sean crossed in front of Lisa, ducking and peering around the boulder on the end, back at the Bronco. Its lights were still on. The vehicle, now in the distance, didn't appear to have moved. Sean must have punctured the tire. The men were likely somewhere along the hill, or perhaps at the bottom of it moving parallel to them. At some point, the hill and its steepening base would converge, but for now there was a clear intermediary.

Sean's gaze floated along the land below, hoping to catch a glimpse of the men—any kind of disruption. Nothing came into view, but he held up a finger to Lisa and listened intently. He heard nothing at first, but after a few seconds there was a faint hum in the distance. A tiny pair of headlights soon appeared along the highway off to the east. It was the first car Sean had seen since Montoya's arrival. It moved at a normal, constant speed—likely some hapless traveler completely unaware of what was happening to the west.

There was no way for Sean to get the driver's attention from so far away, but that didn't mean the vehicle wasn't useful. Montoya and Hector were assuredly keeping an eye on it from wherever they were, concerned it might be the police. Whether the distraction was a gift from the Big Nudge or just dumb luck, Sean was going to take advantage of it.

"Okay, now," Sean said to Lisa, motioning her forward.

She tottered across the open section of hill. Sean mirrored her pace just a foot or two downhill from her, taking on the protective role of the large rocks they'd just left. His head bobbed between the next row of boulders and the lower part of the hill. Dirt and gravel crumbled under their shoes as they walked, but the noise was no louder than the echo of the car's engine. They made it across to the next line of boulders without incident. The car on the highway disappeared from view, having never altered its course or speed.

"Are we sure they're even following us?" Lisa whispered, taking a moment to catch her breath. She leaned her back up against the second rock in. "Maybe they're still back at their car."

"Doing what? Playing checkers?"

Lisa's face tilted up toward Sean's. Her unseen eyes were likely scolding Sean's sarcasm, the way they used to when they'd argue as a couple. "Maybe they're fixing a flat tire. Did you think about that? Maybe you shot one of them—one of the men. A number of possibilities."

"It's a nice thought," Sean whispered, softening his tone. He glanced back over his shoulder. "But I know I didn't hit anyone, and they're not going to waste time fixing a flat. Not right now anyway." He took a breath before continuing. "Listen, Montoya and his stooge aren't going to give up. Not tonight. They've got us isolated and all to themselves, out here in nowhere-land. What *we've* got is a bullet in me, a kid in tote, and no one around to help us. They're not about to cut their losses and let us get away. This is too personal to Montoya, and too perfect of a situation."

"Perfect?" said Lisa, keeping her voice low. "There were three of them when they got here. Now there are just two."

"Life's cheap to a man like Montoya," said Sean. "I'm betting he spent less time mourning good old *Miguel* than I did. But the same isn't true of his son. That's a life that most certainly matters to him. *El familia,* or whatever the hell he called it. He sure as hell isn't going to turn back."

Lisa said nothing at first, the words probably echoing what she already knew but hadn't wanted to accept. "We'd better keep going then," she finally said.

They continued on, navigating along the west side of the rock wall. Sean's feet were in pain that worsened with each step forward. His shoes, filled with earth and rocks, weren't made for such terrain, and he could only imagine the blisters that now disfigured his feet. His shoulder had stopped bleeding again, but now it had a different problem. It was numb. He wasn't sure if it was from nerve damage or was related to blood circulation from the tape wrapped around it, but he was worried it would hinder his capacity to use the rifle.

Every minute or so, the two would halt for a brief moment, lowering themselves against the inside of a rock, and watch and listen for the men. In each instance, they detected nothing but a dark, still landscape, and heard little beyond the wind and some light snoring from Hannah.

"Could they be working their way ahead of us somehow?" Lisa whispered at the next stop. "From down below?"

"I don't think so," said Sean with a furrowed brow. "We'd be seeing or hearing something down there if they were pushing that hard and fast." He turned to Lisa. "Montoya is nothing if not patient. He spent two years secretly digging himself out of a Chihuahua prison. Real *Shawshank Redemption*-type shit, except Montoya actually *belonged* behind bars. Right now, I think he's keeping his distance and matching our pace. Just waiting for an opportunity to pick us off with a rifle."

Lisa nodded. "Or maybe wait us out—wait for us to run out of steam."

"Yeah. That too."

"How's your shoulder?" Lisa asked after a moment.

"Shitty," he answered. "But not much can be done about that right now. How's your head?"

"I'll live."

Sean nodded.

"Can I ask you a question?" said Lisa, her tone soft.

"You just did," replied Sean.

"Where did you get all that money—the money in your bank account? You said it was from security work, but—"

Sean sighed. "You don't think that—"

"No, no . . . I know you have nothing to do with what Kyle stole. I just—"

"You're *just* wondering how a working-class stiff like me ended up with a quick $200K to his name, especially since that's what got this whole ball rolling?"

Lisa's silence answered for her.

"It's fine," Sean said, his voice even. "I said I'd tell you later anyway." He took a breath before continuing, voice remaining low. "You know that gig I had at the missile silo, back in Colorado—the one I was working when you saw me on the news?"

"Yes," she said, suspicion in her voice. "That the *armed cult* tried to take over," she added, evoking Sean's earlier phrasing.

Sean explained how the leader of the group had a secret agenda, unbeknownst to the others. His real reason for being there was to unearth a collection of diamonds, worth millions, that had been hidden there by a former silo operator during the Cold War.

"You found them—the diamonds?" said Lisa. "And then you *what*—sold them?"

"Yes and no."

"What does that mean?"

"Yes, I found them. But no, I didn't sell them. People died that day for those diamonds—innocent people. I wasn't going to cash in on their memories, their lives. It would have been blood money."

Lisa hesitated before pressing. "Then how . . ."

"I returned the diamonds to their rightful owners, the family of the silo operator's wife. They were sort of . . . family heirlooms, long ago." He chuckled and added, "Insanely valuable family heirlooms."

Lisa said nothing. Sean wasn't sure if she was skeptical of his words, or if she was still processing his story. He could only imagine how crazy it must have sounded to someone who wasn't there, and was hearing it for the first time.

"The family was very appreciative. They're still filthy rich, so a couple extra million wasn't exactly life-changing to them, but the diamonds were of sentimental value. They wanted to reward me for returning them."

Lisa continued listening, not saying a word.

"I told them I didn't need any reward, because I didn't." Sean said. "But they wouldn't drop it. I finally gave in, figuring I could put the money to good use. It seemed to make them happy . . . or maybe less guilty for being so rich, who knows?"

"Are you?" Lisa finally spoke up.

"Am I what?"

"Putting it to good use."

"Well, I haven't had it long, but I'm trying to. Remember Toby?"

"That kid in Winston, the one with autism? The one who looks up to you?"

"Yeah, much to his mother's ongoing dismay."

"What about him?"

"He's been having a lot of trouble over the past year or so. With school. With teachers and the other students. He's a special kid, and he's not getting what he needs. It's causing him problems at home too. Diana's helping me set up an education fund for him, to get him set up in a private school, where the teachers and staff are better trained for . . . for kids like him, and others like him . . ."

Sean suddenly felt something brush against his wrist, something soft. It was Lisa's hand. She wrapped her fingers around his and guided him toward her a bit. He guardedly let her.

"You're a good man, Sean," she said warmly.

His stomach tightened. "*A man with the weight of the world on his shoulders,*" he answered, quoting words he knew she'd recognize—words that felt like they'd come from a lifetime ago. " . . . *who can only lift that weight himself.* You were right about that."

When she tightened her grip on his hand, a tear began to build in his eye.

The snap of wood and what sounded like a grunt suddenly brought their attention back to the situation. Their hands whipped free of each other. The noise had come from somewhere below them. They both lowered themselves and leaned deeper into the rocks. Sean brought up his rifle into both hands, his finger on the trigger.

One of their pursuers had likely tripped over a branch or some scrub. The sound hadn't come from terribly close by. There was still some breathing room between them. An additional relief, as small as it may have been, was that he now knew the men were taking the low path and weren't behind them on the hill. He and Lisa weren't in any less danger, but at least they knew which direction that danger was coming from. He could only imagine how infuriated Montoya must be, knowing that their relative position had just been broadcast.

Whether or not the men knew where Sean and Lisa were hiding was a different story. They assuredly had a general idea; maybe more than that if the wind had carried the whispers of their conversation down the hill. Either way, it didn't constitute a change in tactics. Montoya and Hector were still the hunters. Sean and Lisa were still the prey. Their only realistic option was avoidance and escape.

Sean turned his attention to the terrain above them. He and Lisa had gradually made their way higher on the hill, the natural placement of the rocks facilitating the ascent. But the closer they came to the top, the smaller and more spread out the rocks were becoming, replaced with patches of brush that could barely absorb water, let alone bullets.

He leaned into Lisa. "What do you know of this area?" he whispered.

"What?" she whispered back. "Nothing. I've never been up in these hills."

"More generally," Sean clarified. "The road down there. The guys in the van said it was Highway 95. We're west of it and probably ten miles south of Henderson. Do you know what's on the other side of this range, west of here?"

Lisa's gaze lowered to the ground. "I'm not sure."

"Come on," pressed Sean. "You *live* here."

Lisa scoffed. "I live in the city. West is California. East is Arizona. The rest is just . . ." She stopped, organizing her thoughts.

Sean peered around his rock, watching for signs of the men. He saw nothing.

"Interstate 15 runs parallel to 95," she finally said, pointing west. "Sloan Canyon is between them. That's what would be on the other side."

"What's in Sloan Canyon?"

"Not much. It's a conservation area. Federally owned."

"Like a national park?"

"Basically. But it's just desert, like here. A few trails. No camping, if I remember right. They close the place down at night."

"Is there a visitor's center? Or ranger station?"

Lisa nodded. "I think. Somewhere. I haven't been down that way in a few years, but I remember there being a road and a couple of buildings alongside it. That stuff may be quite a bit farther north, though. I'm not sure. I thought you wanted to keep going towards Henderson."

"As long as we can, but . . ." Sean stopped talking when he heard a hum in the distance. He twisted his head to the south, keeping low and peering around the rocks.

"What is that?" asked Lisa.

Sean listened for a moment. "An engine, I think."

"A car?"

"I don't know. We're a ways from the road, and—"

Some light flickered across an area of land to the south.

A loud pulse suddenly overtook the sound of the engine. Seconds later, music blared, echoing across the valley from the same direction. It had to be the Bronco, its PA system blasting out what sounded like a rock station. Staggered beams from a headlight and spotlights soon appeared over a ridge, bouncing up and down. They were far away but moving closer.

"Were they fixing their car this whole time?" Lisa whispered. "Were they not following us until just now? And why the music?"

The song was Iron Butterfly's "In-A-Gadda-Da-Vida," its haunting guitar riff adding an extra chill to the air. The vehicle bobbled over the terrain, slowly coming closer as Sean struggled to make sense of what was happening. The sound they'd heard below a minute earlier wasn't just part of their imagination. It wasn't made by the wind or an animal. The men must have split up. One had stayed behind to fix the flat while the other was on their trail. But Lisa had a good question: *why the music?*

Sean gasped and pulled himself upright, peering over the top of the boulder. "It's got to be a distraction."

"What?" said Lisa. She got to her feet beside Sean.

When the Bronco's lights spread across the hill for just a moment, Sean watched in horror as the outline of a large, broad-shouldered figure quickly made its way up the slope toward them. The man's legs pumped forward like a mountain lion coming after a deer.

Montoya.

"Shit!" Sean snarled, drawing his rifle up over the rock.

Another stray beam exposed what looked like a long rifle strapped behind Montoya's back. His right hand was clasped around something, probably a pistol. He was less than a hundred and fifty feet away but making quick ground.

Sean could barely raise his left arm. There was no feeling in it from his shoulder to his wrist. He turned to Lisa.

"You need to go. Now."

"What?" she gasped.

"Now. Go straight up to the top of this hill with Hannah. Go down the other side. Don't stop and don't look back. Just go. Find that ranger station."

"No," she said firmly.

"Yes!" he roared. "We're out of time!" He knew her only chance was the remaining cover of night, and that opportunity would disappear the moment the Bronco reached the bottom of the hill.

Sean turned back toward Montoya, the darkness now cloaking his ascent. Sean struggled, with one hand, to line up a shot with where he'd last seen the man. He listened for the movement of dirt and rocks to try and triangulate his position, but all he heard was Lisa working her way up the hill with Hannah, rocks and dirt from her ascent bouncing off his back.

With the rifle resting on the boulder in front of him, Sean squared his jaw. When he thought he saw movement, he fired a shot. Then another.

Chapter 23

A clerk at Vesper was more helpful than Lumbergh and Holman could have hoped for. The thoroughly pierced teen, with black and teal bangs dangling just above his eyes, not only remembered selling the Halloween costumes to a man who was "in a big hurry," but also recognized the individual as a regular customer.

"Yeah, he buys shit here all the time," said the clerk. His badge read "Brad." "Lots of diet soda. He likes Cool Ranch Doritos too."

Amidst wide shelves of lottery tickets, cigarettes, and chewing tobacco, Brad described the man as being in his late thirties with dark hair and a bit of a gut. He always paid in cash, so digging through the rolls for credit card information would be a waste of time. But according to another employee on duty—a pudgy twenty-something with a crewcut who was stocking one of the refrigerators with energy drinks—the man's first name was "Vic," a nugget of information that had once come out in casual conversation.

Neither knew what Vic did for a living, but he was at the store often enough that they assumed he either lived or worked close by.

"Have you ever seen him pick up a prescription?" asked Holman with a head nudge toward the pharmacy counter at the back end of the building. Its security gate had already been pulled down for the night.

Brad hadn't, but did know that Vic drove a dark van. He'd seen him pull up in it a number of times. However, he wasn't sure of the make or model—something that irritated Lumbergh, though it didn't surprise him; youth of the modern era didn't take the same notice of cars that his generation did. He hoped he'd get the information soon enough, however, as the stocker was on his phone calling their boss for access information to the store's security cameras.

Holman further questioned the clerk.

"Did he say why he was in a hurry, or why he needed the costumes?"

"I figured they were for his kids or something," said the teen, rubbing his eye. "I mean, those costumes are made for kids and all." He pointed down an aisle where other Halloween masks and props were hanging on hooks. "Maybe his sons were late for a Halloween party or something, but hell, we're only a few days into October, so I guess probably not. That would be weird."

"Have you ever *seen* him in here with any kids . . . or any adults for that matter?" asked Lumbergh.

"No, he's always by himself. I was just guessing about the kids. You know, because of the costumes."

"And he was by himself today too? He wasn't in here with an older guy?"

"He was by himself. I guess there could have been someone out in his van, but who knows, you know? He just came blasting on in here, like he was three seconds from pissing his pants. I figured he was zooming toward the restroom, but then he did a ninety-degree over to the hat rack." The clerk pointed to an aisle at the other side of the store. His finger traced the remainder of his account. "And then he said, 'fuck,' or something, and I guess he decided that he didn't need a hat after all, but needed some Halloween clothes instead. So, he grabbed a couple of costumes and paid for them."

"In cash?"

"Always in cash, man. Like I said."

"Did you—" started Holman.

Lumbergh talked over her, drawing from her an annoyed glance. "And you didn't bother asking him why he was in such a hurry?"

"Well, no man," said Brad, shrugging. "Who am I to judge? Whenever *I'm* in a hurry, I don't need some jackass slowing me down by asking me why I'm in a hurry. You know, a man's gotta get places and all."

Both Lumbergh and Holman sighed.

Holman turned to Lumbergh and pointed to the security camera above the clerk's head. "If we can get some good angles off these cameras, that may be all we need. If we're *really* lucky, the outside one picked up the van's license plate."

Lumbergh nodded, digging into his front pocket, and then reaching into his back one. His eye twitched.

"Got it," said Holman, backing up from the counter and gazing over the gum section.

Lumbergh twisted his chin over his shoulder and cupped his hand to his mouth. "How are we coming with those cameras?" he shouted, his patience wearing thin.

"Getting there," came the stocker's voice from the open door of a small office down the hall. "He's having to look up the password. We don't review videos very often."

Holman paid the clerk for the gum. She dug out a stick for Lumbergh.

"Okay, we're in business!" shouted the stocker.

Lumbergh and Holman joined him, with Brad following closely on their heels. The bell from a customer entering the store drew a sigh from Brad, who returned to the counter.

Inside the small room comprised mostly of file cabinets and wall certificates and posters was a desk with an old PC. There were numerous stickers and sticky notes attached to the monitor. Its screen was split, showing shots from two different cameras—one from behind the counter and one from the parking lot. The back end of Holman's car was visible on the latter, meaning the shot was either live or recorded within the last few minutes.

"Brad, how long ago did he come in?" the stocker yelled. He flashed a quick grin at Holman.

"Don't know, dude," Brad shouted back. "Couple of hours, maybe. I wasn't looking at the clock. Just rewind until you see the van. It was right out front."

The stocker grunted. "Okay, this could take a few minutes. I hope that's okay."

"We're not going anywhere," assured Holman, grinning back.

Lumbergh's eyes slid back and forth between the two. Holman seemed to be working on maximum cooperation.

The three sat through a good ten minutes of cars and shoppers quickly departing before arriving at the store. The stocker used that time to repeatedly emphasize his appreciation for law enforcement, his eyes landing on Holman a number of times. When a dark van appeared on the right side of the screen, Holman nudged the back of his chair.

"Hello!" the stocker said excitedly, a groan coming from his chair as he leaned forward.

Lumbergh and Holman leaned in as well.

"Okay, is this him?" asked Lumbergh pointing to the picture

on the left, where a man with dark hair and dark clothes moved quickly from one aisle to another.

"Yes!" confirmed the stocker. "That's Vic!"

Vic was every bit as out of sorts as Brad had described him, his movements quick and seemingly desperate. He jogged over to the Halloween costumes, skipping over the half masks and other props, and choosing two that he assuredly believed, in his hurried state, would do the best job of concealing their identities.

"There's someone in the van," said Holman.

Lumbergh's eyes slid to the other shot. Though the camera was pointed toward the driver's side window, there was clear movement from the passenger seat. The picture, however, wasn't tight enough to capture details of the man's face. What appeared to be cigarette smoke lingered around him.

Everyone's attention turned back to the indoor shot. When Vic approached the counter, the stocker hit the pause button. "Boom!" he yelled, having captured a clear, close-up shot of the man's face.

"That's him!" snapped Brad, causing everyone to jump. He had moved in behind them without warning. "Sorry. But yeah, that's Vic."

Lumbergh turned to Holman. "Recognize him?"

She shook her head. "No, but this is good. This will get us an ID. I need a printout if you can get me one," she said, placing her hand on the stocker's shoulder.

The stocker blushed. "You've got it. One print screen coming up." He pressed a key and then turned on a printer to his side. It appeared even older than the PC.

"Okay, let's keep going on this," said Lumbergh. "We need a license plate on that van."

The stocker turned to Holman, as if to ask for confirmation. Lumbergh's eyes narrowed.

"Yes, go ahead please," she said with a wink.

The stocker grinned and resumed the video. Vic exited the store and returned to his van, opening the door, tossing the costume over to the passenger, and positioning himself in his seat. His face grew animated as he seemed to be arguing with the passenger. The van reversed out of its spot, the back end of the vehicle beginning to twist toward the camera.

"Here it comes!" said Lumbergh. "We'll need you to pause again once the plate's visible."

The stocker nodded, tensing his body with his finger on the mouse.

Just as the plate was about to enter the picture, another vehicle—a light-colored pickup truck—pulled up to the front of the store, directly between the van and the camera.

Holman and Brad gasped.

"Oh Jesus, who's this idiot?" Lumbergh bemoaned.

The stocker grimaced, his head tilting back toward the others.

"It's him," said Brad.

"What? Who?" asked Holman.

Brad leaned forward and shoved his finger into the stocker's shoulder. "*He's* the idiot."

The truck's door opened. The stocker slid out, dressed in his store uniform. He lowered his head and glanced into his driver's side mirror to check his appearance before shutting the door and entering the store.

"It was the start of my shift," he moaned, collapsing in his seat and covering his face. He spun toward the others. "How the hell was I supposed to know that—"

"Moron," said Brad.

"Screw you, Brad!"

"Easy gentlemen," said Holman, her voice calm. "All is not lost."

Everyone's eyes returned to the monitor. The van had veered to the right, the driver turning to get back on the road. When the back of the van emerged from around the truck, farther away now, but still in view, Holman reached forward and clicked on the mouse, freezing the shot.

"Zoom in," she said.

The stocker, seemingly inhaling the scent of Holman's hair that now dangled over his shoulder, clicked a button a few times and drew the shot of the van in closer.

"212 . . . before the hyphen," Lumbergh said, squinting. "Right?"

Holman nodded. "That looks like ZGZ after it."

"It is," Brad agreed. "212-ZGZ."

The stocker breathed a sigh of relief. He swiveled in his chair toward the others, nodding in self-satisfaction. "Hey," he said, tilting his head toward the police officers. "Have there been any updates on Roy?"

"Who?" Holman asked.

The stocker's face tightened. "Roy . . . You know, Siegfried's partner. You guys are working that case, right?"

Chapter 24

H is rifle was empty, lying on the dirt beside him. The only rounds left were in the pistol he'd taken from Hector, a Glock 29 with six shots remaining. He had it pinned to a large rock about eighty feet down the hill. Montoya had taken cover behind it during their last exchange, his position exposed by the approaching headlights. Montoya hadn't switched back to his rifle yet, still using a small arm, but it was only a matter of time before he whipped it back out.

Music continued to blast from the Bronco as it reached the base of the hill directly below them. The racket was originally meant as a distraction, and was now probably intended to intimidate, but unbeknownst to the men, it was actually serving to Sean's benefit—or more precisely that of Lisa and Hannah. It was drowning out any sounds the two were making above as they continued their way up the hill.

Sean hated sending them off on their own, but it was the best option at the moment for keeping them safe. The men knew where he was, but they didn't seem to have a clue that Lisa and Hannah had left his side, and may have already reached the top of the mountain. Sean pictured them in his mind, cautiously making their way down the other side in the dark, cooling air. And for the briefest of moments, he also thought of the words he had repeated to Lisa as they held hands behind the rock.

They were *her* words, from the letter she'd rested on his

nightstand all those months ago, the morning she'd left his home in Colorado and never returned.

He'd do everything he could to get back to her, but for now, the best he could manage was buying her and Hannah more time and distance. That meant leading the men in a different direction, hopefully without getting himself killed.

There were still some spots for cover along the mountainside to the north. The rocks mixed in with brush weren't as large as the one he currently knelt behind, but they would hopefully suffice now that he was on his own. He'd need to stay mobile, using the boulders and slabs the best he could as he worked his way farther along the ridge. Where it would take him, he wasn't sure. All that mattered was keeping the men off-step and oblivious to the fact that he was now alone. The best way to do that was to stay in the dark.

Hector was positioning the Bronco to spread its remaining lights up the hill. Turning off the music, he reversed and pulled forward again, navigating a chunk of rough terrain. Soon, Sean would no longer have the darkness on his side. If he was going to make his move, he needed to do it soon.

Montoya hadn't fired a shot in nearly a minute, nor had he uttered a word. Sean couldn't know if he was reloading, waiting for Hector, or lying in wait with his rifle, just salivating over the thought of Sean sticking his head out long enough for him to blow it off.

Sean closed his eyes and drew in a deep breath, hoping for a little guidance from the Big Nudge. Unfortunately, none came . . . and he couldn't wait any longer.

He clenched his teeth and tightened his grip on his pistol. A second later, he bolted out from behind the boulder. Adrenaline pumped through his body, keeping the pain at bay as his legs drove him forward along the ridge. His left arm flopped at his side as brush tore and earth crumbled beneath him.

Gunfire tore through the night. It echoed across the turf as muzzle flash flickered along the mountainside. Montoya may not have seen Sean, but he'd definitely heard him, and was now pummeling the area with lead. Sean slogged his way toward a slab of rock. When his foot hooked something, and his momentum caused him to falter forward, he let himself crash flat to the ground. Dirt and gravel from the bullets pelted his face and body as he squirmed along the ground through brush and stone.

A few more rounds blasted out before the gunfire halted. Montoya yelled something in Spanish, probably calling on Hector to move the Bronco again. Sean crawled over some rock and a mound of earth, rolling to the other side and planting his foot on the downward slope to keep his large body from sliding down it. It wasn't an ideal hiding spot, but it would have to do as he rested his pistol on his stomach and pressed his right hand over his left shoulder. He felt warm, wet blood again.

"There is no escape!" shouted Montoya. "Everything you're doing . . . It is for nothing!"

Lying on his back, feeling as though energy was being drained from his body, Sean tilted his head toward the sky, his eyes transfixed on the thin moon above. He wished he had never placed that call to Lisa. He wished he had never left his friends back in town. If he hadn't, none of this would be happening. But it *was* happening, and what he couldn't do was give up. The longer he held them off, the safer Lisa and Hannah would be.

He grabbed the gun and turned to his side, keeping low

as he crawled over dirt and scrub. He used his legs and right
elbow, unable to do much with his left arm. Just as he reached a
smooth slab of rock about four feet high, a disturbance behind
him heightened his senses. He quickly pulled himself over the
slab and down to the other side. Kneeling with most of his
body now behind the rock, he aimed his pistol in the direction
of the noise. Montoya had left his own rock and was on the
move again.

Sean gazed across the ridge, watching for him. He fired a
blind shot, hopefully dispelling any bold notion Montoya may
have had that he was out of bullets. He quickly pulled himself
lower behind the rock, hearing some sliding and shuffling
several feet in front of him; Montoya had likely dropped low,
assessing Sean's new position.

Out of the corner of his eye, Sean noticed new light.
Another set of headlights had appeared in the distance along
the highway. They were headed in the same direction as the
previous car. Sean wished there were some way of getting the
driver's attention, and for a second, he even considered taking
a shot at the vehicle in hopes the driver would place a call to
the authorities. But the car was too far away, and if it hadn't
been, Sean's luck may have resulted in the driver being shot.

Sean was about to divert his eyes back to the ridge when he
noticed the car's headlights begin to flip on and off. It continued
on for several seconds. Sean wasn't sure what it meant, but the
car had also started to slow down.

Could it be Lumbergh? Sean wondered. *Has he somehow found
me?* It didn't make sense how.

A second later, the Bronco's headlights began switching
on and off as well. Sean gasped, his eyes shifting back to the
highway where the vehicle subsequently left the road and was

now bouncing across the desert floor in the direction of the Bronco.

It wasn't help for Sean who'd arrived. It was reinforcements . . . for Montoya.

Chapter 25

Sean stumbled along the ridge, keeping his breathing low as sweat poured from his face. He could no longer exercise caution, not with another vehicle of men soon to join the hunt. He was already outgunned. The situation was about to get far worse. With larger numbers, they'd ascend the hill together, using each other's gunfire for cover rather than rocks and earth. A full-frontal assault.

A glance over his shoulder captured the vehicle much closer than before, bouncing across the terrain, finding air at times. Its engine roared with haste.

Ahead was a small stretch of sagebrush sprouting out from the mountain, the headlights exposing it for just a moment. Sean lumbered toward it, losing his balance as he twisted through their branches. He collapsed to his knees behind one of the shrubs, quickly turning on his backside and dropping to his good shoulder along the incline. Digging the tread of shoes into the earth, he aimed his pistol through the needles. His chest pushed in and out as he sucked in air.

The ridge had begun to curve inward a bit, the edge of the mountain now blocking his view of the Bronco. Still visible were the beams from the incoming vehicle's headlights. They brought a bright glow to the section of mountain Sean had just crossed. Long shadows pressed toward him. Sean watched them like a hawk. If one moved at a different pace than the others, he'd start shooting.

It didn't happen. The beams slowed and stopped, and the sound of the vehicle's engine was replaced with car doors slamming and multiple voices excitedly conversing in Spanish. He waited a few extra seconds before pulling himself back to his feet. Staying low, he pushed forward.

His head flipping back and forth between the areas in front of him and behind, he heard more commotion from the base. After a minute or so, while working for a foothold along some steepening rock face, he watched a couple, more narrow beams of light glide across the land. The new arrivals had brought flashlights.

The farther north Sean moved along the ridge, the steeper and rockier the incline became. It wasn't the terrain he'd expected, continuing to curve inward, to the northwest. What he stood on weren't like the mountain ranges back in Colorado that went on for miles and miles. This one was steadily shaping into what felt like the face of a cliff. Several times, Sean needed to shove his pistol into the back of his pants to grip onto coarsening rock slabs with his hand. They scraped his palms and knuckles, and his footing was getting harder to maintain with each step. He prayed it wasn't the same type of terrain he'd directed Lisa toward.

It was too dark to see much of the mountain below him, but with the contour of the rock sharpening and its bend bringing him toward the other side of the ridge, it was clear that *down* was now the direction he needed to go.

Sean had little faith in his ability to either climb or descend a steep rock face, especially not at night and with just one arm. But the situation left him little choice.

He heard a car's engine in the distance. One of the vehicles sounded to be on the move, though there was no chance it was headed directly toward him. Not even a major four-wheel drive could make it up the mountain's eastern slope.

Sean felt his way around the next slab, clinging to it while he dropped his leg low to search for a foothold. He found a crevice in the rock and shoved his shoe inside it, wincing from the pain it brought his whittled-down foot. His other foot soon joined it as he pressed his back and hand up against the side of a boulder behind him. He slid himself down about a yard, then another, his feet working the crevice. When the boulder began to spread away from him, he pried his right foot loose and lowered it to search for another foothold. His shoe slipped twice before he found an impression in the rock, dug his heel into it, and straightened his leg to hold himself in position.

A man's muffled voice bounced across the rocks behind him. Soon came a second one, a bit deeper in tone. They weren't right on top of him, but they had made quick ground. Neither sounded like Montoya; more likely two of the new arrivals, though Montoya had to be close by. When the beam of a flashlight lit up some rock face above him, Sean stayed as still as he could until it moved.

Sean's body trembled, his taut muscles keeping him suspended above a small portion of rock of which he couldn't see much. He could only make out its outline in the dark a few feet below, and hadn't a clue how sharp of an angle it sat at. He lowered his leg, searching for any kind of surface. He found none, so he slid down lower across the rock behind him. His heart paused when he felt the pistol slide up from under his pants, against the swell of his back. He quickly flattened himself against the boulder to sandwich it and keep it from dropping.

"Fuck!" he mouthed, nostrils flaring.

He couldn't reach behind his back and grab it without losing his leverage and falling; his elbow and hand were all that were keeping him balanced. But if he didn't grab it, it would likely topple down the mountainside the moment he shifted his weight. If that happened, the noise would give him away, and he'd likely lose track of the weapon entirely, even if he managed to descend the slope in one piece.

The one thing he couldn't do was stay in his current predicament. His muscles were straining and the top of his head was still slightly above the decline, visible to anyone with a flashlight within twenty feet of him.

When the sound of dislodged rocks and earth tumbling down the mountain echoed across the bluff, he understood he had even less time than he'd thought.

Sean needed the gun. He couldn't afford to lose it, not with so many men on his heels. He also needed to go down. His strong preference was to do so slowly and carefully, but that option no longer seemed viable.

He took a breath and shoved his arm behind his back, leaning forward a few inches to snatch the pistol by its grip. His body began swaying apart from the rock face. He tightened his hold on the gun and recoiled his legs from the rock across from him. Doing his best to stay vertical, he fell several feet before his shoes landed on loose rock along a slope so sharp, his momentum immediately carried him forward. With a death grip on his pistol, he toppled and crashed through unseen branches. His shoulder slammed against a boulder, twirling his body and dropping him to his side onto dirt and gravel that carried him further down, face forward, as if he had been swept up in a miniature avalanche.

Pain shot up his shoulder as he slid off a small crag. He

dropped a few feet straight down before thick, course branches from some kind of pine shrub stopped his propulsion.

He gasped for air, the wind having been taken from him. He tasted blood in his mouth. Needles from the shrub brushed along his face as he painfully pulled his body behind the branches. He rolled to its other side where the ground wasn't quite as steep. There, he concentrated on getting air back into his lungs.

A flashlight beam from somewhere above suddenly lit up the shrub, slicing its way through Sean's dust trail and the still swaying branches. Eyes wide, Sean rolled behind a four-foot boulder to his side.

A man shouted and gunshots followed. Bullets tore through the pine. Earth pelted Sean's face; he quickly covered it with his arm. He crawled in deeper behind the rock, moving his legs away from the gunman's line of sight.

More gunfire erupted, a second shooter and another beam of light having joined in. Sean was safe among the chaos for the moment, but it wouldn't last long. Once the others caught up, they'd get braver and begin working their way down the rock face toward him.

There was an area of ground below that was unlit. The flashlights couldn't penetrate it through the tall rocks Sean hid behind. If it was blocking the lights, it would block bullets too . . . at least until the men repositioned themselves.

Sean wasn't going to give them time to do it. He snarled and dropped to his chest, rolling across the ground before he felt nothing but air beneath him. He fell several feet before the side of his body struck a mound of earth. He continued tumbling forward along dirt and scrub, his momentum carrying him forward, shoulder over shoulder. The gun almost fell from his hand, but he reworked his grip. His shin bounced off a rock, sending a sharp wave of pain up through his leg. Its only mercy was the curtailing of his momentum, letting him pull himself somewhat vertically to dig his heels into the ground.

Eyes watering, he twisted his focus back toward the ridge where the two beams of light were now scrambling to catch up with him. He drew in more breath, his hand going to his shin where his pantleg had torn open. Warm blood oozed out.

A third beam switched on from farther down the same slope the men stood on, a couple hundred feet away. One of Montoya's people, maybe even Montoya himself, had anticipated Sean's descent. The light slid across the incline, searching for its target. Sean knew there was nothing to stop it from finding him.

He turned toward the source of the beam, digging his knee into the hill and grunting from the pain it caused. He raised his pistol. It shook in his hand, but he took a breath and steadied his arm as best he could. He lined up the flashlight in his sights. A half second before the beam reached him, Sean began firing.

The flashlight went flying. Two seconds later, an agonizing cry let out across the land, fluctuating between high and low pitches. The other men shouted, confused as to what had just happened. Sean resumed his descent with a limp, working his way farther west as the buzz up top continued.

One thing was for sure from the injured man's voice: it wasn't Montoya. *Where was he?*

Sean hobbled his way down the gradually loosening slope until it nearly flattened. He was at the base, or so it seemed, limping and feeling as though he had just been in a car accident. The man Sean had shot was now sobbing. Multiple flashlights on the ridge joined his. After a few seconds and some more shouting, the beams began to spread back out along the slope. Sean found a close patch of sagebrush and collapsed behind it.

He was exhausted, not wanting to go any farther, but he knew he wasn't even close to being out of the woods. For now, the men after him were unsure of where he was, and distracted by the howler on the ridge. Still, it was impossible to know if there were others in the group still closing in, perhaps without flashlights, under the cover of night. *Who knows how many men were in that second car?*

Sean suppressed a dry cough with his wrist, his throat feeling as if he'd swallowed more sand. Lifting his head and peering through long grass and plants, he watched the flashlights continue to trace the land. He had exactly two bullets left in his pistol. He thought about lining up a shot at another beam, but things had changed. He was farther away, and even if he managed with luck to take another man out, this time the others would see the flash of his gun.

In the distance, the sound of a car engine returned, somewhere beyond the men. A couple of flashlights switched directions, pointing north. Brighter lights soon appeared to the northeast, out from behind the edge of what appeared to be the bottom of the mountain or close to it. There was enough light that Sean knew it belonged to the Bronco. The driver had found his way to the other side, taking a lower route. He was now headed in Sean's general direction, the lights up top bobbing from side to side as he crossed the desert basin.

The pit in Sean's stomach took on more feeling than the pain in his body. The closer the Bronco got, the more the area would light up. They'd eventually find him.

With a loud pulse, the vehicle's PA system flipped back on. Instead of music this time, Montoya's deep, distinctive voice filled the air with a Spanish diatribe. He'd gone back to the Bronco and had sent his men ahead to draw Sean's fire and flush him to the other side of the ridge . . . where he'd be an easier reach. The boss was now giving them additional in-structions.

"Smart son of a bitch," Sean muttered.

When Montoya stopped talking, the cries of the injured man returned. A sudden gunshot silenced them.

"Jesus," Sean gasped, closing his eyes.

The Bronco carefully continued on, veering a bit north from Sean but growing closer. Montoya's men descended the ridge, their lights tracing their routes until they began switching them off one by one.

At least Lisa and Hannah are still safe, or so Sean hoped. By now, they had likely descended the other side of the mountain, farther south of all the action, with their pursuers none the wiser. Hopefully, she was well on her way to finding a ranger station, or maybe just a maintenance building—somewhere from which she could place a call. It was most certainly wishful thinking on Sean's part, yet the imagery came as easily as a daydream. But when Sean lifted his head to pan the area southwest of him, his body shivering from a sudden chill, all he could see was dark, barren land with the black outline of another mountain range in the distance. No lights. No signs of civilization at all.

He worried for a moment that Lisa might see the beams of the Bronco from afar and mistake them for a park vehicle. But if she could see the headlights, she would have also assuredly heard the gunfire and Montoya's voice through the speakers, and know to stay away.

It felt like a sick joke that the safest direction for Sean actually would have been back toward Lisa, the path of least resistance. For that reason, he knew he couldn't take that path. It would draw the danger back to her and Hannah. For now, he'd need to continue edging north, as best he could . . . to keep the others focused on him. If he could make it until daybreak, the park would re-open and hopefully he'd find a road or a person—someone to flag down who had a car or a phone. All of that required him to get back up and move, no matter how much his beaten body protested.

Chapter 26

According to the van's registration, "Vic," as the drugstore employees knew him, was Victor Rizzo. He had a bit of a rap sheet, mostly minor offenses: assault and battery that were settled out of court, small-time theft, check bouncing, and a DUI from a decade earlier. He was thirty-seven years old, and lived alone in an apartment south of Vegas. It wasn't until Lumbergh and Holman arrived at the building that they learned through the radio that Rizzo worked at a local locksmith business owned by his father, Victor Sr.

"The older man in Wendice's video," Holman had said as they left the car, guns drawn.

They'd pounded on the front door of the unlit apartment until neighbors emerged, one explaining that he hadn't seen "Vic" all day, and that his van hadn't been in the lot since the previous morning. Without a warrant, Lumbergh and Holman decided to check out the locksmith office, which was a five-minute drive. According to public records, it was also Victor Sr.'s residence.

Detective Dennis Corbett, Holman's partner, had wrapped up the crime scene at the Dusty Nickel. He confirmed over the radio that a prioritized fingerprint search on the man Lumbergh had shot in the hotel driveway had turned up nothing. He wasn't in Nevada's database, and the national search would take longer. Corbett had planned to meet up with his partner and Lumbergh at the locksmith office.

There had been clear agitation in Corbett's tone over the radio, and when the detective pulled in front of their car in the alley adjacent to the building, Lumbergh understood why. Dusty was still with him, excitedly waving at Lumbergh from the passenger seat.

Corbett exited the vehicle, his face rigid as he slammed the door. He appeared to be scolding Dusty, pointing his finger through the open driver's side window. Dusty held his hands up in the air, presumably expressing compliance through appearing as though he were a bank teller being held up. Corbett shook his head in disgust, telling Dusty to stay in the car. He walked over to the passenger side of Holman's vehicle.

"The hell's with this guy?" Corbett asked in a gravelly voice. His head leaned through Lumbergh's window with his thick, dark tie dangling inside the vehicle from an open sportscoat. "He won't shut up . . . about anything. He kept interrupting my interviews back at the casino, asking idiotic questions of the witnesses. I thought I was going to have to handcuff him to a slot machine inside. And then in the car, he kept trying to touch the radio and everything else, and carrying on about Roy and the tiger, and—"

"I'm sorry," said Lumbergh, noticing a strong scent of cheap cologne oozing off Corbett. "He has some issues, and he's upset about Sean, and—"

"Well, he's riding back with you two when we're done, not with me," said Corbett, matter-of-factly.

"Why is he even still with you?" Lumbergh countered. "Why didn't you just leave him at the hotel?"

Corbett took a step back, his body straightening as he shifted a confused gaze between Lumbergh and Dusty. "He told me you wanted him close to the case," said Corbett. "He said he's done some consulting work for your office, and that you wanted him along as an advisor. I thought I was doing you a professional courtesy here."

Lumbergh's eyes closed in irritation. When he opened them and turned to Dusty, Dusty was looking back at him with a shrug and a cringe across his face.

"The only consulting work he's ever done for me was on party balloons for my daughter's birthday," said Lumbergh, shaking his head. "Again, I'm sorry."

Lumbergh and Holman stepped out of the car. Lumbergh walked over to Dusty's window. Noticing that his travel partner was still wearing his red outfit, he lectured him on lying to a police officer and told him, as Corbett had, to stay in the car.

When he noticed Dusty's eyes sagging and his gaze floating away, Lumbergh lowered his tone. "Corbett kept you in the loop?" he asked.

Dusty nodded, sniffing before lifting is eyes back to Lumbergh. "We're going to get Sean back, aren't we?"

After a few seconds, Lumbergh answered. "Yeah. We will. And when we do, the three of us are going to get back to celebrating you and your final days as a single man." He forced a grin across his face.

Dusty nodded, his eyes wandering.

"Just hold tight," said Lumbergh. "We'll be back before you know it." He bounced the back of his knuckles off Dusty's shoulder and returned to the detectives.

"Ready?" asked Holman, adjusting a small police radio on her belt.

Lumbergh nodded and the three crossed the darkened alley, approaching the two-story building from its rear. A streetlamp on the sidewalk in front of the building lit up part of the brick structure's side wall, revealing a banged-up metal dumpster and some graffiti. A telephone wire, with a pair of old sneakers dangling at its center, drooped from the building's sagging roof to a wooden pole on the other side of the alley.

A metal shed sat in the dark behind the building. It looked about ten by twelve feet with a large, tilt-up door at its center.

"A van could fit in there," whispered Lumbergh.

Corbett nodded and quietly jogged over to its door.

Lumbergh nudged Holman's shoulder when he noticed some light flickering from a small window on the second floor, just above a metal fire escape. Inside, a television looked to be on.

Corbett jogged back. "It's padlocked shut. I can't see inside."

"Cover the back?" whispered Holman, nudging her head toward the building.

"Yeah," Corbett said, pulling his pistol from a holster inside his sportscoat.

Holman nodded, and she and Lumbergh carefully made their way across the side of the building, guns drawn but at their sides.

A small neon sign in the shape of a large key at the front of the building was turned off. It read "Rizzo" across its head and "Locksmith" vertically across its blade. Three cement steps led up to a small wooden porch and the front door. A window beside the door displayed several certification and branding stickers, but there wasn't any visible light beyond them.

The two waited for a couple of cars and their headlights to pass by before moving up onto the porch, the wood creaking a bit from their weight. Lumbergh took a position to the side of the door, holding his gun up in front of his chest. Holman nodded and knocked hard on the door.

"Mr. Rizzo!" she shouted. "Las Vegas Metro! We'd like to—"

There was a crash inside. It sounded like something ceramic hitting the floor. Eyes wide, Holman raised her gun and stepped back from the door, pressing her shoulder against the building.

"Mr. Rizzo!" she shouted again. "We'd just like to get a word with you involving a case."

The two listened, bodies tense and still as they waited.

"Sean, are you in there?" Lumbergh yelled out. "Lisa!"

A woman's voice cried out. It was faint, as if it had carried from a long distance. Dramatic, orchestrated music immediately followed it.

"I heard a scream," said Lumbergh, swinging in front of the door and backing up a couple steps.

"No!" whispered Holman. "That was from the television."

"We don't know that," said Lumbergh, holding his Glock with both hands. "Someone may be in trouble."

"Yes, we *do* know that," Holman asserted. "Don't even think—"

"I'll take point," said Lumbergh, knowing full well that Holman was right, but also understanding the legalities of probable cause. "Fall in behind me."

Lumbergh lunged forward, clenching his teeth and driving the bottom of his foot hard into the door, just underneath its metal knob.

The door cracked but only went in about an inch. Pain shot up Lumbergh's leg, drawing expletives as he stumbled along the porch, nearly collapsing to a knee. Holman's face tightened, glaring angrily at Lumbergh before turning her attention to the door. She squared her jaw and tightened her grip on her pistol.

"Fall in behind me," she instructed, clenching her arms, taking a step back, and sending a wicked kick just above the knob.

The frame splintered and the door flew open, hitting the opposite wall. What sounded like glass frames collapsed behind it, shattering when they landed on the floor. Holman darted inside with Lumbergh hobbling in after her, quietly impressed. Their guns were drawn as they walked along a linoleum that heightened the sound of each step forward. The smell of cigarettes filled the air.

"Victor Rizzo!" Holman shouted again. "Las Vegas Metro. We heard screaming and have entered the premises. Please come out with your hands up, so we can bring this situation to a peaceful end."

Lumbergh swung his arm over the front counter to his left, checking behind it. He found no one, but it was dark. He reached along the wall behind him.

"I've got a light switch," he said. "Are you ready?"

"Yeah," answered Holman, a few feet in front of him. She lowered herself to a knee, her gun pointing deeper into the building.

Lumbergh flipped the switch. Fluorescent lights along the ceiling flipped on, row after row. They blinked before exposing a small office setting, cubicle panels at the front leading to an enclosed room in the back. The room's wooden door was half open. The noises from the television lay somewhere beyond it.

Behind the front counter was a wall of hooks with hundreds of uncut keys hanging on them. A metal key-cutting machine sat beneath it, arms and levers sprouting out from it in multiple directions. An old-school cash register and credit card reader sat next to it.

The two slowly edged forward, covering each other as

Holman repeated her call to Rizzo. Lumbergh looked inside the first cubical, spotting a shattered plate of what looked like spaghetti across the floor. The meatballs among the mess were so small, they probably came from a can. Sauce-stained paw prints led away from it and down the hall.

"That crash we heard—" said Lumbergh. "I think we spooked a cat chowing down on Chef Boyardee."

Holman glanced at the mess, before returning her focus to the back office. "Whoever made that plate left in a hurry."

Lumbergh knelt down and ran his finger through the sauce. It was room temperature. "A while ago. Probably off to Vespers Drugs from here."

Holman nodded. Her gun still pointing forward, she brought up her radio with her other hand. "Dennis, we're inside. Stay put. Keep your eye on the back."

Lumbergh noticed what looked like recording equipment along the cubicle's metal desk—speakers, with some kind of switchboard device with a dozen or so input and output plugins. Half of them were filled, and some wires in the back looked to be spliced and directed into a phone jack in the wall.

"Let's get the rest of this place secured," said Holman.

The two searched each cubicle and a small bathroom while whatever movie was playing on the television continued. The dialogue sounded contrived, and the music old, perhaps something from the golden era of cinema. When they reached the back room, they found an office full of file cabinets. A large desk sat at its center in front of a swivel chair. On top of the desk was a lamp and a large magnifying glass on a retractable arm. Some glue and cotton swabs sat between them, along with an ashtray and a stack of passport booklets. It was evident that the Rizzo family had business dealings that went well beyond keys and locks.

A narrow doorway to their right, beside a raised white shade that looked like a photo ID backdrop, led to a U-shaped wooden staircase. Holman led as the two carefully made their way up it, guns angled at the upper floor. The television grew louder with each step. When a loud creak rose from below Holman's foot, the two stopped. Holman took a breath, listening for a few seconds before she carefully proceeded. Lumbergh skipped the step all together to avoid another alert.

They entered a short, carpeted hallway. Pictures of people lined the wall all the way to an open door with a large wooden dresser along the only visible wall. It appeared to be a bedroom. To the left was a small bathroom and shower. Lumbergh quickly peeked inside, smelling mildew but seeing no one. They proceeded toward the bedroom, the television growing louder as its screen flickered. An actor on the screen stated, "I told you not to wander off."

Holman swung inside the room, with Lumbergh close behind her. They pointed their guns at a full-sized bed along the adjacent wall. It was empty, loosely made with a thin spread. Lumbergh quickly checked under the bed, then the closet.

"The building's clear," Holman said into her radio.

The television on top of a short nightstand was decades old, a large box with a power knob that Lumbergh twisted to the off position. He noticed it was plugged into an electrical timer on the wall. Maybe it was part of a domestic routine. Maybe it was for security purposes.

"You know anything we find is now compromised without a warrant, right?"

Lumbergh glanced back at her.

"Of course, you know," said Holman, her eyes aimed upwards. "Remember what I said to you earlier, about who's leading this investigation?"

Lumbergh's eyes dropped. "Yeah," he said. "Listen, I'm sorry but—"

She cut him off. "But you're not concerned with building a case. You're concerned with finding your brother-in-law. I get it. I really do. But it's my ass. Don't let it happen again. You're here because I'm allowing it—because of who you are. If you disrespect me and my job again, I'll radio a black-and-white to take you back to your hotel."

Lumbergh nodded. "Fair enough. You're right."

Loud footsteps rose up from the floor below.

"Dennis?" Holman called out.

"Yeah!" Corbett confirmed. "I could see into the shed from a little hole in the back! No van! Just an old sedan!"

"Dammit," she mumbled, gazing across the room.

In the closet was nothing but clothes. Same with the drawers, as Lumbergh found rifling through them. On the top of the dresser was an old family photo of a middle-aged couple kneeling beside a young boy with dark hair. Above the bed was a classic Dogs Playing Poker painting inside a wooden frame painted gold.

"Let's take a closer look at the guy's office," said Holman, flipping on the hallway light as she walked back toward the stairs.

Lumbergh followed her, glancing at some more photos along the wall. They were more recent than the ones in the bedroom. "This has got to be Rizzo Sr.," he said, pointing at the image of the son standing next to a much older man who was thin and bald, with a cigarette in his mouth.

"Probably," said Holman.

Lumbergh continued glimpsing over the photos as Holman descended the stairs. He stopped when he reached the second to last. It was the image of the father alongside a young man who wasn't his son—a slender man with short blonde hair. The individual's face rang with familiarity.

"What is it?" asked Holman from the stairs, her head turned over her shoulder.

"I know this guy from somewhere," he said, glancing back at her.

"What?"

"Yeah, I've seen him before." His eyes narrowed as Lumbergh closed in on his face. It suddenly struck him. "Holy shit."

"Who is it?"

Lumbergh twisted toward the detective. "Kyle Kimble, Lisa's dead husband."

Holman's face recoiled. "Rizzo knows the Kimbles?"

"He knew the husband, anyway, because that's sure as hell him. I've only seen the guy in photos. Well, sort of."

"What do you mean, *sort of?*"

"I saw his dead body when it turned up in a reservoir in Colorado a little over two years ago."

Holman nodded. "Same day as the Montoya shoot-out."

"That's right. Of course, he was all bloated from being in the water a couple of days, and he had a bullet in his head. But I saw pictures of him in court, and some that Lisa had. This is definitely him, but he looks younger in this shot. This might pre-date his marriage to Lisa. Hell, probably even their relationship."

"Are you thinking Sean may have not been the target after all? That they were after Lisa for some reason?"

"I don't know," Lumbergh said, shaking his head. "None of this makes sense. It seems we have two moving parts here. Let's take Montoya out of the equation for a minute. The Rizzos live here in Vegas. So does Lisa. They could have snatched her up anytime they wanted. But it didn't happen until she was with Sean. There has to be a reason for that."

Holman nodded. "That begs an obvious question, of course."

"Yeah. How did the Rizzos *know* they were together, or *would* be together?"

Holman raised a brow.

"Could Wendice have known?" questioned Lumbergh. "He acted as if he didn't know Sean was coming over that night, prior to seeing him on camera. Maybe Lisa *had* told him."

Holman shook her head. "You think Wendice would consciously put his daughter in the middle of a situation like that? Men barging in with guns?"

Lumbergh's head swept to the side. "That's a good point."

"I think your police instincts are working overtime on Wendice, Chief," said Holman, her face loosening.

"Guys?" came Corbett's voice from below. "Come hear this!"

The two quickly descended the stairs. By the time they reached the bottom, they heard a familiar voice filter out loudly through what sounded like a speaker. It belonged to Wendice.

"Working overtime, huh?" said Lumbergh, raising an eyebrow.

Holman's eyes narrowed. They joined Corbett at the first cubicle, all three listening to the machine Lumbergh had noticed earlier.

"I don't know how to tell you this," said Wendice. "But Lisa's missing. It . . . it seems she was kidnapped." His voice was shaking.

"What?" came an older man's. It was deep and gravely. "What do you mean, kidnapped? Is this a joke?"

"No, sir. It's not a joke. Listen, the police are here, and—"

"The police?"

"What the hell is this?" asked Lumbergh, speaking over the conversation.

"It just started playing," said Corbett. "There were some clicks, and then there was a dial tone and buttons being pushed. It's a phone call." He moved his finger to a small red light on the face of the machine. "And it looks like it's being recorded."

"*Being* recorded?" asked Holman.

"Yeah," said Corbett, scratching his ear. "I think this is live. I heard Baker's voice in the background, right at the beginning. Last I checked, he's still at Kimble's house."

"The Rizzos have Lisa's phone bugged," said Lumbergh.

"They could have set up something to conference calls in, on maybe something in the phone itself," said Corbett.

"They heard Sean call her earlier tonight and make plans to meet her," said Lumbergh. "That's how all of this started."

"Who's Wendice talking to?" asked Holman, looking at Corbett.

"I'm not sure. He called the guy 'Mr. Nelson' at the beginning."

"That's Lisa's maiden name," said Lumbergh, pushing some air from his lungs. "That's got to be her father. Wendice is just catching him up to speed. This isn't going to help us. Can you turn it down?"

Corbett reached over and twisted a dial to the left, lowering the volume. Lumbergh's eyes shifted to Holman, who met his gaze with a raised eyebrow and the hint of a smirk.

"Working overtime indeed," said Lumbergh, conceding Holman's point. While Wendice had some character issues to work on, he had nothing to do with what had happened at Lisa's home.

A quick whistle suddenly rang out from the front entrance. Everyone in the room spun toward it, guns drawn and aimed.

"Wait!" Dusty screamed, dropping to his knees on the porch, both arms raised high.

"Jesus, Dusty!" yelled Lumbergh, lowering his gun and drawing in a deep breath.

"I told you to wait in the goddamn car!" snarled Corbett.

"I'm sorry, I'm sorry!" Dusty pleaded, carefully lowering his arms. His wide eyes bounced between the others. "You were taking so long, and I was worried you might need help!"

"Help?" said Holman, shaking her head and holstering her gun.

"What kind of help would *you* give us, Red?" asked Corbett, his tone sharp. He holstered his gun. "Distract the bad guys with some balloon animals?" He turned to Lumbergh.

"Come on," said Lumbergh. "There's no need for that."

"There's no need for *him*," countered Corbett. "He's just getting in the way."

"I said I was sorry," said Dusty, climbing up. "What was that you guys were listening to?"

Lumbergh looked at the detectives, before shrugging his shoulders and replying. "These guys have Lisa's phone bugged. It looks like they've been recording her calls." He nudged his head toward the machine.

"Really?" said Dusty with some unexpected perk in his voice. He stood up straight and walked inside.

"No," cautioned Corbett, raising his hand. "You have no business in here. This is a potential crime scene. Just go back to the car."

Dusty peered over Corbett's shoulder at the machine. "Wow, look at all those wires."

"Dusty . . ." Lumbergh cautioned.

"Hey," said Dusty. "Do you think they also record calls coming in and out of *here*? The office?"

Lumbergh opened his mouth, but nothing came out. Digesting Dusty's words, his eyes slid to the detectives. Their faces had tightened as well.

"I mean, if they do . . ." Dusty continued. "Maybe there's a recording of them talking to Montoya."

Chapter 27

He didn't know if the temperature had suddenly fallen or if his body was shutting down, succumbing to the punishment it had taken. His teeth chattered and his body trembled from the chill that spread through his skin. Yet, sweat still slid down his head. He'd have guessed his shoulder was infected, but the injury didn't seem old enough for that. Maybe it was just some kind of general shock.

Sometimes his shoulder hurt. Sometimes it was numb. Whenever he sensed that it was bleeding again, his opposite hand would confirm that it wasn't . . . or at least didn't seem to be. It was a surreal sensation that didn't make sense to him.

As he moved forward, each step felt heavier and more painful than the last. Whenever he'd go low to the ground in response to the Bronco's lights sweeping in a new direction, it was twice as hard to get back up after they'd passed.

The darkness was all Sean had going for him; that and the low sagebrush that had grown a bit denser. Though he'd lost track of time and felt disoriented, he'd estimated that he had a few more hours of night before the beginnings of a new day would lend his pursuers stronger visibility. Hopefully by then, Lisa and the child would be long gone from the wasteland, nestled safely back in the arms of civilization. With luck, Sean would later join them, but the premise felt less likely by the minute. For now, the best he could do was stay alive and continue to draw his pursuers in the wrong direction. That involved keeping them on their toes.

Fifteen minutes earlier, Sean had found a good-sized rock along the desert floor. He'd gone to a knee behind it, waited for the Bronco to turn away from him, and then fired a single shot toward the men on foot . . . or at least in the direction in which he'd heard occasional voices. He knew the chances were low that he'd hit anyone, but it would send them the signal that he was still northwest of their location. A couple of the men had reflexively returned fire. As Sean had hoped, Montoya sped toward them in the Bronco, thinking the action was closer to them. Sending dust and scrub into the air and blinding them with his headlights, the distraction allowed Sean to pull farther ahead, at a faster pace, without detection.

But Sean's energy was winding down and the stunt had drained his arsenal to a single bullet. The more he thought about the situation, the bleaker he felt, especially after Montoya started off again from the rest of his group.

The Bronco circled around the outside of the brush-filled desert plain. Its engine roared as its lights exposed more of the same type of terrain. Its brake lights flared up to the north of Sean, and the vehicle slid to a stop. Sean heard a door slam, and then the Bronco took off again. They were trying something new.

Had he just dropped someone off?

Sean's fears came to light when the Bronco halted once more. The door slammed again before the vehicle began to veer south. Montoya was completing a half circle, correctly banking on Sean being somewhere in the middle between him and his men. They'd come at Sean from all sides, squeezing him into the bullseye of a very large target. They kept their flashlights off, not giving away their exact positions, but Montoya's remaining men were assuredly spreading out to the west to complete the circle—a circle with about a 250-yard radius. Maybe the others had started out on foot minutes earlier and were already in position. It was impossible to know.

Hunkered down behind some sagebrush, Sean took quick inventory of his surroundings, watching and listening. He gripped his pistol, worried he'd find himself having to expend its last bullet sooner than he'd hoped.

The unexpected screech of tires brought his focus back to the Bronco. The vehicle was suddenly swerving, its brake lights on and its headlights exposing a sliver of what looked like blacktop beneath them. Montoya had pulled up onto a paved road that he probably hadn't seen until he was right on top of it. His headlights lit up a metal road reflector a second before the Bronco clipped it, creating some sparks. Montoya regained control of the vehicle and then carefully left the road, pulling the front half of the vehicle onto the dirt shoulder. His lights lit up the area.

He shut off the engine, leaving the lights on. The cab bobbled, and a second later Sean heard a car door shut.

"Amigos," came Montoya's voice over the PA. "I must admit that I am impressed. And I'm not a man who impresses easy. Between you and me, I never thought you'd make it out of those sun panels back there. But you did. I underestimated you."

He's buying time, Sean thought to himself. While Montoya was working on drawing his attention, his men were moving silently in the dark, closing the perimeter with each cautious step forward.

"Never underestimate someone who's got nothing to lose," Montoya continued. His tone had turned sober, almost pensive. "My brother used to say that . . . But he underestimated Lumbergh, didn't he? So did I, I suppose."

Sean closed his eyes, pushing through his pain while he struggled to clear his head. He tried to form a realistic picture of how many men he was dealing with. There were two, including Montoya, before the second car arrived. There couldn't have been more than four or five people in the other car, and one of them was now dead. That left six tops; hopefully fewer but it felt wise to err on the conservative side.

Sean thought of the tightening circle around him as the face of a clock, with Montoya's position being midnight. If Montoya had directed some of his people south, even before dropping off at least two of them to the north, there was a chance there was still some breathing room around the ten o'clock hour. That person would have had to travel the farthest, on foot, while still trying to remain discreet. They might not have reached their position yet.

Sean stayed low and moved southwest, half crawling around sagebrush as Montoya continued his monologue. He quickly discovered that he couldn't move effectively that way with his gun drawn, so he shoved it back into his pants. His injured arm was mostly useless, and he needed the use of his good hand to push off the desert floor.

"You know what surprises me?" said Montoya. "How quiet that little girl has been."

Sean stopped, his stomach forming a knot.

"My son. The one Lumbergh shot. He was never that quiet. Not at that age. None of my children were." Some silence followed.

It seemed that Montoya was beginning to figure out that they had split up. Sean squared his jaw and continued through the brush, moving more slowly.

"First things first," Montoya finally said, his voice returning. It was followed with a click.

A door slammed and Montoya's large body crossed in front of his vehicle, casting long shadows across the land. Sean went to his knee and reached for his gun, but Montoya's outline had only appeared for another second before he dropped down off the bank on the side of the road. Sean was sure the outline had included a long rifle held in his arms, probably the same one as before.

Sean gritted his teeth, pointing his gun below the front of the Bronco. He watched for the top of Montoya's head to pop back up into the beams of the lights. It did a couple of times, but each was too brief for Sean to line up a shot, especially with his hand shaking as it was. If he could take out Montoya, he'd have a straight shot toward the Bronco and a quick ride out of the area. Perhaps Montoya understood that, and was baiting Sean by distancing himself from the vehicle. Either way, with only one bullet left, and thus just one opportunity to take down a man with Montoya's cunningness and firepower, it was a game he couldn't afford to play. Losing would have meant Sean dead, and the men's attention turned back to Lisa and Hannah.

Sean continued in the same direction. The course would bring him marginally closer to Montoya, at least for a little bit. But unless Montoya suddenly darted off to the south, Sean believed he'd be able to avoid a direct confrontation. At least he hoped he would. He kept his gun drawn and ready, just in case.

Sean thought about the road. From what he'd seen under the Bronco's headlights, it traveled north and south, which meant he'd reach it on his current course. Lisa had mentioned a road with a couple of buildings beside it when she'd described her trip to the park years earlier. Maybe it was the same one. Maybe the buildings were somewhere north or south of where he was. Either way, getting to the other side of the road, hopefully undetected, would mean that Sean had escaped the search perimeter and the men . . . at least for the time being. But he hadn't made it there yet.

The crack of a branch splitting arose in the night. Sean carefully went down. It couldn't have come from Montoya; he was on the other side. It must have been from the *ten o'clock* man. Sean planted both of his knees firmly in the dirt, his gun raised and his eyes peering through the brush in the direction of the sound. He kept his eyes focused above a section of scrub, hearing faint footsteps from somewhere beyond it. When the outline of a figure appeared from the night, Sean slid his tongue to the corner of his mouth and steadied his gun as best he could.

The individual suddenly gasped and dropped down low, disappearing from sight. Sean's eyes shot wide. *He saw me. Fuck!* Adrenaline raced through his body as his finger hugged the trigger.

A flicker of light in the distance suddenly grabbed Sean's attention. It was off to the south, appearing once again. Two lights. Headlights. They were traveling north on the road . . . coming straight toward them.

Chapter 28

"There!" said Lumbergh, hearing a man answer in Spanish. He stood on the opposite side of the desk, along with detectives, to keep his shoes out of the spaghetti sauce.

The machine used a single cassette but recorded multiple phonelines. One of them, as Dusty had theorized, tied into the building's local area network. Having rewound the tape and listened again to Sean's conversation with Lisa from The Mirage—this time from both ends—Lumbergh hoped the next call had been placed from Rizzo's office to Montoya. It seemed he was right. According to the digital time stamp on the display, it had gone out less than five minutes later.

"*Habla inglés?*" the caller asked in broken Spanish when someone picked up. The man's voice was a bit frail. He sounded old.

"That's got to be Victor Sr.," said Holman.

A few seconds of Spanish dialogue could be heard in the background, seemingly from a television set, before the man on the other end responded.

"*Qué?*"

The caller grunted. "Dammit. Do you speak English?"

"*Sí.* Yes."

"Okay. Good. This is uh . . . Victor. Victor Rizzo. I uh . . . I need to talk to your boss. ASAP."

"Rizzo?" said the man. "We're waiting for that package."

Rizzo grunted. "That was dropped off this morning."

"Normal spot?"

"Yeah, normal spot. It's there. Now listen, I'm calling about a separate matter. It's uh . . . It's about that matter involving . . . uh . . . restitution."

"Involving what?"

"*Restitution*. Just tell him that, okay? He'll know what I'm talking about."

"Hold on."

Footsteps could be heard. The sound of the television gradually faded. The footsteps grew louder, now producing a reverberating echo.

"Stairs?" hypothesized Corbett.

"We need the number he called," said Holman. "See if we can trace it back."

"An *hombre* like Montoya probably uses a burner," said Corbett.

Lumbergh nodded.

"Maybe," said Holman, "but maybe we'll get lucky."

"What's a burner?" asked Dusty.

"A pre-paid phone," answered Lumbergh. "They're hard to trace back to the purchaser."

Holman checked over the machine, looking for a digital readout on the number. There didn't seem to be one for outgoing calls.

"Just check the phone itself," suggested Lumbergh, glancing at the office-style phone beside the machine. "The redial button ought to pull it up on the display. Check the time stamp, but it's likely the last number dialed."

Corbett nodded and began tracing the buttons on the phone with his finger, looking for the right one.

"Don't actually call it though," said Lumbergh. "Not yet, anyway."

"Yeah, thanks. I'm not an idiot," muttered Corbett. He pushed the redial button and wrote down the number that appeared on the display.

Lumbergh turned to Holman. "Why would Rizzo record his own calls? Connections to organized crime, phony passports . . . I'm sure a hell of a lot more, not even including tonight. Recordings are evidence against him."

"Leverage," answered Corbett, earning Holman's nod. "If he ever goes down, he's taking the bigger fish with him, maybe for a plea deal. Another angle is blackmail. Get the right person to say the wrong thing on tape. Makes for a quick payday."

"A renaissance man," said Lumbergh, shaking his head.

"Or . . ." added Dusty from behind them, "Maybe it's like a study tool. You know, to have a better business rapport with your clients. You replay the conversation and listen to how you came across to others. Then you work to improve the customer relationship by being a more effective communicator."

The other three slowly slid their gazes to him, their faces deadpan.

"What the fuck are you talking about?" Corbett finally said.

Dusty's eyes lowered. "I just . . . I've been reading some business books. You know, for my entertainment business, and—"

"What . . ." a deep voice poured from the recording machine, drawing everyone's attention back to it. Dusty swallowed.

"That's Montoya," said Lumbergh, leaning forward and placing his hands on the desk.

"Hey, uh . . . This is Rizzo."

"I know."

"Okay, I'm not going to beat around the bush, because

we have a very short time window here. I think we've got a breakthrough on Kimble's money."

Lumbergh and Holman exchanged glances.

"What money?" asked Dusty.

The others shushed him. Corbett added an angry glare and a finger toward the door.

"Not Kimble's money," said Montoya, his tone sharp. "My brother's money."

"Of course," Rizzo said nervously. "Of course. Your brother's. Listen, do you remember the name Sean Coleman?"

After a pause, Montoya answered, "No."

"He was boning Kimble's widow for a while," said Rizzo. "Real piece of work. He's also the guy who saw Kimble blow his brains out in Colorado. The sole witness. The last man to see him alive."

"The security guard," said Montoya.

"Yeah, yeah . . . the security guard. We, uh . . . We hacked his bank records a while back, to . . . you know, cover the bases. We have access to his statements. We didn't think it would ever lead anywhere, but we figured it was worth a try. Get this. The dude was dead broke until just last week. That's when nearly a quarter of a million dollars shows up. Straight deposit. No explanation for it."

The detectives directed their gazes to Lumbergh. He shook his head and mouthed, "I'll explain later."

"Tonight, lo and behold, he shows up in Vegas," continued Rizzo. "He just called the widow. Says he wants to meet and talk about things. She invited him over. He's on his way to her house . . . *right now.*"

"Now that Moretti's out of the picture . . ." said Montoya.

"Exactly! Exactly! Three weeks ago. The trial's over. The man's in prison for life. No more feds snooping around.

Coleman's been sitting on that money, goddamn it! It probably burned away at him for the last two years. Now he's ready to spend some of it. Maybe he's ready to disappear with the rest and take the widow with him."

"How did he get his hands on it?"

"He must have figured something out from Kimble. A hidden account. A safety deposit box. Maybe Kimble dropped a copy of a ledger out there in the forest somewhere, before he offed himself. He always was a sneaky bastard."

"Or Coleman killed Kimble."

"What?" Lumbergh mouthed, just as Rizzo said the same thing out loud.

A strange, fluttering noise in the background drew everyone closer to the machine to better hear the ensuing conversation.

"He was the only person who saw Kimble die . . . from a bullet," said Montoya, raising his voice. "Maybe it was no suicide. Maybe it was murder."

"Murder," Dusty mouthed, his eyes wide.

"Well . . ." said Rizzo, doubt in his voice, but seemingly afraid to contradict Montoya. "Either way, we've got a chance to get your brother's money back. But we've got to move, and move now. She's in Henderson."

Montoya shouted something in Spanish, seemingly away from the receiver.

"What did he say there?" Lumbergh asked the room, the fluttering noise gradually fading away.

"*Saddle up*, basically," answered Holman.

"Go there now," ordered Montoya.

"What?" asked Rizzo.

"You're much closer. Less traffic. Go there now, and keep them there until I arrive."

"I'm sorry," said Rizzo, his voice shaky, "but I don't think—"

"Don't think. Just do it. And don't let me down." Click.

Two seconds later, Rizzo gasped, "Shit!" Another click followed.

Chapter 29

Montoya's man had seen the headlights before Sean had. That's why he'd gone down so quickly. He didn't know Sean was squatting in the dark with a gun no more than twelve feet away.

Sean's pulse raced. His eyes darted from the approaching lights to where the man had ducked. He glanced over his shoulder, seeing nothing but the Bronco to his right. Montoya had probably gone low as well.

Whoever was driving toward them likely worked at the park. Lisa had said the gates were closed every night. No overnight camping. *A park ranger out enforcing that rule?*

What Sean knew for sure was that all eyes were now on the vehicle. Montoya and his men had to know that Sean would see the opportunity as a lifeline. They'd be watching for him to pop up and try to wave down the vehicle. When that happened, they'd blow off his head and take out the driver for good measure. It was a maddening situation, but Sean knew the answer wasn't to just sit there, out of sight, and let the vehicle pass. It likely wouldn't pass anyway, not with the driver seeing Montoya's Bronco.

Sean decided he had to go for it. He had to do exactly what Montoya and his men were expecting, but that didn't mean he had to do it on their terms. He'd take out the man on the other side of the scrub—the one who'd otherwise see him first, the moment he ran toward the road, and not hesitate to put him down. With that obstacle eliminated, he'd stand at least a fighting chance of getting out alive.

Sean crawled across the sand as quietly as he could, using his elbows and knees. As the approaching engine came into earshot, he circled around the patch of grass and shrubs he'd seen the man disappear behind. Gun shaking but still pointed forward, Sean slid around the edge of the patch, extending his arm but seeing no one in front of him. The man had changed positions.

Some sagebrush to his left rustled. Sean swung his gun toward it. He heard a gasp just before the butt of a rifle shot out from the branches. Sean tilted his shoulders to avoid a headshot but the butt connected with his wrist, knocking the pistol from his hand. Sean grunted and grabbed onto the rifle with his now empty hand, yanking it toward him.

Sean had surprised the man, turning up just a couple feet from him and not allowing him time to swing his rifle around for a shot. Now he was locked in a tug-of-war contest with only one good arm, knowing his opponent would cry out for help the moment he found his breath. Sean couldn't let that happen. He tightened his grip and snarled, yanking savagely at the gun. It slid from the other man's hold with each jerk. Perhaps knowing he was about to lose the weapon whole, the man lunged forward. His face smashed into Sean's, and they both fell to their sides.

Arms tangled together with the rifle somewhere in the middle, the two kicked at each other. Sean's opponent was much smaller than he was, but he was putting up a fight, knowing that if he lost his weapon, it would quickly be used on him. But that wasn't what Sean had in mind. If he could finish things quietly and remain hidden from the others, he would.

Sean gained some leverage and yanked the rifle to his opposite side. He dropped it on the sand, grabbing the man's collar and pulling him in close for a huge headbutt. He arched his back and sent another one into the bridge of the man's nose, hearing it crack.

Before the man could scream in pain, Sean's hand went to his throat, his fingers digging in deep. The man snorted as Sean swung a leg over his body, straddling and pinning him to his back on the dirt. The man's legs continued to kick, now finding only earth and air. Sean's teeth showed as he leaned forward and poured on the pressure, pure adrenaline fueling what was left of his strength.

It was the same situation he'd found himself in earlier with Hector, just outside the solar farm. Only this time, Sean wasn't going to let the man break free. He couldn't. He raised his head above the grass, watching the vehicle draw in closer. It was growing near, its headlamps lighting up the sky above his head.

A gurgling noise bubbled out from between the man's lips, blood from his broken nose flowing over the remaining air draining out of his mouth. Seconds later, the man's legs stopped moving, along with his arms and the rest of him. Sean kept up the pressure for a few more seconds to be sure.

He spilled off the man, drawing in deep breaths as he gazed down at his lifeless body. He checked the man's pulse, finding none. What little light there was had exposed short curly hair on the man's head and a mustache under his nose. Sean wanted to vomit but focused on his breathing and reached for the weapon.

It felt like a hunting rifle. He didn't know how easily he'd be able to fire it with his other arm out of whack, but at least the weapon was light. Body trembling, he searched the ground for his pistol. That's when the area behind him suddenly lit up with red and blue lights, swinging Sean's attention back to the road.

There were emergency lights above the vehicle. They'd just turned on. Sean could now see that it was a white SUV—a Chevy Tahoe with a thick green pinstripe across its side. The vehicle was gradually slowing. It had to be a park ranger. Sean had to move.

His knee bumped into something heavy when he crawled forward. It was the pistol. He laid his rifle down just long enough to snatch it from the ground and shove it into the back of his pants. He painfully pulled himself to his feet, slogging toward the road with rifle in hand.

A spotlight switched on from the driver's side of the Tahoe, pointed past Sean. He followed its beam down the road to Montoya's Bronco. Sean slowed when he saw Montoya casually walk out from behind his vehicle. He raised his arm and waved a greeting, a broad smile eclipsing most of his face as he walked onto the road.

What the hell? Sean stopped and lowered to a knee, wincing from the pain it brought to his leg. *Is this another of Montoya's men? It couldn't be. Montoya has to be playing him.*

It was the first real glimpse Sean had caught of Montoya. Though he stood far away, the spotlight lit up the pronounced features of his face. His sunken face left his eyes dark, but his wide grin above a chiseled jawline displayed teeth so large they could have belonged to a small horse.

Montoya's rifle was nowhere to be seen. He had no visible weapons on him at all. That didn't mean he wasn't armed. Whether or not the ranger was, Sean couldn't know.

Sean was close enough to the road and had just enough time to climb up onto the blacktop and get the driver's attention. *But then what?* He was within rifle range of the others.

The ranger might be so confused and disoriented by the sight of a bloodied-up man rushing his car that they'd both find themselves under heavy gunfire before Sean could so much as open his mouth. Maybe that's what Montoya wanted. If this opportunity wouldn't draw Sean out of hiding, what would?

Sean had to be smart and fast about it. He couldn't give the ranger a chance to think through the situation. He'd have to get to the road, wave his gun, and make the driver stop. He'd have to whip the passenger door open and jump inside. The others would start shooting, but a quick U-turn and a pedal to the metal might just get both of them out alive.

He crawled back to his feet, the muzzle of his rifle dragging across the ground for a moment before he lifted it higher. His legs felt like spaghetti but he bit his lip and continued on, keeping his head low, and knowing that the moment he hit the road, he'd be visible to all under the headlights.

The vehicle suddenly seemed to speed up, Montoya's perceived cordialness perhaps lowering the ranger's reservations. Sean sucked wind, grunting with each lunge forward. He started to worry that he wouldn't catch the vehicle in time, his legs feeling as if they were about to collapse beneath him.

He'd almost reached the shoulder when he suddenly felt nothing below him. He dropped down an embankment just shy of the road's shoulder, crashing face-first against dirt and rock. Pain shot up his shoulder and his rifle fell from his grip.

The vehicle passed by unfazed.

He'd only fallen a few feet, but it was enough not to be noticed. He cursed under his breath, wincing from his wounds and reaching beside him to grab the rifle. He hadn't realized the slope he'd watched Montoya drop down would continue so far down.

The vehicle's brakes squeaked as it slowed to a stop in front of Montoya. Sean had blown his best chance, but he couldn't give up. The ranger was no more than a hundred feet away from him. He'd soon step out of his Tahoe to engage Montoya. If Sean yelled at him to get his attention, it would only get both of them killed. He needed a new plan and fast.

As Sean had discovered the hard way, the road was elevated above a short embankment on its east side. The same was likely true of the other side. If Sean scurried across the road, he might be able to get in close to the two without being detected. It would also give him some physical cover from the rest of Montoya's men.

He waited until the ranger put the vehicle in park and the brake lights went off. Then he pulled himself from the ditch and hobbled his way across the road, keeping low in the dark. He dropped down to the other side, negotiating a short hill before sliding to his knees.

His fingers traced the grip of his rifle until he found its safety, confirming it was off. He knew then and there that he had to make sure he could support the rifle with his left hand. If not, he'd have to rely on the pistol, and that would only allow him a single shot. Holding the grip in his right hand, he placed his left on the weapon's forearm. He clenched his teeth, slowly lifting his left arm. For now, there was more pain than numbness. Under the circumstances, having some feeling was preferable, but the agony that shot up and down his bicep was almost unbearable. His entire upper body trembled as he slowly and painfully drew the rifle up. The moment he held it level, his arm dropped back down like a puppet with its strings cut. He fought the urge to cry out from the pain, taking in deep breaths to ease himself. It wouldn't be pretty or easy, and he wasn't going to win any sharpshooter contests, but he was sure he could fire it.

The Tahoe's spotlight went off but the headlights and engine remained on. When the door opened and a figure stepped onto the road, Sean began making his way along the embankment. Careful in his movements and staying low, he watched the stalky figure in a wide-brimmed hat and green jacket walk toward Montoya; pistol holstered on one side and a radio on the other.

"Good evening," came a female's voice. The ranger was a woman. "Or good morning, I should say." Her voice had some rasp to it. She sounded older, maybe in her fifties or sixties.

"Good morning," said Montoya, his tone eerily casual.

The ranger stopped a few feet away from him, her thumbs tucked into her belt. Her body partially obscured Sean's view of Montoya. Uncomfortable seconds ticked by before either of them spoke another word.

"So, can I ask what you are doing here?" said the ranger. "This NCA has been closed for hours. Overnighters aren't allowed."

"Is that right?" said Montoya, nodding. He chuckled. "Yeah, I guess I shouldn't be here then." He offered no further explanation.

"Sir, have you been drinking?"

Montoya again chuckled. He slid his thumbs into his pockets, seemingly emulating the ranger. "Drinking? Maybe a little. Who's to say?"

"I'm asking *you* to say, sir. You're here illegally. And you've been driving."

Sean knelt in the dark, just a few feet below the road. His body shook as he propped the nuzzle of the rifle up against some higher earth on the embankment. The ranger still stood in his way of a clean shot. If Sean hadn't been injured, he could have maybe laid in a shot over the ranger's shoulder, as Montoya stood at least a foot and a half taller than her. But in his current condition, he was afraid he'd hit the woman instead.

Montoya was drawing out the exchange, hoping for Sean to reveal himself—to try and get her attention. But the stalemate wouldn't last forever. The ranger was growing more suspicious of Montoya by the second. Before long, things would escalate. And when they did, it likely wouldn't be good for her, who'd yet to unholster her pistol.

"Are you here with anyone else?" she pressed.

"No. Looking for someone."

Sean's face tightened.

"Who are you looking for?"

"My wife."

"Your wife?" said the ranger, some concern in her voice.

Montoya nodded, raising his hand from his pocket and scratching the side of his cheek. His eyes lowered to the pavement. "We got into an argument earlier, back home. She was angry. She left our house and took our little daughter with her. She has problems, my wife. Mental problems. Post-pardon something."

"Depression? Postpartum depression?"

"Yeah," he said, the grin no longer on his face.

"And you think she's out here somewhere? Why?"

"She comes here to think sometimes. To be among nature. I thought maybe she came here tonight . . . with our daughter. So, I drove around the gate, and I came in . . . to see if I could find her. Have you gotten any reports? Reports of a woman with a little girl? A woman saying crazy things?"

It was clear from Montoya's ham-fisted story that he had

indeed figured out Lisa and Hannah were no longer with Sean. He was trying to gauge from the ranger's reaction whether or not they'd been picked up.

"No," she said, uneasiness in her voice. Her hand slid discreetly closer to her pistol. It seemed he'd set off her B.S. detector. "Sir, I'm going to have to ask for some identification."

Move! Sean said in his mind, trying to will the sentiment into the ranger's brain.

"I'd also like to take a look inside your vehicle," the ranger added. "We got a report earlier, from a construction crew. They thought they heard gunfire."

"Gunfire?" asked Montoya, folding his arms in front of his chest.

The ranger nodded. "We sometimes run into problems with poachers out here, so we keep an eye on things. We don't allow guns on this property—any kind, per orders of the United States Bureau of Land Management."

Montoya's eyes lowered to the deputy's hip, his arms still folded in front of him. "*You* have a gun," he said matter-of-factly.

She lifted her hand from her belt and tapped its grip. "Federal NCA personnel excepted. Now let's see some ID."

"Do you have a warrant?"

"I don't need one to ask for your ID."

"You need one to search my Bronco."

The ranger tilted her head, taking a step back.

That's it, Sean thought, raising the rifle up another inch. *A few more steps.*

"The way you're acting," said the ranger, "makes me think I need to call this in. Is that what you want?" She unstrapped the top of her holster.

"Whoa," said Montoya, slowly raising his arms in front of

his chest. "Are you placing me under arrest, officer? Do you even have that authority?"

She grunted in irritation. "I'm not trying to be a hard-ass here, sir," said the ranger. "You show me your ID, and the inside of your vehicle, and we can get you on your way out of here. It'll be that simple. Maybe your wife's already back home."

Come on, move. If Sean got any closer, to try and shoot around the ranger, Montoya would surely see him.

Montoya shook his head, slowly turning on his feet partway toward the east where his men were hidden. His arms remained in the air. "Sean Coleman!" he shouted out, startling the ranger.

The ranger placed her hand on the grip of her pistol, prepared to draw it. She raised her other hand in front of her, urging caution. "Sir, what are you doing? Let's just calm things down."

Montoya ignored her. "I thought this would be an easy decision for you! Your means for escape are right here! What are you afraid of?" He laughed.

The ranger drew her weapon, reaching for her radio with her other hand. "Sir, I need you to get down on the ground right now!"

Montoya lowered his right arm a few inches, straightening his hand out, his fingers pointed toward the woman.

Sean's eyes bulged. "He's got a gun!" he yelled, standing straight up. "Get down!"

The shocked ranger spun around toward Sean just as a loud pop pierced the air. She wailed, her body spinning in the opposite direction before crashing to the pavement. Sean snarled and pulled the trigger, adrenaline pumping through his veins as his gunfire woke up the night. Montoya ran to the other side of the road as Sean fired a second round, diving low and sliding across the dirt shoulder on his chest. He disappeared down the embankment.

Sean didn't know if he'd hit him, and he couldn't take the time to figure it out. He climbed onto the road just as shots started coming in from the desert. With their boss out of the line of fire, Montoya's men unloaded. Bullets cut through metal and glass along the side of the Tahoe. Sean went down behind its fender.

He wished he'd recognized it sooner—what Montoya was doing. His late brother Alvar had a known affinity for novelty weapons. Among them was a spring-loaded sleeve gun, wrapped and concealed around his forearm by a leather cast. The affinity must have run in the family.

Sean peeked around the bumper. His eyes widened when he saw the ranger crawling toward him. She was still alive. He dropped his rifle and reached around to grab her by the collar of her jacket. He planted his knee against the tire and moaned with effort as he dragged her along the pavement toward him. He almost had her around the corner beside him when a trail of bullets bounced off the pavement. The last one caught her in the swell of her back. White down from her jacket jetted upward under the light of the headlamps.

"Fuck!" Sean grunted, giving her another good yank until she rolled and was lying beside him.

Her body was twitching, eyes wide with fear and confusion under the red and blue lights as she stared up at him from her back. With a gaped open mouth and blood streaming from her nose, she was unable to get a word out.

"I'm sorry," Sean gasped.

Seconds later, her body went still. Face frozen. Eyes still wide.

Another volley of bullets yanked Sean back into the

moment. They skipped off the roof of the vehicle, destroying the emergency lights up top and sending shards of metal and plastic off the other side onto Sean's shoulders and head.

The headlights were still working. In their glare, Sean spotted the ranger's pistol still in her hand. He pried it from her warm fingers and crawled on his knees to the driver's side door. He tossed the pistol through the open window then grabbed onto the handle and pried open the door.

The engine was still running, warm air blasting out through the vents and a country song playing at low volume on the radio. A CB radio was lit up under the dashboard.

He crawled over the broken glass that now littered the vehicle's cab, remnants of the shattered side window. It crunched under his hip as he lay low on his side, yanking the gearshift into drive. He whipped his head up just a couple of inches to get his bearings through the windshield. In the corner of his eye to the right, he saw movement—a figure emerging from the embankment. It was Montoya, working his way back up. Blood rode the side of his pants as he hobbled toward the Bronco's driver-side door, reaching for the handle. His rifle had to be inside. He must have shoved it in there when he'd seen the ranger approaching.

Sean ducked back down when bullets from farther out hit the grill of the Tahoe. He yanked the steering wheel to the right and slammed his foot on the gas. The Tahoe leaped forward, the momentum slamming his door shut. Sean squared his jaw as the vehicle lunged ahead. He lifted his head again a half second before he smashed into the rear of the Bronco. Metal cried as it jolted forward, off the side of the embankment. Montoya spun and fell to the dirt. More bullets struck the Tahoe as Sean popped it into reverse. There was a shooter somewhere in front of him.

Sean stepped on the gas, skimming the cab for the ranger's pistol. It had to be on the floor somewhere.

He straightened the wheel, only able to imagine where the road fell behind him as he continued in reverse. Bullets were still coming but fewer were connecting. He popped his head up and shot a glance through the back window. His eyes bulged when the reverse lights revealed he was about to drop off the shoulder. He quickly turned the wheel, a tire screeching and metal rattling before he straightened out.

Back in front, only one headlight was still working. It caught Montoya hobbling across the road to the other side. Montoya picked up the rifle Sean had dropped and began firing it at him. Sean lowered his head, but continued to watch over the steering wheel. Montoya grew smaller and less significant in the distance, along with the other men who were now joining him on the road.

Air streamed from Sean's nose and his eyes narrowed as the corners of his mouth formed only the slightest of curls. The half grin lasted only as long as a subtle, thumping noise beneath the car became more pronounced. One of the tires had been shot.

Chapter 30

"Yep, burner number," said Corbett, reentering the building as he shoved his radio back on his belt. "We might have some luck tracking down how and where Montoya's phone was purchased, but that will take time."

"Which we don't have," said Lumbergh. He turned to Holman. "Once these assholes figure out that Sean isn't sitting on the fortune they think he is, they'll have no reason to keep him alive."

"Let's hope they haven't already," said Holman.

Lumbergh reluctantly nodded. "Listen, we can't just sit here waiting for the Rizzos to come back here."

"We don't have to," said Corbett. "I've got a couple of officers in route. Unmarked car. They'll park across the street and keep an eye on the place. Let us know the second anyone shows up. We've got an APB out on the van registered to junior, along with the Suburban, but we're running out of leads."

"Maybe if we . . ." Dusty began.

Corbett interrupted, turning to him and pointing a finger. "And I've got a black-and-white on its way to pick *you* up. To take you back to your hotel."

"Oh, come on," said Dusty, pouting and turning to Lumbergh.

"The detective's right, Dusty," said Lumbergh. "This is

police business, and you're a civilian. You should have stayed at the hotel."

Dusty's eyes fell to the floor. "I want to help you find Sean."

"I know. And I appreciate everything you've done tonight . . . especially for me, back at the hotel. But it's time."

Dusty's lower lip eclipsed his upper.

"Come on," Corbett grunted, rolling his eyes.

"I'll keep you in the loop," Lumbergh told Dusty. "And when this is all over, I'll be writing you up a citizen commendation from my office."

Dusty's eyes widened.

A call came through on Corbett's radio signifying that the patrol car had pulled up out front.

"Come on, kid," said Corbett, nudging Dusty toward the door. "Your ride's here."

Dusty's gaze tilted up to meet Lumbergh. He nodded. Lumbergh nodded back. Corbett escorted him outside.

"Montoya's guy," said Lumbergh turning back to Holman. "He was watching television when Rizzo called. Then he walked up some stairs."

"Yeah. So?"

"He and Montoya weren't in a car, and it didn't sound like they were out in public. They were in a home or some other building where they're probably staying. Montoya also said that the Rizzos were closer than he was—apparently by a lot, which is why he sent them ahead."

Holman nodded. "And that it would take Montoya longer because of the traffic."

"Right. So, let's think about that. Lisa's place is pretty much a straight shot east of here. The high-traffic areas would be . . ."

"North of here. Northwest of Kimble's house."

"Basically, around the strip or the downtown area. So they'd either be in the middle of it somewhere or on the opposite side of it."

"Which is a hell of a lot of ground to cover. What are you getting at?"

"I don't know yet. I'm just walking through this in my head, so bear with me." Lumbergh leaned up against the back of the cubicle desk, folding his arms in front of his chest. "My thought is that someone of Montoya's potential recognizability wouldn't be holed up in the heart of the city. Too many people, including law enforcement, plausibly recognizing him. Also, fewer escape routes if someone ever dropped a dime on him."

"Makes sense," said Holman. "But we're still talking about . . ."

"Only . . ." said Lumbergh, raising a finger. "Someone already *did* recognize him . . . a month ago . . . at a gas station. That anonymous call. Where did that come in from, again?"

"North of the downtown area. Northwest, really."

"Which would indeed be the opposite side of Henderson."

"Okay," said Holman, shrugging. "I can buy into that theory. But how much closer does that get us to these guys? We need an address, not a district."

Lumbergh nodded. "Let's rewind that call."

He stood up and moved out of Holman's way as she worked the recording machine, pushing buttons and adjusting the volume. It took her a couple of tries to get it to the beginning.

"I remember there being some kind of noise in the background after Montoya got on," said Lumbergh.

"Like a fan, right?"

"Maybe. Some kind of machine, anyway."

Corbett walked back in as the phone conversation played. "What's going on?"

Holman raised a finger with a quick, "Shh."

"Yes ma'am," Corbett said sarcastically, clutching his tie like Rodney Dangerfield.

The sound returned just after Montoya had floated the idea that Kimble's death wasn't suicide. After a few seconds, Holman hit the pause button.

"What does that sound like to you? That pulsing noise?" Lumbergh asked the room. "Construction equipment?"

"It was loud and definitely on Montoya's end," said Corbett. "He had to raise his voice to talk over it. It had to be coming from somewhere close by."

"And something that wasn't under his control," said Holman. "I can't imagine one of his men making that kind of racket while he was on a call."

"Agreed," said Lumbergh. "Maybe it was something right outside the building they were in."

Holman leaned forward and pushed the play button. The sound resumed as Montoya and Rizzo continued talking, and then gradually faded in the background.

"Whatever it is, it's mobile," said Holman, raising an eyebrow. "It was moving away at the end. A vehicle?"

Lumbergh's eyes widened. "Shit. Could that be a helicopter?"

The detectives looked at each other, silently listening until the sound completely disappeared.

"Give that man a cigar," said Corbett, slapping Lumbergh's shoulder. He turned to Holman. "The hospital? Flight for life?"

She shook her head, eyes averted. "No. An airport, and I think I know which one."

Corbett's eyes narrowed.

"Which one?" asked Lumbergh.

"The North Las Vegas Airport." She turned to Lumbergh.

"The name says it all. It's a lot smaller than McCarran. No airlines. General aviation and scenic tours."

"Including helicopter tours?" asked Lumbergh.

"Absolutely."

Lumbergh nodded. "And Lautaro just happens to be a pilot. He could have some sort of operation set up there, transporting contraband."

The detectives' surveillance backup soon arrived, and within minutes Lumbergh and Holman were speeding north on Interstate 15 with Corbett following closely behind. They cut onto the highway, the traffic having dwindled enough to avoid lights and sirens. Holman wrapped up a radio conversation with a county official as they pulled onto the business loop. She'd woken him up, a fact the official reminded her of twice before he reluctantly pledged a call to airport security to meet them at a side entrance, southeast of the terminal. The three were granted vehicle access to the tarmac, but couldn't, as expressed emphatically by the official, enter any of the couple dozen private hangars without explicit permission, a warrant, or probable cause.

The term "probable cause" had earned Lumbergh a cold stare from Holman.

"If they're not here, we're back to square one," said Holman. "And on paper, this isn't much of a lead. Not even enough to warrant some backup unless we spot one of the APB'd vehicles, one of the Rizzos, or Montoya himself."

Lumbergh nodded as they turned a corner and found themselves on a side street running parallel to a long steel fence. A couple of vehicles were parked on the shoulder, none of them the ones they were looking for. On the other side of the chainlink were dimly lit silhouettes of small airplanes of different shapes and sizes, parked uniformly across the pavement. A set of runway lights could be seen well beyond them, but it didn't appear as if any planes were arriving or departing. It may have been too late in the night.

Lumbergh twisted his chin over his shoulder, glancing through the back window, verifying that Corbett was still behind them. When he returned his gaze forward, he noticed the time on Holman's dashboard clock. Nearly two thirty in the morning.

"They've had them over five hours now," Lumbergh said dispiritedly. "Sean's a tough bastard and a five-star bullshitter, but that's a hell of a long time. The things the Montoyas did to people in Mexico . . . It was inhuman. The torture. The maiming . . ."

"You never called your wife, did you?" asked Holman, probably seeing some wisdom in changing the subject. She turned right into the airport, then took another quick right per the county officer's instructions.

Lumbergh shook his head. "I'll call her when we have something."

Ahead was a lone guard booth and mechanical arm lit up by a single overhead lamp. They grew brighter from Holman's headlights as the car approached. A portly, uniformed figure emerged from the booth, his hands adjusting his belt or the waistline of his pants. A pistol was holstered on one side and a flashlight on the other. The man had very short hair along with a narrow mustache that took up only a small fraction of his upper lip.

Holman slowed down, lowering her window as they pulled up beside him.

"You Detective Holman?" the guard said in a voice that seemed unnaturally high for a man his size. He wiped his meaty hand on the front of his shirt before extending it through the window.

"Yes," she said, leaning back a few inches and shaking his hand. "I'm here with Police Chief Gary Lumbergh and the car behind us is my partner, Detective Dennis Corbett."

"Pleasure," he said, gripping Holman's hand a few extra seconds before letting go. "I'm Brian. Brian Fowler. I work security here."

"Is this the only gate for vehicles entering and exiting the tarmac, Brian Fowler?" asked Holman.

Fowler smiled, probably tickled that an attractive woman had just called him by his full name.

Lumbergh's eyes shifted back and forth between the two. As was the case with the stocker back at the drug store, Holman seemed to find some benefit—when she needed something quickly—in some harmless flirtation. Lumbergh appreciated her pragmatism.

"Pretty much," Fowler answered. "There's a service gate on the other side of the terminal, but only airport employees have the access code."

"What about the people who lease the hangars? Non-airport employees."

"They come and leave right here."

Lumbergh leaned into Holman. "Have you been stationed right here all night, Fowler?"

"Been here since eight," he said shoving his hand back through the window to shake Lumbergh's. Holman turned her head to the side to allow it some room. "Pleasure. I shift out at six."

"Anything strange happen tonight?" came a voice from behind Fowler.

The security guard jumped, spinning around to see

Corbett, who'd quietly exited his car.

"Jesus!" Fowler exclaimed, taking a step back.

"I'm Detective Dennis Corbett," said Corbett, extending his hand.

Fowler swallowed. "Pleasure," he said, stepping forward and shaking Corbett's hand. "Brian Fowler."

"Okay," said Lumbergh, losing patience. "Now that we've gotten the introductions out of the way, can you answer the detective's question? Has there been any odd activity? Anything out of the ordinary."

Fowler pursed his lips, tilting his head back. "Well, I mean, there was that whole thing with Siegfried and Roy. It's all over the news."

Lumbergh collapsed in his seat, shaking his head.

"Here," Holman said sharply. "At the airport. Have there been any weird comings or goings?"

"Ah. Gotcha," he answered with a wink. "No, not really."

Lumbergh leaned forward again, his tone sharper. "Did a dark van pass through here? Specifically, a GMC Savana, license plate 212-ZGZ?"

"No," Fowler said with a shrug.

"How about a late-eighties black Suburban?" asked Holman. "With tinted windows."

Fowler's eyes widened. "Wait. Are you talking about the Cardozo people?"

Lumbergh's face tightened. "Who?"

"Cardozo," said Fowler. "It's a company name. I mean, it's probably named after one of them, since it sounds Spanish, and they're pretty much all Hispanic or whatever. But it's the name of the outfit. I'm not sure what all they do. It's probably in the records somewhere. They lease a hangar over on the west side. Got a private plane."

"And they have a black Suburban?" confirmed Holman.

"Yeah . . . with tinted windows like you said. Of course, a lot of people in Vegas have tinted windows. Sort of the culture along with how bright it is. The Cardozo people got a couple of SUVs, actually, but one of them is a black Suburban. The other's a white Bronco. They come in and out of here pretty often. Not big talkers, those guys . . . I can tell you that much."

"Are they here now?" asked Lumbergh, his tone serious.

"Well," he said, folding his arms in front of his chest. "At least a couple of them are. That Suburban came back through here a few hours ago. Ten thirty, I think. It might have been eleven."

"How many people were inside?" asked Lumbergh.

"I only saw two when the driver—one of the regular guys—rolled down his window to sign in. It's procedure. The guy in the passenger seat . . . I'd never seen him before. A pale face. I guess there could have been someone else behind them. There was a dog or something whimpering back there."

The police officers exchanged glances.

"Are they in trouble or something?" asked Fowler.

"Yeah, Brian," said Corbett, pulling out his gun and checking its action. "They're in trouble."

Chapter 31

Montoya and his men now out of sight and range, Sean backed onto the shoulder of the road, skidding to a stop. His hand went for the CB radio, twisting its volume dial to the right. Static blared. He pulled the speaker-mic to his lips and held down its side button.

"My name is Sean Coleman," he said, his voice hoarse. "I'm inside the Sloan Canyon Conservation Area. A ranger on duty has been shot and killed. I'm in her vehicle. The man who shot her is Lautaro Montoya. He's a federal fugitive. He and his men are after us. We need help!"

Static returned when he released the button. He waited for seconds that felt like minutes, the static remaining consistent. He tried a second time, again hearing nothing but more static. He began switching channels and only found more of the same.

"What's wrong with this thing?" he growled, punching the dashboard. His eyes rose upward in thought. "Shit!"

He reached across his chest and opened the door, his knee pushing it wide. He grunted and swore as he dropped his leg outside the cab. With his adrenaline petering out, every movement brought with it a varying level of pain. Still, he managed to stand up straight and peer over the roof. Among the destroyed framework of the emergency lights was what appeared to be the chipped remains of an empty antenna base, wiring sprouting out from its top. The gunfire had taken out a lot of things. The stench of antifreeze suddenly caught Sean's attention as well.

He wasn't going to spend another second assessing the damage, nor trying to change the tire. He also wasn't going to dwell on not thinking to grab the ranger's handheld radio from her hip before jumping inside her vehicle. He didn't have the time or energy for that.

Sean had knocked Montoya's Bronco over the embankment, but he very much doubted he'd disabled it. With four-wheel drive and a number of men with him to push the vehicle out of a tight spot, they'd be back on his trail not long after they figured out that one of their guys was lying dead behind some brush, the life strangled out of him. Sean needed to get back on the road, flat tire or not, and put as much distance between him and the others as possible. He'd go as far as the engine and rim would take him. Hopefully, it would be far enough to find help—whatever it took to place a call and flood the area with well-armed officers and choppers.

He understood that south was the direction he'd been trying to avoid. It would bring the action closer to Lisa, but he'd been left with little choice. The road he was on was likely the only one in and out of the area, and heading north meant another head-on confrontation with Montoya and his men. He wouldn't be able to call in the calvary to stop them, and to help find Lisa and Hannah, if he was dead.

The situation had changed now that he had a vehicle. The best option was no longer for Sean to lead his pursuers away, but bring in new players to change the rules of the game. And the more Sean thought about Lisa, the more he worried he wouldn't be able to find her and Hannah without those reinforcements.

She hadn't made it as far as the road, or so it seemed, despite having more time to get there than he did. If she and Hannah had reached it, the ranger would have seen and stopped for her, or at least would have been aware of someone else having picked them up—like the construction crew the ranger had mentioned to Montoya.

But the ranger had known nothing about them or their plight. If she had, she wouldn't have been oblivious to the situation she had come across.

Maybe Lisa *had* seen the ranger's vehicle, but because it was a white SUV it may have looked like Montoya's Bronco from a distance. So, she'd remained hidden. Or maybe she had found shelter—somewhere to hide out or escape the cold for a while. He wanted to ignore the thought of Lisa falling and injuring herself on her way down the mountain. But from his own experience, the incline had grown steeper and rockier on the other side. He held the darker thoughts at bay the best he could.

Sean glanced at the spotlight mounted to the driver's side of the Tahoe. It had been mostly protected from the gunfire and likely still worked. When he reached behind him to grab his pistol—the one with a single shot left—it was gone, probably having fallen out while he was trying to help the ranger. Fortunately, he wasn't without a weapon.

On the floorboard, under the dome light, was the ranger's pistol sticking out from under the seat. He picked it up and quickly looked it over. It was a Colt Anaconda with a four-inch barrel. He leaned forward and laid it on the passenger seat.

His eyes lit up when he saw a clear plastic bottle sticking up amongst some glass, wedged between the seat and the side console. He climbed back inside, took a seat, and grabbed the bottle by its throat. He pulled it up from the debris, finding it two-thirds full of water.

Shoving the bottle between his legs, he popped the trans-
mission into drive. He yanked the steering wheel all the way
to the left and released the brake, finding just enough room
to get turned south. His foot went to the gas and the vehicle
lurched down the road. The door swung shut from the momentum.

He pulled the vehicle straight. Holding the wheel steady
with his knees, he grabbed the water, spun off its plastic cap
with his teeth, and spit it out before bringing the bottle back
to his lips. He gulped down nearly all of it, letting out a heavy
cough afterwards from how quickly it had entered his throat.

He poured the remainder over his wound, barely feeling it,
which probably wasn't good. He popped open the side console,
looking for more water. Instead, his fingers found a metal flask.
It had some weight, so he shook it, hearing liquid slosh inside.
He scoffed and set the flask on the passenger seat beside the
pistol. There had to be other useful items in the SUV, including
medical supplies, but they'd have to wait.

Cold air blew through the open windows. Sean turned up
the vehicle's furnace to counter it, then turned off the FM radio
whose signal, unlike the CB's, was still loud and clear. Finding
a switch for the spotlight, he flipped it on, then crossed his
right arm over through the open window to twist it toward the
desert. It lit up the rugged terrain as he increased his speed.
The thumping noise picked up in volume and rotation.

If Lisa was close to the road, maybe he'd be able to spot her
. . . if she wasn't afraid to show herself. It wasn't lost on him
that both he and Montoya now had only one functioning
headlight. That similarity, along with the color of their vehicles,
might keep Lisa far away.

He stared out his window, his eyes scanning the dirt, rock,
and scrub. He hoped at any moment the two would suddenly

appear, but it wasn't happening. Sean also kept checking behind him, looking for headlights. He saw none.

Sean's heart skipped a beat when something large darted across the road in front of him. When a second figure crossed, he saw that it as a male deer—an adult buck with full-grown antlers well above its head. There were others standing just off the shoulder of the road, staring at him like the proverbial deer in the headlights. Among them was a small fawn, seemingly more transfixed on Sean than the others. Sean watched its eyes as he passed the herd, finding a certain surrealism in life going on as normal around him.

The tire was getting louder with an intermittent grinding noise. The engine had risen in volume too, as if it was working harder than it needed to. Sean could only imagine what was happening behind the shot-up grill, under the hood. The thought crossed his mind that with the vehicle mechanically falling apart, Lisa may hear him before she saw him. That's when his eyes flashed to the CB under the dashboard. He leaned forward, squinting and reading the lit-up labels of each knob and switch. When he saw the text, "PA," he took his foot off the gas and started to brake.

The CB's reception may have been shot, but the PA system wouldn't require it. If working, it would be wired in directly. He hadn't noticed any speakers on the roof, but one may have been behind the grill. He flipped the switch on, hearing a loud pulse from somewhere in front of him. He brought the SUV to a halt and grabbed the speaker-mic. He pulled it to his lips.

"Lisa," he said, hearing his voice echo outside the vehicle. He glanced through his side mirror, then turned the CB's volume all the way up. "Lisa . . . this is Sean. I'm still alive." He swallowed before continuing. "Listen, Montoya and his men are still out there. They're here in the park. I have a car, and I need to leave—for now—to get help. I hope to God you can hear me, baby." He reached up and brushed some sweat from his forehead with the back of his wrist before pulling the speaker back to his mouth. "If you can . . . if you can hear me, know that I'm going to bring a hundred cops back with me. If you're safe for now, and you're somewhere out of sight, stay there. Don't let yourself be seen unless it's a police car—something with a light flashing on its roof, okay?"

He listened through the open windows for a moment, giving her a chance to call out to him if she was somewhere close. He heard nothing but the loud idle of the engine. When his remaining headlight suddenly dimmed on its own, and the engine and RPMs on his dashboard lowered with it, Sean popped the vehicle into park and stepped on the gas to keep the engine revved. He lifted his head to the cracked rearview mirror. Two pinpricks of light glowed in the distance.

Montoya.

"I've got to go now," Sean added, his voice cracking. "Both you and the kid will be back to your lives before you know it. I promise." His face tightened. "I won't let it go down any other way."

Chapter 32

The two police vehicles moved slowly behind the terminal to the west side of the tarmac, headlights off. They passed by more parked planes and some storage units, Lumbergh and Holman scanning the area for signs of activity. As they closed in on the first row of metal hangars, each looking between sixty and eighty feet wide, Fowler directed them left.

"There's a big set of lights between their hangar and the one next to it," he said, leaning forward from the back seat. "They aren't on now, but they're triggered by motion. If we come in from behind and stay right up against the building, we won't set them off. It's the last one on the end, nearest the fence. Facing west."

"Thanks," said Lumbergh as Holman made the turn. "But you'll be staying where you are. Understand?"

Fowler's face went blank. "Are you serious?" he asked. "If someone's breaking the rules in here, it's my responsibility to deal with it. That's what they pay me for."

"He's right, Brian," said Holman. "We don't doubt that you're trained for a lot of things, but we're talking about serious criminal activity. Serious people. If these individuals are who we suspect they are, which we're about to try and confirm, they're heavily armed. You do security here, but you're a civilian. We can't put you in that type of situation."

"I'd be happy to sign a waiver or something," Fowler pled. "You know, so you all aren't responsible or me."

"No," said Lumbergh.

Fowler sank back into his seat, grunting in frustration. "But you all don't even know for sure these are the guys you're looking for."

"Not yet," said Lumbergh, pulling his Glock from his holster and checking its action. "But as far as *your safety* is concerned, we *are* assuming it's them." He turned to Holman. "You got an extra radio?"

She nodded. "Glovebox."

"That doesn't mean we don't need your help, Fowler," Lumbergh continued, opening the compartment. He pulled out the handheld radio and synced up its channel with Holman's. "Stay low, and if you see anyone approaching from the outside while we're checking out the hangar, you let us know ASAP."

Fowler sighed, reluctantly nodding. "Okay, right over here," he said to Holman. He pointed to a spot in front of a hangar whose large doors faced them. "It's the hangar that backs up to this one, on the opposite side."

Corbett pulled up beside them, slowing to a stop and turning off his engine. He carefully exited his vehicle. Lumbergh rolled down his window to let the detective in on their conversation.

"What's the layout like?" asked Holman. "How many ways in and out?"

Fowler described a long bifold door in front, similar to that on the hangar in front of them. On the south wall of the building was an automatic side door for a car to pull in and out. Next to it was a pedestrian door. Both would likely be locked, according to Fowler.

"If you're looking inside from the big bay door in front,

there's a straight set of stairs on the right leading up to an elevated office area. Beyond the office is a conference room. The rest is all bay."

"You've been inside?" asked Corbett.

"Not since the Cardozo people started leasing it. It was before that, and there are a couple of hangars in here with the same layout. It's a nice model. Full bathroom and shower. Even a wet bar. They keep that door closed pretty much all the time, but I doubt they've done any big-time remodeling in there since I last saw it."

Holman nodded. "We ready?"

"Almost," answered Corbett, retreating to the back of his car.

Lumbergh and Holman stepped out, pistols in hand. Corbett popped his trunk, reached in, and pulled out a twelve-gauge shotgun. The three trotted across the pavement, Lumbergh glancing back at Fowler before returning his eyes forward. Holman took the lead, sliding around the corner of the first hangar. Her back drifted along its wall. Lumbergh was close behind her with Corbett taking up the rear, holding his shotgun in front of his chest.

When they reached the end of the first hangar, Holman peered around the corner. She nudged Lumbergh in front of her, and he crossed by her shoulder, pistol in front of him. He jogged to the back of the Cardozo hangar. There was a communal metal dumpster sitting behind it. Another one was farther down the alley. There wasn't much else besides some cardboard boxes. As Fowler had said, there wasn't a back door.

Lumbergh twisted his head around the south wall of the building. He checked for security cameras—something he'd forgotten to ask Fowler about—but he didn't see any. He did see a narrow sliver of light along the pavement, just a few feet down the wall. It came from under the pedestrian door. A couple of yards past it was the garage door. Both were shut.

Lumbergh looked back and nodded. Holman and Corbett jogged across the alley and around him. Corbett stood between the two doors with his back against the wall. Holman kept going, moving to the opposite end of the wall. She poked her head around the corner before jogging back toward the men.

"Front door is shut," she whispered. "No cars."

A faint voice suddenly crept out through the wall. The three officers tensed up. Holman raised her gun. The voice sounded far away, as if the man talking was at the far end of the building. He sounded angry, speaking what sounded like English but with a strong accent.

Lumbergh slid his hand along the wooden pedestrian door, reaching for its metal knob. He tried carefully to turn it but found it locked. The talking inside continued, a new voice adding to the dialogue. Lumbergh placed his ear up against the door.

"Please," said the other man, his voice frantic and loud with fear. "I keep telling you this is all I can do for him!"

Lumbergh's eyes narrowed. He waved the detectives over to the door. Holman came in under Corbett. They both listened intently.

"Yes, the bleeding's stopped for now, but just for now! That's not enough. He needs to get to a hospital! Why won't you listen to me?"

"No!" came the other man's aggressive voice. "You help him! No hospital!"

"You don't understand!"

"*Cállate!*"

"Who is that?" whispered Holman.

"I don't know, but it sure as hell isn't a television set this time," said Lumbergh, taking a step back. "Someone in there is in need of medical attention. It could be Sean, but we've got to get in there either way."

Holman turned to Corbett.

"Come on. Are we okay on this?" pressed Lumbergh.

Holman nodded.

"Fuck yeah," said Corbett. "Get behind me. I'll take the hinges. We'll have about three seconds before they'll know what's going on."

"I'll take lead," said Lumbergh.

Holman's eyes narrowed.

"It won't be like last time. Promise."

"Fine," she said, raising her gun. "I'll be right behind you."

They all stepped back. Corbett lifted the barrel of his shotgun, aiming it toward the upper edge of the door opposite the knob. He fired, the loud blast rippling through the air as the door and the frame around it splintered. He pumped the gun, a cartridge flying as he lowered it to the second hinge. He fired again. The moment he stepped away, Lumbergh launched forward, ramming his shoulder into the center of the door. It cracked loose from its framing and crashed to the floor inside. Lumbergh stumbled forward over the top of it.

"Police!" Lumbergh shouted, gun forward.

The others funneled in behind him as his eyes quickly traced the contour of the hangar. A small white business jet was parked at its center. The Suburban sat deeper inside, its rear wide-open doors facing them. As Fowler had described, a staircase led to an elevated office on their right. Its large windows oversaw the bay. Lumbergh saw no one inside.

He suddenly caught movement on the other side of the jet behind what looked like some furniture.

"Freeze!" he shouted. "Hands in the air!"

"Let me see your fucking hands or I'll blow your head off!" Corbett yelled, sounding much more intimidating.

Lumbergh spread out to the left, hunching low. He tried to get a better visual around the jet. Corbett moved steadily forward, using the thickest section of the fuselage above the wheels for cover. Lumbergh could hear Holman's more nimble footsteps somewhere to his right.

The furniture was made up of some folding chairs and a long L-shaped sofa, its back facing the officers. Beside the sofa was a vertical metal rod, an IV hook with a bag of fluid hanging from it. A muted television sat on a card table beyond the setup. When the top of someone's bald head bobbed up above the top edge of the couch, Lumbergh again demanded to see hands.

"Please!" came a frantic voice. A man's terrified eyes and white, unshaven face steadily rose above the couch. He looked in his early thirties and seemed to be kneeling. "He's got a gun to my back! He says he'll shoot me if you don't lay down your weapons. Please, I . . . I don't want to die."

"Shit," Corbett muttered, having taken position directly behind the jet. He quickly glanced through its open side door, confirming no one was inside.

Lumbergh tucked himself under the jet's nose. Out of the corner his eye, he saw Holman moving up the stairs toward the office, reaching for her radio.

"You're surrounded!" shouted Lumbergh. "The only way anyone's getting out of here is if we see some hands right now!"

"No!" came a voice from behind the captive. "Guns down!"

The captive closed his eyes.

Lumbergh swallowed, trying to better estimate the position

of his captor. "No one needs to die," he said. "And no one will, if you do what I say."

The captive's eyes shifted to his side. "Listen . . ." he said, voice trembling as he spoke to the man behind him. "I know you want to save your friend's life . . . These policemen can have an ambulance here in three minutes. It's his best chance, believe me."

Lumbergh's face tightened. His eyes shifted to the Suburban. On the bay floor below it was a thin trail of blood, smeared with footprints, all the way over to the couch. A tube from the IV rod led to the front of the couch. An injured person had to be lying there on top of the cushions in front of them. It had to be the man Lumbergh had shot in the stomach in front of the Dusty Nickel. Montoya knew that taking him to the hospital would have meant an arrest and a line back to him.

Lumbergh hoped the hostage-taker was more persuadable. "That's right," said Lumbergh, glancing up at the office. There he saw Holman peering through the lower part the window pane, talking quietly into her radio. "If you want to save your friend, we can make that happen fast."

The hostage's mouth shaped into an *o*, seemingly forcing himself to breathe. He stared desperately at Lumbergh, his eyes pleading for help. When he tilted his head up and to the left, Lumbergh knew he had spotted Holman in the window. She was carefully sliding the window pane up. Lumbergh shook his head at the man, signaling him not to draw attention to her. His face turned back to Lumbergh.

The captor had stopped talking, hopefully weighing the offer in his head.

"Come on," said Lumbergh, his tone lighter to guide him along. "This doesn't—"

"Get up!" shouted Montoya's man.

The hostage's face twisted in defeat. He slowly rose to his feet behind the couch, his clothing revealing itself to be pale blue medical scrubs, the shirt portion smeared with blood. He appeared to be some kind of medical worker.

His captor rose up behind him, switching a silver revolver from the hostage's back to the side of his head. His was shorter, his face peering over the medical worker's shoulder. He had olive skin, a black handkerchief covering his head, and a tattooed teardrop above his right cheek. When his eyes met Lumbergh's, they burned with recognition.

"*Marranito*," the man said sharply, nostrils flaring.

"Hands in the air!" ordered Lumbergh.

The man shook his head. "I leave him here for you!" he shouted, nodding his head sideways at the couch. "You call. You fix him up." He pressed the muzzle of his gun harder to the hostage's head. "*You*, come!"

He guided the hostage to their left by a handful of the back of his shirt, his eyes shifting between Lumbergh and Corbett, who had moved under the jet's tail.

"You leave him right where he's at!" shouted Corbett. "You're not taking him anywhere."

The captor's lips twisted into a confident smile. "What you gonna do? You shoot me, you shoot him!"

His eyes bounced between the cops and the Suburban. He drew closer to the vehicle. It seemed he knew he couldn't get his partner out, and was trying to save his own skin using a human shield.

Lumbergh slid his eyes to Holman. She hadn't been spotted yet and was lining up a shot with her pistol. It would be a risky one if she took it. At least forty feet separated them, though he and his hostage were inching closer to her as they made their way to the van.

"Please," pled the medical worker. "I have kids."

"Oh, *you* have kids," sneered the man with the gun. "Lumbergh. He *shoots* kids! He shot *that* kid." He glared at the police chief. "He'll never forget shooting *that* kid."

Lumbergh wasn't sure of his meaning, but it mattered little at the moment. His eyes and gun followed the two. The gunman was standing so close behind his hostage that it was becoming clearer with each step closer to the vehicle that Holman wasn't going to take the shot . . . not until they got to the Suburban, where they'd have to separate to get inside. Lumbergh hated letting it go that far, but it was the safest play for the hostage. Corbett seemed to recognize this as well, staying under the jet with only his aim moving.

"He's going to kill you, you know! If you're lucky!" shouted the gunman, grinning at Lumbergh. "Sweet revenge!" he said, laughing.

Keep talking, asshole, Lumbergh thought to himself.

The hostage's eyes bulged, a tear running down his face. "Please," he kept whispering as he was pulled around the frontside of the Suburban.

The vehicle now between them and the policemen, the captor yelled at his hostage to open the passenger door. The hostage complied.

"Slide through! You drive!" ordered the gunman.

The hostage lowered his head and climbed inside. The moment he did, a shot rang out from above. The gunman cried out, his body spinning and bouncing off the door. Holman got another one off before he returned fire, his blasts shattering the office windows. She went low as he continued firing.

Lumbergh and Corbett moved in. The driver-side door sprung open and the medical worker dropped back out. He ran toward Lumbergh, hands in the air, inadvertently putting himself in the police chief's line of fire.

"Get down!" yelled Lumbergh, grabbing him by the shirt-sleeve and pulling him down to the floor.

The Suburban's engine cranked as Corbett got to the back of the vehicle. He fired through its open rear doors. The wheels spun in reverse and Corbett lunged to the side, one of the doors slamming into his shoulder. It spun his body around, and he crashed to the cement just inches from the tires that sped past him toward the closed garage door. Lumbergh fired at the windshield, the driver ducking low. Holman fired through the remains of the office windows, more glass dropping from the panes as her rounds sent sparks off the vehicle's hood.

The Suburban crashed into the garage door, knocking it from its tracks and tearing off the vehicle's rear doors. More metal cried as the driver backed over what was left of the mangled door, triggering the outside motion light. Lumbergh ran toward the vehicle, sidestepping Corbett and jumping over his dropped shotgun.

Holman bolted down the stairs, skipping every other step.

"Cover the southeast gate!" she yelled into her radio, presumably to officers arriving at the scene. "Black Suburban! Driver is armed!"

The vehicle bobbled over more debris as it turned in the direction the police officers had originally come from. Tires peeled, and the Suburban sped away just as Lumbergh left the hangar. He fired at the vehicle, aiming for the left rear tire. Sparks bounced off the pavement around it.

"Fuck!" Lumbergh grunted, turning back toward Holman. "Is your backup here? We can't let him get away!"

The howl of screeching brakes drew his attention back to the Suburban a split second before a second vehicle slammed into its side, clipping its rear fender. It was Holman's car. Fowler had to be behind the wheel. The Suburban fishtailed and crashed into the front of a small plane parked close to the fence.

"Jesus," Lumbergh gasped. He sprinted toward the collision, Holman close behind him.

"Fowler, if you can hear me," Holman, out of breath, shouted into her radio, "do not engage that driver! Get out of the car and run! Find cover!"

A gunshot rang out just as Lumbergh reached the side of Holman's car. He dropped low behind it. Holman did the same. A strong stench of gasoline filled the air.

"Fowler!" Lumbergh yelled, reaching for the handle on the passenger-side door.

The door suddenly popped wide, drawing up Lumbergh's pistol. Fowler grunted as he crumbled half way out of the cab, his knees dropping to the pavement.

"Heard you on the radio," he said.

Lumbergh grabbed him by his sweat-drenched sleeve and yanked him the rest of the way out. He fell to his side and clumsily rolled toward Holman.

"You okay?" she asked when he fell into her knee.

"I think," he said, out of breath.

The faint sound of police sirens was quickly upstaged by another gunshot. It struck the other side of the car, dropping Lumbergh and Holman lower.

"Drop your weapon!" shouted Lumbergh, reaching out and slamming the car door shut. He crawled forward, carefully making his way toward the front of the car. "You're not getting out of here! Just give yourself up!" He peeked around the car's bumper.

The smell of gasoline was growing stronger. The plane's fuel tank must have been sliced open from the collision.

"Fuck you!" the man shouted, firing off another couple of rounds.

Holman quickly returned one over the trunk of her car.

"Careful!" Lumbergh gasped. "Gas!"

Lumbergh spotted movement behind the right rear fender of the Suburban. It's where the gunman was taking cover, hunched down behind it. He watched the man's head flip back and forth between the southwest fence and increasing volume of the police sirens. Lumbergh didn't want the man dead. He wanted to know where Sean was, and the man likely had the answer.

The memory of what happened back at the Dusty Nickel was still fresh in Lumbergh's mind. The man's partner had chosen death over arrest. If he saw no other way out, the man behind the Suburban might do the same. Lumbergh would have to incapacitate him to keep him alive . . . and do it carefully.

Lumbergh snapped his fingers to try and get Holman's attention. She didn't hear him but Fowler did. With his broad back pressed against the car and his gun at his side, he reached over his chest and tugged on Holman's sleeve. Her eyes went to him and then to Lumbergh. Lumbergh signaled with two fingers pointed to his eyes that he had a visual on the man. Then he held up five and pointed at her. She nodded, signifying that she understood. Lumbergh widened his stance, planting a knee and steadily edging his body from around the front of the car. One eye closed, he lined up the Suburban's fender in his sights. When Holman fired her gun in the air, the man immediately swung his arm from behind the vehicle to return it. Lumbergh fired first.

The man's arm snapped in the opposite direction. He

barked and dropped to his side. Flashing red and blue lights peered above the row of planes behind him.

"Cover me!" Lumbergh shouted, climbing to his feet and darting around Holman's car. His gun in front of him with both hands, he jogged toward the fallen man. "Don't you move!" he said as the man slithered around on the ground. "Both hands out in front of you!"

Lumbergh could see the man's right hand. It shone from blood, his arm stretched out in front of him. His other arm was folded and tucked under his chest. The pavement below the man was wet. Lumbergh slowed his pace when he got within twelve feet. Gun pointed, Lumbergh could hear the trickling of fuel from the plane.

"Lumbergh the hero," the man said with eerie calmness, his face pointed down at the pavement. "Always gets his man." The side of his body was doused with gasoline.

"Slowly slide your other hand out in front of you, palm pressed to the ground," said Lumbergh.

The man chuckled. "I think you should make me famous, hero." He snarled and spun to his shoulder, his left arm swinging toward Lumbergh. He held the gun so awkwardly that Lumbergh was sure he could disarm him without firing. Lumbergh lunged forward and sent the toe of his foot into the man's wrist.

"No!" he heard Holman yell.

There was a loud pop from Holman's direction. Sparks flew off the propeller of the plane behind them.

A large flame rose up from the pavement, quickly spreading in multiple directions. It shot up from under Lumbergh's feet, sending him toppling backwards against the Suburban. His shoes were on fire. His gun fell from his hand as he worked to kick them off his feet. The man on the ground was engulfed in flames from his head to his knees, wildly screaming and swinging his arms as he tried to roll away. No matter what he did, he couldn't shake the fire. Lumbergh frantically kicked off his shoes and circled around to the back of the Suburban. He spotted what looked like a bloody, bunched-up sheet inside. He grabbed it and ran around the vehicle back to the man.

Sirens blared and flashing lights lit up the area. Police cruisers screeched to a stop. The man's screams grew higher in pitch. When Lumbergh reached him, he threw the sheet over the man and tried to help him roll, but the fire was on him like glue. The smell of burning flesh shot through Lumbergh's nose as the flames bounced off the man's hands and face. Lumbergh's sleeves lit up, and he stumbled backwards from his knees to his backside, slapping at them. Holman ran in with a fire extinguisher, probably from the trunk of her car. She struggled with its release lever as the man's piercing screams suddenly went silent. After a pop, carbon dioxide sprayed loudly from its nozzle. She doused Lumbergh's arms and then aimed it at the man on the ground, who'd stopped moving. She covered his body from head to toe.

"Get the plane!" an officer yelled from behind them.

Flames were dancing up the front of the plane. Holman ran toward them, spraying them with her extinguisher.

Lumbergh's eyes fell back to the man on the ground. Smoke and white residue from the carbon dioxide floated up off his body. Uniformed police officers rushed in. One of them was calling for an ambulance while another kicked the man's pistol away from his crisp hand.

"Jesus Christ, I'm sorry!" shouted Fowler in distress. "Oh, God." He looked down at Lumbergh before his hands went to his own face. "Are you okay? Please tell me you're okay. Jesus Christ!"

Lumbergh suddenly understood what had happened. It was Fowler who'd fired, having seen the man whip out his gun. Holman had tried to stop him.

Lumbergh's palms and forearms felt as if they'd been raked with broken glass. His hands were red from burns. His sleeves were singed and torn. He gazed at the unconscious man on the pavement as officers attended to him.

"He's breathing but he's out," he heard one of them say. "Probably in shock."

"Chief?" Holman's voice came from beside him. "You okay?"

In a haze, he tilted his eyes up to her. He wasn't sure how to answer. All he could think about was Sean, Lisa, and the girl.

Fowler was beside himself, pacing back and forth, hand to his forehead.

A single gunshot suddenly popped off in the distance. Officers spun around, going for their weapons. Eyes wide, Lumbergh scrambled to his feet, looking for his gun.

"That was from the hangar," yelled Holman.

Chapter 33

Sean had turned off his lights the moment he'd seen Montoya's, relying on the straightness of the road and its loud gravel shoulder to keep him on track. Without visible taillights, he hoped it would create the illusion that he was long gone, well on his way outside of the park in an operational vehicle. If Montoya and his men felt that he was out of their reach, or believed he'd used the ranger's CB to call the police, maybe they'd flip a U-turn and quickly head north back to the city before help arrived.

No such luck.

Montoya's headlights slowly but steadily grew closer, even as Sean pressed his gas pedal farther down. The front right tire flopped wildly, intermittently producing the crunch of metal on pavement. The racket it made, joined by a new grinding noise from under the hood, consumed Sean's thoughts. When the engine light went on behind the steering wheel, quickly followed by another whose symbol Sean didn't recognize, he knew something was about to give. Even if the engine held, the wheel wouldn't. He wasn't going to make it out.

His head flipped from side to side, eyes desperately searching for a rock formation or any kind of barrier to pull off the road behind. It was tough in the dark, relying only on the limited moonlight for visibility, but the land looked flat as far as the eye could see. He thought about veering off the road, across the dirt and scrub. If he didn't use his brakes, they might not see him. But with his tire almost gone, he worried he'd make it only a few feet across the desert before the bare rim got him stuck in the dirt. And if it didn't, there'd assuredly be a lingering dust cloud, visible under Montoya's lights as they drew close. They'd get him either way.

He glanced in the mirror again before returning his eyes to the road. For the briefest moment, he made out a diamond-shaped road sign to his right. It was too dark to tell what was on it, but the shape usually represented some type of warning. Maybe it was about crossing deer or an upcoming intersection; the former seemed more likely than the latter. When it occurred to Sean that it may be alerting drivers to a sharp curve in the road, he lifted his foot off the pedal.

The last thing he wanted was to lose ground with Montoya closing in, but if he wound up getting stuck in a ditch off the shoulder of the road, things would get much worse.

His eyes were glued to the darkened pavement as he slowed. When he suddenly made out the outlines of guardrails to his left and right, he realized he was crossing over a bridge. The ravine below couldn't have been very deep, not with how flat the rest of the land around him remained. It likely crossed over a stream.

The Big Nudge.

"Okay, okay, okay . . ." sputtered Sean, sitting up straight and trying to catch a glimpse over the side.

He didn't hear water from the window but decided it didn't matter. With his vehicle on its last legs, he couldn't afford to pass on the opportunity. He reached across his body and grabbed the shoulder strap of his seatbelt, pulling it across his chest and buckling it. Next he grabbed the revolver and slid it under his thigh.

His foot remained off the brake. If he so much as tapped it, the lights at the rear would immediately alert Montoya to exactly where he was. No matter what, he couldn't let that happen.

When the guardrails came to an end, he knew he was still going too fast for what he had in mind next. He also knew he had little choice. He steadily turned the steering wheel to the right, gradually guiding the vehicle onto the shoulder. Then he pulled the wheel sharply to the left, a rear tire screeching as he crossed the road and dropped off the opposite shoulder.

The lower front of the vehicle bounced hard off dirt and rock, sending glass and other debris through the cab. It pelted Sean's face as he gritted his teeth and clenched the steering wheel. The momentum pushed him forward as he held the wheel left. Sagebrush smacked the vehicle's grill. Rocks and uneven ground bobbled its frame. Metal barked and everything on the floor and seats slid to the right. As the ground dropped again, and the vehicle with it, it took every ounce of discipline Sean could muster not to brake.

He guided the vehicle as best he could toward the bottom of the bridge. It bounced savagely before falling again and smashing against something so solid that everything was brought to an immediate stop. Sean grunted as the seatbelt strap dug into his shoulder.

The vehicle was wedged at an angle with its rear probably at thirty-five degrees. The engine had stalled on impact. Sean unfastened his seatbelt, gravity dropping him up against the steering wheel. He reached under his leg for the gun. He then unlatched his door and shoved it open with his knee. When the dome light flipped on, he quickly drew it back shut. He twisted his body toward the open window, gun drawn.

Above, the contour of the bridge lit up and grew in definition by the approaching headlights. Sean heard Montoya's engine, sickly rattling—probably caused by damage from the earlier collision. He prayed the babble wouldn't be followed by the sound of brakes. If the men inside had caught a glimpse of his vehicle leaving the road, or noticed a trail off to the side, he was done.

The Bronco passed over without hesitation. If it had slowed even a little, it wasn't apparent. The red glare of its taillights bounced off the bridge's guardrail before things began to fade back to darkness. The rattling fled with it. Sean collapsed his head across the top of the steering wheel, drawing in a deep breath before letting out a couple of coughs. Sweat poured down his temples.

Before long, his attention sank back to the pain throughout his body. He felt it in all of his limbs but especially his shoulder. His throat was dry and strained and even his chest burned, though he didn't know why. He tasted blood in his mouth.

Still, his mind wandered well beyond that of his wounds. The help he'd promised Lisa wouldn't come as soon as he'd hoped. And as he sat there, head pressed against vinyl, he also thought of what Montoya would find when he reached the end of the park. He remembered the conversation between him and the ranger. What had heightened her suspicions was Montoya's tale that he had driven around a gate to get inside and search for his wife. Maybe such a thing wasn't possible. They were on federal land. There was likely better security at its entrances and exits that some mechanical arm or mere semblance of a gate that someone could easily drive around it. If the feds were concerned about poachers and people coming in after dark, it was hard to imagine there wasn't a solidly secured gate and restrictive fence that made that type of vehicle access difficult or even impossible.

When Montoya would eventually reach it and find things still locked down, he'd know that Sean never made it out. *What then?* If he believed the police were on their way from a radio call from Sean, he might be desperate enough to try and plow down the fence with his Bronco and leave. Or if that wasn't feasible, he'd return to the area where he'd found his way into the park in the first place and get out that way.

The thought suddenly crossed Sean's mind that the police may not have even been a concern for Montoya. If he or one of his men had seen the SUV's stripped antenna in the road, and noticed the ranger's handheld still fastened to her hip, Montoya may have been fully aware, or at least heavily suspected, that Sean hadn't been able to call out.

There were too many possibilities and Sean didn't know which ones were more likely. What he did know was that it would be foolish to stay where he was. If Montoya returned, he'd have a better view of the east side of the bridge, where the ranger's vehicle was sticking out. Sean needed to put some distance between himself and the road but also not lose track of it. It was the only landmark he had back to civilization, and his best eye on Montoya's whereabouts, as well as on any help that may eventually arrive.

Sean shoved his pistol back under his thigh and opened the door. He used the above light to find the flask. He arched his hips, wincing from the aches it caused as he shoved the flask into his pocket. He leaned forward across the passenger seat, the vehicle creaking as he did. There, he popped open the glove box, his eyes lighting up with the bulb inside at a folded-up map. "Sloan Canyon Conservation Area," read its face.

He grabbed it, uncovering a half-sized Mag flashlight. He snatched this as well, along with a small, unopened bag of mixed nuts he found beside it. The rest of the compartment was home to miscellaneous paperwork and a few pens and pencils. He ignored them, painfully twisting his torso and using the flashlight to expose the area of the cab behind the front seat. The beam slid over a small fire extinguisher fastened behind the passenger seat, along with what looked like tow ropes on the floor.

When he guided the beam right, he spotted the corner of a red duffle bag.

"Let it be . . ." he muttered, twisting his head as best he could around his chair.

When he spotted white print and a cross on the bag, he breathed a sigh of relief. Lifting some fingers from the flashlight, he reached back and grabbed the first aid kit. It bounced along the seat and console before it settled on his lap. He unzipped it, knocking away shards of glass from the side window as he did. He shone the flashlight through the opening. The sight of pain relievers, gauze, tape, and antibiotic ointment was welcome, but he scoffed at the ample supply of band-aids that he felt pretty well beyond. A couple of plastic boxes surely had other goodies, which he'd sort through later.

He shoved the pistol and other items into the bag for easier carrying and then zipped it back up. The last thing he wanted was the weapon slipping out of his pants like the last one. He needled his good arm through the bag's straps and wrapped his fingers back around the flashlight, lighting up the terrain outside his window. Beneath the bridge was a dry riverbed. Smooth, almost beach-like sand laid a path between shoulders of spattered rock, gravel, and brush. He spilled out of the vehicle onto some rocks, stumbling forward down a short slope toward the front of the bumper that was bent around larger rock. The stench of antifreeze was stronger than before, and

Sean could now see fluids running from under the vehicle and out onto the sand.

It made sense to Sean to travel along the riverbed, at least for now. It would keep him low and out of site until he put some distance between himself and the road. He chose west where there were more rocks cobbled together along the side, and he'd be able to walk on them without producing obvious tracks.

He spread his beam along their trail for a few seconds, then kept the image in his head after switching off the light. He wouldn't turn it back on unless he was certain it couldn't be seen from the road.

Chapter 34

Flanked by three uniformed officers, Lumbergh and Holman ran back to the hangar, Lumbergh without his shoes.

"Freeze!" one of the officers yelled, gun drawn as a bloodied figure darted out through the garage.

"Wait!" shouted the man in scrubs, dropping to his knees. "Don't shoot!" His hands were high in the air.

"He's okay!" shouted Holman. "He was the hostage."

"You've got to stop your friend before he kills him!" said the man, eyes desperate.

A voice from inside cried out. It didn't belong to Corbett. The uniformed officers rushed inside around debris with Holman close behind. Lumbergh stayed back, his gun still holstered. The burns to his hands were so fresh and painful that he could barely hold his weapon.

"Come here," Lumbergh said to the man who'd been held hostage, motioning him to the safety of the wall.

The man climbed to his feet and jogged over as Lumbergh peered inside. Lumbergh watched the officers work their way around the plane. Holman quickly ran around them toward the furniture, holstering her gun.

"Dennis, stop!" she yelled.

Corbett angrily barked back. Lumbergh was unable to make out his words.

"What's going on in there?" asked Lumbergh, turning to the hostage.

"The kid I'd been treating . . . He woke up as I was explaining things to the detective guy. He must have had a gun stashed in the couch. He pulled it out and took a shot at the detective."

Lumbergh's eyes widened. "Is Corbett injured?"

"No. Well, he'll want to get that shoulder looked at. It could be dislocated, but the kid missed clean. The detective snatched the gun from his hand, but then grabbed him by the throat and started choking him. I guess he was pissed off."

"All clear!" shouted Holman.

"Come back in with me," said Lumbergh. "And if you could keep what you saw with the detective between me and you, I'd appreciate it."

The two reentered the hangar, walking quickly.

"What's your name?" Lumbergh asked him.

"Karl. Karl Jacobs."

"How did you get mixed up in this?"

"I'm an ER nurse over at Aliante. I was getting out of my car . . . in the parking lot. About to start a shift. This guy pulls up in the Suburban, sticks a gun in my face, and yells at me to get inside. Says his friend's been shot. I was scared out of my mind. We grabbed some things out of an ambulance parked out front, and I did what he said. He drove us back here, me and the kid with the bullet wound. I've been trying to treat him, but—"

"You okay?"

"Physically, yeah. Mentally, I'll probably be fucked up for a while."

Lumbergh nodded. "Was anyone else held here, besides you? A tall guy . . . or a blonde woman with a baby?"

"No. No one. He kept talking to someone though."

Lumbergh stopped just in front of the plane. He latched onto Jacobs' arm, quickly releasing him when the pain from his burn flared up. With a wince he asked, "What do you mean? You're saying the *driver* was talking to someone?"

"Yeah," said Jacobs, blinking. "On his cell phone. In Spanish."

"Where's his cell phone?"

"He had it in his pocket whenever he wasn't using it."

Lumbergh's shoulders deflated. "It's probably half melted," he mumbled.

"What?"

"Nothing. Any idea what they were saying?"

Jacobs crossed his arms in front of his chest, tilting his head. "A little. I haven't taken Spanish since high school, and I got a C in that class, but—"

"We're desperate here. Anything could help."

Jacobs explained that there'd been frequent calls over the last few hours, status updates that included the condition of the kid, and on the other end, some kind of operation that was taking longer than expected—one that was keeping others from meeting them back at the hangar. When Lumbergh pressed him for details, Jacobs drifted into thought, then recalled hearing "Highway 95" mentioned a couple of times.

"Oh," Jacobs snapped his fingers. "There was something about how they were looking for someone, and I heard the word *colinas* a few times, which I know means hills. It sounded like they needed to find someone before they could come back."

Lumbergh's face tightened, his eyes floating to the side.

"Maybe they're after the guy who shot the kid."

"No, it's not him," Lumbergh said dismissively. "But I think I know who."

"Chief?" Holman said.

Lumbergh nudged Jacobs and the two made their way around the plane toward the officers. Corbett stood in the corner of the room, cooling off. One of his shoulders noticeably hung lower than the other, but if he was in pain, he was hiding it well. His eyes shifted to Lumbergh, probably wondering if Jacobs had hung him out to dry.

One of the uniformed officers was on his radio, voicing directions; it sounded like he was talking to a paramedic crew. The other two were still securing the area, one headed toward the stairs. Holman was on a knee next the couch, eyes etched with concern.

She lifted her head. "Can you come here please?" she asked Jacobs, her tone direct.

In front of her lay a young Hispanic man whose features matched up with the man Lumbergh had shot earlier. At the middle of his long dark hair were scared brown eyes. He wore no shirt, revealing some tattoos on his shoulders. An IV tube led into his wrist and an oxygen tube was stuck to his nose. Bloody gauze was taped over his abdomen. The blood at its center looked fresh.

"Oh, dammit," said Jacobs, hurrying in beside him. "He's bleeding again." He placed his hand over the bandages, applying pressure.

The kid flinched upon his touch, letting out a moan.

Jacobs glanced back at Holman.

"What do you need?" asked Holman, taking a step back.

"What I need is what he's needed for the past few hours: a hospital." He turned to the officer with the radio. "How much longer on that ambulance?"

"They just arrived at the gate," the officer answered. "It'll be a couple of minutes though. They've got to divide resources because of the burn victim."

"*Victim*," Corbett scoffed.

"Can you radio your men by the plane to check the perp's pockets for a cell phone before he's taken away?" asked Lumbergh.

"Yes, sir."

Jacobs returned his attention to the kid. Lumbergh circled in behind the medic, his eyes shifting between the kid's eyes and wound. When the kid noticed Lumbergh and met his gaze, he began to shake. His eyes thinned and his teeth clenched with unmistakable hatred.

"You really want to kill me, don't you?" said Lumbergh.

"Chief," said Holman, urging caution.

"He'd kill all of us if he could," said Corbett from behind them, drawing in closer. "I was checking on his injury when he tried to off me."

"Guys, cool it," said Holman.

The kid continued glaring at Lumbergh, nostrils flaring and eyes burning.

"But it looks like he's got a particular hard-on for you, Chief," said Corbett.

"That's because I'm the one who shot him," Lumbergh blurted.

Jacobs's head swung over his shoulder. "*You* shot him?"

"Not that I wanted to. He didn't give me much choice."

Jacobs turned his focus back to the kid, whose eyes suddenly shifted from Lumbergh's to his. The kid shook his head a little, as if issuing a silent, subtle warning.

"Why is he looking at you like that?" asked Holman.

Jacobs looked back at Lumbergh. "I don't think he wants me to tell you that you're the man who killed his uncle."

"What?" asked Lumbergh.

"F-f-fuck you," grunted the kid, his hand latching onto Jacobs's wrist.

Lumbergh reached in and pried his fingers open, letting Jacobs break free. He glared at the kid. "You're Lautaro Montoya's son?"

The kid glared back. His feelings for Lumbergh made additional sense.

"Well, shit," said Corbett, moving in. "*And* he speaks English. Where's your daddy, asshole?"

A screech of tires and some flashing lights drew everyone's attention to the hangar door. The front of a police cruiser was visible. Two doors slammed shut. A second later a young woman in an EMT uniform rounded the corner with a medical box. An officer was close behind her, wheeling a collapsed stretcher behind him.

Corbett reached over Lumbergh, knocking over the IV bar with his arm and gripping the kid's jaw in his hands. "Where's your daddy?" he yelled, intent on getting some answers before the patient was taken away.

"Fuck you!" yelled the kid, spit spraying from his mouth. His eyes rolled to his head from the pressure on his jaw.

"I said 'cool it,' Dennis!" said Holman, pulling his arm back.

Corbett let loose and spun around. His elbow inadvertently bumped off Jacobs's forehead. With a finger pointing at Holman, he said, "The kid knows where these missing people are!"

"And your plan is to beat the answers out of him?" Holman fired back, getting up in his chest.

"Listen!" he barked.

"No, *you* listen!" Holman persisted as the EMT, trying to remain professional, squeezed in between Corbett and the couch. "I know the stakes. You don't have to remind me. And I shouldn't have to remind you that the only reason you're still on this job is because of how many times I've gone to bat for you when you've made stupid, hot-headed mistakes like the one you're trying to make now."

Corbett's face turned red. He grunted and sneered, hands clenched into fists. His eyes shifted from side to side, realizing that the heated exchange had every other officer's attention.

Lumbergh gave them room, letting them sort things out but silently sharing Corbett's sentiment more closely than he did Holman's. The kid may have been in severe pain, and drifting in and out of consciousness over the past few hours, but he had to have some knowledge about what was happening with Sean and the others. He'd been in the hangar as his partner coordinated over the phone with Montoya or his men. Surely, he had better information than Jacobs and his high school Spanish lessons. But even Corbett sticking a finger in the kid's wound may not have done the trick. Montoya's other two men were willing to go down in a blaze of glory for their boss, and his son had even more reason to protect his father. Then again, with youth came weakness and stupidity.

The officer with the radio informed Lumbergh that they had indeed found a cell phone on the man who'd been burned, but it was damaged and inoperable. They might be able to pull something off it back at the department, but it would take time. It was an ongoing theme of the night.

Holman and Corbett bickered some more before Corbett backed down and paced off in the other direction. He ran his fingers through his hair in frustration, shaking his head.

The EMT had given the kid a shot of something in his shoulder and was holding a clean cloth over his wound, continuing to apply pressure. She was working in conjunction with Jacobs, who pulled the IV tube from the needle, helped set up the stretcher, and hooked the oxygen tank on its side.

Holman took a breath and returned to the side of the couch. "We already have you for attempted murder—two counts," she said to the kid. "You'll be tried as an adult, regardless of your age, along with a whole slew of accessory charges once we've put together the rest of what's gone down tonight. You're set to spend a hell of a lot of time in prison."

The kid glared at her, ignoring the paramedics as they and one of the uniformed officers prepared to hoist him onto the stretcher.

"I know you value family, and I respect that," continued Holman. "Unfortunately, the same is not true of your father."

The kid's eyes narrowed, his scowl twisting tighter.

"I mean . . ." she said, shrugging. "He's not here, is he? He knows his son is severely wounded—a bullet in his stomach— but he's nowhere to be found. Off chasing money. It's like you're no more important to him than any of the others. Hell, he wouldn't even let his men take you to a hospital when he knew it was the only way to save your life."

Lumbergh fought back a smirk. Holman was good at this.

"Okay . . . one, two, three," said the EMT.

The kid was lifted onto the stretcher by a thin sheet under his back while the men held his legs. He whimpered and cried out when they rested him flat. A tear streamed down his eye before his focus returned to Holman.

Holman wrapped her fist around a bar at the bottom of the stretcher, preventing the EMT from pulling it forward.

"Ma'am?" said the EMT.

Holman ignored her, turning toward Jacobs. "How much longer would he have lived, had we not shown up here tonight?"

Jacobs glanced at the blank look on the EMT's face before

meeting Holman's gaze. "He wouldn't have made it to morning. Not without going into surgery. Not with this bullet in him."

"You were never going to see another sunset, *amigo*," said Holman, turning to the kid and feigning sadness in her eyes.

"Ma'am, please," said the EMT, her eyes shifting between Holman and Jacobs.

"Listen," Jacobs told the detective. "The same still holds. He'll die if we don't get going."

Holman's grip didn't loosen. She turned back to Jacobs. "And the moment he would have died on that couch . . ." she said, nudging her head toward the kid, "they would have killed you—a man who did nothing but help him, just for being a witness to all of this." She paused for a moment. "But at least your father would have given a shit about you." Her eyes went back to the kid.

"Shut up, bitch!" the kid sneered.

"Or what, *pendejo*?" she asked, placing her other hand on her hip. She leaned forward over him. "Your daddy's going to do something to me?"

"He will!" he shouted, his face cringing from the pain.

She smiled. "Honey, Chief Lumbergh over there put your big bad uncle down like a dog over two years ago, and your daddy has done exactly dick about it."

Air rushed in and out of the kid's nose. She had clearly struck a nerve.

"He's doing something tonight!" he said, trying to grin but the pain making it difficult. "You'll see!"

"Oh, that's cute," she said with a giggle. "What he *did* is send his *three stooges* after the chief here. Now one of those stooges is in the morgue. Another's being scraped off the tarmac like a charred burger. And the little baby stooge . . . Well, he was left behind to die, like the weakling that he is, while his pussy-ass daddy hides from pride of his hometown. So much for *familia*." Her grin widened.

"Fucking bitch!" he screamed, his body buckling on the stretcher.

"Ma'am!" the EMT yelled, leaning forward. She and Jacobs tried to keep him pinned. "We need to keep him stabilized."

"He's gonna kill Coleman!" said the kid, his eyes straining toward Lumbergh. "He's gonna catch him and kill him . . . slowly and painfully . . . as he begs. Then he'll leave him in the sand for the buzzards . . . to pick out his eyes."

"Where is he?" said Holman, leaning forward.

The kid's glare went back to her, his lips curling. He shook his head.

"Highway 95," said Lumbergh. "In the hills."

The kid's eyes shot wide, jumping to Lumbergh. His mouth straightened. It was the confirmative reaction Lumbergh was hoping for.

Holman turned to Lumbergh, eyes narrow. Corbett did the same.

"We have to get him to the hospital," said the EMT, her eyes stretched with concern. "You can't just—"

"Take him," said Holman, removing her hand. "You get yourself looked at too," she told Jacobs, pressing her hand on his shoulder.

He nodded.

"Hey, wait up," said Corbett, tapping Jacobs on the same shoulder. "I need something else from you."

Jacobs's face was etched with confusion. He walked over.

Holman turned to the uniformed officer next to her. "Help her," she said told him, nodding toward the EMT. "And escort the ambulance. We need the son under tight security at the hospital. Despite what I said, his father or his people might try and come for him."

The officer nodded as he and the EMT whisked the kid away on the stretcher.

A subtle buzzing noise drew Holman's attention back to the living area.

"Where did you come up with Highway 95?" Corbett asked Lumbergh.

"Jacobs overheard it. Also, something about *hills*."

Jacobs nodded in confirmation.

"I don't think they have Sean," Lumbergh continued. "I don't know about Lisa and Wendice's girl, but it sounds like Sean got loose and they're looking for him. That talk from Montoya's son about leaving him in the sand for the buzzards? They've got to be somewhere in the desert. Where does Highway 95 go?"

"*Shh!*" said Holman. "Do you guys hear that?"

"Hear what?" asked Corbett.

"That buzzing!" her voice echoed across the hangar.

The men stopped talking, trying to follow the intermittent sound with their gazes. Lumbergh pressed the back of his hand to the bulge in his pocket before remembering that he'd turned off Dusty's cell phone when the battery light had started blinking.

"Wait, that buzzing. . ." started Jacobs.

Holman's eyes homed in on the bloodied couch the kid had been lifted from.

"Listen, the son had a cell phone with him earlier," said Jacobs. "I heard it buzzing in the van on our way here—on vibrate, I guess. When he woke up later, he talked to someone on it, I think his dad!"

Holman dropped to her knees and began yanking cushions off the sofa. Lumbergh joined her.

"I didn't see the phone after that," continued Jacobs. "I figured the other guy took it."

"I padded him down after he took that shot at me," said Corbett, the buzzing now louder. "No phone."

Holman shoved her arm under the back pillows, sliding it from left to right. Her eyes lit up when her hand stopped.

"You were looking in the wrong spot," she said, pulling out a silver flip phone, its face decorated with dry blood. It continued to vibrate. She raised her head to the others. "It's got to be him. Montoya. He's calling right now."

Chapter 35

He sat with his back against a large slab of rock that edged the riverbed. It was about six feet high and ten feet wide, nestled up against the raised earth of the bank among smaller rocks and brush. For the moment it was an ideal spot, low and probably four hundred feet from the road, facing away from it. There he could use the tight beam of the flashlight on his shoulder without anyone on the road noticing the glare.

Unwinding and peeling off the long strands of duct tape from his shoulder was a slow, painful process. It pulled at his skin and hair, and the wet and dry blood made it difficult at times to assess what he was prying at. When he lifted back the last strand, it brought with it the soaked handkerchiefs his captors from the van had placed there hours earlier. Sean winced when the cloth clung to his wound. Once they were free, he dropped them to the ground and drew in a breath.

With his head twisted and his sweat-drenched sleeve pulled up to his collarbone, it was the first solid look he'd gotten of his shoulder since Lisa's house. It was pretty swollen, the flesh protruding over an inch. At its center was the dark crater from where the bullet had entered, outlined with torn flesh with a glaze of fresh blood, yellowish pus, and somehow even some dirt.

He'd realized earlier that he wasn't going to bleed out, but the pain and immobility in his arm demanded attention. Every bump and scrape his shoulder had taken was further inflaming the injury, and he worried it was digging the bullet in deeper.

He stuck the base of the flashlight in his mouth and pulled the first aid kit onto his lap, unzipping it. He grabbed some packets of aspirin he'd seen earlier, along with the gauze, tape, ointment, and plastic boxes. He also arched his hips and pulled the ranger's flask from his pocket.

When he heard some rustling across the riverbed, his eyes widened and he pulled the pistol from the bag. He lifted his head to light up the bank. Two small eyes, low to the ground, reflected back at him. It was a small fox of some type, its oversized ears casting shadows behind it. The animal darted up the bank, glancing back over its shoulder before trotting off.

In one of the boxes, Sean found a pair of metal tweezers. Pliers would have been better, but he hadn't thought to search the SUV for a toolbox. He searched the bag and boxes for something to cut with, any type of blade. There wasn't one. There was, however, a shard of glass three inches long that had fallen inside from the Tahoe's window.

He dropped the flashlight onto the bag and tore open a couple of packets of aspirin, popping four pills into his mouth. He swallowed them whole. They'd kick in later, but for now all he could do to manage the pain was suffer through it. That or take a long swig of whatever was in the flask, like a movie cowboy from a bottle before some Old West doctor began digging around in his flesh.

But even in his current situation, Sean wasn't about to give up months of sobriety and self-work. As desperate as the circumstances were, the notion of submitting to such an impulse brought sickness to his stomach. He thought about Lisa and the soft look in her eyes back at her house when she understood that he was a changed man. He thought about her hand on his, back on the hill, and how he'd need his wits about him if he was going to get through the night and see her again.

He stuck the flashlight back in his mouth and unscrewed the flask's lid. He gave its contents a quick sniff. Whiskey. Biting down on the flashlight, he carefully poured it over his shoulder. He gasped from the burn, his body trembling until it started to ease.

The flask went to the ground and Sean retrieved the shard of glass. He couldn't remember the specifics of how such moments were handled on television shows, but he did recall a relevant anecdote that his father once told. He'd served in the US Army a few years before Vietnam, and sometimes spoke of a fellow soldier who'd accidentally shot himself in the forearm during an exercise. To spare himself disciplinary measures, as well as a good deal of embarrassment, he'd asked Zed to perform some field surgery to extract the bullet. It was a task his youthful, spirited father was not only up for but eager to take on.

"Two small cuts. Either side of the wound."

Those exact words from his father had managed to survive in Sean's head for over thirty years. There were more that had immediately followed, but Sean couldn't remember them. He repeated the former in his head as he glared at his wound, the tip of the sharp glass trembling just an inch away in his hand. As the wound glistened under the light from the alcohol, he repeated the words again. This time, their meaning stoked confusion.

"Is that two cuts on each side?" he mumbled unintelligibly with the flashlight in his mouth. "Or two total, with one on each side?" A third possibility quickly entered his mind: four cuts, each covering one side in the shape of a square. That one didn't make as much sense. "Fuck," he grunted in frustration.

Whichever technique he'd settle on, it occurred to him that once he spread the wound, the tweezers, which were much better suited for removing splinters, wouldn't be wide enough to grip the bullet.

He set down the glass and retrieved the tweezers, wedging his thumb between the tips and sliding it toward the base to spread the metal wider. With a sudden snap, one of the prongs broke off. It fell to the dirt beside him.

Sean froze, the other prong flopping out of his hand. His eyes lifted to the darkened sky. His arms shook and his hands tightened into fists. He wanted to curse God, and may have if there wasn't a chance the wrong people might hear him.

Gritting his teeth and nearly biting the flashlight in half, he chucked the glass and grabbed the tube of ointment, squeezing it onto the center of the wound before dumping the rest to the ground, and grabbing the gauze. He ripped the square gauze from its package and slapped it to his wound with a grunt. He then dropped the flashlight back to his lap and tore into the tape with his teeth. He yanked a long strip off the spool and then wrapped it over the gauze and around his arm twice.

Spitting out the spool, he leaned forward and worked on controlling his breathing. "I can only control how *I* act."

He pulled the map from his bag and shoved everything else that he could conceivably still use inside. He unfolded the map and positioned it in his lap. With the help of the flashlight, Sean confirmed that there was only one main road traveling north and south within the area, with some short offshoots and a couple of small lots. He looked for bridge symbols, finding only a couple. The only one along a long stretch of straight road was about three miles north of the south entrance, according to the scale. The north entrance was much farther away, and there was nothing but rocks and hills to the east and west. The decision was easy.

He lassoed the bag's straps over his shoulder. It wasn't until he staggered forward and picked himself up off the dirt that he felt the pain return to his feet and shin. They could have used attention too, but he'd wasted enough time.

He turned off his flashlight but kept it in his hand as he climbed up the bank and back onto level land. He continued south, the direction he was headed in until he'd had to ditch the vehicle. He kept his eyes on where he believed the road was, ready to drop down low the moment he saw light or movement.

A cold breeze pushed against him as his body ached and his mind wandered. Thinking of his father had brought back other memories from his past. He recalled, as a child, getting lost in the Colorado mountains while hunting for Bigfoot, a journey inspired by a PBS special on the mythological creature. It was his father who'd found him hours later in the middle of the night, deep in the forest in a rainstorm, shivering with a toy bow over his shoulder as he clung to a rotted pine.

Up until that point, it had been the worst day of Sean's life. He'd had many since. From each of them, he believed he'd ultimately grown stronger, even if it had sometimes taken a while to recognize such. He hoped the same would be true this time, but it was a tough outcome to imagine with Lisa still missing.

Guilt and more second-guessing pried their way into his thoughts. Maybe he should have never told her to cross to the other side of the mountain. Maybe he should have insisted that she stay put with Hannah behind the rocks while he led the others away. *Would that have even worked?* Sean didn't know the answer.

Lisa was tough, far tougher than probably even she realized. He saw it in the way she'd dealt with what happened to her husband. He saw it in the way she used to stand up to Sean himself, getting in his face when he'd sell himself short or portray himself as a victim. He saw it in the way she eventually left him.

Sean had made a lot of mistakes in his life, but chasing her away was near the top of the list—a regret he still hadn't moved on from. He hadn't had a meaningful relationship with a woman since, and he sometimes wondered if he ever would.

Back when Sean was twelve or so, when he still knew his father Zed as an uncle, Zed would tease him about how "good looking" he was—how he'd be a "lady killer" one day, and how he'd have to beat women off him with a broom. He'd say it with a smile and one of those long toothpicks angled out of the corner of his mouth. The remark would crack a grin from Sean too—lifting up a face that exhibited few grins. Sean's lips curled from the memory.

He wished his father could have met Lisa, and she him. *They'd have liked each other.* The two had consumed more of Sean's thoughts over the past couple of years than anyone . . . usually when he was home alone at night, unable to sleep, with nothing but those thoughts to keep him company.

"Two small cuts," Sean mumbled. "Either side of the wound."

A gust of wind narrowed Sean's eyes and brought a chill up his back. In the distance, he heard a clamor of coyotes, howling and singing for a moment. They were well to the west, and Sean knew from growing up in Colorado that the racket was mostly harmless, not the celebration of a kill as was a popular misconception. He also knew that coyotes very rarely attack humans, which brought him ease in regard to Lisa. It was the other predators he mostly worried about—the human kind.

He walked for what felt like a mile, sometimes stumbling over unseen rocks and snagging his pant legs on brush. It wasn't smooth traveling, but he was he making decent progress. He'd grown almost indifferent to the pain, though at no point did it leave.

For a few seconds, he thought he heard a buzzing noise in the distance, almost as if someone far away was cutting wood with a chainsaw. But it soon went away and Sean wondered if he had just imagined it.

When his arm bounced off some tall brush, and he had some physical cover from the road, he took a moment to stop and relieve himself. It wasn't easy with one hand, but he managed. He zipped back up and continued on.

The wind was slowly picking up, the breeze turning to prolonged gusts. He hadn't a clue what time it was. He felt as if he could see more of the landscape around him than was the case earlier. He couldn't imagine it was the mark of the beginning of a new day—not yet. More likely, with the benefit of not being chased for a little while, his eyes had just grown more accustomed to the dark.

His gaze aimed southeast where it remained a challenge to keep track of the road. He saw what he thought was a mile marker, or maybe just a reflector of some type sticking up from the shoulder. It was his only guide for a while as he kept his distance, steadily moving south. The wind grew stronger and colder. He could see his breath. Ahead, some tumbleweeds cartwheeled across the land. Each time, the movement would tighten his stomach before his eyes would catch up and lessen his anxiety. It became a more frequent exercise as the scrub grew thinner, fewer obstacles to block rolling weeds' momentum.

He had just about convinced himself that Montoya had left the land and was long gone when the wind lessened, and he sensed a murmur in the air. He stopped. Seeing nothing ahead, he glanced behind him before returning his gaze to the road. Faint lights rose above a small ridge. Sean went to his knees immediately, dropping his bag off his shoulder to the ground. His shoved his flashlight in his pocket and retrieved his gun. There wasn't much of anything to take cover behind, so he went low to his chest, wincing as he turned to his side to take some pressure off his shoulder.

More lights appeared. They formed the familiar pattern that decorated Montoya's vehicle. He was back.

Chapter 36

"You got a number?" asked Lumbergh. "On the display?"

"*Unknown*," Holman read aloud. She turned to Corbett. "We're not set up to trace this."

"He's probably already tried his other guy's phone," said Corbett. "If no one picks up, he's going to know something's happened to his boy."

"Is that a bad thing?" asked Lumbergh, drawing the attention of both of them.

"It is if we hope to catch him," said Holman. "This is the only location we've got on him. He'll never come back here if he knows we've found this place—if he knows that we snatched up his son."

"He'll figure that out if no one answers too, and then he'll stop calling," said Lumbergh. "Listen, he's not going to let that thing ring many more times. Let me talk to him. I've done research on this guy. I know things about him. I can get somewhere with him. We don't have much else to go on."

Holman and Corbett exchanged glances.

"Please. He's going to hang up."

Holman bit her lip and handed the phone to Lumbergh. He winced from the pressure on his burn but managed to press the "Talk" button. Raising the phone to his ear, he said nothing at first, only listening. There was a loud rattle of what sounded like metal, and some rustling in the background. It was accompanied by Spanish chatter. The voices all belonged to men. They were overtaken a second later by a lengthy screech of what sounded like a car's brake.

"Hugo?" came Montoya's deep voice. It had taken him a second to realize the call had been picked up.

Lumbergh looked at the detectives. He nodded his head, drawing them in closer. He waited a couple of seconds, listening and hoping to hear something helpful. "Si," he finally said, sensing suspicion on the other end.

It would have been a miracle if his voice convincingly passed for Montoya's son, but the objective was to draw out the call as long as possible in hopes of gaining a clue as to Montoya's location. For a few seconds, all Lumbergh heard was more rattling.

"*Aquí!*" a man abruptly shouted in the background. The voice didn't belong to Montoya. "*El coche!*"

The audio was quickly muffled. It sounded as if Montoya had put his hand over the phone. He said something else, but it was unintelligible, directed away from the phone. What sounded like howling wind and the slam of a car door was followed by silence.

"That you, Lumbergh?" came Montoya's voice.

Lumbergh's eyes narrowed. "Yeah," he said. "It is."

"I take it you have my men in custody?"

"Your *men?*" answered Lumbergh. "That's kind of an impersonal way of saying it, isn't it?"

A few seconds floated by before Montoya chuckled. "So . . . You know that one of them is my son."

"Well . . ." said Lumbergh, putting on his best performance to sound confident. "He's kind of a chatterbox. Not the calm, collective type like his old man."

After a few seconds, Montoya responded. *"Calm and collective* is what's kept you alive for the last two years, *marranito*. It's kept your tall wife happy and your little girl growing up with a father. It's let the good people of Winston go to bed at night with a warm feeling in their bellies, with their fearless police chief on patrol. You should be thanking me."

Lumbergh's stomach tightened. He quickly covered the phone with his other hand, fighting past the pain it drew from his burn. He quietly rattled off his home phone number to Holman, asking that she call his wife and office back in Winston. "They need to be moved to a motel until further notice, right away, under guard," he added, speaking of his wife and daughter.

Holman nodded and moved away from him, digging into her pocket.

Lumbergh didn't know how far of a reach Montoya had in the states, but after hearing the details of his family life described to him over the phone in eerie detail, he wasn't going to take any chances. He let some air escape his lips, composing himself before uncovering the phone. "It sounds like I've been living rent-free in your head for a while."

"Not free," said Montoya. "There'll be a price to pay."

"Why don't we talk about *your* family for a minute?" said Lumbergh. "In case you've forgotten, we have your son. By the way, I'm sure he'd be touched to know that you haven't bothered to ask how he's doing."

"Do you still need me?" Jacobs mouthed to Corbett.

Corbett nodded, pulling him aside.

On the other end of the phone, Montoya sighed. "If the police are there, he's already under medical care. Probably on his way to an emergency room right now. American law officers are so sweet that way. Much more humane than those Mexican pricks. And if Hugo had told you anything, you would not have felt so desperate as to answer his phone and pretend to be him. You wouldn't be engaging in this friendly little chat, trying to figure out where your brother-in-law is."

Lumbergh glanced at Corbett. He was still occupied with Jacobs. A dozen feet away, Holman had gotten through to someone on the phone, hopefully Diana.

"Well, I know a few things," Lumbergh said to Montoya, lowering his voice. "I know that *you* don't know where Sean is either. And that doesn't bode well for that *restitution* you're after."

Restitution was the term Rizzo had used in his phone call to Montoya—the word he'd relied on to get Montoya to take his call. Though Lumbergh didn't know the context of "Kimble's money," as Rizzo had described it before Montoya corrected him, he hoped it would push the right buttons. The silence on the other end suggested that it had. All that remained was the wind and the rattling. He could only imagine the amount of uncertainty bouncing off the inside of Montoya's head as he worked to reconcile how Lumbergh knew as much as he did.

"What do you know about that?" said Montoya, his voice steady.

Holman held a thumb up to Lumbergh as she continued her phone conversation, signifying that his family was okay and were being taken care of. Lumbergh's lips curled as he nodded back.

Lumbergh lowered his voice and quickly walked away from the others, his footsteps soft in his socks. His lips moved quickly. "I know that Sean's not the best way of getting to that money. You think he had the smarts to pull this off himself—a fucking security guard? The guy can't even read a book without moving his lips. That quarter of a million was to keep him happy and quiet. I've got the rest of Kimble's money, and since we both know that *I'm* the guy you *really* want, I'd say I have some bargaining chips."

After a couple of seconds, Montoya said, "You're full of shit, Lumbergh."

Lumbergh reached into his pocket, cringing as he pulled out Dusty's cell phone. "Shit is what you've got right now. I'm offering to change that if you call off the search for Sean and meet me. Understand?" He read the phone number off the sticker on Dusty's phone. "If you want me and the money, call that number in fifteen minutes so I can assure our conversation will be private."

Lumbergh repeated the number and hung up.

Chapter 37

It had been about fifteen minutes since Montoya's Bronco had passed by, engine loudly rattling but the vehicle moving slowly and steadily without event. The men inside had assuredly strained their eyes through the vehicle's windows, their flashlight beams gliding across the terrain, hoping to catch a glimpse of him or the SUV. But Sean had put plenty of distance between himself and the road. Even with minimal cover, just lying flat on the ground in his soiled clothes was enough to provide ample camouflage. He could no longer see the Bronco's taillights to the north.

If they hadn't found the Tahoe yet, they soon would. Of that, Sean was sure. They'd only missed it the first time because they were moving fast and driving on the opposite side of the road. Neither would be the case upon their return. From there, they'd look for his tracks in the dirt and try to figure out which way he'd gone on foot. Though he'd stepped on as many rocks as he could to avoid leaving a trail, there was no guarantee it would work. Still, he'd have a good head start on anyone trying to come after him on foot.

He estimated that he'd walked almost two miles from the riverbed, maybe a bit less. That meant roughly one mile to go. He wasn't expecting much just inside the gate, maybe just a single-man station for collecting entrance fees. No one would be on duty at that hour, but if there were a phone inside, that's all he'd need.

Every ten seconds or so, he'd glance over his shoulder, watching for lights. Even if Montoya and his men weren't able to track Sean, they might surmise that he was moving in the same direction as before. But none were to be seen, so he pushed on.

His shoulder was no longer numb. It seemed that changing the dressing back at the riverbed had alleviated whatever friction or pressure was causing it. The downside was the pain, though it had lost some of its bite, probably from the meds he'd taken.

After twenty minutes, he crossed a short ridge and spotted a weak orange light in the distance. It was pointing down from what looked to be a wooden post. A small section of pavement was lit up beneath it. He cautiously drew closer, stumbling a couple of times but collecting himself as he worked his way down the ridge. There were no vehicles and no people, at least that he could see.

A stop sign came into view just beyond the streetlight. The back of a much larger wooden sign was beside it. He almost didn't see the fence, as it was much different than he had pictured, no more than five feet tall, made out of rustic wooden posts that spread out in both directions from the road. He followed it to the west with his eyes, brows arching when he spotted the contour of what appeared to be a small metal shed.

The long gate in front of the road looked to be made of metal. It was no taller than the fence and appeared as though it opened and closed on a single set of hinges. It was likely secured with nothing more than a padlock and chain, but that's all it would have taken to let Montoya know that Sean had never made it that far in the Tahoe.

Sean crept closer to the gate, gun in hand, his body low. No other structures were visible until he spotted what looked like the overhang of a roof on the other side of the larger sign. It was a fee or information station of some kind, as Sean had hoped to find. Though he didn't see a telephone wire, that didn't mean there wasn't some means of communication inside it, even if it was just a radio.

A flash of light in the corner of Sean's eye drew his attention to the north. Lights appeared in the distance along the road, their, pattern consistent with the Bronco. It was returning, traveling fast. Sean changed course, returning some distance between himself and the road. He found some low-lying sagebrush and ducked around it, licking his dry lips as he watched the vehicle move closer, along with the rattle of its engine.

Whatever traces Montoya and his men found of Sean after he'd left the Tahoe had led them back, or so it seemed.

The Bronco slowed as it approached the gate, about two hundred feet away from Sean. Its brakes squeaked and body rattled. It halted in front of the stop sign. Sean's heart stopped when the remaining headlight lit up a figure with a rifle stepping out of the small station, wooden door pounding shut behind him. Montoya had left one of his men at the gate. If Sean had snuck up to the station in search of a phone or radio, he would have been greeted with semi-automatic fire.

Two other men piled out of the bashed-up Bronco, dents in the vehicle's backside and part of the grill caved in. Their rifles pointed down as they approached their companion. Montoya stood taller than the others, limping as he approached his lookout from the other side of the Bronco. The two spoke in Spanish, their demeanor surprisingly casual. Sean recognized the other man's voice. It was Hector, from back at the solar farm. If the two believed Sean was somewhere in the vicinity, possibly even watching them, they sure weren't acting like it.

Sean could see four in total, though it was possible someone was still in the Bronco. Montoya and Hector broke off from the other two, one of whom appeared to be lighting a cigarette. They walked up to the gate, and a few seconds later, there was a metal clink of chain links grinding against each other. It was followed by what sounded like a metal spring being released. The gate popped open wide. There must have been a key to the lock inside the station. Montoya spoke more with his lookout, his voice rising at times but still unintelligible.

The other men chatted, one handing his lit cigarette to the other. It didn't make sense to Sean how carefree they appeared, confident even. It was as if the last few hours had never happened. *What had changed?*

Sean's heart sank when he wondered if they had found Lisa. *Are she and Hannah being held in the Bronco? Is Montoya's next move to use them to lure me out, like with the ranger?*

He turned to the Bronco, listening carefully as he watched for any kind of movement from the vehicle. All he heard was the men talking. The cab didn't look to bobble an inch.

Montoya limped back to the vehicle as Hector subtly reentered the station; the door closed softly behind him. The other two peeled off, one tossing his cigarette to the ground as they climbed back inside the Bronco. Montoya didn't join them at first. Instead, he gazed down the stretch of road he'd just driven in on, the vehicle's lights casting his long shadow through the open gate. He just stood there, for a good fifteen or twenty seconds, before Sean heard what sounded like a deep chuckle over the wind and engine's rattle.

Sean's face tightened as Montoya shook his head and returned to his vehicle. He slid inside, put it in gear, and drove forward through the open gate. The noise from the engine grew fainter as his lights followed the road around a bend. They soon disappeared and the night was as dark and calm as it had been just a few minutes earlier.

It was foolish to conclude that Montoya had given up, especially with the amount of time he'd invested in Sean. Leaving a man behind assured that he hadn't. Still, he and his other men were gone.

Sean knew he could easily avoid Hector's attention. All he had to do was discreetly continue south, slide through the fence, and follow the road from a distance until it eventually reached a highway or the interstate. It would take some time, but with the men seemingly no longer on his heels, he could do so safely.

It was tempting, and the Big Nudge couldn't have offered him a better opportunity, but the situation wasn't sitting well with Sean. He needed to know what had changed. He needed to know if Montoya had Lisa and Hannah. It was important for him to understand why the search had been abandoned. And a man who had all of those answers was hiding out in a little park station just two hundred feet away. So was a possible means of communication to the outside world.

Sean waited a couple of minutes, scanning the area as best he could. Hector stayed inside, and it didn't appear anyone was returning. Sean took in a deep breath and let his bag slide off his shoulder to the ground. He didn't want it to get in the way for what he had to do. Gun still drawn, he kept low and carefully made his way closer to the road. Once the entrance sign was between him and the station, he made a beeline for it, hobbling a bit from the pain in his feet. The sign had obscured his earlier view of the small building, and it would do the same for him as he drew in closer to Hector.

The nearer he got, the more he worried the lamp above would cast his shadow along the ground and alert Hector. When he was close enough to see that the station's wall facing away from the road was solid wood from top to bottom, he scurried to the right and took up a position behind it. A half second later, his heart froze when he heard its door swing open.

He winced and took a step back, raising his gun and ready to pull the trigger the moment Hector swung his body around toward him. But that didn't happen. Instead Sean heard steady footsteps along gravel and dirt, heading in the other direction. When he saw Hector's shadow appear on the road, he steadily moved to his left to keep the station between the two of them.

Hector grumbled under his breath, his pace sounding so nonchalant that Sean was convinced the thug hadn't a clue he was there. Sean continued stepping to the left, moving in a half circle to stay out of sight behind the station.

Hector cleared his throat then stopped. When Sean heard a zipper, and what sounded like fluid streaming into hollow metal, he squared his jaw and peered around the corner of the station. He saw the outline of Hector's body, standing less than twenty feet away with his legs spread in front of the gate's metal post, relieving himself. The stock of his rifle was pinned between his forearm and ribcage. Hector was making things easy, but having learned from last time, Sean wasn't going to cut him any slack.

Arms straight, Sean lowered his aim, closing an eye and firing two rounds, one into each of Hector's thighs. Hector cried out above the shots' echoes that still filled the air. His rifle dropped to the ground and bounced to the side as he buckled forward into the post. Sean moved in and kicked the rifle across the dirt, watching Hector's chest and shoulder slide down the wet pole as he collapsed forward.

Hector howled, rolling to his back. His hands went to the back of his legs.

"Hands in the air!" Sean ordered, his voice sending another jolt through Hector.

Hector moaned, his hands bouncing back and forth from his legs to the air above his chest.

"Wait . . ." he barked confusingly, head shifting as he struggled to absorb what was happening.

"Now!"

"I'll bleed out!" he screamed, "P-please!" He was making a case for letting him put pressure on his wounds.

"No!" shouted Sean. "None of you fuckers gave that lady ranger a time-out! Now get on over here into the light." He motioned Hector with his wrist.

"I . . . I . . . can't," he whimpered. "You shot me!"

"In the legs, cupcake." Sean said dismissively. "You can crawl. Get started."

Hector was on the verge of sobbing as he rolled to his side and then his stomach. He dug his elbows into the dirt and pulled himself along the ground, knees helping only a little as he worked his way onto the road. Sean walked steadily behind him, gun pointed between his shoulder blades.

"That's it, Hector," he said tauntingly.

The road lamp lit up more of him, giving Sean a better look at his body. He had short dark hair and an undersized jean jacket that rode up so high on his body that Sean could see he had no side holster, nor even a bulge in his clothes suggesting a handgun.

Sean stepped forward and pushed him onto his back with is foot. Hector grunted as he flopped onto his back, hands going back under his legs for his thighs. Sean saw no weapons on the front of him either. The rifle must have been it.

"Why don't you just go!" shouted Hector, his voice trembling. "Now's your chance! Just go!"

"Where's Lisa and the kid?" asked Sean.

Hector's face tightened, his eyes thinning. "What?"

Sean stared at him. The puzzlement in his glare appeared genuine.

"Don't fuck with me," Sean said, extending his pistol to make sure.

"No!" said Hector, his voice jumping an octave as his hand went in the air. "We don't have them! We thought you hid them somewhere! Montoya was pissed!"

Sean pushed air out through his nose, holding his glare on Hector. "Where did the others go just now? Why did they leave?"

Hector said nothing, his chest moving in and out as he drew deep breaths.

"You want me to mess up your arms too, asshole?" asked Sean, straightening his aim. "Because I've got plenty of bullets to spare."

"No!"

"No what? No, you don't care about your arms? Let's find out." Sean walked in close, leaning forward and training his pistol on Hector's bicep.

"He'll kill me!" screamed Hector, arms defensively in front of his face.

"*I'll* kill you!" Sean shouted back. "That's what your other buddy back down the road chose! To die for your guys' boss! Is he really worth it?"

Hector whimpered, his arms still covering his face. His body shook. Blood trickled onto the pavement beneath him.

"I guess he is," Sean said coldly, pulling back the hammer on his revolver. "Let's get started."

"He's going to meet Lumbergh!" Hector shouted, body tightening.

"What?" Sean asked, taking a step back.

"They're meeting! They talked on the phone and they're going to meet!"

A dozen questions rushed through Sean's mind as he digested Hector's words. Until that moment, he wasn't sure that Lumbergh even had any clue of what was happening. All he knew was that his brother-in-law had somehow shot Montoya's son.

"Does Lumbergh know where I am?"

Hector shook his head.

"Why are they meeting?"

"To . . . negotiate," answered Hector, his voice turning raspy. "For you. For the money."

Sean's face recoiled. *The money?* There was no reasoning with a man like Montoya. No room for negotiation. If the two really were meeting, it would only be used as an opportunity for Montoya to kill Lumbergh. Sean knew that Lumbergh had to know that, and wondered what kind of angle his brother-in-law was playing. Whatever it was, Lumbergh had likely bitten off more than he could chew.

Sean glanced at the station behind him. There was a plexiglass window at its front with sticky notes plastered to its inside toward the bottom. He backed up toward it, keeping his eyes on Hector. He pulled the door open with a couple of fingers before sliding his foot inside to keep it propped. He searched for a light switch, flipping it on once he found it.

He took his eyes off Hector just long enough to glance over a small podium where paperwork, a stack of maps, keys, and lots of pens and pencils rested. On top of them was a short key on a ring, its head made of hard black plastic. He looked back at Hector before following a curly cord from just below the podium to the floor. In front of the chair inside lay a small CB radio smashed to pieces.

"Son of a bitch," said Sean, returning his focus to Hector.

"He told me to!" Hector asserted. "Didn't want you using it to call out! In case you came this way!"

Above the chair, Sean noticed a couple of green windbreakers hanging on a hook on the wall. One was much larger than the other. He let the door close and returned to Hector.

"Why did he leave you here?" asked Sean. "To keep an eye out for me?"

Hector didn't reply at first. When Sean took a step closer, he said, "Yeah! We didn't know which way you went, but he thought maybe I'd get lucky."

"Do you feel lucky?" asked Sean.

Hector didn't answer.

"*Then* what?" Sean pressed.

Hector glared back. "Then . . . I would kill you."

Sean nodded. "Bummer that things didn't work out for you, Hector. But I know your heart was in the right place, even though Mother Nature called and loused things up."

Hector glanced to the side, saying nothing.

"Where are they going to meet—Montoya and Lumbergh?" asked Sean.

"I don't know," said Hector. "He didn't tell me."

"Bullshit," said Sean, raising his gun again.

"He didn't! I swear!" yelled Hector, backing up on his elbows. "I was just supposed to meet them . . ." Hector stopped himself, his eyes quickly sobering.

"Meet them?" Sean said. "How?"

He panned the area around the gate again, looking for an automobile he might have missed from the ridge. Seeing nothing, he peered over his shoulder to the west, past the station. The only thing visible was the shed he'd seen before. He suddenly remembered the buzzing sound he'd heard on his way there. At the time, it had sounded like a chainsaw. A different explanation soon came to mind, supported by the key he'd seen in the station a minute earlier. Its black head was the tip-off.

"You guys found a motorcycle over in that shed, didn't you?"

Chapter 38

Was this a dream or some distant memory? Either way, the image of a dark-haired, brown-eyed boy in shorts and a white T-shirt drew the man in closer. The sun above was bright and dazzling. The man felt its warmth on his face and chest as he chased the boy through a field of tall, flowing wheat. Everything was gold in color except for the two, though the boy exuded an unmistakable gleam that outlined his small body. The boy laughed and urged his pursuer forward with his hand.

Running through the tall grass that nearly came up to his chin, the boy wore a smile almost as bright as the sun itself. His giggle grew louder; more jovial as the man's arms, freckled and hairy, reached for him. The boy playfully swatted them away, a reflection bouncing off a gold wedding band on the man's finger.

The boy continued running, but the man suddenly found himself unable to keep up; his chest tight and his breath leaving his body. He stumbled through the grass over clumps of white sand that weren't there a second earlier. When he raised his head, the boy was far ahead—at least fifty yards, running with his back turned.

The man collapsed to his knees. They sank into the sand as he cupped his hand to his mouth and yelled, "Victor!"

The boy stopped, his head spinning around to meet his

father's gaze. The boy's thin eyebrows furrowed in concern, but when his father called his name again, the smile returned.

"Bye, Pops!" his tart voice echoed. He raised his arm and waved. Then he turned and ran deeper into the field.

"Victor!" the father shouted one last time. He suddenly couldn't breathe. His eyes bulged and he gasped for air, letting out a sick cough from the dust that filled his mouth.

The field was gone. In its place was a dim sky. The faint outlines of sparse clouds floated above. A cold, whistling wind rushed across his face. His chest burned and he turned to his side. Something cracked beneath him as he let out another cough that shot more pain to his chest.

He felt something under his shoulder, and when he reached for it, he found his glasses. He pulled them in front of his face. Both lenses were cracked and a temple had snapped off. Still, he managed to drape them over his nose and rotate onto his elbows.

Before him was the lifeless arm of his son, the edge of his jacket sleeve flapping around in the wind. Blood stained the rocks beneath him. He closed his welling eyes over the body and groaned in sorrow. He sounded like an injured animal, the wind spreading his grief across the desert.

Rizzo pulled his knees in and slowly rose up, his joints grinding. His trembling hands went to his own chest where his dust-covered fingers found two small holes sliced into his jacket. He grunted and pulled at them, enlarging the holes into one before moving up to his zipper and sliding the jacket open. He lowered his head, his neck aching as he glared through the large tear at a small piece of metal surrounded by some shredded cloth from his protective vest. The other bullet had to be lodged in there somewhere too. Otherwise, he'd be dead.

The night before, his son had grabbed the bulletproof armor

as the two rushed out the door. Speeding toward Lisa Kimble's house, with a quick stop at a drug store after the two decided they would need masks, he'd pressed his father to put it on. It had been a gimmick purchase months earlier, mostly for grins. Victor Jr. had picked it up at a gun show downtown. The father didn't think for a second either of them would actually need it that night. He figured the chances of Sean Coleman bringing a firearm to a meetup with his old girlfriend were pretty slim, but because he wanted his son focused on the task at hand instead of his father's safety, he'd given in.

"Under your jacket, Pops," his son had told him. "You don't want him aiming at your face instead."

It was his son's persistence that had spared his life, not from Coleman but Montoya. He only wished, at that very moment, that it was his son who'd been wearing the vest. Victor Jr. had had many years ahead of him, or at least he should have. His father, on the other hand, was near the end of his journey. He'd had a long, albeit not always honorable, life. He'd made plenty of bad decisions, all kinds of mistakes, but the one thing he never regretted was marrying his son's mother. He'd loved her, from the day she said "I will" to the day she lost her long battle with cancer. He also loved his son, far more than he ever managed to express with words. As he knelt on the gravel, his gaze panning across the desert horizon to the north, the withholding of those three words filled him with remorse. *I love you.*

He leaned over his son, tracing his dead eyes that he soon put to rest with the brush of his hand. Still, the words didn't come. Instead he said, "I'm sorry."

His body shook when something bumped against his ankle. His head spun to the left where he found the plastic Halloween mask he'd worn the night before. The ugly alien's face was dented in. He couldn't remember the character's name, but he wanted to. He wanted to hear his son's voice speak it once more.

The old man lifted his head toward the road they'd driven in on hours earlier. It ran parallel to the hill range west of Eldorado Canyon. Beyond it was Arizona. There was no traffic and the sun had yet to rise.

Montoya and his men were gone. Probably long gone. He didn't know if Coleman and Kimble had gotten away, and there wasn't much of him that cared.

Over his shoulder, he saw the van. Its side door was still open. He hoped the inside light hadn't drained the battery all the way down. He dug through Victor Jr.'s pockets before recalling his son tossing the keys over the fence to prevent Coleman and Kimble from leaving. The light above the payphone lit up some of the area. It would help him find the keys, though he had trouble picturing himself first climbing the fence and getting over the barbed wire to find them.

It was then that he remembered the bolt cutter, a tool of his trade. It was with some other items in a box in the back of the van. It would take a number of snips to pry open a hole in the fence. He just hoped he'd have the strength left to do it.

His will heartened him, and twenty minutes later he was crawling, out of breath, back out through the sharp metal mesh with the van's keys clenched in his fist.

His joints cracked as his body straightened. His shoulders low, he crossed in front of his van and closed its side door. That's when he heard a child's babble.

He gasped and spun around, reaching for his pistol. The sight of it pointed at his face from a few yards out reminded him that it had fallen from his grip when Montoya shot him.

Now it was being held by the hand of the woman he'd taken from her home several hours earlier.

Lisa was on a knee next to his son's body, her face and clothes dirty, her hair frazzled, and her boyfriend's child folded in her other arm. She said nothing, her body shivering as her chest pushed in and out. Dry blood outlined a knot on her forehead. The light above the phone exposed the intensity in her eyes. The child looked up at her, the tips of her fingers brushing against Lisa's soiled jaw.

He slowly raised his hands. "You have every right to pull the trigger," he said with little emotion in his voice. "Part of me even wants you to." He was half surprised she hadn't done it already. The girl in her arm may have been the only thing preventing it—a conscious decision by Lisa not to etch such imagery in the young child's mind.

Lisa offered no other clues, glaring back, not saying a word.

"If you're not going to do this," he continued. "I've got something I need to do . . . to make things right. And I need my van."

She shook her head, keeping him in the crosshairs. "No," she finally said, her voice hoarse. Hannah moved from playing with Lisa's face to twisting her hands in her hair.

Victor Sr. swallowed. "Listen, I'm going to slowly lower my left hand," he said, doing exactly that.

Lisa's arm straightened, her eyes growing larger in warning. "No."

"I promise I'm not going to hurt you," he said. "And I keep my promises."

Banking on the child's presence keeping him alive, he pushed his thin fingers into his pants pocket. Something inside jingled as he lifted them back out. He began dropping quarters onto the dirt beside him.

"For the phone," he explained. "Call the police. Call whoever else you want. You and the girl are safe now. My name is Victor Rizzo Sr. Tell them that. Tell them I'm the person who took you. My son was only doing what I told him to." His eyes went to his son's body. "He's not to blame. He's dead because of me."

Lisa remained still, jaw square as she kept her eyes pinned to him.

He thought about telling her that he had known her late husband once, years before she and Kyle had ever met. Years before Kyle had gotten tangled up with Moretti. But he didn't know how she'd take it in her current state, and he didn't want to press his luck. She'd find out soon enough.

"I'm going now," he said, keeping his hands in her view. He carefully walked to the front of the van and around it, a chill running up his spine when he left his back prone to her for a few seconds. "I'm sorry," he added before opening his door and climbing in.

Lisa's face tightened, her hand trembling. Her eyes bounced to Hannah for a second before returning to Rizzo.

He pushed the key into the ignition and cranked the engine. It turned hard but lit up. He flipped on the headlights and placed the vehicle in reverse. He gently pressed on the gas and reversed away from the phone and Lisa, stealing another glance at his son as he did. Lisa followed the van with her aim until he turned around in the dirt lot and moved forward back toward the highway.

In his rearview mirror he watched her slowly lower her gun and turn toward the payphone. He nodded, and then turned his eyes to his own reflection, sickened by the sight.

Chapter 39

His Glock reloaded and a couple of extra clips in his pocket, Lumbergh glared through the windshield of the speeding sedan. His face was taut as the vehicle exited off I-15, tires screeching with the merge onto a frontage road that ran parallel. Picking up speed again, he watched for the next road sign.

"You sure you're going to be able to fire that weapon?" asked Holman from the driver's seat, glancing in the mirror at the police cruiser, lights blazing, following closely behind them. A body-armor vest over her shirt came into view from a passing street lamp.

"Jacobs spotted me some Tylenol," said Lumbergh, a wet towel wrapped around ice between his bandaged fingers. He was wearing a similar vest.

"Oh, that ought to do it," Holman said dryly.

"I'll be fine," said Lumbergh. "Lucky for me, Jacobs also shares my shoe size." He glanced down at the white sneakers below his Dockers, one of them still stained with Montoya's son's blood.

Corbett spoke into his hand radio from the back seat, holding a cold compress similar to Lumbergh's against his shoulder under his jacket. Per Corbett's request back at the hangar, Jacobs had managed to pop his shoulder back in place. Holman insisted that Corbett stay back and rest, but her partner wouldn't have any of it.

"Okay, over and out," he said into the radio. He leaned forward. "The feds are almost at the north entrance. They'll shut down anyone who comes through that way. They'll also be sending a couple of cars south behind us, but they're farther out. May not get here in time."

Holman nodded.

"Here!" said Lumbergh, leaning forward and pointing through the windshield.

A brown-and-white sign on the left read, "Sloan Canyon National Conservation Area."

Lumbergh was convinced they had the right place. The lead began with Jacobs's account of hearing Montoya's man talk about "Highway 95" and "hills." Though the highway also picked up north of Las Vegas, its mountainous region fell along its route just south of Henderson, where Sean and Lisa had first been taken. It was a logical escape path if the Rizzos' goal was to get out of the city and get away from people long enough to meet up with Montoya and hand over their captives.

The three were already speeding down I-15, prepared to head east toward the 95 exit when Montoya called back on Dusty's phone, insisting that he and Lumbergh meet in thirty minutes in Sloan, a town about fifteen miles south of their location. The spot and timing didn't make sense if Montoya were still somewhere off 95. His pursuit of Sean had to have brought him west. Lumbergh assured Montoya that he would come alone, still playing the role of a crooked cop who'd gotten his hands on some of Vincenzo Moretti's fortune. But he planned on running into Montoya sooner than that . . . and with backup.

The land between the highway and interstate was mostly

made up of the conservation area, miles of rugged terrain with a single road leading in and out. A call to the area's local office had revealed that one of their rangers, looking into a report of gunfire in the southern region, hadn't reported back and wasn't answering her radio. The three police officers feared they knew why.

Already on route and with a head start that wouldn't be expected, the three believed that the best play was to stop Montoya and the people he was with before they ever reached Sloan or even the interstate. It would eliminate the chance of innocent bystanders being put in harm's way like back at the Dusty Nickel.

With Holman catching the feds up to speed, the north exit was being sealed off. Lumbergh, the detectives, and the two local officers in the cruiser behind them planned on doing the same with the south exit. Since it was miles closer to Sloan, it seemed the more likely route Montoya would take.

Holman followed the sign left onto a paved narrow road. The cruiser followed closely behind them. She pulled her radio to her lips and hailed the officer behind the wheel, telling him to turn off his emergency lights as to not announce their arrival. He complied.

"There's a chance Montoya and his crew already left the area," said Corbett, wincing as he pulled his shotgun onto his lap. He dropped his icepack to the floor.

"Possible but not probable," said Lumbergh, disposing of his ice as well. He carefully slid his hand around the grip of his gun, biting the inside of his lip from the pain it brought. "They were inside a stopped vehicle both times I talked to him. His guys were getting out the first time. They were climbing back in the second. Doors slammed. They weren't on the move, and we got here too fast for them to have gotten much farther."

"That's all assuming he didn't find another way out," said Holman.

"Off-road?" said Lumbergh.

Holman nodded.

"Maybe," said Lumbergh. "But if the terrain is as rough as you both say, and if his engine is in even half as bad of shape as it sounded over the phone, my guess is that he'll stick to the road."

The landscape around them grew more desolate as they drove, tall grass turning to rock and sparse scrub. Large orange rock formations emerged on the left, yards of broken shale at their base. The rocks grew in size as they drew closer.

A wooden sign sprouting out from gravel on the shoulder announced three more miles until they reached the natural area's entrance, but for all intents and purposes they had already entered no-man's land. Other than the modest road beneath them, there wasn't a sign of civilization anywhere.

"There!" Holman suddenly said, drawing both men's attention forward.

Staggered lights from a vehicle had appeared over a ridge, moving quickly toward them. Seconds later, its brake lights flared up at the rear. It seemed a reaction to the sight of approaching vehicles.

"Showtime," said Corbett, clenching his shotgun.

Lumbergh drew in a deep breath, squaring his jaw as he painfully clenched his gun.

Holman was back on her radio. "Okay, this could be our guy," she said. "Let's block the road and see if they come closer or try to turn back around."

She guided the steering wheel left, pressing on the brakes and slowing to a stop once the front of her car crossed onto the gravel shoulder. She put the vehicle in park.

Corbett held his radio to his mouth and reported the incoming vehicle to the federal officer he'd been talking to. He ended with, "About to engage the suspects."

"Chief?" Holman said, holding up a pack of gum.

Lumbergh pushed some air from his nose. He reached over and pulled out a stick. Two seconds later, the gum was taking a beating from his teeth.

The police cruiser flipped its emergency lights back on. Red and blue lit up the area around them, casting new shadows off rocks and sagebrush. The officer pulled the vehicle right, emulating Holman's position on the other side of the road. Only a couple of feet separated the cars' rear fenders.

The approaching vehicle continued to slow, but it hadn't stopped or changed directions. Only one of its headlights was working. The other lights were coming from its roof. Its driver and occupants were processing the situation. Holman opened her door, leaving it wide as she stepped out. Pistol in her hand, she quickly retreated behind the vehicle and joined the uniformed officers by their car. Lumbergh exited and jogged behind Holman's sedan. Corbett joined him from the other side.

The rattle of the approaching vehicle sent a chill up Lumbergh's spine. "It's him!" he said, hand cupped to his mouth. He went low behind the car, gun pointed straight over the angled trunk. "That's the engine I heard over the phone!"

The other four officers quickly followed suit, the two uniformed taking up a position behind their doors. The officer on the far side held a rifle. Corbett shuffled his way behind Holman's door on the driver's side.

"Light him up!" Holman shouted from behind the trunk of the cruiser.

The officer by the wheel switched on his spotlight and

aimed it at the vehicle. It was an eighties Ford Bronco, white in color like the one the airport security guard had described sometimes leaving and entering the grounds. The windshield above a smashed-in grill was heavily cracked and covered with dust. That along with its dark tint allowed only outlines inside to be seen. The large, broad-shouldered individual behind the wheel was likely Montoya. It was difficult to tell how many more were inside—at least one in the passenger seat and one sitting behind them.

Lumbergh kept his aim sharp, half expecting Montoya to slam on the brakes and then slip the Bronco into reverse. Instead he kept approaching, gradually slowing until he came to a stop less than eighty feet away. Lumbergh hoped it was a sign the men inside were confused and unsure of what to do, but he feared it meant boldness. There was almost no movement inside.

"Give me the radio," said Holman, leaving her position and moving up behind the officer at the spotlight.

He handed her his receiver. She brought it to her mouth over his shoulder, eyes pinned on the Bronco.

"Lautaro Montoya!" she shouted, her steady voice blaring through the cruiser's PA system. "We're with Las Vegas Metro! Carefully turn off your engine and come on out with your hands up! One at a time, and do it slowly!" She tossed the radio back onto the seat and again concentrated both hands on her pistol.

The Bronco's engine continued on, its eerie rattle heightening the already tense night air. Dust that floated by in a breeze between the vehicle's headlights was all that visibly moved.

"Shit or get off the pot," Corbett muttered under his breath. Seconds ticked by. Nothing happened.

"What next?" asked the officer on the far side of the cruiser. "Move in?"

"No," said Holman. "Stay put."

Above the noise from the engine, there was the subtle sound of a latch. The Bronco's cab shuffled a little.

"They're coming out," said an officer.

Lumbergh wasn't as confident. "Get out of the fucking car!" he yelled.

Before the words had even finished leaving his mouth, there was motion near the bottom of the splintered windshield. When Lumbergh saw an oversized muzzle, he yelled, "Gun!"

Deafening gunfire screamed through the windshield, shattering glass to pieces from inside the Bronco. Lumbergh and the others returned rounds, ducking lower as bullets tore through their vehicles. The firing from the Bronco was relentless, so rapid and steady that it had to be coming from an automatic. Other rifles joined in from the Bronco, sweeping back and forth across the police vehicles. They shredded metal and glass, sending debris crackling down around Lumbergh's body as he shuffled behind the car to find a better position.

They may not have been outnumbered, but they were grossly outgunned.

Lumbergh spun on his heels behind Holman's car. He popped his head up from the other side of its now missing window just long enough to see the passenger-side door on the Bronco pop open. He fired a couple of rounds into it, glass exploding before another sweep of return fire pinned him back down. His hands burned from his tight grip on his gun, but he wasn't about to loosen it.

One of the policemen to his right cried out. Lumbergh saw his body hit the pavement from under his car. In between a couple of blasts, Montoya shouted something to his men.

Lumbergh moved to his left to get closer to Corbett, who was still huddled on one knee behind the open door of the sedan. There was a blood spatter along the broken window above him. He had to have been shot but hadn't gone down.

A thin man with long dark hair slid out from the Bronco's passenger seat. Rifle in hand, he fired at the sedan as he sidestepped to the shoulder of the road. Lumbergh pointed his weapon but Corbett popped up between them, shoving his arms through his broken window to make it wider. He blasted and pumped away with his shotgun.

Montoya's man buckled violently backwards, his chest open and blood spraying before he collapsed to the pavement. Corbett lowered himself back down.

Another man immediately sprung out from the passenger side of the Bronco. Lumbergh lifted his arms back up, firing two shots over Corbett's shoulder. They didn't connect. The man, rifle in hand, disappeared behind the Bronco.

Holman shouted something. Lumbergh couldn't hear it over the gunfire, nor could he see her. Pops from someone's pistol launched a new volley of gunfire, this time centered on the police cruiser. Lumbergh crawled back the way he'd come, taking a couple of seconds to reload behind the sedan. Bullets bounced off the trunk above him as he slammed in his clip.

"He's coming!" he heard Holman yell.

Lumbergh lifted his head above the trunk. Montoya was limping toward the police cruiser with the boldness of a military tank. He held a huge rifle in front of his face, pointed toward Holman and the officer as they scrambled toward the rear of their vehicle. Lumbergh swung his arm over the sedan's trunk just as Montoya unloaded fire into the back of the uniformed officer.

The officer barked, blood spraying across the cruiser beside him. He stumbled forward over his own feet and crashed to the pavement. Holman tripped over his arms as he fell. She went down hard in front of him. Lumbergh fired at Montoya, his hands shaking. At least one bullet connected, slicing through Montoya's jacket near his ribs. Montoya swiveled his attention to Lumbergh, sending a new stream of bullets as he faltered to his left.

Lumbergh went back down, his eyes shifting to Holman as she squirmed free of the police officer's limbs. She broke loose and rolled closer to the car.

Montoya's man from the back of the Bronco jogged across the road, keeping on the heels of his boss. He fired his rifle at both police vehicles, swinging it back and forth indiscriminately and yelling obscenities.

Lumbergh went down low, peering under the sedan with his gun just as loud blasts rang out from his left. Bone and brain flew off the head of the man, bringing his yelling to an immediate halt. He stumbled around on random footing before crashing face-first to the pavement. Corbett had gotten him.

Montoya snarled, leaving Lumbergh's view as he crossed in front of the cruiser. He unloaded on Corbett's position, shouting in fury as metal popped and more glass broke. Lumbergh bobbed up, trying to line up a shot through the cruiser, but Montoya dropped off the road's shoulder on the other side.

Holman crawled across the pavement toward Lumbergh, eyes intense and breath heavy. He motioned her in, noticing blood on her shirt. He didn't know if it belonged to her or the officer on the ground next to her. Lumbergh held his aim above the cruiser's trunk to give her cover. He shoved her behind him and followed her, hunched over, back to the driver's side of the sedan.

There, Holman gasped at the sight of her longtime partner, lying motionless on the ground. She crawled to his side and reached for his neck to check his pulse. She found nothing but blood. Lumbergh peered over the open door above him, watching for anyone else exiting the Bronco. It appeared empty. There'd been three inside, total. Montoya was the last remaining.

Gunfire started up again, sparking off the pavement beneath them. Holman screamed, pistol falling from her hand as she fell to her side. Lumbergh's thigh buckled out from under him. He crashed to his back beside her. He gasped, heart racing as he felt for his wound. Montoya had fired underneath both of the police vehicles and tagged his remaining targets.

Holman searched for her gun as Lumbergh lifted his in the air. He was barely able to hold onto it, shifting his aim from the back to the front of the vehicle. He didn't know what direction Montoya would be coming from.

From the corner of his eye, he saw Holman rolling off the shoulder of the road, hands attending what looked like two separate wounds on her leg. Lumbergh gave her cover as best he could, sliding along the pavement across his backside as she spilled over the dirt and rock. Lumbergh positioned himself on the other side of Corbett's body, using the fallen detective as a shield against another low attack from Montoya. Corbett had given his life for his colleagues, taking out both of Montoya's men. In death, he was still protecting a fellow officer, and Lumbergh knew it was what he would have wanted.

"How are things feeling over there, *marranito*?" came Montoya's voice with heavy breath, echoing off the land. "I must admit to underestimating you. Even with all the superhero bullshit down south, I figured that in the end, you were just some hillbilly who got off a lucky shot that day."

Montoya sounded stationary. He probably wasn't back on the road yet. Lumbergh figured he was either reloading or switching weapons . . . otherwise, he'd still be shooting instead of talking. He was buying time.

Lumbergh twisted his head over Corbett's chest, looking for his shotgun with no luck.

"But you took out my men at the hotel," Montoya continued. "You found my son. Then you found me. Maybe there's a little truth to the folk-hero tale of Chief Gary Lumbergh."

Lumbergh said nothing, feeling along the ground. If Montoya was arming back up, he needed to do the same. The shotgun missing, he shoved his hand under Corbett, looking for his handgun. He found the detective's radio instead, but it was a mishmash of wires and broken plastic.

When something flashed out of the corner his eye, Lumbergh peered across the shoulder beside the road. In the dark he made out Holman hunched down behind some sagebrush, one leg out straight behind her and the other pulled in against her chest. She held Corbett's shotgun in her hands. It must have been knocked from his grip and fallen down the bank when he was shot.

Holman signaled Lumbergh with her hand in a spinning motion. She wanted him to lure Montoya back to the road, to draw his head up above the vehicles. Using Lumbergh as bait was a risky play, more so for her than him. The only cover she had was visual, and not even that was great. The brush wouldn't stop anything stronger than a light breeze.

"You still alive, Chief?" asked Montoya, responding to Lumbergh's silence. "I know you're a man of short stature, but I didn't think enough for me to sink in a head wound from underneath a car." He chuckled.

When Lumbergh found Corbett's pistol, he pried it from

his holster and checked its action. It was clean out of bullets. Lumbergh swore under his breath and dropped it. Then he propped himself back up against the open car door.

"The good thing about being short . . ." yelled Lumbergh, drawing in a breath. "When I shot your brother in the head, his brains flew high into the sky behind him. Like fucking fireworks. And it wasn't even the Fourth of July."

If that doesn't draw Montoya out, nothing will.

The Bronco was still running, its rattle challenging Lumbergh's focus as he listened. His body tensed up when he heard the scuff of pavement. He slid his aim back and forth between the open door to his right and the rear fender, unsure of Montoya's approach. When he saw Holman tense up, staring at the road, he knew Montoya was coming from the rear. Lumbergh held his gun steady just above the roof, his eyes shifting between it and Holman. He could see her breathing in the dark, waiting for her moment.

Holman suddenly lunged to a knee. Teeth clenched, she swung the shotgun horizontal, pumping it and pulling the trigger. Nothing happened. Her eyes shot wide. Two bullets fired from the other direction. Holman's body flew backwards, legs swinging in the air before she crashed to the dirt and rock behind her.

A buzzing noise held in the air as Lumbergh gasped and swung his arm up. He fired through the back window, working only on trajectory. He unloaded his clip. His heart punished his chest as he shoved his hand into his pocket for his last one. A quick whistle drew his attention back to the rear of the car. Standing above him was the towering frame of Lautaro Montoya, large pistol drawn and pointed directly at him.

The buzzing continued as the Bronco's lights lit up

Montoya's large teeth below sunken eyes. He wore a grin that grew wider with each passing second.

"Oops," Montoya said.

Lumbergh glared back, saying nothing. His mind was firing on blanks until it latched onto images of his wife and daughter. The buzzing grew louder and sharper, taunting Lumbergh. When Montoya lifted his eyes to the road, Lumbergh realized he could hear it too.

Montoya's face lit up brighter, another beam of light joining the Bronco's. It cast a longer shadow behind him, forming an almost spiritual presence. His grin remained as he lifted an arm, motioning someone closer. It had to be another of his men, perhaps from the park, showing up to assist; a late arrival.

Montoya's head twisted toward Lumbergh, but his eyes were quickly pulled back to the road. His grin faded. Loud pops rang out. Something whizzed through the air. Projectiles battered Montoya's upper body, hitting his shoulder and chest and sending dust and shredded clothing through the air. He grunted, stumbling backwards. His gun fell to the road. The buzzing consumed everything.

Chapter 40

Sean fired his pistol until he was out. He dropped it to the road and shoved his fingers back around the motorcycle's handgrip, drawing it straight again. The windbreaker he'd taken from the ranger station formed a bubble at his back from the speed.

He knew he'd hit Montoya. He'd seen the gun fall from his hand and the way his body lumbered backwards. But the man wasn't done. Sean watched him scuttle to the other side of the police cruiser, limping with his arm folded across his chest.

The Bronco's headlights revealed carnage along the bloodstained road. Multiple bodies, at least one belonging to a uniformed police officer. Shot-up vehicles. Glass everywhere. Sean didn't know how things had gone down, but the gunfire he'd heard and the flashes he'd seen in the distance as he drew closer made it clear that Montoya and his men had met police resistance.

Sean veered to the right side of the Bronco, the old Honda dirt bike skidding to a stop on the shoulder just in front of another body. It was one of Montoya's men—the one he'd seen smoking earlier. The man's eyes were wide and lifeless under the cycle's lamp. With the Bronco between him and Montoya, Sean swung himself off the cycle. As it fell to the side, Sean pulled Hector's rifle from where he'd wedged it between the cycle's fork and front fender. The Honda toppled into the ditch and into the shoulder. Sean kept low, moving behind the Bronco's front wheel.

He'd seen jeans and cowboy boots on a body on the other side of the Bronco. It was likely Montoya's other man from back at the station. It seemed Montoya was now on his own, but he probably wasn't the last person alive. He had pinned someone down on the other side of the sedan when Sean had begun firing.

"Whoever's on the motorcycle . . ." came a familiar voice from beside the sedan. "Stay where you are! This is a police situation!"

"Yeah, no shit!" Sean shouted back, his eyes shifting between the sedan and cruiser.

"Sean?"

"Yeah."

"Thank God."

"Gary, are you okay? Are you hit?"

Lumbergh took in a breath. "Down but not out. You?"

"Same. Is it just Montoya left?"

"Yeah," said Lumbergh, out of breath. "Federal officers are on the way. Can you see him from where you are?"

The slam of a door and the crank of an engine interrupted the conversation. Sean popped his head up over the Bronco's hood. Gunshots fired, hitting the opposite side of the vehicle, sending Sean low again. The police cruiser roared to life.

"He's in the police car!" Sean shouted. "He's trying to leave!"

"That means he's badly hurt," shouted Lumbergh.

Tires squealed on the pavement. There were two loud thumps and the grinding of metal. Sean lifted his head again, seeing the cruiser reversing quickly down the road. Sean left the Bronco, stepping around the body and heading for the sedan. He was breathing hard by the time he reached it, skirting past its open door and another body, this one dressed in a sports jacket. He saw Lumbergh on the ground, crawling toward the rear of the vehicle, and dragging his leg behind him. The police cruiser was about a hundred feet away, in the middle of a wide turn to try and straighten out in the other direction.

"We can't let him get away and disappear again!" Lumbergh shouted, sucking wind. "He'll come after my family!"

Sean dropped to a knee beside Lumbergh. He tried to pull the rifle horizontal. "Fuck!" he shouted, his arm making it too painful.

Lumbergh twisted back toward Sean. He grabbed the rifle from his grip and went back to his chest, positioning it forward with both hands. He began firing at the cruiser as it fled in the other direction. He heard as it made contact, sparks flying, but the cruiser only picked up speed.

"Dammit!" Lumbergh snarled, slamming the rifle down on the road.

Sean collapsed to his rear end. He drew in a breath and then let himself fall to his back. "Tell me you picked up Lisa— Lisa and the girl," he said. "And that they're safe and sound."

Lumbergh twisted his head back toward his brother-in-law, saying nothing.

"Shit," said Sean, interpreting his silence. "We've got to call everyone. They're out here still. We've got to find them."

A loud gasp of air jolted both men.

Lumbergh swung his rifle in its direction but dropped it the moment he saw a figure topple forward between some brush. "Holman!" he yelled, latching onto the back door of the sedan to try and pull himself up. "Sean, she's a cop."

Sean jogged over to the woman, who was still mostly

concealed in the dark. She coughed and gasped some more, propping herself up against a rock and reaching for her chest. Sean went down to a knee beside her.

"She has a vest!" Lumbergh grunted as he planted a foot. "Check her!"

She moaned some as Sean pulled at a strap of Velcro in front of her stomach. She worked on the area above her chest, wincing with each stretch of her arms. They peeled off the armor, and her hands went up and down her torso.

"It stopped the bullets," she muttered.

"You're bleeding," Sean said, pulling back his hand.

"My leg," she said. Her eyes turned to her car where the dome light inside still exposed her partner's body. Her face tightened and she leaned back on the dirt, eyes welling up. "Oh, Dennis."

Sean looked over his shoulder in the opposite direction. The cruiser's taillights disappeared over a ridge.

Chapter 41

A pinprick of sunlight emerged over a range of rocky hills to the east. Seconds later, a wider ray followed it across the land, exposing the terrain's orange, rugged tone. A couple of tumbleweeds skipped along in the breeze, crashing into the bumper and undercarriage of a mid-nineties Honda Accord as it drove along a weathered road.

Cold air rushed in through the vehicle's open driver-side window, lowered down to hide the fact that its glass had been broken for entry. The rest of the shards were hidden under the floormat a couple of feet below a busted open steering column where the ends of stripped wires were twisted together. Local news radio played on an a.m. station.

The large man behind the wheel dropped a dry cough, his face refusing to register the pain it brought him. When he tucked his square jaw to glance down at his shoulder, he noticed that blood had started to soak through the undersized jacket that covered his chest. He grabbed a towel from the passenger sheet, balled it up, and stuck it up under the jacket against his wound. He shook his head and returned his gaze to the road, holding the towel in place for a couple of minutes.

Twelve miles northwest of town brought him to a raised marquee about half the size of a billboard. It was run-down with age and abandonment, and missing some big black letters from the phrases "Thank you" and "Closed." Its metal supports were either rusted or stained orange by blowing sand; it was hard to tell. Above the marquee, in neon letters that hadn't shone in years, read the words, "Holiday Twin Drive-in." The first part of the business title was presented in the same cursive font as a popular motel chain of a similar name.

The driver turned left at the marquee, sending dust into the air behind him as he drove over a dirt road with wire fencing on both sides. Ahead was a tall, curved metal arch like an upside down *U*. Its sides connected to chain-link fences that spread out in both directions. He drove through the arch, passing by a boarded-up and graffitied ticket booth on the left.

He crossed past the edge of the projector and concession building and pulled the wheel right through the second of two large, propped-open gates. Beyond it was the parking area where a dozen or so raised rows of dirt and gravel were decorated with metal posts with closed soundboxes at their top. A few steel trash barrels still littered the lot, most having been knocked over by wind. A large screen—dirty, weather-faded, and missing panels—hovered in the background.

He'd never been to the drop-off point. He'd never had any reason to go. It was low-level work, the kind his men had been more than capable of. But many things had changed since the night before. Most of his men were dead. So were a couple of associates. Others including his son were in custody. He didn't know the extent of who and what had been compromised, including funds and aliases. He just knew there was enough in the office back at the hangar to open a slew of leads. Drug related. Hit related. The works. He couldn't go back, which also meant he couldn't fly out.

He wondered if this was how Moretti had felt when things were closing in on him. Not knowing who was turning on him. Not knowing which operations were safe and who and what was a liability. The one person who remained loyal to the casino and crime mogul was his brother, Alvar.

He gave his life for Moretti, *like a good son would do for his father.* Moretti may have been the closest thing that Alvar ever had to one, but in the end, he was *no better than the one we never knew.*

Moretti's high-priced lawyers got him into a white-collar country club detention facility to serve out his time. It came from successfully pinning two murders on Alvar that Moretti himself had personally committed. *Dead men tell no tales.*

To Alvar Montoya's criminal history, it was nothing more than a footnote at the bottom of a long list of egregious actions that included several provable and suspected murders. To Lautaro, it was an injustice—a betrayal of the loyalty his brother showed his boss. An injustice that demanded restitution.

It wouldn't come from exacting revenge on the inside. Lautaro didn't have that kind of reach; not inside that kind of institution. Instead, it would come from what was left of Moretti's fortune, the portion not frozen and confiscated by federal agents—the portion Kyle Kimble had stolen before his death. Only then would there be restitution for Alvar's name, and only once Lumbergh was dead would there be restitution for his life.

He had delayed the latter for too long, and it had cost him. Even if his son recovered from his injuries, he might never see him again. Lumbergh needed to pay. *And pay he will.*

To do it, Lautaro would need to travel. Once on the mend, he'd drive to Winston, Colorado, where he'd deliver to Lumbergh a painful death and wipe his seed from the earth. His wife. His brother-in-law. His little daughter. He'd done worse. From there, it would be back to Mexico . . . at least for a while. He knew of hiding spots and had associates. He'd lay low until things settled down. Then he'd return to the United States—the land of opportunity . . . and begin anew.

For that he would need a new identity and new identification. A new past. And just hours before he'd received the phone call letting him know Sean Coleman was meeting with Kimble's widow, those very things had been left for him at a retired drive-in movie theater as part of a separate transaction just a dozen miles away. He just hadn't envisioned needing it so soon.

He pulled up to the third parking row, checking his mirror and gazing through his windows before he pushed open the door. Broken glass jingled in the door panel. He shoved a pistol into the pocket of his jacket and grabbed onto the outside roof of the car, pinning a screwdriver between his fingers and the metal. He grunted as he pulled himself outside of the vehicle, seething as the bullet lodged in his trapezius muscle sent nerve pain through his neck. When it passed, he walked stiffly down the row, his foot dragging across dirt in a limp.

He counted down the numbers sprayed through a stencil on the outside of the sound boxes. When he reached number 17, he lifted his screwdriver and began loosening the box's lid. He let the screwdriver fall with the screw to the dirt, and he opened up the box. Inside was a beige cloth wrapped around a passport, driver's license, social security card, and birth certificate. He thumbed through the documents, half of which bared the only photo he'd allowed taken in years, showing him with a collared shirt and a thick mustache he no longer had. His eyes traced the seals and paper gradients, admiring the handiwork.

"Jorge G. Padilla," he read aloud, wincing at the new name.

He turned around and took one step back toward the car when a quick series of pops sent him toppling backwards into the sound box behind him. The torn chest of jacket oozed blood. He reached for the pistol in his pocket, but two more pops dropped him to the dirt before he could get his finger on the grip. His back propped up against the pole behind him, he gasped for air as his wide eyes searched for his assailant. They landed on a couple of steel trash barrels that stood side by side two rows over.

A frail, freckled hand cupped the top rim of one of the barrels. It was soon joined by the weathered face of an old man. He had a mostly bald head and glasses sitting on his sharp nose. He emerged from behind the barrels, pistol drawn. He spit some phlegm off to his right and walked toward Montoya.

Blood streamed out of the side of Montoya's mouth, a twisted grin forming upon recognition of Victor Rizzo Sr., the man who'd forged the documents and the man he'd believed he'd killed hours earlier.

He walked slowly and steadily toward Montoya, gun pointed and face emotionless. He kept an eye on the fallen giant's hands. If they moved again, he'd empty his pistol into him. He'd worried that his older set of glasses would muck up his vision enough that he'd miss, but his will had kept his aim sharp.

"Killing me won't bring back your son," said Montoya, blood outlining each of his large teeth.

"I know that," said Rizzo, stopping a few feet away. He reached his trembling hand into his pocket, pulling out a pack of cigarettes. He tugged one out and dropped the box before sticking the cigarette in his mouth.

Montoya stared at him, eyes narrowing.

Rizzo reached back into his pocket, this time retrieving a lighter. He brought it up and lit his cigarette, casual in his movements. He returned the lighter and took a long drag. Pinching it from his thin lips, he blew smoke from his mouth and nose.

"Truth is," said Rizzo, "I don't even blame you for what happened to him." He cleared his throat before continuing. "I blame me. I blame myself for bringing him into this world—for giving him a job in it. I set him up for what happened and I'm going to have to live with that."

"You don't blame me?" asked Montoya, eyes swimming.

"No . . . I don't." He took another drag, his eyes still glued on Montoya's hands. "I don't believe in that *restitution* bullshit. That's why I'm not going to do to your son what you did to mine. Assuming he lives, I'm not going to call in any favors on the inside, and believe me . . . I've got guys in there who *owe* me favors. Guys I've kept secrets for. Guys whose assets I watch over."

Montoya stared back.

Rizzo continued. "I kept Kyle Kimble's secrets. I did for a long time. He used to work for me, you know. This was back when he still spoke like a dirty-faced Kentucky hick fresh from the train tracks. This was back when he went by his birth name. The kid was making ends meet by picking tourists' pockets outside casinos. One day, he picked the wrong guy's pocket." He chuckled. "I sure as hell ain't a tourist. But I recognized some talent and I put him to work. Gave him a place to stay. Hell, I even came up with the name 'Kyle Kimble.' Before long, he was involved with nearly all of my business operations. I drew him into the underground like I later did my own son, which is how Kimble later hooked up with Moretti, the way your brother did."

Montoya's eyes floated off to the side.

"When you look at it that way," said Rizzo, "you could say that *all* of this is my fault."

"Then why did you come here, *pendejo*?" slurred Montoya, his head slumped over and his eyes settling back on Rizzo. Blood continued to trickle from his chest. "If it's your fault, why not just shoot yourself instead of me?"

Rizzo took another drag and then glared back at Montoya. "Because I'm a man who keeps his promises."

The second Montoya's arm whipped toward him, open sleeve aimed at his face, Rizzo fired and kept firing until his gun was empty.

Montoya collapsed flat to the dirt, a plume of dust rising up around him in the glare of morning. Multiple bullets were lodged in his head. A small gun was sticking out from his sleeve.

Rizzo dropped his cigarette to the dirt. He put it out with the tip of his shoe. "Adios."

Chapter 42

S ean gazed out his hospital room window at a kid shooting baskets on some blacktop across the street. He couldn't have been more than thirteen, but he was good, sinking most of them. A couple of times he even seemed to surprise himself, smiling from ear to ear when a shot would bobble its way on in. He was by himself but was having a blast.

It looked hot outside; glaringly bright. The kid retreated to a bench on the sideline every few minutes to grab his sports bottle and take a swing. It was a stark contrast from the heavily air-conditioned room Sean was in, seated in an elevated bed propped up in front of a mounted television on mute.

Beside him was some monitoring equipment that occasionally beeped, attached to a Velcro strap around his arm and an oxygen meter clamped down on his finger. An IV was planted in his forearm, delivering much-needed fluids. Whatever drugs they had him on kept him from feeling anything under the thick bandages wrapped around his left shoulder. The rest of his arm was elevated in a sling.

He'd been told before going into surgery that Lisa and Hannah had been picked up and were safe. It was a huge relief, though Sean felt embarrassed over the look on the nurse's face when she noticed him tearing up from the news.

Lumbergh and the woman detective, whose name Sean had forgotten, were out of surgery as well. Both would pull through fine. The same wasn't true of the male detective. He'd been killed in the line of duty along with one of the uniformed officers. The other officer from the shootout was still in critical condition, last Sean had heard.

Police officers roamed the hallway outside of Sean's room. He heard them talking from time to time, mourning the loss of their colleagues. With Montoya still on the loose, there was concern for Lumbergh's safety at the hospital. Sean's too, he supposed, though he wasn't worried . . . at least not for the time being. He knew he'd left Montoya in rough shape, to the point that he could no longer wage a fight. If he survived his injuries and came back for vengeance, it wouldn't be that day or even that week.

Sean thought about the reunion between Hannah and her father, and the image brought a smile to his face. The smile faded when he thought of the same with Lisa. As he'd told her the night before, before the men with guns and masks showed up, he was happy that she had a good life. But at that moment, as he gazed across the room, he felt empty that her good life wasn't with him.

"Mr. Coleman," a woman's voice came from the hallway. "Are you feeling all right? Is there anything I can get you?" It belonged to nurse who had checked on him twice in the last thirty minutes.

"Still good," he said. "Thanks."

"Well, you have a visitor if you're up for it."

Sean's stomach tightened. "I do?"

She nodded.

"I thought this wing of the building was locked down."

"Your brother-in-law cleared it," she said. "If you'd rather not—"

"No," said Sean. "It's fine. Thank you."

When she left, Sean used his bed control to bring himself more vertical. He wished he could fix his hair, but a sling on one arm and an IV in the other made it impossible.

He heard a bobbling noise in the hallway. It grew louder as footsteps slapped their way across vinyl. Sean's face tightened. A cluster of colorful balloons was suddenly shoved through the doorway, screeching off the sides of the doorframe. In behind it popped the white, makeup-covered round face of a stocky man with a red nose and enormous smile. The curls of a green wig bounced above his head.

"Surprise!" yelled Dusty. He followed up the greeting with a laugh that rose up from his belly.

Sean glared at him. "Are you fucking kidding me?"

Dusty laughed again and shoved the rest of his body into the room, displaying the same red getup from the night before, minus the hat. "God, it's so great to see you, Sean!"

A nurse and a passing doctor poked their heads in from the hallway, looking over the spectacle. The doctor had a half grin on her face, unsure of what to make of the scene before ducking back out. A cop took her place, checking in before exiting as well.

"Why?" Sean said, shaking his head.

"Why what?" said Dusty, tying the balloons to the bottom of Sean's bed.

"What do you mean, *why what?* Why are you wearing makeup and—"

"This is what I do for a living. It's my profession. You know that. I bring smiles to people, especially when they're feeling down."

Sean glared back for a few seconds before lowering his head. A chuckle finally escaped from his mouth.

"Mission accomplished!" shouted Dusty, smiling and

throwing his hands into the air. His hand tagged one of the balloons and popped it. "Son of a bitch!" Dusty shouted.

The cop hustled back in, face tight with his hand next to his holster.

"False alarm, officer," said Dusty, his hands back in the air, keeping them away from the balloons this time.

Sean nodded the cop off. "Sorry. He's . . . he's got problems."

"Ouch!" said Dusty as the officer left. His eyes were pinned to Sean's shoulder.

"Are you going to be okay?"

"That's what they tell me," said Sean.

Sean recalled the relief he'd felt when his surgeon explained the nature of the wound and how trying to remove the bullet himself, as he had attempted to back at the riverbed, would have been a colossal mistake.

"If it ain't bleeding . . . ," the surgeon had told Sean in common speak, "don't mess with it."

It was only then that Sean remembered his father saying something similar at the end of his army story from thirty years earlier. It seemed that the Big Nudge was talking to him after all back in the desert but he had only half listened.

The bullet had mostly caused muscle damage, and though it didn't come out easy, it did come out. The wound had been cleaned out and pumped full of antibiotics. He'd be on the mend for a few weeks, most of it at home. There should be no permanent issues . . . at least on the outside.

Dusty toned things down after a while, taking a seat beside Sean's bed and exchanging details from the night before.

"So, they haven't released anything new on Roy's condition?" asked Sean, just as a knock came from the door.

Sean straightened his body when he saw Lisa standing in the doorway, in fresh clothes with her hair again pulled back.

Her face was scraped up a bit and she had a bandage under her chin.

"Lisa . . ." he said.

Dusty's eyes widened and he immediately jumped to his feet, nearly stumbling over his chair in the process. "Lisa!" he shouted, causing her to jump.

Her eyes darted back and forth between him and Sean, trying to wrap her mind around his appearance. "Uh, yes," she said.

"Oh, I've heard so much about you!" said Dusty, smiling broadly and slapping his hands on his knees. His voice, again, was uncomfortably loud. "I mean, not before yesterday . . . until we were watching you at the school. I didn't know anything about you before then." He turned and offered Sean a wink that was met with a scowl. "It's just . . ." he added, turning back to Lisa. "It's just great to see you and meet you."

He walked up closer, opening his arms, brazenly wrapping them around her in a hug.

"Jesus Christ," Sean muttered, shaking his head. "I'm sorry," he mouthed to Lisa, who was staring back at him with wide, confused eyes.

Dusty finally released her and tilted his head back toward Sean. "Are you going to . . .?" he said, motioning his hand toward Lisa. "That's fine," he answered, turning back to her. "I'm Dusty."

"Oh," she said, her face loosening. Dusty had left a little of his paint on the side of her cheek. "The guy who's getting married."

Dusty's face straightened nervously. "Yeah . . ." he said, glancing over at Sean before closing his eyes, taking a deep breath, and turning to face him directly. "I've been meaning to say something about that. Um . . ."

"What is it?" asked Sean, taken aback by the change in Dusty's demeanor.

"Well . . ." he said. "I might not be getting married after all."

Sean's eye widened. "What happened? Did you guys break up?"

He shook his head, clenching his teeth. "A few months ago, actually."

"A few months ago?" Sean said, his voice elevated.

"Yeah, I mean . . ." Dusty began, looking back and forth between Sean and Lisa. "We weren't really . . . technically . . . engaged in the first place."

"What?" Sean shouted, clenching his fist. "That's the whole reason we came here! That's what started all of this!"

"I know! I know!" Dusty pleaded, his hands out in front of him. "I'm sorry! I just wanted to hang out with you! I don't have many friends and—"

"Oh my God," Sean groaned, his eyes lifting to the ceiling. "Dusty . . ." Sean could barely catch his breath. "I can't . . . Out!" He pointed to the doorway.

"What?"

"You have to leave. Now. I can't . . . I can't deal with this right now. You have to go."

Face turning to that of a sad clown, Dusty nodded. He turned to Lisa. "Once again, it was really great to meet you," he said, extending his hand.

"Out!" Sean yelled, causing Dusty to jump.

"Okay, okay," he said, hands in the air. "I'll just . . . I'll just check in later, and . . ." He stopped himself and nodded again before leaving the room.

Sean's eyes went to Lisa. "I . . . I don't know what to say. I . . ."

She shook her head, easing him. "It's not important now. What happened . . . we can't blame your friend. It was Kyle's ghost that brought this back into our lives—the world he was part of; the bad men he worked with." She moved in beside Sean's bed, pushing the chair away with her calf.

Her eyes began to moisten as she placed her hand on the side of Sean's face.

"I'm so glad you're okay," she said with a sniff. "I thought they'd killed you. I kept hearing the gunfire and I saw that other car pull up with more men. And I just—"

"You saw that?" Sean asked.

She nodded, her face shriveling as a tear rolled down her cheek. "From the top. We got to the top, and there was no safe way down the other side. It was like a cliff and it was so dark. All I could see were lights. Lights from cars. Lights from the city. I could see the whole strip from up there." She swallowed before continuing. "I held out hope for you. I prayed for you. I saw the men's flashlights. They kept north along the ridge, after you. You drew them away from us, farther and farther. They kept moving north and then to the west, and when we saw no one to the east, we began making our way back down the way we'd come. Slowly and quietly—as quietly as Hannah would let me, anyway."

Sean nodded. "And she's okay? Hannah?"

"Yeah." Lisa nodded, flashing a quick grin. "She came out of this better than anyone. Anyway, after a while, I heard shooting again. Lots of shots. It sounded like a war zone. And then I heard nothing. It all stopped." Her face started to shake as she leaned forward over him. "I thought that meant you were dead." She kissed him on the forehead. "I'm so glad you're still here, Sean."

His heart skipped a beat upon hearing her say his name,

and the tenderness with which it had come. He nodded. "Me too." He swallowed. "I'm glad you're here too."

She leaned back and wiped a tear from her eye, a smile forming across her lips. Sean smiled back, though he doubted he was hiding the sadness in his eyes.

"I bet Greg's on cloud nine right now, having his daughter back," said Sean. "Having you back."

She nodded. "I can't imagine how scared he was. We've got some things to work out though."

"What do you mean?"

"Some things he told me about this morning. Some things I didn't know. Some things, like you said with your friend Dusty, that I still need to process."

Sean didn't pry any further and Lisa seemed eager to change the subject.

"Does that hurt?" she said, nudging her head at his shoulder.

"No, not that," he answered. After some silence between the two, Sean asked, "I take it they have a cop or two watching you? Police protection."

"One," she said, nodding. "For the time being. Let's hope they catch Montoya quickly." Her eyes shifted away before rejoining Sean's. "You know, speaking of the police . . . I don't know why this popped back into my head on the way over here, especially with everything that's happened since then . . ."

Sean squinted. "What is it?"

She shook her head, as if wanting to dismiss the thought, but she powered through nonetheless. "When I inferred back at my house that you reminded me of a character on *NYPD Blue*, I'm worried that you thought I was talking about Dennis Franz's."

"You weren't?"

She grinned a little. "I mean, I get why you would have

thought that. Sure, there are some similarities. But I was talking about David Caruso's."

Sean's eyes widened. "Really?"

She nodded. "Sean, I meant what I said before. You *are* a good man. I've seen you with the weight of the world on your shoulders, and I've seen you lift that weight. When I look in your eyes, I don't see bitterness. I see kindness. I see sincerity. I see a man who wants, and tries, to do the right thing. I see a man who others should aspire to be."

Sean listened with softness in his eyes.

"I'm proud of you," she said, her voice cracking. "And I will forever be rooting for you, regardless of where I am in my own life. Do you understand? I need you to understand that."

Sean nodded. "I do."

The two spoke for another thirty minutes, mostly avoiding the events of the night before. Lisa talked about needing to reschedule her Michigan flight. Sean spoke of his sister flying out that afternoon and everyone heading back to Colorado in a few days, after they had the medical okay and the police procedures were wrapped up. They kept things light and casual, even though the burdens of the past eighteen hours still weighed heavily on their minds. When the conversation dried up and Lisa glanced at her watch and stood up, Sean believed in his heart that it would likely be the last time he'd ever see her. She seemed to recognize it too, leaning in close, gently pinching his chin with her fingers and pressing her lips against his. Lisa closed her eyes. Sean left his open, engraining the image of her face, and how she looked just then, in his memory.

Seconds later, she left his sight as quickly as she'd come into it at the school a day earlier.

"Life's a journey," Sean remembered Lisa saying back at her

house, shortly before the men with guns arrived. "It's all about experiences and learning and growing." The words hung in his mind.

With a dryness in his throat and a tenderness in his heart, he let his gaze drift back to the window. The kid playing basketball was still there, but he'd been joined by an older man with a similar-looking face and build. The two horsed around and smiled, and the older man took it easy on the kid a few times . . . the way only a father would.

Sean watched them until he fell asleep.

About the Author

A lifelong Coloradoan, John A. Daly graduated from the University of Northern Colorado with a business degree in computer information systems. He spent the next sixteen years developing accounting software and Internet-based solutions. With a thirst for creative expression that went beyond the logic and absolutes of computer programming, John developed an interest in writing. He currently writes political, cultural, and media analysis columns for multiple news publications, when he's not working on the next Sean Coleman thriller.

Other Books in the
Sean Coleman Thriller Series

by John A. Daly

There are times when the truth invites evil, and there are times when the truth can get you killed. Few residents in the secluded mountain-town of Winston, Colorado, have kind words to say about local troublemaker Sean Coleman. He's a bully, a drunk, and a crime-show addicted armchair detective with an overactive imagination. After a night of poor judgment, Sean finds himself the sole witness to the unusual suicide of a mysterious stranger. With the body whisked away in the chilling rapids of a raging river, no one believes Sean's account. When his claim is met with doubt and mockery from the people of Winston, Sean embarks on a far-reaching crusade that takes him across the country in search of the dead man's identity and personal vindication. He hopes to find redemption and the truth—but sometimes the truth is better left unknown.

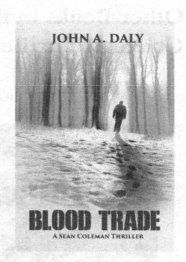

Sean Coleman is back in the latest thriller from John A. Daly, set in the mountains of Winston, Colorado. Six months after the murder of his uncle, Sean is trying to get his life together. He's stopped drinking, he's taking better care of himself, and he's working hard to keep a fledgling security business afloat. At a blood plasma bank Sean frequents to earn extra income, he meets the distraught relative of Andrew Carson, a man who went missing weeks earlier on the other side of the state, with a pool of blood in the snowy driveway of his home as the only clue to the man's fate. Sean decides to help in the search for Carson and quickly finds himself immersed in a world of deception, desperation, and danger—a world in which nothing is what it seems, and few can get out of with their lives.

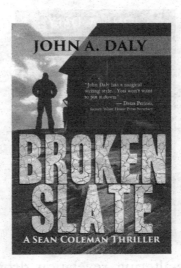

Thirty years ago, Sean Coleman's father abandoned his family in the Colorado mountain town of Winston, and was never heard from again. The reason for his disappearance was always a mystery, but a lifetime of blaming himself put Sean on a rough, dark path that took him years to return from. Now content in his life, Sean receives unexpected word that his father has finally reemerged, on the other side of the country in Pawleys Island, South Carolina . . . as a murder victim. At the wishes of his sister, Sean flies out to retrieve the body, and hopefully find answers to why his father left, and the life he went on to lead. What Sean discovers is a second family, a web of deception, and a brutal killer who's still on the loose . . . and isn't finished killing.

Months after a life-altering revelation drove Sean Coleman from his mountain hometown of Winston, Colorado, the longtime security guard has found stable work as the sole caretaker of a retired nuclear missile site along the Eastern Plains. The desolate Cold-War-era facility now serves as a rarely visited museum and records archive and provides perhaps the perfect job for a lonesome, headstrong man working to erase the painful memories of his past.

But as Sean soon discovers, the forgotten compound has piqued new, unwelcome interest. A mysterious group of armed individuals, frighteningly cultish in their methods, work to cut off communications with the outside world and take over the facility by any means necessary. Though their dark purpose is ultimately exposed, Sean suspects their charismatic leader is guided by even more sinister motivations—motivations that can prove more deadly than anyone could possibly imagine.

What was supposed to be a lazy Monday evening turns into a savage battle of survival and a close-quarters race against time as Sean fights for his life, liberty, and the things he'd left behind.